Into These Eyes

Darcy Daniel

ISBN-13: 978-0-9924004-5-3

Cover Art by Tristan Partic-Gray

DEDICATION

To everyone I know who puts up with my passion for writing. You have no idea how amazing you are. Thank you for allowing me to drive you crazy!

Chapter 1

DARRYL KIRK'S NIGHT keeps going from bad to worse. First, his mother had scolded him for failing to shave before leaving home. Then, three hours into his night-shift, he'd grabbed a Quarter-pounder meal from Macca's, only to have the freaking gherkin shoot out from between the buns. Of course it'd landed on his pristine security shirt, leaving behind a fabulous smear of tomato sauce and beef patty juices. *Brilliant.*

After devouring the traitorous burger, he skilfully extracts a single fry from its warm home. Long and lean, and with a golden tan, he slips the crisp potato past his lips, enjoying the sensation of the grains of salt gradually dissolving in the grease between his thumb and forefinger.

When he glances at the dashboard clock, he groans.

After wiping his fingers on his dark slacks, he starts the cheap four-cylinder shit-box provided by the security company and drives through the Sharman Grove Estate entrance. Cruising around the rabbit-warren of peaceful suburban streets, he passes McMansion after McMansion, all displaying strictly enforced manicured lawns and hedges.

For the millionth time, he wonders if patrolling a community that's about as dangerous as heaven will ever see him fulfil his dream of becoming a cop.

As he takes a bend on a street like all the others, his headlights sweep across a parked car, and illuminate a startling scene behind its bumper.

Darryl stomps on the brakes, not quite believing his eyes.

On the nature-strip, a woman lies sprawled on her back, a teenage boy kneeling over her. He's gripping the handle of something protruding from the woman's chest while he strangles her with his other hand.

The teenager's head snaps up. Squinting, he freezes in Darryl's headlights.

Then, like a movie unpaused, the kid bolts, leaving the object imbedded in the woman's chest.

Darryl flattens the accelerator. Tyres screech as he hunches over the wheel, heart pounding, knuckles white.

The kid's head snaps side to side, looking for an escape route. Darryl can't go after him on foot, not when he has a gut full of burger, fries and a chocolate shake. Besides, the kid seems to run like the fucking wind.

But he *can't* lose him. This is the chance he's been waiting for. The chance to be more than just a security guard. The chance to be a *hero.*

Forcing the shit-box to mount the kerb, Darryl speeds along the footpath in hot pursuit.

The terrified kid glances over his shoulder. And trips on the only piece of footpath in disrepair, going down like a sack of spuds.

Darryl stomps on the brakes, losing all control as the car sails into a sideways skid on the nature-strip. For a horrifying moment, he thinks he's about to run over the kid. Then the car comes to a jolting stop.

High on adrenalin, Darryl scrabbles with his seatbelt and flings open the door as the kid clambers to his feet.

With a speed he never knew he possessed, Darryl lunges, tackling the kid. They both go down, breath exploding as they hit the footpath.

Beneath him, the kid wheezes as Darryl grins with victory, pries a set of cuffs from his utility belt and snaps one onto the boy's wrist.

"No!" the kid gasps. "It's not … what you … think."

Darryl scoffs at the clichéd words. Leaning his weight on the perp to hold him in place, he extracts his radio from his utility belt.

"Please," the kid sobs.

Darryl grins. This night just went from dismal to fucking festive.

He presses the talk button on his radio. "Home base, come in. Over."

Brief static, then, "Home base. What's up, Darryl?"

"I've got a woman down, possibly stabbed. Location, halfway along Sacramento Place. I have the perp in custody. Repeat, I have the perp in custody. Over."

"Are you shitting me, Darryl?"

A moment of fury shoots through him. "One hundred percent serious, Mr. Johnston. I need an ambulance and police assistance immediately. Over."

Pressing more weight against the struggling teen, he waits.

A sharp crackle pierces the night air. "Ambulance and police are on their way. But if you're screwing with me, Darryl, I'm gonna fire your arse."

Beneath him, the kid stops struggling. He's given up. Knows he's done for.

Darryl beams with elation. The only way this night can get any better is if that woman is dead.

More than being a cop, he dreams of something bigger. He can already see the news, see himself being interviewed while the banner at the bottom of the screen reads: *Local Hero Catches Killer.*

One Hour Earlier

Chapter 2

Gavin

I SIT ON the edge of my bed and pull on a fresh pair of sports socks. The last thing I feel like doing is going for a run, but once I'm out there and my heart's pounding, lungs protesting, I'll disappear into the mind-numbing rhythm. It's an escape I need, even if only for an hour. Besides, as captain of our high school soccer team, I have to keep in top shape to lead them to victory when we play in the grand final in a few weeks.

Although I'm sure no one would blame me if I failed them, the weight of obligation falls heavy on my shoulders all the same. Dad's taught me the meaning of responsibility my whole life. So, whether my heart's in it or not, I won't let my teammates down.

Funny how things change. A little over a year ago, all that mattered in my world was soccer, training, and getting scouted by the professional teams in our state. Now three scouts have put in offers to take me on next year as a fully paid professional player. Everything I've been working for my whole life.

And now, I couldn't give a shit.

Letting out a heavy sign, I shove my feet into well-worn runners. As I tie the laces, my gaze settles on the bedside drawer.

I shouldn't, it'll only tear my heart out all over again, but I can't help myself. Leaning over, I open the drawer. Guilt hits me when I'm forced to shove aside junk I've thrown on top of the framed photo of me, Mum and Dad. I'm disgusted with myself for treating this memory with such disrespect. I'd love to keep it out in the open, but I just … can't. Not yet.

I stare at us all smiling for the camera after I led the school soccer team to victory last year. At least Mum got to share that moment. If only she was still here. It would've been something special to see her face light up when she learnt I had my choice between three teams. But all the joy and enthusiasm I once experienced through the sport I love has gone.

Gone because Mum died a month ago. After her ALS diagnosis, the cruel disease had given her a year and some change with us before taking her. We'd hoped she'd be one of the rare people who lived a decade or longer. She wasn't. I'm grateful Dad and I gave it our all while caring for her, even though the pain of watching her deteriorate before our eyes shattered us. At least we were there for her. At least we had each other to lean on.

When the time came to hand her over to palliative care, everything changed between me and Dad. While I spent every spare moment I had at Mum's bedside, Dad grew distant, rarely visiting her. I want to know why he changed during that time. I want to talk to him about everything, but he's still so damn closed off.

The only comfort—as painful as it was—is that I was there, looking into Mum's eyes and holding her hand when she took her last breath. She didn't die alone. My final gift to her. And hers to me. Dad missed it, and I'm not sure if he feels bad about that or if he's relieved he wasn't there.

Mum might not have been alone when she passed, but I was.

I needed him.

I still do.

Staring at Mum's smiling face, my heart lurches as my eyes fill with tears. How long will it take until I can look at her without crumbling? Another month? A year? Never? To push aside all the decimating emotions her death has brought into my world, to try and move on, feels like a sickening betrayal.

I desperately need to talk to Dad about that. But, when it comes to me, he seems incapable of communicating anything other than mundane orders.

I didn't lose just one parent the day Mum died, but two. Nothing's the same. We were always a close, tightknit family unit. My parents were best friends. And Dad used to look at me with such pride … pride that meant everything to me. Now, I may as well be a ghost.

Wiping my eyes with the back of my hand, trying to get a handle on the pain coursing through me, I tenderly place the photo back in my drawer.

Outside my window, the streetlights glow as light fades from the sky. I love running at twilight while the final strand of illumination on the horizon vanishes into pure darkness.

Standing, I raise my arms over my head, lengthening the muscles in my back, then my sides. As I begin calf stretches, the door swings open.

Dad stops short at the sight of me. "I thought you were at training tonight."

"Got cancelled. Coach had to move it to tomorrow night."

"Shit." He leans against the doorframe and crosses his arms, lines furrowing his brow.

"Why? What's the problem?"

He checks his watch before staring at my chest. Never my eyes. Not since Mum died. He won't let me in and it's killing me.

Dragging a hand down his face, he hesitates. "Listen, Gav … you're a mature kid. You understand what it means to be an adult, right?"

Has he forgotten my eighteenth birthday a few days ago? I suppose, if he's feeling anything like I am, it's possible, so I don't poke him about it. "I guess. Why?"

He sighs heavily, turning as if he's about to leave. When he stops, his fingers thrum against the doorframe before he faces me again. "I've invited someone over. I thought you'd be at training."

"So?"

"It's just, well … I suppose it's time you know. I'm seeing someone."

I freeze mid-stretch. If I hadn't observed Dad so closely over the last few weeks, waiting for a moment to open up to him, I might believe he's joking. But more and more, I've noticed his melancholy act slip. When he thinks I'm not around, I hear him humming, even singing along to the radio. I've tried to understand, to rationalise that maybe Mum's death has eased something inside him. That maybe he's relieved she no longer has to suffer. Those thoughts are hurtful enough. I haven't considered that he has another reason to feel good.

"Look," he says, "I know it's a shock, but—"

"Mum's only been gone a month!" I yell, hating the high pitch to my voice.

"It's not that simple," he says, staring at the floor.

"Bullshit!"

"Lower your voice, Gav." Even though he refuses to meet my lethal stare, he keeps his tone gentle, cajoling.

"Who's gonna hear, huh? Mum? Because I hope she can!"

"Don't be ridiculous."

My hands ball into fists. "Far as I can tell, you're the ridiculous one. What is it? Can't handle being on your own for two seconds?"

He straightens, filling the doorway.

"Are you sleeping with her?" I grind out.

"That's none of your business."

"That's a *yes*!" My jaw clenches so hard, I'm surprised my teeth don't crumble to dust.

"Listen, Gavin. You don't understand. If you'd just let me ex—"

"No! You're a pathetic fuck!"

While my chest feels like it's being constricted by a python, he's calm. Maybe if my heart stops, I won't feel anything. That'd be better than this.

"Maybe so," he says softly. "And if that's how you want to see me, then go right ahead. But my life hasn't stopped because your mother died, and neither should yours."

I scoff, wanting to let fly, but something in his posture stops me. *Now* he wants to talk? Why? Because he's desperate to get laid?

As I push that revolting thought aside, his words finally register.

"My life hasn't stopped either," I spit, "but at least I have the decency to grieve like a normal human being. What's your excuse? Did you even give a crap about Mum?"

He advances into the room. "Quit it. Right now," he warns.

I square my shoulders. Just because Mum's dead doesn't mean I can't stand up for her. "I hope you're ashamed of yourself. And I hope your … your *slut* is too, because I can only imagine what sort of bitch jumps into bed with a man when his dead wife's body isn't even cold."

Eyes flashing with rage, his face reddens. "Watch your mouth, Son."

I'm pushing him to the brink, and I don't give a fuck. I'm already over the edge.

Who the hell does this new woman think she is? Is she trying to replace my mother? Is that why he's pulled away from me instead of being the supportive father he's always been? Was he cheating on Mum … while she was *dying*?

If I ever find that woman in this house, *near* this house, my father better be standing in the way, or I don't know what the fuck I'll do to her.

Apparently, I don't need to go running to make my heart pound. I take a step right into his personal space and jab a finger into his sternum. "Or were you screwing the whore behind Mum's back all along?"

"Enough! Don't *ever* talk about her like that again." His palms slam into my chest, knocking me back. My legs hit the edge of the bed. The moment my arse hits the mattress, I bounce up. I don't even think. My fist smashes into his face, my knuckles cracking with the force.

Clasping his cheek, he staggers back. I shake with a rage I've never known. Heart jackhammering, I grab his shirt and pull back my throbbing fist, ready to strike him again.

His stunned eyes lock with mine.

Finally, he sees me.

Right when I don't want him to.

A fleeting moment of guilt washes over me, but I tamp it down. That punch was for Mum. He deserved it.

"Gavin …" he breathes, shocking me with the look on his face.

He's afraid. Of me.

I shove him away and back up. I want to tell him I hate him, but I hold back. Mum's right here with me, a reminder that I'll never know when it might be the last time I see someone, the last words I say to them.

Hand burning, I catch a different look on his bruised face. Disappointment.

Fuck that. *He's* the disappointment.

I shoulder past him, desperate to get away.

Storming through the house, fury racing through my veins, I fling open the front door. And run.

Chapter 3

Jamie

I STAND IN the doorway of my parents' bedroom and watch my mother, Matilda. Mattie to everyone who knows her. She sits at her dressing table in a silk robe, hair freshly blow dried into a new, elegant style she's adopted lately. At thirty-four, she's stunning. If I look as good as she does when I'm her age, I'll be pretty freaking happy. I suppose it doesn't hurt that there's only eighteen years between us.

At seventeen, Mum accidentally found herself pregnant with me. My dad had done the honourable thing and married her, and against all odds, they're still together.

Now that I'm only a year away from seventeen, I find it impossible to imagine myself in the same situation. I'm in awe of Mum having the strength to handle such a life-altering event. I only care about which boys I like at school, what to wear each day and what party I'll be allowed to attend next. The thought of raising a baby sends chills down my spine. Though I'm sure I'll want one in the future, now definitely isn't that time.

"Jamie, honey? What're you doing there?"

I snap out of my thoughts and catch Mum's eye in the mirror. Remembering what brought me here in the first place, I sigh, stomp into the room and flop on my parents' bed.

"Anika again," I grumble.

Mum's shoulders slump a little as she applies foundation. "What's she done now?"

"I'm so sick of her going into my room. Why can't she get it through her head that she's not allowed in there?"

Mum blends the foundation onto her face, then picks up some powder. "She's two, Jamie. That's why."

"I know, but—"

"Hey, hon," Dad says, winking at me as he saunters in. Crossing the room, he stops behind Mum and places a sweet kiss on her neck.

Whenever they're affectionate with each other, I get a warm, gooey feeling. The way they're so happy together makes me feel safe and loved. I can't imagine them ever divorcing like so many of my friends' parents. No, mine are the exception. They might have ruined my standards, though. I'm not sure I'll ever find a man who'll love me the way Dad loves Mum.

Straightening, he gently squeezes her shoulder as he gazes at her reflection. "You look amazing, Mattie. Seems every time one of these girls' nights comes around, you look more beautiful, more alive. Kinda makes me want to tag along."

"That's sweet of you to say," Mum laughs, "but I really doubt you want to be around a bunch of gossiping women."

He drops a kiss on top of her head. "You're probably right. So, you'll be home at the usual time?"

"Yep," Mum answers, watching him in the mirror. "Unless you need me back earlier?"

Dad shakes his head vigorously. "The kids and I are in the swing of things now. We can handle one or two nights a week without you. Right, Jamie?"

I grin. "I don't think so. You've been like a lost puppy the last couple of times."

Dad rushes me, catching me in a playful headlock. I squeal with laughter as he tickles my side. "Take it back!"

Barely able to get my breath, I shriek, "Okay! Okay!"

Knowing I hate it, he ruffles my hair.

"Dad!"

Grinning like an idiot, he backs toward the door. "Oh, by the way, can you clean up Anika? She's got black marker all over her face."

"Can't you do it?" I ask, wanting to talk to Mum.

He gives me a quick shrug before disappearing down the hallway. It drives me crazy the way he never helps with my sister. Mum doesn't like it either, but she never calls him out on it. Which pisses me off even more.

She turns to me, an eyebrow raised. "Black marker?"

"That's what I was trying to tell you. She went into my room—*without* permission—and got my eyeliner. She scribbled all over herself and somehow managed to break it in half. It's not fair that she gets to destroy my things. Can I *pleeeease* have a lock on my door?"

"Come here."

I reluctantly rise and shuffle over. She plucks a black eyeliner from her own makeup collection and hands it to me.

"That's not the point," I say, but take it. "Anika gets away with everything."

"Because she's two."

I let out a small huff. Smiling up at me, Mum gives my arm a comforting rub.

"I know it's not easy being sixteen and having to deal with a toddler. But Ank loves you. She thinks you're the best, the most special person in the world. Sometimes, I get jealous of how much she adores you."

"That's stupid." Though I'll never admit it, that feels kind of good.

Mum squeezes my arm. "Just think about it, Jamie. In a few years, you'll be off to university. Ank will only be four. She's going to miss you so much. So, for now, just forgive her. No matter how old we are, we all make mistakes. It's part of life. What doesn't have to be part of it, is holding a grudge, especially against someone who's family. It's no good for the person you're accusing, and it's especially not good for you."

"Fine," I sigh.

"Good. Now, do you mind going and checking on her?"

"Okay … but Mum?" I ask, meeting her eyes in the mirror. "You know what'd be really nice? If you, me and Anika had our own girls' night."

She smiles. "That's a good idea, hon. But tonight, it's adult time. I need a break too, and having a laugh with other women, well, it just detangles me. You understand, don't you?"

I shrug. "I guess." Hanging out with my best friends is a huge part of my life. How can I deny Mum the same thing?

"But what about Saturday mornings?" she asks.

"Huh?"

"Instead of a girls' night, we could have a girls' morning. We can cook pancakes in our pjs, do each other's hair and fingernails. What do you say?"

I grin. "Mum, we've always done that."

She gives me a playful frown. "We have?"

From the time I started forming memories, Saturday mornings were amongst some of the best. In a rush of emotion, I hug her. "You're pretty cool."

"Whoa, that certainly means something coming from a teenager." She pulls back and touches my face. "I'm proud of you, Jamie. You're turning into a wonderful woman. Just … open your heart, okay? Forgiveness is a powerful thing."

My mood lighter, I nod, then head out to find Anika. As annoying as my sister is, I do love her. And when I leave home, I know I'll miss the little cutie.

Chapter 4

Gavin

THE FRIGID WINTER air cools the sweat on my face and neck, but does nothing for the slick skin beneath my tracksuit.

After sprinting aimlessly through the familiar streets, my footfalls gradually slow to a walk until I come to a complete stop. Resting my hands on my knees, I suck the cold air into my heated lungs. It hurts. And I like it.

With my breathing under control, I walk on, barely paying attention to where I'm going. I'm too in my head, too caught up in the confrontation with Dad. I fist and uncurl my right hand. Unfortunately, the throb in my knuckles doesn't lie. I hit my father.

Fuck. I've screwed up. I have no idea where that rage came from. It felt like I vanished, went somewhere else while something dark and out of control crept inside me and took over.

I try to reason that Dad put his hands on me first, provoked me, but a shove isn't a punch, no matter how I try to convince myself otherwise. I'd decked the man who, until recently, had been there for me my whole life. The man I love. I guess that's why it happened. If I didn't care about him, I wouldn't have reacted.

But God-fucking-dammit, he's been cheating on Mum. How was I supposed to take that news? How am I supposed to process it *now*? I might've calmed down after running off all that aggression and adrenalin, but that doesn't mean I've accepted what he'd sprung on me tonight.

In fact, now that I can think, I've gotta wonder if it's even entirely Dad's fault. I mean, who the hell is this woman? Can she really be callous enough to sleep with a man while his wife's dying? Or did she seduce him because she had a reason to? We're upper-middle-class, I guess. Maybe she sees Dad as an opportunity to raise her status. He'd been vulnerable and raw during Mum's deterioration. In a volatile moment, had she been there to give him the kind of comfort no one else could?

Shaking my head, I scuff the bottoms of my sneakers on the footpath. It's all speculation. The only way I'll know the truth is to ask him. I suppose that's only fair. I shouldn't jump to conclusions that could be woefully wrong.

As a drop of sweat runs down my spine, I shiver.

I can't let her destroy what's left of my family. I'm an only child. Dad's all I've got. So why am I the one wandering the streets? No one's forcing me out of my home. Especially not some piece of work who's probably after my father's money. Maybe I can put a stop to this before she gets her claws firmly hooked in him.

Fury rushes through me again. Checking my watch, I realise Dad didn't mention what time she's supposed to be arriving.

As I break into a run, I concentrated on the steady rhythm of my feet as they slap against the footpath.

Although I dread facing Dad, I want to confront her more than anything. If she's there, I'm gonna let rip. There'll be no holding back. I just hope I can keep this simmering rage under control long enough to humiliate her. By the time I finish, and she sees how much damage she's done, hopefully she'll flee my home in tears.

Hyped up, ready for a confrontation, I fly along beside the massive golf course that backs onto our house backs. Nose tingling, breaths visible with every exhale, I wipe at the icy tears flowing over my cheeks and try to convince myself they're simply a reaction to the biting air.

As I grow closer to home, I slow to a walk, wanting to catch my breath before I get there.

When I turn the corner, heavy footfalls rush toward me from the shadows the streetlights don't quite reach. A figure wearing all black and a baseball cap barrels into me so forcefully, I bounce off the guy and land on my arse on the damp nature strip.

"Hey!" As I scramble to my feet, whoever the fucker is vanishes around the corner without even acknowledging me.

Prick.

Turning, frantic movements catch my eye. Soft lamplight illuminates the second-floor window of the house that sits on the dogleg bend further along our street. But that's not what has my attention.

It's little Liam Thompson's shadowed figure. He's waving at me.

But is he waving? His silhouette's arms flap wildly, as if he's trying to take flight. He's only six or seven, so at first, I think he's playing some sort of weird game. I stand there, staring up at him with confusion. As suddenly as his arm movements started, they stop. Then his window flies up.

"Gav! Gavin!" he yells excitedly.

He's pointing frantically at something further along the street, closer to his house. Curious, I stride forward, getting a gauge on where he's directing all his attention.

"Gav!" This time, I hear panic in his voice.

That's when I see what's got him so worked up.

I freeze, my breath catching in my throat.

There's a woman a few metres away.

And since I don't recognise her, I'm pretty fucking sure it's *her.*

As I stare at her, all I can think about is my mother.

Heart booming against my chest, I take off.

And run straight at her.

Chapter 5

Jamie

"YES!" I YELL with utter satisfaction.

"You're cheating!" Dad protests, a big doofus grin on his face.

"Park Lane is mine! Now I'm going to bleed you dry, old man."

He laughs, giving me an affectionate wink. It's not like *he* doesn't gloat when he scores the top two Monopoly properties.

On the couch beside him, Anika giggles and claps her hands, her bright eyes glued to the Finding Nemo DVD I'd put on nearly an hour ago. As soon as Mum had left, Dad insisted I take Anika upstairs for her bath. Because, of course, he couldn't possibly do it himself.

While I ran her a bubble bath, I chased her around the bedrooms, playing her version of hide and seek. My motivation might've been to tire her out, but by the end, my cheeks and belly were both aching from giggling so much.

Once her bath was ready, the bubbles and delicious scent inspired me to lock the door and get in with her. Really, it was easier than hanging over the side of the tub for an hour while she played.

We spent so long in there, I had to carefully top it up with hot water twice. My fault, since I insisted on playing her favourite game of creating a bubble beard and shaving it off over and over. Then we moved on to filling her plastic dolly up with water and squeezing it so it looked like she was peeing. That never failed to have my little sister in fits of hysterics.

Despite all my efforts to tire Anika out, she's showing no signs of nodding off. I glance at Dad as he takes a peek at his watch.

"Why don't you take Anika up to bed? It's almost nine already."

I glare at him. "Oh, I get it. Since I'm about to kick your butt, you're ending the game?"

"Can't sneak anything past you, can I?" he admits.

"You suck."

"You suck!" Anika yells, clapping her hands.

"Jamie … she needs her sleep." Dad warns, but he still has a smile plastered on his face.

"Fine," I grumble. "That means you're packing up."

"Deal."

I stand and lift Anika into my arms. She instantly grabs my cheeks with her sticky fingers. "Ow, ow, owwww!" I giggle and tickle her feet. She squeals in delight, lifting my mood when she presses her flat palms against my face and squeezes.

"Fishy, fishy!" she yells. I pucker my mouth and make fish-lips at her before plonking noisy kisses all over her rosy cheeks.

"Go on, you two," Dad reminds me. "And stop revving her up, Jamie. She'll never get to sleep at this rate."

To my utter shock, once I've got her in bed, her long lashes—which I'm forever jealous of—flutter closed. As I lie beside her and watch her drift off, I wonder if Dad will bother coming up to kiss her goodnight.

After ten minutes, I give up on that stupid idea, carefully slip from her bed and head downstairs.

When I join Dad on the couch and see he's watching a boring documentary, I get started on my latest reading assignment for school while I wait for Mum to get home.

The doorbell rings.

I stare at Dad and he stares right back, a frown on his face. "Why's your mother ringing the doorbell?"

I shrug. He's right. She should've pulled her car into the garage and come in that way. Tossing my book on the couch, I get up and hurry into the foyer.

Grinning, I swing the door wide.

And freeze.

Two police officers stand on the other side of the locked security door. One male. One female.

My heart takes off like a rocket. Before I regain the ability to speak, Dad's behind me, resting his hand on my shoulder.

"Are you Brian Evans?" the male officer asks.

"That's me. What's the problem?"

Both officers' eyes swing my way, then return to Dad.

"Do you mind if we come in?" the female asks.

Dad moves me aside, but he doesn't release my shoulder as he unlocks the security door. The policewoman removes her hat as she steps inside, her partner following her lead.

As Dad's hand tightens on my shoulder, my heart doesn't know whether to beat harder or stop altogether. By the look in the officers' eyes, devastation is about to hit my little family.

"Jesus," Dad says, his voice filled with anguish. "Please don't tell me she's been in a car accident."

"Mr. Evans, is your wife Matilda Evans?" the male officer asks.

"Yes," Dad croaks.

Both sets of eyes snap to me. "Maybe we should talk in private?" the woman suggests.

"Mum …" I whisper, my throat slamming shut as Dad's grip on me grows tighter.

"Just tell us," Dad insists.

"Mr. Evans, we're sorry to inform you that your wife Matilda has been killed."

Silence engulfs us all before Dad shakes his head. "No. No, you've got it wrong," he reasons. "She's out. With her friends. That's all."

"I'm sorry, Mr. Evans. She was murdered earlier tonight."

"*Murdered?*" Dad gasps.

The world spins. My knees buckle, slamming painfully into the tiled floor. Dad kneels beside me, crushing me to his chest as I try to draw in air as thick as oil. I think I'm drowning. Drowning on words I desperately didn't and don't want to hear.

"How?" Dad cries, his voice vibrating against my ear along with the thunderous beat of his heart.

"She was stabbed. We have the suspect in custody."

The only thing I hear after that is the wail of Dad's cries as he holds me and rocks me right there on the cold tiles. It can't be real. Things like this don't happen to families like ours.

That's what I keep telling myself all night as I lie in bed, waiting for Mum to come home, waiting for her to apologise for being so late, that she simply lost track of time.

Waiting for someone to tell me it's all been a terrible mistake.

In the early hours of the morning, Anika slips into my bed and snuggles close. I hold her tight and try to absorb her warmth. But when light filters in through the window, winter seeps right through my feather-down comforter and burrows deep inside my soul.

At 9am sharp, Detective Jarrod Reid enters our home. Dad ushers him into the living room, where only last night we'd been oblivious to the horror about to destroy our world.

With Dad still in shock, he doesn't force me out of the living room as I sit beside him and listen to the detective explain what happened to Mum.

He tells us that my mother's murder was captured via a security vehicle's dash-cam. The suspect was recorded holding the knife he'd driven into my mother's chest. He tried to flee the scene, but was caught by the security guard. An open and shut case, the detective reassures us.

"But … but where?" I ask. "She was out with her girlfriends."

Detective Reid hesitates, his eyes fixed on Dad, his expression unreadable. "I'm not sure your daughter should be here for this."

"We're talking about her mother. Whatever it is, she has a right to know," Dad mutters.

Detective Reid nods, his sympathetic gaze lingering on me. "It's come to light that she wasn't out with friends. She was visiting a man. Lachlan Lake. Does that name mean anything to you, Brian?"

What? A man?

That's not possible. Mum wouldn't …

I look at Dad. The small amount of blood remaining in his face drains away. Shaking his head, he glares at the detective. "What do you mean by *visiting a man?*"

Exactly. This detective's got it all wrong. Obviously.

"It's part of his statement. They were in a … romantic relationship."

If I'd managed to eat any breakfast, I'm sure it'd be all over the carpet right now.

"This is bullshit!" Dad roars, leaping to his feet. "Get the fuck outta here with your filthy lies! My wife would never do … anything … like …"

For a terrifying moment, I think Dad's having a heart attack. He sways on his feet, his face bright red, hands fisted at his sides. After a moment, he flops onto the couch beside me. Resting his elbows on his knees, he drops his head in his hands. I stare, one part of me processing the absurdness of Mum cheating, another wondering if Dad might actually pull clumps of hair from his scalp.

Like, just maybe, he believes it.

I force my gaze to the detective, noticing his eyes flicking from me to Dad and back again. I shake my head, unable to force words from my tightening throat.

"I'm sorry," Reid says, giving my hand a quick, gentle pat. "Unfortunately, it's true."

Pushing the idea of Mum doing anything to hurt our family aside, I concentrate on the practical side of the revelation.

Swallowing down my shock, I ask, "This man … he killed her?"

Reid shakes his head. "It was his son, Gavin Lake."

I'm not sure if Dad's listening anymore, but I suddenly have an insatiable need to know every detail. If I know how it happened, *why* it happened, then I can make sense of what seems impossible. "But … why?"

Reid gazes at Dad for a long moment. When he realises my father isn't in any state to take in information, he turns to me, explaining that Gavin Lake had discovered his father's affair with my mother last night before she arrived at their house. His own mother had recently passed away, so when he found out about the new woman in his father's life, a violent altercation took place between father and son.

"Gavin left the premises, but when he returned and saw your mother near his house, he attacked her."

As silence fills the room, Dad sobs uncontrollably into his hands. I hold him close the way he'd held me the night before, but I don't let him distract me. Some *boy* killed my mother?

"How old is this … Gavin Lake?"

"Eighteen."

"So, he'll be sentenced as an adult?" I want to confirm.

Reid blinks at me. "That's right. Pending a thorough investigation, of course. But, like I said, the evidence is highly incriminating. Trust me when I say this, Jamie. He'll pay for what he's done."

I stare straight into his eyes with fierce determination. "I hope he rots in prison forever."

He stares back with utter conviction.

My mind races back to last night. I watched her get ready. I watched her lie.

How happy she seemed. Glowing even. And she'd told me not to hold onto grudges when it came to family. To open my heart.

Had she been trying to soften me up for the news that would break our family apart?

Every muscle in my body tenses. I can't even comprehend Mum cheating on Dad, let alone how I'm supposed to feel about it. But there *are* feelings welling inside me. Feelings I've never dealt with before.

Hate. Anger. Rage.

Those are solid, easily identifiable emotions I can cling to. Focus on.

And I know just where to direct them. Toward a violent thug who took my mother's life.

As Dad continues to fall apart in my arms, I realise in that moment that it's me who'll have to be the strong one. It's me who'll have to keep everything together. It's what Mum would have wanted. Anika's so little. She needs a mother. Had it only been yesterday I'd been so grateful I don't have a kid to look after at my age?

And Dad? He's always been the typical old-school Aussie bloke. I've never seen him cook a meal in his life, let alone make a bed, do laundry, or any type of housework. He works his job in construction, comes home and does whatever needs doing around the yard. That's it. And Mum let him get away with his gender-role beliefs.

The weight of it all comes crashing into my body, threatening to take me to the floor and crush me like a steamroller.

I don't think I can cope with that much responsibility.

But what does it matter what I think?

A boy called Gavin Lake has stolen the future I was meant to live.

One Year Later

Chapter 6

Gavin

AFTER THE CORRECTIVE Services officer places me in the side-dock, I glance nervously around the courtroom I'll soon become accustomed to. For how long, I don't know. What I do know is that it's a far more pleasant environment than the remand cell I'm barely surviving in.

This courtroom, and the twelve people seated in the jury box, are my only hope of freedom. Contrary to what my publicly-appointed defence lawyer believes and has repeatedly explained.

He'd shown me the video footage from the camera mounted in the security patrol car. It looks bad. Due to the lack of context. It shows me gripping the knife handle, while—my lawyer pointed out—it looks like I'm strangling her with my other hand. Then I stare up at the headlights in shock. And flee.

The jury won't see what happened moments before the camera captured me. They won't see the man in black shouldering into me, nor me rushing to the woman's aid.

My lawyer also told me the assault on my father will come to light and that Dad will take the stand for the prosecution.

None of it sounds promising, but I hold strong to the belief that the truth will prevail. That's what court is for, right?

I search the public gallery for my only parent. He's nowhere to be seen. I don't know if that's because he's not here, or if he's not allowed in the courtroom. Either way, it doesn't matter. I haven't seen or heard from him since that night.

He believes I killed his lover. My lawyer won't confirm it either way, but I know. After almost a year, I don't have to be a genius to understand my father's abandoned me.

I'm here alone, with no one on my side. Not even my court appointed lawyer.

Staring at him, I watch as he has a quiet laugh with the two prosecutors seated at the bar table. Apparently, my life hanging in the balance isn't enough to come between mates enjoying a joke. I'm sure he believes I'm guilty too.

My insides shrivel. No one cares what happens to me.

Swallowing over the lump in my throat, I let my gaze drift over the jurors faces. Some glance at me, some drop their eyes as soon as mine meet theirs, and some refuse to even look my way. At this stage, they should be neutral in their judgement. Though, I wonder if their opinions have already been swayed by the mere fact that I'm sitting in the dock.

I scan the gallery again, trying to see if there's a single familiar face amongst the strangers. Maybe a teacher, a friend, one of the guys on the soccer team. Surely at least one person turned up to support me.

Instead of finding anyone I know, my gaze falls on the most beautiful girl I've ever seen. She clutches the inside of an older man's arm. Her smooth, clear skin is free of makeup. Dark auburn hair hangs almost to her elbows as the overhead lights dance on the silky surface with every movement she makes. I stare at her plump lips as she talks to the older man, watch the way they purse and relax while she forms unheard words.

Then she looks right at me.

And our eyes lock.

Her eyes. Oh, *wow.*

Like the emerald in a tall wave right before it breaks.

When that stunning green turns fierce, aflame with utter hatred, I know who she is.

The woman I'm on trial for murdering was a wife and mother. A mother to a two-year-old, and a sixteen-year-old. Both girls. And that teenage daughter is staring at me like I'm the devil himself.

As much as I want to shrink away, I also want to scream at her, tell her I'm innocent, that the real killer's still out there, roaming free.

Of course, I can't do any such thing. I've been thoroughly prepped on courtroom etiquette, and yelling out to the murder victim's family won't go well for me. So, I keep my mouth shut.

That doesn't stop my eyes from constantly finding hers. Even though they're filled with hatred, the intense passion within their depths captivates me.

When I'm returned to my holding cell, I beg for paper and a pencil. And I do something I dismissed when soccer became my life. There's no soccer for an accused killer. There is, however, plenty of time to get creative.

Now, I sketch on the crumpled piece of paper. And as I draw, I disappear. Time vanishes. The cell dissolves. All the fear and hurt and turmoil evaporates. All I'm left with are the strokes of my pencil and the image taking form.

When I'm finished and I snap back to reality, her eyes stare into mine. Although the image is black and white, there's no mistaking the utter disdain I've captured, the loathing that tears at my heart.

It doesn't matter. Whether she hates me or not, I've found a way to escape this nightmare. *She's* given me a way.

Over the course of my trial, through all the so-called evidence presented to the judge and jury, I find myself watching that beautiful girl. All. The. Time. When she glances my way, our eyes clash. And every time, I feel like a piece of my soul's being sliced away.

But I can't stop myself. I've even found a word for her. Compelling. She *is* the definition of that word. She's evoked my interest, my attention, my admiration in a powerful, irresistible way.

I think I might be obsessed. How can I not be? She's my escape, my inspiration.

Her hatred of me is a lifeforce burning within her.

While I sit here feeling dead inside.

Occasionally, I catch sight of such sorrow in her eyes, I can't look at her. Although my grief began a month before hers, it's only intensified with the trial and the loss of my father's belief in me. I need my mother now more than ever, but she'll never be here for me ever again. So, I force myself to look away from Jamie Evans before her heartbreak infects me. I don't want to cry. I need to be strong. I need to be like her.

Throughout the trial, she hears all the damning evidence. The prosecution's ability to make up lies spears dread into my soul while the jury eats every word up as if they're watching a movie.

When the truth is revealed, Jamie Evans will see that we're the same. We're both victims of whoever killed her mother. In a way, I'm jealous. At least she has somewhere to direct her anger. And she's certainly taken advantage of that.

As the days blur, her passionate hatred of me grows into something utterly inspiring. If she can be so zealous about despising me, then I can be just as determined about maintaining my innocence.

When I speak to my lawyer and demand I take the stand and tell my side of the story, he shoots me down, stating in no uncertain terms that I'll be thrown to the wolves. I guess that means I'll be ripped apart by the prosecution. I've relented, but every day after, when I look at that girl, I'm ashamed of myself for letting someone else hold my future in their hands. But what can I do about it? Nothing. Except rely on the professional advice of my lawyer.

The shame of not being able to fight for myself doesn't stop me from watching her. Every time her eyes meet mine, I commit another detail to memory, searing every component into my brain until I can lie in my cell and see them floating above me in the darkness.

I've noticed that her father's attendance has dwindled to non-existent. Yet she's here every single day.

Even when she's all alone, her strength and conviction never waver.

I'm probably deluded, probably latching onto anything I can, but I believe I know who she is on the inside. Simply from observing her body language. And those eyes.

One day I'll change that loathing into something else. Something warm and forgiving.

One day, I'll tell her what she surely must be wondering about her mother's last moments.

As soon as the justice system works its magic.

Because I have faith.

Faith that innocent people don't go to prison.

Chapter 7

Jamie

AFTER ALMOST A year of waiting, the day of closing submissions has finally arrived.

Alone yet again, I seat myself in the gallery and glance around at the others here to gawk. As the trial progressed, Dad's presence had ebbed away until he couldn't bear to attend court. I suppose today isn't the verdict, but his excuse that his employer thinks he's had too much time off work feels like a lie. If he'd told me he was taking Anika out of daycare to look after her himself, I wouldn't have minded so much. But when I need him most, he's not here for me, or her, and that hurts.

When he *was* here, I'd noticed he refused to look at Gavin Lake. I figured, if he took one look at the killer in the dock, he'd leap over the small barrier and murder the guy right there in front of everyone.

Speaking of the devil, the Corrective Services officer leads the vile arsehole into the courtroom and deposits him in the dock.

As they have every day of the trial, his eyes instantly find mine. And once again, I glare daggers at him. He stares back like he truly believes he's innocent, and it drives me wild with fury. Worse still, he's a brilliant actor.

When he looks at me in a certain way, I almost believe him. The devastating pain and utter despair in his eyes occasionally slip through my armour of hatred and tear at my heart. Pathetic.

He's doing it right now. It doesn't come across like he's feeling sorry for himself because he got caught. It comes across as if he's sorry for *me*. Like he empathises with my loss. Even my anger. Which makes no sense, since he's the cause of it all.

Wrenching my gaze from his, I stare straight ahead, ashamed of myself for feeling anything but rage toward him. Still, I feel his eyes on me, just like I have every day. What he hopes to accomplish, I don't know. Though his staring doesn't seem threatening, I hate it. But I don't let that keep me away. There's no way on earth I'd let him deter me from being here. I'm not just here for myself, I'm here for Mum.

After the thug's lawyer raves on with a bunch of lies, the prosecutor addresses the jury. I tune into him, my gaze sliding over to the killer himself. I don't care if he stares at me, I want to see his reactions to everything the prosecutor says.

"Let's begin with what the defence has presented. The word of the accused. The word of a killer, a man whose own father testified against him. That is all they have. Nothing else."

Gavin Lake's jaw clenches, his eyes briefly skittering over to the prosecutor as the man strides closer to the jury.

"Now, let's look at the actual evidence. You all saw the footage from the security guard's vehicle. The accused kneeled over the victim, one hand on the lethal weapon, the other strangling her. He then tried to flee the scene. The accused was covered in the victim's blood and his fingerprints were the only prints found on the murder weapon. All compelling evidence, none of which can be denied. On top of that, we have motive."

The murderer stares into my eyes, pleading with me. It's so ridiculous, I almost laugh. It's like he thinks the evidence against him is a lie. But he's the only liar in this room.

"The accused had a violent altercation with his father over his dissatisfaction with his father's new relationship. Clearly in a rage, the accused obtained a weapon from the kitchen before leaving. Upon seeing the victim outside his family home, the angry young man lashed out, ending the life of an innocent woman, leaving behind a grieving husband and two motherless children. This is an open and shut case, ladies and gentlemen. There is no reasonable doubt here."

When Gavin Lake shakes his head in denial, I want to scream. It's not enough that he'd killed my mother, but he then had the audacity to drag our family through this hell? If he'd just pled guilty to begin with, this trial wouldn't have taken place. I never would have laid eyes on him. Though, truthfully, I needed to see the monster who killed my mother. I need a picture of him in my head, an image I can call upon to keep my hatred for him alive.

The next morning, as I sit in the gallery, Detective Reid seats himself beside me. At least I'm not alone.

Then the jury foreperson announces their decision.

Guilty on all counts.

Utter relief washes through me. Although sentencing might not take place for a few weeks, I've done my research. He should get sentenced to life imprisonment with a non-parole period of twenty years.

I find Gavin Lake's pitiful face and glare at him. Chin trembling, he stares back. When the Corrective Services officer approaches him, he shakes his head, tears brimming in his eyes.

Good.

The officer indicates for him to step down from the dock.

The moment his foot touches the floor, he charges toward the low railing separating the public gallery from the rest of the courtroom.

Suddenly he's right in front of me, leaning over, his eyes locked with mine. I gasp and draw back, clutching at Detective Reid's arm.

"I didn't do this!" the killer shouts. "I didn't take her from you! I would never—"

Reid shoves him back into the officer, who twists Gavin Lake's arm behind his back and takes him down to the floor as the judge calls for order.

Heart thundering, I stand on trembling legs as the officer cuffs him, then yanks him to his feet. As he's marched roughly to the exit for the guilty, he looks over his shoulder. Right at me. My gut twists at the sincerity in his eyes, at the tears streaming down his face.

But I refuse to be fooled by him. Instead, I give him the only smile he'll ever see from me. I know it doesn't reach my eyes, but I force it anyway. As soon as I do, I feel nasty, cruel even. But it's him who should feel that way, not me. He's the one who's hurt me, my family. He's the one who keeps hurting us by refusing to admit what he did.

"The killer's still out there!" he pleads. "You have to believe me!"

Then the door closes behind them, and he's gone from the courtroom. And from my life.

The killer's still out there.

How stupid does he think I am?

When the pain of my nails digging into my palms registers, my knees buckle, and my butt hits the seat I'll never occupy again. Detective Reid places a comforting hand on my shoulder, but I can't bring myself to look at him. It's finally over. I've spent so much time in this courtroom, the lawyers and court officials have become so familiar. But just like them, Reid will leave here and forget I exist.

While the courtroom slowly empties, I sit motionless, trying to figure out what to do now. I'd thought Gavin Lake's conviction would somehow, finally, make him admit his guilt. But he's holding onto his innocence tighter than ever, and the verdict hasn't taken away any of my pain either.

Instead of relief and a sense of justice, I'm numb.

Without the distraction of the trial, reality rushes in.

Am I capable of being a mother to my sister? With almost no help from Dad, I've cared for her for almost a year, and it's been anything but easy. She's only three now. There's fifteen more years to get through before she's an adult.

Fifteen years of a life I didn't sign up for.

I'm an unqualified mother to a toddler I didn't give birth to. I haven't even had sex for fuck's sake. My carefree teenage years are over. I'll never get them back. Time stolen from a life I'll never know.

Being here today should have felt like freedom. Instead, I've been shackled to my own prison sentence.

All because of Gavin Lake.

Fifteen Years Later

Chapter 8

Jamie

AS EVERYONE FILES out of the courtroom for the lunch break, I rise and grab my laptop from the bar table, place it in its leather satchel, and leave.

Finding a table in the corner of my regular café on the next street over, I take out my phone and power it up while I wait for someone to take my order.

The trial I'm working on is going well, putting me in a good enough mood to treat myself to a cupcake for dessert. Though lately, the career I've worked and sacrificed so hard for appears to be losing its glossy sheen. Recently, one of the partners in the firm I've been with for the past seven years has brought his ick-factor son into the fold. The sleaze has tried to crack onto me more than once, so now my days in the office are spent avoiding the creep. Because, apparently, he doesn't take no for an answer, even though I've politely made it clear I'm not interested.

But that's only added to the real reason I'm doubting my chosen career. Having to see the photographic evidence and read about the depraved things people do to each other, in detail, day after day, no longer sparks a fire inside me. It extinguishes it. I'm beginning to consciously acknowledge the unwelcome fact that I might be burning out, that being bombarded with the worst aspects of human nature may very well be darkening my life in a way that borders on unhealthy.

Looking up, jealousy punches me in the gut as the bright, happy waitress practically bounces over to my table. Lucky her. I'd like to feel that carefree and joyful again. Last time I remember that sort of happiness was before Mum's death.

After the waitress takes my order, I check my phone. There's one missed call from a number I don't recognise—no doubt scammers—and one message from Anika telling me she won't be home for dinner tonight. Now that she's eighteen, this is becoming a regular occurrence. For the most part, I don't mind. Why should she stay home with me and Dad? I'll be working and he'll watch TV all night and ignore her like he always does. If I had the chance to relive my teenage years without the weight of all this responsibility, I'd be out every chance I got.

Anika's quite the party girl, and she's tested my limits to no end while raising her. She's never been the type to willingly bend to authority. Which is why it came as quite the shock when she announced she wanted to become a police officer. After she finished her higher school certificate last year, she snagged a job at a local pizza restaurant with no idea what she wanted to do with her life. University wasn't for her, apparently. I suppose witnessing the amount of time I had to put into my studies while raising her, and forsaking a social life, may have put her off.

These days, she's at the gym every chance she gets, training for Session Two at the Police Academy. She hasn't even started Session One yet, which involves sixteen weeks of study via an online course. It's the most committed I've seen her about anything. Not that I particularly like the idea of her being a cop. As a criminal lawyer, I see the horrors the police are hit with daily. I'd prefer she wasn't exposed to that sort of trauma. But she's an adult now, so there's nothing I can do to stop her. Despite my misgivings, I'm incredibly proud of her.

Letting out a long sigh, I switch from messages to my personal emails.

And my heart stops.

Waiting for me in bold lettering, is an email from the State Parole Authority.

I don't want to open it, don't want to deal with it in any way. I already know what it'll say. There's only one reason they're contacting me.

Heart hammering against my ribs, I press my finger to the email and keep it held to the screen, as if removing it will set off a landmine. But, like stepping on a landmine, I'm already screwed. Mouth dry, I remove my finger. The email opens and my eyes fly over the familiar words. Sure enough, just like last year, Gavin Lake is applying for parole.

His sentence for murdering my mother came to twenty years. With an eighteen-year non-parole period. Problem is, as I learnt last year, prisons are full to overflowing, so a lot of convicted criminals are able to apply for parole earlier than their initial mandatory sentence.

My mood plummets as the waitress places a black coffee to the side of my laptop. Hands shaking, that familiar rush of rage bubbles to the surface. Why do I have to go through this again?

Last year, I opposed the killer's application, and it worked. He'd failed and remained locked away. My mother isn't walking around free, so why should he?

And now he's trying again? Will this be my life for the next few years? For the last decade and a half, I've had no reason to think about him, so I didn't. Well, maybe sometimes his face flashes into my mind, along with the last words he ever said to me. But I banish such thoughts almost the instant I recognise them.

"Hey," a deep, gentle voice says from beside me.

I look up to find Peter Pritchard, an Internal Affairs officer, close friend and mentor, peering down at me.

"Mind if I sit?" he asks, his usually friendly face creased with worry. He doesn't wait for a reply before he slips onto the chair opposite.

Giving him a forced smile, I take a sip of my coffee in an effort to compose myself. I met Pete on my very first case as a lawyer for the prosecution. He'd been a detective back then and his help with nailing the accused had been invaluable. Since then, we always take time to stay in touch.

The wrinkles in his forehead deepen as he gazes at me with those friendly, curious eyes. At around sixty-five or so, he's probably well overdue for retirement, but seems in no hurry to get there. He also hasn't been taking care of his health since his wife died a few years ago, evidenced by his belly rubbing against the edge of the table.

"I know for a fact, that look on your face has nothing to do with your current case. Word is, you're annihilating the defence."

I shrug as I move my laptop to the seat beside me to give the waitress room to set down my salad and cupcake.

"How's your father doing?" Pete asks when I glance his way.

"He's fine." I don't tell him that I've noticed Dad going to bed a lot earlier than usual lately. He's not eating much either, which probably explains why he's so tired. I've also noticed the whites of his eyes are a strange, faint mustard colour. Of course, I've questioned him about it, but he says he's been to the doctor and everything's fine. I'm not quite sure I believe him, but all I can do is keep an eye on him.

"Well? What's up?" Pete asks.

I let out a sigh. "He's up for parole. Again." I don't need to elaborate. Pete knows who I'm talking about.

He rubs his chin and leans forward. "It's been a year already?"

I nod as I pick up a fork and move cherry tomatoes around amongst the lettuce and cucumber. "Feels like yesterday," I mumble.

He nods with sympathy. "You going to oppose it again?"

"What I want is to forget about him." I let the fork clang against the bowl. "It's funny … when you think it's all gone away, it's really just lurking around the edges, waiting to stab you in the heart again."

Pete nods, plucks a cherry tomato from my bowl and pops it in his mouth.

"Hey!"

He shrugs. "We both know you hate raw tomatoes." After he finishes chewing, he says, "Maybe the only way to put Gavin Lake behind you is to confront him head on."

"Don't go getting all old and wise on me."

He huffs out a laugh. "Unfortunately, and fortunately, both of those things are true."

"What're you thinking?" I ask, curious.

"Have you heard of Restorative Justice? It's a program the government developed a while back."

"Sounds familiar, but I've never looked into it."

He steals a slice of cucumber this time. If he goes for my cupcake, he's a dead man.

"Well," he says as he swallows, "it's for people like you who've been affected by a criminal offence. And it's for the offender. You can correspond through letters or meet face-to-face."

I screw up my nose at the thought of seeing Gavin Lake again. I want to wipe him from my memory, not bring him to life.

"I don't see the point," I tell him, all too aware that he just eyed my cupcake. With the mood I'm in, salad might not be what I want, but that cupcake is definitely what I need.

"The point is, while it's not for everyone, it does have a great track record of helping both the victim and the offender understand each other's perspective."

Anger flashes through me. Even Pete doesn't get it. "I don't care what his perspective is."

"Fair enough, but he might be able to give you more than you realise, Jamie."

I stare down at my salad, then push it across the table at him. "Elaborate."

Instead of digging in, he keeps talking. "He'll have a chance to express his remorse, and hopefully, give you a sincere apology. I know you don't think it'll mean anything, but I've seen it happen. Giving the offender a chance to make amends for the harm he's caused you and your family might mean more than you think."

Picking up a fork, Pete jabs at the salad and takes a mouthful. As he chews, I let his words simmer while I imagine looking at Gavin Lake when he finally admits what he did.

"What if he still maintains he's innocent?" I ask.

Pete considers my question for a moment. "Then I guess you've lost nothing. You'll just be where you are now. But if it goes the other way … it might help you move on. You're an intelligent woman, Jamie. I believe it's worth a shot. Have a think about it. If you're interested, I can help."

I nod, then eye my cupcake before glancing at my watch.

"Okay," I barely manage above a whisper. Grabbing the cupcake, I take a bite, letting the icing ooze between my teeth and coat my tongue in an effort to dislodge the discomfort that always accompanies thoughts of Gavin Lake.

"Damn," Pete mutters. "I was hoping I'd put you off that little treat."

"Nice try."

"Worth a shot." He winks and digs into my salad.

That night, while I eat Chinese take away and try unsuccessfully to concentrate on another brief, I give Pete's words serious consideration. My stomach twists at the thought of facing Gavin Lake after all this time. But if I oppose his release again, I'll be right back here in a year. That thought makes me nauseous.

I suppose I could do the Restorative Justice program via letters, but I don't like the idea. One, it'll draw out the whole process, and I'll probably develop an ulcer waiting for a reply. Two, if he writes something I don't like, I want to be able to look him in the eye and tell him exactly what I think right there and then, not in a letter that'll take time to get to him and drive me insane while I wait for a reply.

Best to rip the Band-Aid off fast.

Suddenly fired up, I decide that if my mother's killer wants parole, he can damn well look me in the eye and witness the ripple effect of his choices right up close.

Slamming the chopsticks down with resolve, I grab my phone and head out the front door and down the street where Dad can't hear me. Then I ring Pete and ask what I need to do.

He's pleased with my decision, but I'm not so sure it'll do what he thinks it will.

Chapter 9

Gavin

THE LETTER CAME ten days ago.

Holding it delicately, I run my fingertips over the lined white paper, its texture now resembling velvet, the fibres upright and soft after repeating the same action over and over again. The paper remains completely silent as my fingers work on muscle-memory, unfolding it for the one-hundredth or ten-thousandth time.

I know every intimate detail about the page I hold. Every crease, every word, every letter.

She wrote to me. I can still barely believe it as I stare down at her crisp, cursive style. It's simple and to the point. And it fills my soul with hope and dread in equal measure.

Gavin Lake,

I wish to request a session with you under the government's Restorative Justice program. Face to face. Unless you oppose my request, a meeting will be arranged as soon as possible.

Jamie Evans

Of course I accepted. For two reasons: To tell her what really happened that night so she can understand that her mother's killer is still out there. And to see her again. In the flesh.

In less than half an hour, I'll be in a room with her.

Apart from the trial, this feels like the most important moment of my life. No one ever listened to me before. No one believed me. No one cared. Soon, Jamie Evans will be my captive audience. And once I'm face to face with her, I'm certain I can convince her of the truth. As long as she looks at me, she'll see it.

She has to.

Folding her note into the small square that fits neatly in my pocket, I lie back on my bed and stare at the two sketches of her eyes taped to the wall. Eyes I've sketched whenever I felt the struggle of injustice bubbling to the surface, making me want to lose control and destroy everything. I'm positive, if it wasn't for those arresting eyes, I might have actually committed murder in here. As time passed, I began drawing those eyes in different ways. In ways I wanted to see her look at me. I drew them with sympathy. I drew them with sorrow. And I drew them with love.

She's saved me so many times, yet she has no idea. I don't care that she hates me. It's a hatred based on a lie.

Today, that lie ends.

I stare at the first drawing and, next to that, the most recent. Hate and love. Side by side.

I can't wait to see how she looks at me today. When I tell her the truth.

As I imagine her eyes locking with mine, the only other reason I'm still alive walks into our cell.

Benny Carter. My long-term cellmate. He's an old, cranky goat on the outside, but inside, his heart knows no depths. At sixty, he's been in prison for almost forty years. First for killing his stepfather after coming home to find the bastard beating his mother, then again for killing an inmate only a year before he was due for release for his first conviction.

He took me under his wing when I was transferred from remand to Goulburn's supermax security prison after my sentencing. He taught me how to survive without ending up like him. And he became my surrogate father. Benny's done more for me than my own ever did. For one, he believes me.

Out of all the inmates who say they're innocent, he actually believes me. For that reason alone, I'd do anything for the guy.

Only thing is, Benny's the type who won't let me. I've wanted to step in and protect him with my fists on many occasions, but he's always refused, giving me that look that tells me I'll be on his shit-list if I even think about it. So, I've listened to him, I've taken his advice, and I've managed to stay clean and out of trouble right up to this moment.

"You swoonin' over those bloody eyes again?" he asks, leaning against the doorjamb.

"There's no swooning going on. Unless, of course, you want me to move so you can take my spot."

He scoffs, but we both know I've caught him doing exactly that on a few occasions. Swooning. Nothing else. Thank fuck.

"How long 'til ya see the princess?" he asks.

Her visit today is one of the few things we don't agree on.

"Five, ten minutes."

"And ya still goin' ahead with that insanity of yours?"

"It's not insane. It's the truth."

We've had this discussion ever since I received her letter. But, apparently, here we go again.

"Not ta her, it's not," Benny reminds me for the hundredth time.

"Too bad."

Turning away from the sketches, I find Benny looming above me, his face deadly serious.

"You think, after sixteen years, she's gonna listen ta you, nod her head, and thank ya? That, my friend, is fuckin' delusional. As in, *insane*."

"It's my only chance," I remind him. Again.

"If that intelligent brain can absorb anythin' through that thick skull of yours, it's this … She doesn't give a fuck about the truth. All she wants is ta know the cunt who killed her mother has paid the price and he's sorry. You don't act all remorseful when ya in that room with her, she's gonna walk away hurt and gunnin' for ya at your next parole hearin'."

"I know. You've told me all this before, remember?"

"I'm tellin' ya again, because even though ya got your degree in that psycho-babble-bullshit, ya still don't fuckin' get it."

"I'm not letting this opportunity go to waste. I never got to tell my side on the stand. No one's ever heard it. Today, *she's* going to hear it. And I don't give a shit whether she likes it or not. The truth isn't about how it makes us feel." I don't usually lie to Benny, but now I've just told him two lies in one breath.

I do care about her reaction to the truth.

And I know the truth can really fuck shit up.

"You don't wanna get outta here, is that it?" Benny presses.

"Of course I fucking do. But she needs to know what really happened. She's living a lie. The real killer got away with it. Why wouldn't she want to know that?"

"Cause all she wants is closure. She didn't request this Restorative Justice crap ta listen to your side of things. She requested it so *she'd* feel better, not you. Why the fuck can't ya see that?"

As I open my mouth to argue with him, I slam it shut. Deep inside, I know he's right. Trying to convince her of the truth will probably sentence me to another year, but I don't think I can live with the truth locked away any longer. If I follow Benny's advice and show remorse, I might gain my freedom, but will I really be free if everyone still believes I'm guilty?

"Let's go, Lake." Raising my head, I find Janson, one of the friendlier correctional officers, standing in the doorway.

I rise and look the best man I've ever known in the eye. "The truth's about to come out."

As I skirt around him, Benny grabs my bicep and squeezes. A little too fucking hard.

"Don't do it, Gav. Ya deserve ta get outta here. Tell her you're sorry, you regret it, you're as remorseful as fuck. Stick to the plan."

The plan.

The fucking plan I've lied to him about for years. But I can't let him know that.

I wrench out of his grasp, take a step back and shake my head. When I walk out of the cell, he yells after me, "When have I ever steered ya wrong?"

Never.

Fucking arsehole. Just has to rub it in, doesn't he?

Following Janson down the metal steps and through the prison, a war rages within me. I know Benny's right. But I also know, as insane as it is, I need to do this for my own sanity, my own integrity.

A year ago, I applied for my first parole hearing. I refused to admit I committed the murder I'd been charged with. Which in turn meant I refused to accept responsibility. On top of that, a statement from an anonymous victim of the crime demanded I remain incarcerated.

I'm certain that anonymous victim was Jamie Evans.

I never saw the same passionate hatred in her father's eyes the few times he showed up at my trial. I'm pretty certain he wouldn't make an effort to keep me in here.

It was her.

After Janson leads me into the room, I greet Chris, the counsellor I became close with while studying for my degree, and take a seat so I'm facing the door. He's already briefed me on how these meetings usually go. He'll only get involved if things get heated, otherwise, he'll simply sit and listen. He has no idea what I'm about to tell Jamie Evans. Though he's a great guy, I'm sure he'd never allow this meeting to take place if he knew. He doesn't believe I'm innocent either.

But I've made up my mind. Even if it means failing my upcoming parole hearing, I'm going to blast her with the truth and pray that she can find it somewhere within herself to believe me.

When I hear the door unlock with a loud clack, my pulse goes haywire. As my breathing accelerates, sweat prickles my skin, my mouth desperate to spit out my story.

I sit up straight and run a hand over my bald head, suddenly remembering I don't look like the nineteen-year-old kid she stared daggers at in a courtroom long ago.

I look like a scary motherfucking criminal.

The door swings inward. Janson enters first, eyeing me as he holds the door open and waits.

Then in she walks, heels clicking on the lino floor, shoulders squared, her gaze focused on Janson. I devour her in an instant. That fiery auburn hair pulled back in a tight ponytail, the professional pencil skirt and silk top hugging the curves of her figure to perfection. I avoid her legs, because, hell, I'm already losing the ability to think. But I might be too late.

Even from here, her scent wafts over me, filling every cell with the sweet, flowery fragrance of her perfume, awakening something deep inside me that's been dormant for a long damn time. That distinctive feeling of coming *alive.*

Jesus. I'd forgotten all about the amazing scent of a woman, and my body's responding like a fucking freight train.

As I sit there, drawing in a deep breath, she turns.

The moment her eyes lock with mine, I know I'm fucked.

Chapter 10

Jamie

WHEN I STEP past the guard and lay eyes on Gavin Lake for the first time in fifteen years, I freeze.

That nineteen-year-old boy isn't here, sitting in this cold, sterile room.

The man before me is truly terrifying.

Then he stands, by way of being polite, I think, but it only reinforces his menacing presence. At around six-two or three, the combination of his bald head, unkept beard and the muscles stretching his prison shirt, reveals an ominous beast born of nightmares.

I fix my gaze on the table separating us and stride toward the chair waiting for me, the click of my heels on the linoleum completely out of place. I probably should have worn jeans and runners. But, of course, I'd needed to make the lie I'd told my father about going to work convincing. He most definitely would not approve of me being in the same room as the man who killed his wife.

Determined not to let Gavin Lake see my reaction to his appearance, I greet the counsellor sitting at the head of the table, slide out a chair and take a seat. Only then does the monster sit.

Does he think he can fool me by acting like a gentleman? Not a chance in hell. Though, by the looks of him, he might have come straight from there without a trace of bother.

Avoiding his eyes, I notice something out of place. Or, more accurately, the absence of something. I can't see a single tattoo on his bare head, neck or arms. Everything else about him screams cliché prisoner. Except for that little detail.

Maybe he's scared of needles.

I almost smile at the thought, then remind myself why I'm here and who it is I'm looking at.

As he settles in his chair, I meet his steady gaze.

The strangest sensation I've ever had washes over me. Those deep blue eyes seem to penetrate right through the steadfast walls I've erected around myself. His stare leaves me completely and utterly exposed. If that isn't startling enough, I'm not uncomfortable at all. The intensity he's directing at me isn't hostility. In stark contrast to his appearance, it's filled only with kindness.

In fact, as I gaze into the depths of the monster I hate, a wave of calmness blankets me. I should shake it off, but I don't want to let it go. I want to hold onto it and wrap it around my whole body. Snuggle into it and fall into a deep, undisturbed sleep.

What the fuck is wrong with me?

And then I realise, it's simply because he's familiar. I may not have seen him in fifteen years, but those eyes haven't changed since the weeks I spent looking at them in that courtroom. That's all it is.

Placing my hands on the table, I clasp them in front of me. I've thought about how I should sit in this setting and decided on the partially closed off position. Plus, this way, he can't see my hands shake. Though, strangely, they're not doing any such thing.

With a slow, measured movement, he mirrors me. I feel like I should pull back a little, to keep more distance between us, but I don't. I won't give him the satisfaction of believing he's intimidating me.

His gaze finally breaks from mine, but he doesn't look away. Instead, he takes in my forehead, my hair, my nose and cheeks. I watch his eyes move lower, to my chin and throat. To my breasts. And up to my lips.

I suppress the urge to ask him if he's getting a good look, because I'm not so sure he's even aware that he's checking me out in the most obvious way.

Then he's looking into my eyes again and I discover that his previous compassion has been replaced with what I can only describe as a war of conflict so strong, it's almost tangible.

Something in me wants to calm him, wants to reach out and cover his hands with mine. I literally have to clench my fingers tighter to prevent them from doing just that.

Focus!

I drop my gaze to his mouth, then his throat. He swallows. As if it's me who's the intimidating one.

When I meet his gaze, he utters the first words I've heard from his mouth since he screamed that lie at me in the courtroom. The lie he's maintained all these years.

"How are you?"

Low and deep, his voice vibrates through the air, travels toward my body and enters. Once again there's a complete disconnect between the image of the man before me, and the gentleness and genuine care in his tone.

Brushing aside those ridiculous thoughts, I gather the anger that's been with me for sixteen years. "How do you think?" I snap.

If he's offended by my abrasiveness, he hides it well. Which pisses me off. I want to hurt him, make him crawl into a dark hole where he belongs.

Tilting my chin higher, I glare at him. He simply stares back, as if he has nothing to be ashamed of.

He shifts in his seat slightly, then runs a hand over his scrappy beard. "Stupid question," he mutters. "Well, I'm eager to hear why you wanted to meet with me. Please, go ahead."

Like he's giving me *permission*. I glance at the councillor, who simply nods.

"I want you to know how you affected the family members of the woman you killed," I tell him.

He glances at the empty chair beside me, making it clear there are no other family members here. "You mean *you*," he clarifies.

Every muscle in my body clenches. I had this crazy idea that I could distance myself somewhat if I made this about my family, but I won't let him intimidate me. Of course this is personal.

"Yes."

"Did you get my letters?" he asks.

Confused, I try to reel my brain back from what I expected him to say. "What letters?"

"I wrote to you when I first came here."

"No, I didn't get any letters." If he's telling the truth, what the hell happened to them? I suppose it doesn't matter, because I already know what they'd say. And I would have ripped them to shreds.

Studying his face, I see disappointment.

Well, boo-hoo. Fuck him and his stupid letters.

"So that's it?" I ask. "That's all you have to say?"

A physical change comes over him. I watch his throat bob when he swallows, his shoulders slump, the silent exhale that collapses his chest.

He shifts in his chair, hands clenching into fists, then unclenching, his brow furrowing. After a moment, he brings his fingers to the bridge of his nose and closes his eyes. His body starts to vibrate slightly, the result, I realise, of his knee bouncing up and down under the table. Whatever's going on inside his head seems to be a battle. But what do I care?

Is he trying to make me feel sorry for him? Well, fuck him. "You killed my mother! Say something!"

I glare at him, waiting for him to deny it, to make every bullshit excuse under the sun. Because I know it's coming. I see it in his eyes. He truly believes he did nothing wrong.

Nothing!

Taking a deep breath, he focuses on my hands. Too late, I realise my knuckles are white, my fingertips bright red from the crushing force I'm inflicting upon them.

His eyes meet mine, and this time, all I see is pain.

"I'm sorry," he says quietly. "I'm so, so sorry."

Something inside me shifts ever so slightly. "For what?" I almost whisper.

He swallows, his gaze never leaving mine. "I'm sorry about your mother's death. I'm sorry for all the pain you've gone through … for all the pain your family's suffered. I'm sorry she doesn't get to see your wedding, or your sister's. I'm sorry she'll never meet her grandchildren. I'm sorry your father doesn't get to grow old with her. I'm sorry for everything that the loss of her life has taken from you."

Tears well in my eyes. This isn't the man who took my mother's life. A boy who only lives in my memory did that. But, I remind myself, he *was* that boy. His actions as that angry, violent teenager still have the same consequences today as they did then.

"Please, Miss Evans," he continues, "know that I understand, and know that I'm sorry for all of it from the bottom of my soul."

Tears flow freely over my face now, scorching a path I wish he never had the privilege of seeing, but here we are. And somehow, I don't care. Let him see. After all this time, he needs to see.

But that glimpse is all he's getting. Slowly, I unclench my tangled fingers and rise, the scraping of the chair loud in the silence.

I thought I'd want more, thought I'd want details, thought I'd want to know the one thing about my mother's death only he knows. But I don't. I can't. His apology needs to be enough. I have to put all of this behind me.

Swallowing through my tight throat, I manage to croak out, "Okay," before I turn and hurry to the door. As I pull down on the handle, I can't help but look back at him one last time.

And I'm shocked to see tears sliding down his cheeks. The beast is crying. Not sobbing or shuddering. Just weeping tears, his expression and body motionless. It actually hurts to see him in so much pain. I wonder if it comes anywhere close to the hurt my mother felt when he plunged that knife into her chest.

I hold myself together through the prison and out into the bright sunshine of the parking lot. When I slide into the warmth of the car, I start it up, crank the radio and rest my forehead on the steering wheel. Taking gulping breaths, I refuse to cry. Gavin Lake has finally taken responsibility for what he did. That's what I've wanted for so long, so why lose control now? I haven't cried over anything since the night Detective Jarrod Reid came to our door with the devastating news.

Lifting my head, I stare out at the beautiful day and let my visit with *him* wash over me. He understood. He'd clearly thought about what he'd taken from us, from me. And I know without a doubt that he meant every word he said. And I hate that I feel like a weight has been lifted from my shoulders. I hate that seeing Gavin Lake again is the cause of that, that *his* words have done that for me, even though that's the reason I came here.

Because now, I realise, I want to hold onto the hate I've fed off all these years. I want to hold onto it because it gave me the drive to become the person I am today. It gave me the determination to raise my sister when my father was incapable. It's given me the drive to make sure criminals like Gavin Lake are locked away, keeping society that little bit safer. I want to hold onto that hate because it's kept me stoic and put together. It's kept me safe, kept people at arm's length, never allowing anyone to truly know me, and most certainly never love me.

I love that hate.

I don't want to lose it. It's so much a part of me, I don't know who I am without it.

But I feel it slipping away like a breath on frigid air.

I refuse to let it go. It's mine. It's *me.*

I remind myself that only one thing changed today.

He's finally said he's sorry.

That doesn't change the fact that he killed my mother. Do kind, understanding words wipe that away? Fuck, no.

As I sit there, not quite capable of driving yet, a breaking news story cuts through the music.

"The death toll from last night's high-rise apartment fire in The Rocks has unfortunately risen to seven. The devastating blaze started in the historical building situated beside the City View high-rise apartment complex in the early hours last—"

I shut off the radio, suddenly aware that a few stray tears have managed to leak down my face. Quickly wiping them away, I stare through the windscreen, seeing nothing. Instead, I imagine the terror the people in that building endured. The number of loved ones affected by their deaths. The utter devastation and the excruciating grief to come. And the sudden slap to the face that nothing is permanent, that life can change in an instant.

But I don't really have to imagine it. I know all about it.

I also know all about pushing it down and getting on with what needs to be done.

As I sit there and think about my sister starting her journey as an adult and the worry I've tried to ignore about my father's health, my hatred of Gavin Lake seems microscopic in the scheme of things.

I'm pretty damn sure the heartfelt victim's statement I submitted to the parole board last year kept him where he was meant to stay. If it wasn't for me, he could very well have been free a year ago. Without ever getting an apology out of him.

Sighing heavily, I lean into my seat and let the tension flow out of my body.

And I decide it's not worth the effort to fight him again. I already know it doesn't make me feel any better.

Besides, whether he's in prison or not, I can still hate him.

And I will.

To my dying day, he will be a black mark on my heart.

Chapter 11

Jamie

SLIDING MY LAPTOP into my bag, I head straight from the office to the hospital. Life now consists of work and spending every other spare moment with Dad.

My father's pancreatic cancer diagnosis came shortly after Gavin Lake's release from prison six months ago. At first, we were all in denial, positive the doctors had it wrong. But when Dad declined at an alarming rate, the truth had to be faced.

Anika's now almost finished Session Two of the compulsory four-month training course at the Police Academy down in Goulburn, which has left me alone to deal with Dad, who's barely holding on now. I don't blame Anika for one second. The timing couldn't be helped and there's no way I'd ever demand she stay home and risk her career.

Besides, why should she look after Dad when he's never cared about her? That wall he erected between himself and Anika has never come down. Although he changed after Mum's death, he's never treated me with the coldness he's projected at my sister. On more than one occasion, it's crossed my mind that he's only remained caring toward me because he needed me to stay to look after his other daughter.

Even if that's true—and I don't know if it is—Dad's always had my back. He worked hard so I could attend a local university and get my law degree. By living at home, I remained the carer he needed me to be for Anika. I'd come home from uni and collect her from school. Then I'd help with her homework and assignments, make sure she was fed and in bed at a reasonable hour before I finally lost myself in my studies.

With Dad working two jobs to support us, I suppose, in part, his relationship with Anika never deepened because he was hardly ever around.

I'd considered forgetting about uni and settling for a clerical job straight out of high school, but Dad wouldn't hear of it. Even after Mum's death, I poured myself into schoolwork as an escape, keeping near-perfect grades.

Parking at the hospital, I change my heels for runners, head straight to the cafeteria and grab a sandwich for dinner. With Anika gone, I don't see the point of going home to an empty house and cooking. One less thing to worry about.

Picking up my pace, I hurry into an empty elevator. I'm late tonight, which gives me only ten minutes with Dad before the nurses kick out all the visitors. Working for a large law firm in the city has its downsides. Like the expectation of long hours, despite what's going on in your personal life.

After weaving through the corridors, I enter Dad's room. As usual, he's asleep. Quietly putting down my handbag and sandwich, slip into the bathroom.

Even though I'm ashamed of myself, I hide in here for five minutes. Seeing him like this, having to deal with it alone, tears at my soul and takes all the energy I have left.

Staring in the mirror, I remind myself that I've got this. I'm tough. Nothing's beaten me down before and, as bad as this is, it's out of my control. I can't change it, can't stop it. I can only be here for him like he's been there for me. Besides, this is about him, not me. He needs the comfort of family. And I'm it.

After I wash my hands and emerge from the bathroom, I take his cool, bony hand and brush my thumb over the tissue-thin flesh.

"Jamie," he croaks, his throat raspy and dry.

From the bedside table, I pick up a bottle of water with a straw already in place, and press it to his parched lips. He sucks weakly, some of the water spilling from his mouth before I catch it with a tissue.

"Hey, Dad. How's that?"

He barely nods as he cracks an eye open with great effort.

"Jamie," he says again, this time a little easier.

I put aside the water and tighten my hold on his hand. "I'm right here."

His feeble fingers encircle mine. I vividly remember how tight he once gripped my hands when he'd twirl me around, when he taught me how to ride a bike, when he held my hand at Mum's funeral.

I want to cry, but refuse to give in. I'm strong. He doesn't need to see tears, he needs my strength. Breaking down will only hurt him, worry him, make him feel like he's abandoning me. He doesn't need that. There'll be time for tears … after.

Even though he's still right here in front of me, I swallow down the grief welling inside and say, "I'm sorry, Dad."

"For what?"

"That this is happening to you. It's not fair."

He gives his head a slight shake. "It's okay. I deserve it."

I frown at him, confused. But he's already asleep, his breaths rhythmic.

I deserve it?

What the hell is he talking about? He doesn't *deserve* this cruel disease. He's the last person who deserves to suffer like this after all he's been through.

"Dad?" I squeeze his hand but get nothing in return.

After kissing his cheek, I stop at the nurses' station and speak to one of the regulars.

"His obs aren't looking too good, I'm afraid," she tells me.

I blink at her. I should be prepared for this news. But can anyone ever be? "You think he's getting close?"

Her kind eyes find mine and she nods. "Maybe a few more days."

In the car on the way home, the urge to bawl my eyes out almost overwhelms me. Still, I hold on. He's not gone yet. And I'm not a crier. What's the point? It solves nothing.

Once home, I take a few bites of the hospital sandwich before throwing it in the bin. Then I get in a staring match with my phone. I want to call Anika. I need her here with me.

But I don't. She's only a few weeks away from finishing her training. The last thing she needs is to come home. Besides, Dad hasn't asked for her once. The only time they interacted was when I put my foot down and demanded it. Even then, they had nothing to say to one another. I did all the talking between them, telling Dad how amazing she was, what a great police officer she would make. I frown, trying to remember him asking her questions. Trying to remember him even looking at her.

I can't picture it.

Apparently, they don't need each other. It's only me who needs both of them.

The next day, I arrive at work early, thankful I don't have to appear in court. When I return to my desk with a fresh coffee, my phone rings.

I stare at it with dread, hating that it announces who's calling. Nothing good can come from taking this particular call. But I can't ignore it.

"Jamie Evans," I answer.

"Jamie, it's Renee in the palliative care ward. I think you should come in. Your father … he's … well, he's in quite a state, refusing his meds until he sees you."

I'm there in half an hour and what I walk into leaves me shocked. Dad's sweating, his breathing laboured, eyes wide. When they lock onto me, he sinks into the pillows with utter relief. Then his shaking arm lifts slightly and beckons me to his side.

He glances over my shoulder. "Go!" he almost shouts, startling not only me, but the nurse who's lingering at my back.

I nod at her as I grasp his hand, surprised by the strength of his grip compared to yesterday. For a brief moment, I wonder if the nurses are wrong. How can he be this strong if he's so close to death?

Then I remember that pain can do strange things to the mind and body, and if he hasn't had his medication, God only knows how much he's hurting.

"Dad, what's happening? Why won't you take the drugs? You know—"

"Listen," he interrupts, his voice just above a whisper now, all the strength of a few moments ago leaching away. "Closer," he says, tugging weakly at my hand.

I lean down, lowering my head until we're almost touching.

"I have … to tell … you," he breathes. Leaning closer still, his grip on my hand tightens as he whispers to me in fragmented sentences. Words that I want to believe are said because he's in a pain induced delirium. Words that can't be true. Words that devastate.

"I'm … so … sorry," he gasps.

Heart hammering, skin prickling, the shock of his words sends nausea rolling through my stomach as I wrench my hand from his grip.

Gasping for air, he stares at me, and for the second time in my life, I see tears spill from his almost dead eyes. Eyes that plead. Eyes that hold a truth I want nothing to do with. A truth I wish he'd never spoken.

Whirling around, I blindly flee, crashing into a nurse in the doorway.

"Oh, sorry," she says. "Are you okay?"

I nod numbly, desperate to get the fuck out of here before I fall apart.

"Do you think he'll take the pain meds now?" she asks.

"Give him everything you can."

Then I push past her and race for the public restrooms. As I slam through the door, sweat flashes over my skin and saliva rushes to my mouth. I don't even make it to a toilet. I throw up straight into the basin.

Twisting the tap, I squeeze my eyes shut and purge my mostly empty stomach. When everything's gone, only bile remains. After a few more painful retches, I cup water into my mouth, swirling and spitting it out before splashing my clammy face.

Once I'm sure the nausea has subsided, I grab a bunch of paper towels and hold them to my face as I breathe. In and out. In and out. Until the rhythm calms my trembling body. Only then do I lower my hands and look in the mirror.

I'm hot all over, but the face staring back at me is ghostly white. Except for the streaks of mascara beneath my eyes. Although my body isn't vibrating anymore, my hands shake as I reach into my handbag and find the makeup I keep inside.

When I step outside the bathroom, a nurse hurries around her desk and places a gentle hand on my arm.

"He needs you now," she says, before rushing off toward his room.

I remain rooted to the spot. Hesitating, I sway on my feet until my back connects with a cool wall. The urge to run surges through me so powerfully, I push off the wall and stride along the sterile corridor in the opposite direction.

After what Dad whispered in my ear, I should keep walking and never look back.

But I can't.

I stop dead in my tracks, then turn and head to his room.

Feeling like I'm on an ethereal plane where I'm completely numb, I stare at the shadow of a man who was once my father. He's not conscious. The pain meds have made sure of that, but something's changed. Not just physically. He doesn't seem to be here anymore.

His shallow breaths are a mechanical operation that has nothing to do with the man who once occupied his body.

The nurse's words come back to me. *He needs you now.* But does he? Or am I already too late? I wonder if he left the moment I walked out of his room.

Either way, I find myself holding his hand, squeezing and rubbing until his body tenses. With a gasp, he deflates on a final exhale.

And he's gone.

Forever.

Some part of me wants to place a kiss on his wrinkled forehead, while another demands I scream at him.

In the end, I do neither. I let the nurses take over and wait for the doctor to arrive and officially declare my father dead. I'm not sure what happens after that. It's only when I'm standing outside the hospital in the scorching midday sun that I come back to myself.

I haven't cried, and I don't think I will. Even if the urge comes, who would I be crying for? I didn't know the man in that hospital bed. How could I? For half of my life, he's lied to me. To Anika.

As heat penetrates the icy death inside me, my mind snags on something monumentally important. And refuses to let go.

I won't think about the man I once called Dad.

Instead, I'll focus on another man.

A man I no longer have the right to hate.

Chapter 12

Gavin

AFTER SLATHERING MY freshly popped toast with butter and a scraping of Vegemite, I turn it over, take a huge bite and let the salty explosion rest on my tongue for a moment before I chew. As much as I hate my new accommodation, I love the freedom to eat whatever I want, whenever I choose. Hot toast was a rarity in prison, but hot toast with real melty butter, that was non-existent.

Finished with another mind-numbing shift at the poultry factory, I'm home by lunchtime. Which is the sole thing I like about the only job I've secured in the six months since my parole. Although I'm not a fan of the 4am start, knock-off time makes up for it in spades.

Just as I pop the last bite of toast in my mouth, a sharp rap comes from the door. Confident it's Benny, who was released only a few weeks ago, I continue to chew as I swing the flimsy caravan door wide.

And almost choke.

A woman dressed for the corporate world—not this lowly caravan park filled with ex-cons on parole—stands in strappy high-heels two steps down from me. When a wolf whistle lets loose from another caravan, she turns her head in search of the source. But I don't. My attention remains pinned on her. The blazing sun highlights dark red notes in the few loose strands of hair that have made an escape from her severe ponytail. While her eyes aren't on me, I take in her large sunglasses and the fitted green business dress clinging to every curve of her body. When it ends several inches above her knees, my gaze drifts down her smooth, naked legs to pretty, manicured toes.

I shouldn't be checking her out, but fuck, I'm enjoying the view. She's hot, and the last time I'd been privileged enough to be in the vicinity of a sexy woman, had been at the Restorative Justice meeting.

Unfortunately, she's clearly got the wrong caravan.

Turning to face me again, I think she's looking me over, but I can't be sure with her eyes hidden by those large, impenetrable sunglasses.

"What?" I almost bark as I swallow the last of my toast.

"I was told this is where I'd find Gavin Lake."

Okay, so she *is* here for me. On edge, I'm unsure why someone like her is standing on my non-existent doorstep. One thing I do know, is it can't be for anything good.

Then she takes off her sunglasses and squints at me.

Holy *fuck*.

No wonder I think she's hot. I've *always* thought so.

Jamie Evans.

No doubt about it.

I should've known by the colour of her hair, but I've never seen it set ablaze in the sunlight.

"Miss Evans?" I ask, stunned.

Her eyes narrow in confusion. "How do you know my name?"

She doesn't recognise me. I shouldn't be surprised. Six months ago, she saw a prisoner with a shaved head and an unkept beard. That's who she's expecting. But I don't look like that guy anymore.

"Because I'm Gavin Lake," I tell her.

Her eyes widen with surprise. Then she stares into mine, searching, assessing, identifying. Shoving the sunglasses back on her face, she crosses her arms.

"Oh … I … ah … Sorry. Can we talk inside?"

Of all the people in the world, she's the last one I expected at my door. This is going to be anything but pleasant.

"Why're you here, Miss Evans?"

A wolf-whistle pierces the air again. Darting my gaze across the dirt track and grass that separates the caravans, I spot scum-of-the-earth Jake Fletcher sitting on his steps, dragging on a cigarette.

"Gotcha self a high-class hooker there, Lake?"

Shit.

Stiffening slightly, her fingers dig into her crossed arms. "I have some information I think you'll want to hear," she says quickly. "But I'd feel more comfortable talking to you privately."

The woman who's hated me for the past sixteen years, now wants to be alone with me in a cramped space? It makes no sense at all, but I suppose there's only one way to find out what she wants.

As I step back to let her in, Fletcher calls out, "Fuck her hard, man. I wanna see that tin-can rockin'."

Fucking prick.

Retreating to the kitchen, I lean my hip against the counter, hoping to God she puts my red face down to the stifling heat. As much as I've fantasised about fucking her hard—and every other possible way—I most certainly don't want her to know that.

She enters slowly, letting the door spring shut, heels clicking on the cheap linoleum as she takes a few steps inside. With the door closed, the dimness forces her to remove her sunnies.

I wait, and while I do, her uncertain eyes flit around the tiny space, taking in the bed behind me and the small table to the right. She shows no disgust, no reaction at all as far as I can tell. Apart from the way she's clutching her handbag to her stomach like it's some sort of barrier between us.

That delicious scent of Jasmine and spring reaches me as it fills the caravan, spiralling me back to my meeting with her six months ago. Awakening that feeling of coming alive after being dead inside for so long.

Then her gaze is on me, taking in my bare feet, khaki shorts, red t-shirt, my throat, my lips, and finally my eyes. She's never looked at me the way she is now, and this new look has all sorts of nerves jolting through my body and mind.

Worse still, I catch a tremble in her chin. Is she about to cry?

I clear my throat. "Are you okay?"

Her eyes quickly drop to my chest. "No … yes … actually, I have no idea."

I'm baffled by her response. She's always come across as self-assured, not this lost, bewildered woman before me. What can she possibly be here to say that has her so disconcerted?

"Would you like to take a seat?"

She quickly shakes her head, her chest expanding, then contracting before her eyes sweep up to mine.

"I know you're innocent," she says softly.

I wait for her to correct herself. Clearly, that came out wrong. But all she does is watch me.

"I'm sorry, Miss Evans. I'm not sure I understand—"

"I found out a few hours ago," she says, a noticeable quaver in her voice. "You're innocent."

I understand her words, but every ounce of my being rejects them. Continuing to stare at her, I wait for a punch line that'll allow me to make sense of what she's doing here.

"Say something," she says.

"Miss Evans, I don't know—"

"Please stop calling me that." She takes a step toward the table. I don't miss her slight wobble as she places a hand on the surface to steady herself. Then she slides onto the bench seat, puts her handbag aside and releases a long breath. "I think I do need to take that seat after all."

She places her palms on the table in what I presume is an effort to keep them from shaking. Something earth shattering's happened to her, and it has something to do with me.

As I take a seat across from her, the brush of my bare knees against hers sends a jolt of electricity straight to my dick. *Christ.* The first woman I've touched in sixteen years and it's Jamie

Evans. Repositioning myself, I break the contact. I need to get it to-fucking-gether.

"Miss— Jamie. As of a minute ago, there were only two people on this planet who believed in my innocence. Me, and the man I shared a cell with for fifteen years. Explain to me why you deserve a membership to our exclusive club," I say with a small quirk of my lips.

What the hell's wrong with me? Why the fuck am I making jokes? This is serious. Only, more than anything else in this moment, I want to make the incredibly sad woman across from me smile.

She doesn't.

"I don't just believe you're innocent. I know it to be a fact."

Refusing to get my hopes up, I sigh. "Okay. Why? How?"

There's that tremble in her chin again, and this time, tears pool in her eyes. I watch as she blinks fast, getting them under control before they can fall.

"I just heard a dying declaration." She takes a deep breath and stares at her hands. "He said he killed my mother."

The shock of her words rock me to the core. This time, there's no resistance, no disbelief. Someone confessed. "And you believe this person because?"

"Because he's my father … *was* my father."

I fucking knew *it.*

Her eyes meet mine again. We sit like that for a long moment, letting the weight of her words hang between us. And then it clicks.

"Wait a minute," I say. "Did your father die? *Today?*"

She nods. "But you're missing the point. You're innocent. And now that I know, something has to be done about—"

"Jamie," I interrupt. "Slow down. Let's back up a bit, okay?"

She releases a breath, her stiff shoulders drooping.

"It's only lunchtime, so tell me … where were you this morning?" I ask, hoping I can get her to concentrate, to focus on a timeline rather than what's clearly a jumble of emotions she's barely containing.

"I was at the hospital. My father's been ill with cancer. So, this morning the nurse called me and said I needed to get in there …"

I study her hands on the table, the way her fingers press into the chipped surface as if searching for a way to anchor herself. It takes a great deal of restraint not to reach out and hold them so she can squeeze something human, something that can offer comfort.

"So, you went to the hospital," I prod.

"He was refusing the pain meds until he spoke to me. I honestly don't even know how he had the strength … Once the nurse left …" She moves her shaking hands into her lap under the table, takes another breath, and focuses on my chest. "Then, he just said it."

My heart rate accelerates, but I remain silent, waiting until she's ready.

"He said he killed my mother. That he knew about her affair, and he followed her. Stabbed her." She swallows hard and blinks fast again. "He almost took the truth with him. Ten minutes later he was dead."

"Jesus," I whisper. "Fuck."

She meets my eyes. "Yeah. Fuck."

We stare at each other for a long moment. I need to absorb what she's told me, what it means to me, but while I'm looking at her, the only thing my mind's consumed with is the fact that she's sitting here, giving me the best news of my life, when her world's just been shattered. The fact that she's alone with me in this tiny caravan is no longer a mystery. She's too distraught to even recognise the danger she might have put herself in had prison turned me into a real monster.

Even so, what sort of person puts their grief aside to share brilliant news with someone they hate?

"Jamie," I say softly. "I'm so sorry … for your loss."

She waves a dismissive hand at me. "It's fine."

"I'm sure it's not."

Her gaze snaps to the table. "Stop being so nice to me."

"No, I won't stop." Resting my forearms on the table, I lean forward as her surprised eyes meet mine. "What're you doing here, Jamie? Shouldn't you be with family right now?"

She shakes her head. "It's just me and my sister. She's away, training for her career. I know I have to tell her. But I'll wait until she's finished for the day."

"So, of all places, you came here?"

She nods. "You deserve to know. If I was in your shoes … well, I'd want to know as soon as possible."

Dropping her gaze, she slowly traces the Formica's fake woodgrain. Two things cross my mind. One, she's here because she's all alone. And it's better to be with anyone—even me—than to be on her own. Two, she didn't have to tell me about her father's confession. She could have kept it to herself and no one else would ever have known the truth. But she hadn't.

And that makes my heart ache. The woman sitting before me is truly special. As I've always suspected. Now I have confirmation.

"Jamie?" I wait for her to look me in the eye. "Thank you. I know you didn't have to tell me."

She frowns. "Of course I did."

"No, you didn't," I say, shaking my head. "Some people would just let things lie. It can't be taken back, can't be reversed. It's over with. The only way is forward. Why dredge something up that won't change a thing except cause more trouble? That's what some people might think."

She studies my face with confusion. "But I would never … that's not who I am."

"I know. Or you wouldn't be sitting here right now."

"Then why even say that?"

The urge to hold her hand is so strong I drag mine off the table and place them on my thighs. "So you know that I understand what a big deal it is that you've gone out of your way, made yourself uncomfortable—at a time when you've lost your father—to tell me the truth."

She shrugs, fixing her eyes on my chest again. "Well, it's important."

"It's been the most important thing in my life for the last sixteen years."

She slowly meets my gaze, a soul-crushing sadness right there in her eyes.

Then the truth sinks in, washing over me like a tsunami. And as it does, I discover I'm now the one who has to blink fast. But for me, the blinking isn't working, and the tears overflow, spilling down my cheeks.

Embarrassed, I slide free of the table and turn my back to her. I'm on the edge of losing complete control of this enormous rush coursing through me. While I know it's inevitable, I don't want it to happen in front of Jamie Evans. She's got enough to deal with without me falling to pieces.

I lean against the narrow opening between the kitchen and my bed as more tears course down my face. My throat constricts with the effort to keep the emotion from bursting free. It does anyway. My whole body shudders as a sob escapes. Followed by a sharp, hitching breath. And another sob. There's no way she's not hearing this, seeing it. It's fucking mortifying.

But there's nothing I can do. All this time, being hated by her for something I didn't do … and for her to come to me with the truth right after the confession that must have destroyed her world … it's more than overwhelming. Her selflessness is staggering.

Then, as a million thoughts scatter through my brain, something unexpected happens. An explosion of euphoria blasts through my entire being. My heart, my shoulders, my chest, suddenly feel light. Almost like I'm floating. I'd never realised that the burden of carrying that guilty verdict inside my head, has also been weighing down my body. But now, it's fading, and I feel a hundred kilos lighter and ten years younger.

Because Jamie Evans believes me.

Chapter 13

Jamie

I WATCH HIS back, realising that although my father's earth-shattering revelation has left me numb, it's the opposite for Gavin.

I'd seen it on his face. Awe and relief all at once. When tears he couldn't hold back spilled over his cheeks, the enormity of his suffering spiked through me like a spear. I've never given a thought to the incredible pain he's experienced. Why would I? But witnessing his tangible, physical reaction ruptures my heart. An innocent man, hated by everyone. So much so, his own father testified against him. The media, like sharks, tore strips off him piece by piece, used him for ratings, like he was some sort of carnival freak. Then there's the loathing he must have seen in everyone's eyes in that courtroom.

And I'd been the worst of all.

As my own tears spill, his body shudders and I can't miss the sobs he's trying to stifle. Overwhelmed by the news, he needs to physically release the pain he's been carrying all these years.

I should leave, give him privacy. He's clearly trying to control himself because I'm sitting here, invading this personal, highly emotional moment.

As I slide toward the end of the bench seat, a rumble comes from somewhere deep inside him. I freeze, confused by the sound. It's not a hitching breath or a sob.

It's a … laugh?

And it comes again, comes from his core with such force it fills the whole caravan.

He reaches out, steadies himself against the kitchen counter, and doubles over as laughter rolls through his body and tumbles from his mouth.

I stand. I should go. This is his time. He deserves to experience his joy privately.

But my feet refuse to move, the intoxicating cadence of his laughter rooting me to the spot. Before I can check myself, I'm smiling, his sheer happiness a contagious virus that slips right into my body. And suddenly, I'm laughing, too.

Gradually, he gains control of himself, his laughs becoming chuckles, his chuckles tapering off to delighted sighs. Turning to face me, he swipes at the tears on his face.

When our eyes lock, my laughter explodes into sobs as everything that's happened today crashes into me.

Embarrassed, I bury my face in my hands, and just like Gavin Lake, I try to control the whimpers that scorch my throat.

Then his strong arms encircle me and hold me protectively against him. I'm not scared. I don't think I've ever been afraid of him. Just hateful and angry. All built on my father's lies.

But I don't need to be hugged, to be held, to be cared for. I'm strong, resilient. I don't need his comfort. Yet I can't pull away.

What can it hurt to give myself just one moment of vulnerability? Sliding my hands from my face, I lean into him and wrap my arms around his waist. It feels so fucking good. And so foreign. I struggle to remember the last time I was held. Apart from Anika's hugs when she was little, I realise it's been almost as long as Gavin spent in prison.

That thought alone releases something entombed deep inside me. It crawls out of the dark and floods every inch of my being. And I let it.

Burying my face against his warm chest, the sobs shudder through my body, through my soul. His only response is to tighten his hold in an effort to offer more comfort.

Who is this man consoling me when he should hate me? At the very least, resent me. I can't even comprehend what must be going through his head right now.

And here I am, destroying the elation he should be experiencing.

"I'm so sorry," I gulp against his chest, slowly regaining control of myself. "I'm so, so sorry."

He gently rubs my back. "You've got nothing to be sorry about."

I shake my head. "Yes, I do. So much." Sniffing, I take a deep breath. "I don't … I'm not usually … And now I'm ruining this … moment for you."

"You haven't ruined anything," he assures me. "Christ, Jamie. *You* gave me this moment. Do you have any idea how long it's been since I've laughed? Because I literally can't remember. I'll never forget this. There's nowhere on earth I'd rather be right now than here with you."

His words steal my breath. I look up into his face, into those dark blue eyes. "Me?"

He gives me a sweet smile. "Why wouldn't I want to share this with someone who has such integrity and strength? You just gave me the best news of my life, and here you are … after getting the worst news of yours. You have every right to cry, Jamie. You *should* cry."

Of course, his gentle, kind words send me whirling into uncontrollable territory again. I bury my face against his chest, my fingers fisting in his t-shirt at his back. This time, I really let loose, so grateful to have someone to hold on to.

By the time I calm down, the only sense I have of time passing is the ache in my feet and the trembling in my knees.

And I notice something else then, too. He's making slow, soft circles with his fingers at the nape of my neck.

Now that I'm not losing it, I become aware of his body pressed against mine, how tall he is, the firmness of every part of him I'm touching, and the contradiction between his strength and the tender way he's holding me, caressing my bare skin. It's almost as if he knows me intimately. I tell myself I'm only noticing these irrelevant things about him because I'm trying to distract myself from the new reality of my life.

Except, now that I'm quiet, I can hear his heart thudding against my ear. It's not the slow, strong beat I expect from a physically fit, relaxed man. It's beating fast. Much too fast.

Jolted back to reality, I uncurl my fists from his t-shirt and drop my arms to my sides. He instantly releases me. Frozen to the spot, I watch as he takes a couple of steps toward his bed, then return with a box of tissues. Grabbing a wad, I quickly wipe my eyes and give my nose a blow, completely aware that I must look utterly frightful.

Mortified, I avoid his gaze and stare at his chest, only to discover I've left wet patches on his t-shirt.

Reaching out, I press my fingertips to the dampness, realising too late that I'm deliberately touching him, that he's watching me deliberately touch him.

"Sorry," I mumble, pulling my hand back into my own space.

He gives me a grin and shrugs. "I think I'll live."

I grab more tissues and blot at my face, knowing it won't do any good. "God, I'm so embarrassed," I murmur.

"Me too," he says in that deep, gentle voice. "So, I guess, since we both are, we cancel out each other's embarrassment. That's how it works, right?"

Surprising myself, I huff out a laugh and let the tension leave my muscles. Who is this guy?

When I meet his gaze, I find that reassuring calmness I noticed during our meeting in prison. Only this time, I allow myself to sink into it.

"Well," I say, clearing my throat. "I suppose I should get go—"

"How about a drink?" he interrupts.

God, I'd just about kill for one right now. Better it be with him than alone, I suppose. "That might be nice. But just one. I have to drive home."

He scratches the back of his head and gives me an apologetic look. "Sorry, I don't have any alcohol. Not while I'm on parole. I was thinking a Coke, tea, coffee …"

"Of course. I ah … tea would be great." Seems like I'll have to drown in grief on my own once I get home. After I've told Anika. There's still that to deal with.

As he turns on the kettle, I think about how the poor guy can't even have a drink to celebrate, and I suddenly realise something else. "I'm sorry, I didn't even think … do your parole conditions include no contact with the victim's family members? I don't want to get you in trouble."

"No. I was actually surprised it wasn't on the list." He gestures toward the table. "Take a seat."

I do just that, grateful for the relief after standing in my heels too long. As he busies himself with mugs and tea bags, I can't resist the urge to kick my shoes off under the table, freeing my feet from the torturous devices I loathe.

"Sugar? Milk?" he asks.

"Just one sugar, thanks." With his back to me, I study his smooth movements, the way his muscles ripple and flow beneath his tight t-shirt and, with his head mere centimetres from the ceiling, how imposing his size is in this small space.

I close my eyes to stop the thoughts. My father just died. My father, the man who killed my mother and kept it a secret for sixteen years. My father, who willingly allowed an innocent young man to go to prison. That's what I need to think about. Nothing else.

After resting my tired, puffy eyes for a while, Gavin places a mug of black tea in front of me and takes the seat opposite, his bare knees briefly brushing against mine. He frowns slightly and looks under the table, and I realise he must have touched one of my shoes.

"Good," he says simply, and takes a careful sip of his tea. "Do you have someone, Jamie? So you're not alone tonight?"

"I … No. Not really." His curious stare sends heat crawling up my neck. "I work a lot," I explain, though why I need to explain anything to Gavin Lake is a foreign idea, but I don't seem capable of stopping myself. "Raising my sister and building a career takes up a lot of time."

He nods with understanding, though he has no idea what my life's been like.

"And your sister's away, training?"

"She's down in Goulburn at the Police Academy. Only has a few more weeks until she's finished."

"So," he says, turning his mug around and around, "you're alone for the first time in your life?"

I glance up from the large, strong fingers spinning the mug and look into his eyes. That hasn't even occurred to me. The last few months have been a little strange with Anika gone, but I've been busy with work and visiting Dad in hospital every night. Now that he's gone, there's only work left. "Yeah, I guess I am." A lump grows in my throat, but I force it down, focusing my attention elsewhere. "Why are you so good at this?"

He tilts his head. "At what?"

"How you're treating me, how you're keeping me calm, being so kind when I'm the last person who deserves it?"

"Well, for one, you *do* deserve it." He shifts uncomfortably in his seat and his knee brushes mine again. "And secondly, I managed to get a degree in psychology while I was locked up."

I stare at him, seeing him through new, thoroughly astonished eyes. I'd never put any thought into what he'd been doing in prison. If I had, I don't think getting a degree of any kind would have been on my list of possibilities.

"Is that what you're doing? Shrinking me?"

He shakes his head. "No. What I'm doing, is just being here for you."

Those expressive eyes of his tell me he means it.

He lets out a long breath. "Besides, I'm a convicted murderer, which means my degree is useless. I'll never be able to practice."

As his words sink into my muddled brain, without any thought at all, I reach across the table and gently wrap my fingers around his wrist. His busy hand stills on the mug, my touch snapping his eyes from mine to the grip I have on him.

"Gavin. I'm going to change that. I'm going to make sure you'll be able to do whatever you want with your life. Without restrictions. As a free and innocent man."

With a reassuring squeeze, I let go and wait for him to acknowledge what I've just said. But he can't stop staring at his wrist, leaving me wondering if he even heard me. Until his eyes swing up and meet mine.

"You?" he asks. "You'll do that?"

"Of course. You're the reason I became a criminal lawyer."

He blinks at me, and when his hand comes up to his neatly trimmed stubble, I notice the tremble in his fingers. He seems completely rattled. "You don't have to," he says quietly.

"No one's going to fight harder to clear your name than me."

The way he looks at me in that moment sends my temperature skyrocketing. There's something I can't read in those blue eyes. Even though I can't name it, whatever it is, whatever he's thinking feels … special.

Breaking eye contact, I clutch the front of my blouse and fan it against my skin. "It's so hot in here. How do you stand it?"

"I'm used to having no choice in the matter."

"Sorry," I say, "I must sound so pathetic complaining about—"

"Don't do that, Jamie. Don't sensor yourself because of me. Just be you."

He's smashing every belief I ever had about him. He's not a pig, a stupid bum, a piece of shit like I always imagined. He's shown me no contempt. Why does he have to be so fucking nice? And why does that hurt so much?

"I should go," I say, standing before I remember my shoes are under the table. Plonking down again, suddenly physically and emotionally wiped out, my feet search the floor until I find them and kick them out past the table.

He rises, looking down at me while I slip on the uncomfortable heels.

"I still don't like the idea of you being alone tonight," he says, his voice thick with concern.

What choice do I have? Ignoring him, I grab my handbag and fish my phone out. "I'll need your number."

After he rattles it off, he escorts me out of the stifling caravan.

"Didn't see no rockin' goin' on, Lake. She suck you off instead?"

Slipping on my sunnies, I ignore the piece of filth staring at me with a lecherous grin, but I can't ignore the gentle, protective hand on my back as Gavin guides me along the worn dirt path between the caravans.

When we reach my car, his hand slips away as I open the door to let the heat dissipate.

"If you … ah," he says, hesitating. "If you, by some miracle, come back here, please let me know when you arrive. I'll come and get you. I don't want you walking through this … minefield on your own."

"I'm not a snowflake."

He lets out a huff.

"What?"

"This place is full of some vile criminals. I don't trust that it won't just be words they attack you with. Not when it comes to someone like you."

I blink at him. "Like me?"

His eyes shift to my car as he rakes one hand through his light brown hair and shoves the other in his pocket. After all the measured confidence he's projected, he's suddenly uncomfortable.

"What does that mean?" I push, curious about his change in demeanour. So curious, I slide my sunnies up to my forehead.

His eyes snap to mine and hold there. "Because I don't trust a single one of these animals when it comes to a … gorgeous woman walking through here."

I let my sunnies plonk back to the bridge of my nose, desperate to hide my startled expression. Though there's nothing I can do about the burn in my cheeks. I didn't imagine it, did I? He just called me *gorgeous*.

With his words and the scorching sun ratcheting my temperature up to furnace levels, I slide into the car, start it up, and crank the air conditioning.

"Shit. Sorry. I'm really out of practice at this. Ignore me," he says, stepping into the gap between me and the open door.

I shake my head. "It was just … unexpected, I guess."

"There's been a lot of that going around today."

I can't argue with that, so I don't. Instead, I stare up at him. Now that he's outside in the glaring sun, the tiny dots of his pupils reveal the incredible depth in his blue eyes. With the sky enhancing their colour, they're not light and icy, but a deeper blue, one that reminds me of denim. Different shades of gold and chestnut highlight his mussed brown hair and closely trimmed beard. I shouldn't even be noticing any of those things. I should be grieving, reeling over the turmoil of the last few hours, but with him looking at me with concern, looking the way he *does*, he's one hell of a distraction.

He's fucking devastating.

A flutter of fear shimmies through my gut. Maybe I've made a mistake offering to help clear his name. I'll have to be careful when I'm working with him. I can feel it right down to my toes.

He rests a forearm on top of the door and leans down. "Will you promise me something?"

"Well, that depends on what it is," I say, pretty sure he's worried about my vow to clear his name.

"Promise me, that if you don't feel like you're coping tonight, you'll call me. No matter how late it is. At the very least, you should have someone to talk to."

I blink at him, surprised again. He shouldn't be worrying about me. He should be celebrating his good news.

"I'll be fine," I tell him as I click on my seatbelt. I want to reach for the doorhandle, but he's in the way.

"Promise me, Jamie."

"Sure. I promise," I answer quickly, needing to get out of here before I have another complete meltdown.

Apparently satisfied, he takes a step back and gently closes the door for me.

As I drive away, I glance in the rearview mirror to find him standing where I left him, watching.

When I turn out of the caravan park, a strange sense of loss overcomes me. I scoff. Is it really a surprise? I lost my father today. My only parent.

And I've lost the sixteen years of hate I held in my heart for a man who never deserved it.

Can it simply be redirected to a man I loved my whole life? Because I haven't just lost my father, but every single memory of him.

All of them were nothing but lies.

Chapter 14

Gavin

AS I MAKE the trek back to my caravan, I pretty much want to punch myself in the face. From the brief glimpse I had of her eyes before she shielded them with those dark sunnies, I knew I'd said the wrong thing. Even though it's the truth. Of course she's gorgeous. But I should know better than anyone that the truth can backfire spectacularly.

Now I've probably scared her off for good.

Approaching my personal oven, I notice Fletcher's still sitting on his steps. I feel sick that she came here on the worst day of her life and had to deal with his disrespectful comments. So, I barrel over.

"She comes back, Fletcher, I don't want to hear a word out of your mouth. Leave her alone."

He stands and puffs his chest out, but doesn't move closer. He's a good five inches shorter than me and probably forty kilos lighter. Though he's not the sharpest tool in the shed, he's not completely stupid.

"Can say whatever the fuck I want. Ain't nothin' you can do about it."

I don't even bother squaring my shoulders. He's all talk. "Don't test me on that."

He scoffs, sits on the step again as he plucks out another cigarette and clamps it between his teeth. All in an effort to convince me I don't scare him.

"Ya wanna end up back in the clink, be my fuckin' guest," he grumbles before lighting up and taking a deep drag.

I stride over to my caravan and barge inside, letting the door whack shut behind me. The arsehole is fucking right. I get into any sort of altercation that leads to assault, I'll be right back in a cell.

Letting out a long breath, I lean against the kitchen counter and stare at the little table where Jamie Evans sat. Where she flipped my worthless life on its head.

And once again, her life has changed forever, too.

Only difference is, this time, she doesn't hate me. This time, she's going to help me.

Or so she says.

I have no reason to believe she won't, but I also don't have a reason to believe she will. Especially after my little fuck up in the car park.

When she gets over the shock of her father's revelation, and his death, she'll probably change her mind. She might find it's far too painful to be reminded of why I need her help. After all, she owes me nothing and I'm sure that whatever work is required to clear my name, won't be a straightforward path. Like I told her, it'd be far easier for her to keep quiet and do nothing, to forget about me and get on with her life.

I won't blame her if she soon comes to that realisation. Even if it crushes me.

Taking a seat at the table, I miss those captivating eyes I'd devoured for nowhere near long enough. Like the copper around her irises, that I now know gets swallowed when her pupils dilate just enough. I wonder if the stunning green left behind changes with her emotions, their depth of colour altering like the ever-perpetual motion of a wave.

I didn't want her to leave. My shitty life and the suffocating confines of the caravan all disappeared the moment she stepped inside. Her presence was like a holiday from reality.

But more than that, I didn't want her to be alone. If I'd been a normal person in a normal home, I would have tried to convince her to stay a while longer. But who in their right mind would want to spend more time than necessary baking in this tin can?

Besides that, just a few short hours ago, she hated me with every fibre of her mind and body. Though, when she'd been sitting here, it seemed like all of those negative emotions melted away. Can that really happen so quickly? From hate to … well, I don't know what. As long as it's not hate, I'm happy.

Getting up, I reach into a cupboard above my head and pull down my sketchpad. After I flick through all the drawings I've completed of her eyes over the years, I turn to a new page.

Today, she'd looked at me with so many different expressions, I couldn't decide which one I wanted to immortalise on paper first.

Not until I turned around and saw her eyes dancing with the first genuine smile I've ever seen from her. Happiness not for herself, but for me. While her world was falling apart.

How long have I waited to see joy in her eyes? No guesses needed. But I hadn't counted on her compassion. Her selflessness. Which can't be drawn, but only held deep inside.

As my pencil moves over the page at different angles and varied pressure, I recall how her happiness turned into what it should have been hours before. She could no longer contain that intense emotional pressure. She'd crumbled.

And it felt so natural to ease her into my arms when that moment hit her.

I almost hadn't, terrified she'd cringe at my touch and shove me away. When she'd not only let me hold her, but held me, too, I seriously wondered if I was fast asleep, having the best dream of my life. That's how much I distrust affectionate human contact. It's not easy to accept. Not when the only form of touch I've experienced for the last sixteen years has been either brutality or indifference.

Even with the unbearable heat inside the caravan, I'd welcomed the warmth of her body against mine, the feel of her clinging to me as she shuddered. When I accidentally made contact with the bare nape of her neck, I knew I should have stopped touching her. But the sensation of her soft skin beneath my fingertips insisted I do what I shouldn't. The slow circles I made calmed her, and something invisible changed. I became aware of not only the physical aspect of holding her, but how emotionally right it felt to do so. With crazy thoughts like that coursing through me, my heart took off.

She either felt or heard it thundering in my chest. That's the moment she chose to let me go, as if realising who she was clinging to.

Coming back to myself, I study the emerging eyes now staring at me from the pad. There's still a hint of sadness that's been there since the moment I first saw her, but the happiness shines through.

I grin like a fool. After that hug, she hadn't fled like someone I'd repulsed. Instead, when I gave her the tissues, she'd touched my chest where her tears had dampened my t-shirt. I run my hand over that spot, but it's evaporated in the heat.

She'd reached out and touched me when there'd been absolutely no need to.

She'd clutched my wrist when she said she'd help me get my life back.

Did that mean anything, though? Really, I can't judge any of her actions. She was in shock. Nothing she did or said should be in any way taken as a truth about her.

Even so, as I use the green and brown pencils to work on the irises I know so well, I find my smile slipping.

I need to tell Benny about her visit, though I already know what he'll say. He'll tell me I'm an idiot, that I shouldn't trust her offer to help me, that I'll never see her again.

My jaw clenches as the harsh spike of truth spears through my euphoria. I don't want to listen to Benny's voice of reason inside my head right now, let alone in person. Problem is, he's more than likely right. I gave her my number, but she didn't give me hers. She holds all the power. If she never contacts me again, there's not a fucking thing I can do about it.

It won't be the first time I've been abandoned.

Leaning back, I stare at her half-finished eyes. They watch me with a truth I desperately want to believe.

A truth I've probably projected into them with wishful thinking.

But when I picture her holding onto me, apologising for ruining my moment of joy, I see it there. She cared more about me and my happiness than she did about her own devastation.

That's someone special.

Chapter 15

Jamie

I TAKE A SEAT at the stone-topped breakfast bar and once again pick up my phone. Like every other time I've tried to do this, my hand shakes. This time, I promise myself, I'm calling my sister.

Bringing up her contact, I press the dial button. The urge to immediately hang up is so strong, I almost do, then I hear her voice.

"Hey, what's up?" She sounds so damn happy amid the loud background chatter.

"You're not in your room?"

"Nope. Just hanging with some of the other cadets at the pub. Why?"

"Are they good friends?" I ask, remembering Gavin's words about dealing with this alone.

"Sure. Jamie, what's going on?" Her light tone has taken on an edge. We know each other too well.

I'd love nothing more than to say I'll speak to her later, but I don't want her to get the news while she's sitting in her room alone. Better she's surrounded by friends. At least I can give her something I don't have.

"There's no easy way to say this, Ank. I wish to God I didn't have to do it over the phone."

"It's Dad, isn't it? He's gone?"

"Yeah," I choke.

She's silent for a long moment, the only noises reaching my ear are those of the other cadets. Happy people enjoying their lives.

"You okay?" she finally asks.

I blink back the threatening tears. "I'm supposed to be asking you that."

"Well," she says carefully, "it's not exactly a shock, is it? Were you there for him? At the end?"

"I was … he … he didn't die alone." How do I tell her that's not what has my throat constricting? That he may be gone, but he's left behind a fucked-up mess?

More silence for a long moment, then she says, "You didn't answer my question."

"Didn't I?" Does she know I'm hiding something?

"I asked if you were okay."

Swallowing, I plaster a smile on my face, knowing she can't see it, but hoping she can hear it. "Of course. Like you said, we've known this was coming. I suppose it's a bit of a surprise that it's actually happened."

"Should I come home?"

I really should tell her *yes*. One benefit of family is that we're there for each other. Right? Except when you're a liar who killed your wife. Fuck. Now that I have her on the phone, I realise I can't tell her what he did until she's here with me. This isn't news you blurt out over the phone. He didn't just kill my mother, he killed hers too.

"No," I say, "No, don't do that. I'm fine. I've got work and everything that comes with a death to sort out."

"He didn't want a funeral, Jamie. You remember that, right?"

The reality of why he'd been adamant about that sinks in. How could a man who killed his wife and lied to his children about it for sixteen years expect anyone to gather to mourn his loss?

"There are other things that need to be dealt with," I tell my sister. "No point in you being here. I'll barely see you anyway.

Plus, there's the shit timing. You've only got a few more weeks until you graduate."

"Yeah, almost done. It'd really fuck everything up if I had to leave now, but if you need me, I'll be there."

"I'll send you straight back if you turn up. Graduate, Ank. Don't let him take that away from you. It's not like he was your favourite person in the world."

Another long silence.

Finally, she says, "As long as you're sure. Just ring if you need me. I'm only a couple of hours away. I mean it, Jamie."

"Thanks, but like I said, I'm fine. More than anything, I want you to be happy. Be with your friends, Ank. That's what'll make me feel better."

"Yeah … I will."

"I love you."

"Love you, too."

She hangs up and I sit there staring at the phone, my whole body shaking. God, I need her. I should have told her to come home. She needs to know the truth, needs to know about all the lies we've been told. But I refuse to let our father's actions throw a spanner in the career she's working towards. I won't allow him to hurt her any more than he already has.

Hitching in a sob, I clamp down on it. I'm fine. I'll call her in a few days when my mind is in a more cohesive state and nail down her graduation date. That'll give me a deadline. I'll let her celebrate her graduation, then I'll tell her who our father really was.

But there is someone I can tell right now.

Scrolling through my contacts I find Detective Jarrod Reid's number and dial. He answers after two rings.

"Well, well. Jamie Evans. It's been a while," Jarrod says, his tone overly friendly.

I cringe a little, remembering the last time I saw him. Five years ago. I'd already been on one date with him, and was a little hesitant to accept his offer of a second date, but Dad talked me into it. Jarrod took me shooting at his pistol club. I'd surprisingly enjoyed learning how to handle and fire a few different guns. What I didn't enjoy was the kiss he'd tried to force on me afterward. There was something about the way he seemed to think it was his right to take what he wanted. Not to mention the look in his eyes when I stopped him. That alone made me realise I most certainly did not want a romantic relationship with the man, no matter how attentive he'd been toward us after Mum's murder.

"Jarrod. How are you?" I ask, though I couldn't care less.

"Couldn't be better. And you?"

"Dad died," I tell him, my voice flat.

"Shit, Jamie. I'm sorry. The cancer?" I have to give it to him, his condolences sound genuine. I'm also surprised he knows about my father's cancer. Obviously, they'd kept in touch.

As much as I don't want anything to do with Jarrod anymore, I find myself feeling sorry for him. It'll come as quite a shock to learn he locked away an innocent man while staying in touch with the actual killer. I suppose he'll be embarrassed, especially now that he's worked his way up to Detective Inspector.

"Yes, but there's something else. Something he told me right before he passed. It's a bit of a shock, but you need to know."

He pauses briefly before he says, "Okay."

"He told me he's the one who killed my mother."

Absolute silence.

I wait. I wait way too long. "Jarrod?"

"Yeah, ah … you know that's not right, Jamie."

My heart accelerates as my anger rises. "Except it is."

A long sigh travels into my ear. "It was an open and shut case. You know that. You sat through the whole trial. Maybe your father was confused. He must have been on a lot of medication, so he—"

"No, he wasn't. I believe him. It makes sense. The man who went to prison for a crime he didn't commit always maintained his innocence. Remember?" I certainly do. I remember the way Gavin looked at me in the courtroom, how he pleaded his innocence before they dragged him away.

"You saw the evidence, Jamie. Besides, he's out now. I'm sure he just wants to put it all behind him and get on with his life."

What the fuck? That's not what I expected him to say at all. I thought he'd be as stunned as I am. Outraged, even. He had, after all, been completely outsmarted by my father.

"That's a little dismissive," I say through clenched teeth. "Gavin Lake may be out of prison, but he's still a convicted murderer. He doesn't deserve to go through the rest of his life slapped with that label."

"Jamie, seriously, just let it be. You'll only stir up a hornet's nest. And for what? It's over. Let your father's memory remain untarnished. You don't want to go creating a problem where there isn't one. Why dwell on the past? It's behind everyone now. Keep it there."

I hang up, every hair on my body standing at attention. Detective Inspector Jarrod Reid just told me exactly who he is. He used to be the man who gave our broken family comfort and reassurances during the worst time of our lives. Now he's exactly the type of person Gavin spoke of in the caravan today.

Nearly jumping out of my skin when my phone rings in my hand, I stare at the screen. It's Jarrod. I reject the call, then block his number. Five years ago, I trusted my instincts. I'm glad I did. The man has no integrity. I can't believe that he's risen so high within the police department. Shouldn't a man so invested in the law also be invested in the truth? Instead, he views the truth as an inconvenience.

Shaking with anger, I slide off the barstool and hurry into the kitchen, suddenly remembering the bottle of vodka I hid behind the cleaning products under the sink. I'd bought it the day my father was diagnosed with pancreatic cancer and hid it from him so he wouldn't be tempted while undergoing treatment. Although I've barely touched it, I feel like making quite a dent in it now.

From the fridge I find a bottle of lemon, lime and bitters, pour a couple of fingers of vodka into a glass and top it off with the fizzy liquid. I manage to swallow the whole lot in one go. Then I pour myself another and take it into the bathroom.

After I undress and step under the shower, I wash the sticky humidity from my skin, wishing I could wash everything else away just as easily. More tears want to come, but I clamp down on them. I'm not a crier. I've done enough crying today to last me another sixteen years.

Besides, the alcohol's already working its magic. I'm no longer shaking, and there's a nice fuzziness creeping into my over stimulated brain.

When I'm done, I plonk on the couch in front of the television, but as hard as I try to concentrate, my mind keeps drifting back to that caravan.

To Gavin Lake.

The very thought of him used to make my skin crawl and my blood pressure rise. No more, apparently. He's an innocent man my father stole sixteen years from. Well, that's an understatement. My father's still stealing from him. Even though Gavin's out of prison, he's not free. He can't go wherever he wants, can't have the career he deserves, can't even have a fucking drink.

It's up to me to get his conviction quashed, to put his life back in his own hands. I don't for a second regret promising I'll do that for him. But it's another burden I have to bear on top of everything else right now.

And although I'm a lawyer, I'll have to conduct some research into how to go about reversing a conviction. That's not part of the law I've studied. Doesn't matter. I'm a fast learner and I know people who can help. But it does fall to me. I'm the only person on this planet who heard my father's confession.

I take another long swallow of the liquid that's starting to numb me. As it slides down my throat, I remember Gavin's words again. I shouldn't be alone. I suppose I shouldn't be drinking on my own either.

As I glance around the empty living room, I realise that apart from the flickering TV, it's dark. When did that happen?

Agitated, I get up, head to my bedroom and stare at the bed. One part of me wants to collapse onto it, fall asleep and disappear into oblivion. Another part knows I'm not anywhere near drunk enough to do that yet. I'll just lie there going over everything. Round and round and round until I want to scream.

I need more alcohol, but I shouldn't sit here and drink alone.

After booking an Uber, I change out of my pyjamas and put on a summery white dress and a little makeup. I consider letting my hair down, but I'm not in the mood to try and tame it, so I neaten up my ponytail instead.

My reflection tells me I'm not good enough, but it also tells me I don't give a fuck.

Once I get to the leagues club I've been to with a couple of colleagues, I find the classier cocktail bar at the rear of the venue and position myself on a tall stool at the bar.

I'm not drunk. Yet. So I have no problem ordering a Long Island Iced Tea from the young bartender. By the time he places it in front of me, I tell him to start making another. And so begins my mission to obliterate my problems.

Chapter 16

Gavin

IT FEELS LIKE I've only just drifted off to sleep when my phone buzzes beside my head on the tiny nightstand.

Prying my eyes open, I stare at the screen. Not a number I recognise.

Pissed at being woken when I have to get up for work in a few hours, I'm more than ready to let whoever's on the other end of the line have it.

"What?" I snap.

"This Gavin Lake?" a man asks.

"Who wants to know?"

"Jamie Evans."

What the fuck? "You don't sound like Jamie Evans."

"Yeah," he says, "I mean, this's her phone."

Heart racing, I sit up. "Where is she? Is she okay?"

"I don't know, man. She just handed me her phone and told me to call you. That she'd promised you or something. She's pretty wasted. I wouldn't wanna leave her unattended much longer, if you know what I mean."

After a short conversation regarding her location, I book an Uber, pull on jeans and runners and slip on the only button-down shirt I own, hoping the club doesn't discriminate against wrinkles.

Once in the car, I realise I now have her number. Scrabbling with my phone, I quickly add it to my contacts. Sitting back, my chest relaxes a little. Not that I'll abuse the honour of having her number. It simply makes me feel better knowing she's not completely out of reach.

When I arrive at the leagues club, the receptionist signs me in and directs me to the cocktail bar.

As I enter and lock eyes with the barman, he takes a few steps over to a woman in a flowing white dress that gently hugs her figure, her hair up in a messy auburn ponytail.

Slowly turning on the barstool, she takes me in, her eyes dancing with delight before her mouth curves upward. My breath catches and I stop in my tracks. I'd give anything to have her look at me like that when she's sober.

She's clearly drunk, clearly happy to see me, yet obviously in a world of pain she's been trying to drown.

But I'm not here to take in how beautiful she is. I'm here to help her. She hadn't forgotten the promise she made me. And the smart girl that she is, she kept it. All while wasted on grief and alcohol.

When I move up beside her, she points at me and says to the barman with a giggle, "He thinks I'm gorgeous."

An uncomfortable heat races up my neck. Christ. Even while drunk, she hasn't forgotten my slip up.

Gripping my shoulder, she leans all her weight against my side. I wrap an arm around her waist before she topples off the stool.

"Thanks for coming, man. Time to get her outta here before she gets herself in trouble," the barman says.

"Oh, Sammy-whammy, don't be a big party pooper," she slurs with a grin, then looks up at me. "He's mean."

Sammy-whammy rolls his eyes at me. It's definitely time to go.

When I look down at Jamie pressed against my side, she grins at me with glazed, yet happy eyes. It's evident she's achieved her mission to forget. I'd been worried my presence would bring it all rushing back. Apparently not.

I pull my phone from my pocket so I can book an Uber, but realise I don't know her address.

"Got your phone?" I ask her.

"Course I do, silly," she giggles. "How'd you know I was here otherwise?"

Well, at least she still has some rational thought processes going on in that alcohol-soaked brain.

"We'll need it to book an Uber and get you home."

She slaps her palm against my chest and laughs, like I've said the funniest thing she's ever heard.

"Okay," I say, trying to ignore how warm her hand is through my shirt, and how fucking good her body feels pressed against my side. "What's your address?" I ask, figuring it might be easier to book it on my phone.

"I can't remember," she slurs, letting her fingers slowly trail down my shirt's buttons. When I give her a questioning look, she says, "Oh! Maybe it's on my phone?"

Her fingers pause above my navel. "Wait a minute," she says as she flattens her hand and rubs her palm across my torso. "Are those muscles?"

"Phone, Jamie."

"Oooo … I can feel them getting all tense. Can I see?"

When she tries to undo a button, I flatten her hand with mine.

Jesus, this isn't the woman who came to see me today. The warmth of her body pressed against me, and the touch of her hand on my stomach, is driving me crazy. Only one problem. None of it's real. It's the alcohol, not her. I know that. Well, at least my brain does.

I take her purse from her shoulder and place it in front of her on the bar. I really don't want to dig around in there, but I will if I have to.

Fortunately, she gets the message, removes her hand from my abdomen, and fishes out her phone. Unlocking it with fluid swipes, she hands it to me.

I quickly find the app, book a ride to the destination she has saved as *home*, then haul her off the stool and wrap an arm around her waist, tightening my grip when she stumbles in her heels. After making it through the club without an incident, we wait outside the entrance for the Uber that's only a few minutes away.

At the kerb, I close my eyes and take it all in. The warm, gentle breeze caresses my skin and ruffles my hair, reminding me how freedom feels. Six months ago, along with the sixteen years that preceded it, I'd have been locked in a cell for the rest of the night, with no possibility of experiencing heavenly fresh air. Such a simple thing. Sometimes it's these tiny moments that hurt the most. But that's not all there is tonight. Now I have a beautiful woman clinging to my side and resting her head against me.

Shifting, Jamie takes a step in front of me, trips on my feet and stumbles. When I haul her flush against me to keep her from going down, she wraps her arms around my waist and holds on tight. Her cheek gently rubs against my chest, her hair brushing my jaw and catching in my whiskers as that amazing scent of hers gets sucked into me with my next breath. It's intoxicating and surreal, so completely the opposite of my experience in prison, it's hard to wrap my head around.

Of course, I'm left with no choice but to continue to hold her. I wouldn't want her to fall and crack her head on the concrete. Getting her home safe is my only priority.

She takes a deep breath and lets it out on a long, pleasant sigh. "I like this," she says so softly I almost miss it.

I barely manage to stop myself from touching my lips to the top of her head. But I don't manage to keep my mouth shut. "I like it, too."

She looks up at me with a smile that lights up her stunning face. Then she releases her hold on my waist and slowly runs her hands over my pecs before letting out a little groan of pleasure. *Christ. I'm in trouble here.*

"You're so strong and hard," she murmurs. "I think you're turning me on, Gavin Lake." She quickly covers her mouth and giggles. "Oops. I'm not supposed to say that, am I?"

Fuck.

In the nick of time, our Uber pulls up alongside us.

Extracting her hands from my chest is excruciating, but I do it before she feels just how hard I'm getting elsewhere. I reach around her and open the door, helping her in before I climb in beside her while she moves over.

But she doesn't move to the other side of the car. The moment I settle in beside her, she cozies up to me. I'm not sure I can survive all this touching.

"Seatbelts," the driver says, turning to look at us, his eyes grazing over Jamie's bare thighs where her dress has ridden up a little too high.

I glare at him as I tug it down before snapping on our belts.

As the car pulls onto the road, her head drops against my shoulder at an awkward angle. Without thinking, I raise my arm and stretch it across her shoulders. She snuggles into me, her hand reaching across my stomach and resting against my side.

Instead of staring at her alluring bare knees, I turn my gaze out the window and keep it there.

And soak in everything. I honestly never thought I'd be in the position I'm in now. With a beautiful woman's arm draped across me, her body pressed to mine. I thought I'd lost any chance of this forever. She's drunk, and the moment she's sober, this goes away. But for now, I'm going to enjoy it.

She's tucked her shoulder under my armpit and twisted into me, her heartbeat knocking against my ribs. Her soft breath skims over my shirt, creating a barely detectable movement over the fabric. Strands of her hair tickle my jaw, catching in my beard again.

I'm so sensitive to touch, to *her* touch, I literally feel the rush of endorphins spike in my brain.

When the hand against my side uncurls and starts a meandering exploration up my torso, I place my palm on her forearm, stopping her. The touch of my skin against hers takes me by surprise. Sparks shoot up my arm and settle in my stomach. All on their own, my fingertips brush over her skin in small, featherlight circles. She lets out a tiny groan that transfers from her body to mine.

Goddammit, I'm so hard it's painful. Not that it matters. Even if she was mine, I wouldn't be doing anything more than what I plan to tonight. Not while she's in this state. If I ever get to *really* touch her, I want her undivided attention.

Trying to get some semblance of control, I concentrate on the scenery outside. Within minutes, the car pulls up in front of a neat brick home with a welcoming porch light.

I grip her shoulder and give her a little shake. "Wake up, sleepy head."

She grumbles before snuggling closer.

"Jamie?" I persist, unbuckling my belt, then hers. "We're here. Well, at least I think we are."

The driver looks over his shoulder at Jamie. "You know him, love?"

I glance at Jamie, who's staring at me with confusion.

"You safe with this guy?" he asks with concern.

As her gaze flicks to the driver, I lean in and whisper in her ear, "Tell him I'm your boyfriend."

Coming to life again, she giggles. "He's my boyfriend. Gavin Lake, the man I hate, is my boyfriend."

My whole body stiffens.

"You hate your boyfriend?" the driver asks.

"Oh!" she says, turning to me with sudden excitement. "That reminds me of something."

"What's that?" I reluctantly ask before I open the door.

She squints against the dim light cast by the overhead lamp as I offer her my hand. Drawing her bottom lip between her teeth for a moment, she sighs heavily. "Now I can't remember."

Good. I already know why she hated me. But after her father's confession, I'd hoped she'd changed her mind.

Taking my hand, she clumsily extracts herself from the car, trips on the kerb and falls hard against me. I hold her tight and shut the door. A few steps into our journey toward the welcoming porchlight, she stumbles again, almost twisting her ankle in those crazy heels she's wearing.

Sweeping her off her feet, I realise my mistake too late when she snuggles in tight and presses her face into the side of my neck.

"Mmmm," she murmurs, "you smell so good."

"Where's your keys, Jamie?" I ask, barely able to form words as I take the three steps up to her porch.

Keeping an arm slung around my neck, she pulls her purse into her lap. With fumbling fingers, she undoes the clasp, digs out a small bunch of keys and dangles them in front of my face.

"I'll need to set you down," I tell her.

"No. I don't think I can stand up," she grumbles, pouting her bottom lip. It takes everything I have not to pull it into my mouth and nip it.

"Then how do we get the door open?"

Grinning, she forces the keys into my hand gripping her thigh. I awkwardly hold her while I separate one key from the rest. Bending a little, I fumble around until the key slides into the lock. But it doesn't turn.

As I feel for the next key, she presses her face into my neck and makes no secret of the fact that she's inhaling my scent again.

"Do you taste as good as you smell?" she mumbles.

Before the words even sink in, her lips brush my skin. I freeze.

"Hmm … salty," she whispers in my ear.

Trying to ignore my body's reaction, I shove the next key into the lock. Still no bloody luck.

Then her damp lips kiss my neck, and I almost drop her when she gives me a little nip. Just enough to send a solid flow of blood straight to my dick.

And she does it again. A little harder. When she releases my flesh from between her teeth, she covers the spot with her open mouth. I remain motionless, all reason leaving my brain the moment her tongue touches my skin and swirls.

I can't control the rumble escaping my throat. Her lips are soft and wet and hot against my neck, and all I want is more. I want everything I can't have and it's goddamn torture.

Before I can dwell on that thought, I suddenly feel suction. She's giving me a fucking love bite.

Jesus.

And I don't do a single thing to stop it. I should jerk away, put her down, get some distance between us, but I can't. I stand rooted to the spot, trembling a little, though whether from the strain of holding her so long or from the effect she's having on me, I'm not sure. All I want right now is to enjoy her lips and tongue on me while I wonder what that suction might feel like on my cock.

As suddenly as she latched on, she releases me with a giggle. "Why're you puffed?"

It's only then I realise I'm breathing like I've done fifty laps of the exercise yard.

"I'm trying to find the right bloody key," I grumble.

Doing just that, I shove another one in the lock and, thank Christ, it turns. As the door swings inward, I stride inside and close it with my heel. Coming to a stop, I take in the soft light glowing from a lamp beside the couch. The open plan living area contains a big-screen TV, a cozy, thick-pile rug and an assortment of paintings on the walls. Further in, a dining table rests to the right of the couch and a breakfast bar separates the kitchen from the rest of the room.

Even though cool air-conditioning caresses my skin, the atmosphere is warm. Jamie clearly takes pride in her home.

"Oh! I remember!" she suddenly announces.

"What?"

"The rhyme I made up when Anika was little."

I stand there like a fool, waiting.

"It goes," she continues, gazing up at me, "*Gavin Lake, the man I hate*

Gavin Lake, never my mate

Gavin Lake, is a total fake

Gavin Lake, I hate, hate, hate."

She grins. "Isn't that funny?"

"No," I growl, my gut clenching at the thought of her despising me so much she made a goddamn hate-poem out of me. "Bedroom?" I snap, and for some reason, that sets off a blast of sexy chuckles from her throat.

"Well, aren't you sure of yourself?"

"No … I didn't mean—"

"There," she interrupts, pointing past the kitchen.

I hurry forward and as I reach the dark hallway, her fingers slide into my hair. Almost tripping over my own feet, I steady myself, close my eyes for a moment, and let the sensation of her touch against my scalp wash over me. I really need to get away from her. This is all too much.

Following the dim light coming from further along the hallway, I step into her bedroom, taking in the illuminated lamp on the nightstand and her neatly made bed. As I move forward, she tugs on my hair.

"This's so much better," she breathes. "So hot … or handsome? Are they the same thing?"

I'm about to die. Alcohol definitely loosens her inhibitions, both physically and mentally.

When I gently lay her on the bed, her hands slide from my hair to the sides of my face, her fingers gliding through my short beard, exploring. Goddamn that feels good.

She frowns in concentration, then smiles. "It's both," she murmurs.

"Both what?"

Her fingertips soften, testing the hairs on my face as her eyes meet mine. "I was wondering if this was soft or spikey. It's both."

"You were wondering, were you?" I shouldn't encourage her, but how can I resist? I'm pretty certain she'd never say anything like that while sober.

She gives me a slow nod. "I like it. I didn't like your other beard. I couldn't see your lips properly."

Then she brushes her thumb right along the seam of my mouth.

"They look yummy," she breathes, tightening her hold on my face and pulling me in so close I feel the warmth of her lips just below mine.

Nope. I can't let that happen. I've already allowed her to cross too many lines I'm certain she never would when not intoxicated. Very gently, I extract her hands from my face, place them on her stomach and step back.

She watches me with hooded eyes, as if she's about to drift off to sleep. Or pass out. Surprising me, her gaze drifts from my face in a slow, lingering inspection of my entire body. Reaching my feet, she trails her scrutiny back up again, in no hurry whatsoever. When her eyes meet mine, she smiles.

"You are so …" Her words fall away as she bites her lip, apparently trying to come up with the right word. And I'm holding my breath, waiting for it to escape her lips.

When she stretches both arms toward me, I think she wants me to embrace her. Of course I want to. But I won't.

"I need to pee," she sighs.

Ah, well, that's different.

First, I slip off those sexy, dangerous heels and place them out of the way. As I lean over her, she snakes her arms around my neck as if she's done it a thousand times. The moment I lift her, she instantly snuggles her face into my neck again. Damn. If only I was someone who deserved to be burrowed into.

Sighing, I carry her into her ensuite and gently place her on her feet with her back to the toilet. When I try to move away, she grips my shoulders.

"Everything's spinning," she whispers.

Shit. Here we go.

"You'd better hurry up and pee," I tell her.

She looks up at me, the pressure of her fingers on my shoulders increasing. For the first time tonight, she doesn't look happy. She looks humiliated.

"I don't think I can get my undies down," she slurs.

Oh, fuck.

And now I can literally see the colour draining from her face. I don't have time to stop and think about how inappropriate this is. I'm just thankful she's wearing a dress and not pants.

With her grip still firm on my shoulders, I drop to one knee, slip my hands beneath the hem of her dress and quickly glide them up the outside of her silky thighs. Christ, how I'd like to take my time, but for more than one reason, I don't. When my fingers hook into the lacy underwear, I slide them down her thighs, my dick straining with the knowledge that she's naked behind the thin material right in front of my face.

Once I've drawn her underwear down far enough, I stand up and grip her waist. "Sit," I tell her, and her knees unlock.

Gently lowering her to the toilet, I place her hand on the vanity beside her so she can steady herself, and quickly help bunch her skirt into her lap. Now that's out of the way, I discover her pale face has taken on a green tinge.

Scanning the bathroom, I spot a rubbish bin on the other side of the vanity, grab it and place it on her lap. She leans over it, hugging it with her free arm. Except for the tinkling coming from the toilet bowl, nothing happens.

That's when I notice her underwear have migrated to her ankles. I try not to look at the lacy garment, but it's impossible to miss the damp swatch of material resting between her feet.

Jesus Christ. My dick is so hard I'm sure it'd shatter into a million pieces if someone took a hammer to it.

So, she *had* been telling the truth about being turned on. Doesn't mean it had anything to do with me, of course. More likely a side effect of the alcohol.

She groans, yanking me back to reality right before she throws up into the bin.

Well, that brings my dick back under control.

There's not much I can do for her except make sure she doesn't topple off the toilet seat. My stomach doesn't roil at the sounds of her retching. I'd heard much worse from my cell many, many times.

I grab a washcloth from the shower, douse it in cold water, wring it out and fold it. She lets out a small moan as I press it against her forehead. After a few moments of stillness, she turns her tear-streaked face up to mine.

"That feels better," she mumbles.

"You think you can sit here for a little bit without falling off?"

She nods and I make sure she's got a firm grip on the vanity beside her before I take the bin from her lap and hurry into the hallway.

It doesn't take long to find the laundry. After placing the bin in the tub and reminding myself to deal with it later, I find a bucket and return to her.

While she still seems to be steady, I grab a large towel, head into her bedroom, and spread it over her pillow and down the side of the bed. She might think she feels better now, but that probably won't last long.

When I re-enter the bathroom, I freeze. She's wiped the streaks of mascara from her face, but that's not what has me captivated. She's let her hair down. It's soft and wavy and flowing and messy. And it's sexy as fuck. The dark, shiny tangles tumble almost to her waist. But it's how it frames her face that has my lungs on strike. The deep red brings out the green in her eyes and softens her stunning bone structure.

My legs want to buckle. *Gorgeous* no longer carries enough weight when it comes to how she looks right now. It's not just her beauty, it's the utter vulnerability she's letting me see.

"I'm sorry," she says, trying to force a smile.

"Don't …" I take a breath, reining in my reaction. "Don't be sorry. I'm happy to be here for you."

A shudder passes through her as she places the bucket on the floor, crosses her arms over her stomach and grips her waist. "No one, except for my mum, has ever taken care of me. Until now. Thank you."

Tears pool in her eyes, then slip down her cheeks. She's sobering up a little, which only serves to make her words sink deeper into my heart. No one's ever done anything like this for her? How is that possible? I'd give my soul to be by her side whenever she needs me. Why hasn't anyone snatched her up and given her everything she clearly deserves?

I move forward a few steps, take the washcloth from her fist and carefully wipe the tears from her exhausted face.

"Ready to get up?" I ask.

Holding out her hands, she nods. I toss the washcloth on the vanity and bring her to her feet. She doesn't sway. Instead, she trembles.

"Hold onto my shoulders," I tell her, then bend to my knee. When I feel her tentative hands on me, I gently free her feet from her underwear. Quickly shooting the lacy garment into the corner of the room, I rise, but her eyes aren't on me. They're on her lacy panties. Then they sweep up and meet my gaze.

Mortified, she places her hand over her face and groans, "Oh, God."

"Hey, I didn't see a thing. Now, time to rinse." Trying to make her forget her embarrassment, I guide her to the basin and run the cold water. Filling a glass, I hand it to her.

"I need to clean my teeth," she whispers.

"You don't want to do that after you've ..." I don't want to say the word in case it triggers her. "Just a good rinse."

"But I'm gross."

"Trust me, you'll still be gross in the morning."

She chuckles, meeting my eyes in the mirror. I'm unsure which is worse; the glassy drunk look she had not long ago, or the sadness and humiliation in her eyes now.

Before I do something stupid like pull her into my arms, I ask, "Do you have any Panadol in here?"

She opens the medicine cabinet, sending our reflections careening away. I spy the box, pluck it from the shelf and pop out three capsules. She takes them from my palm with shaking fingers, swallows them down with the water, then rinses her mouth a few times. They might come back up a little later, but at least I know she has a good supply.

Closing the cabinet, we lock eyes, her fatigue and grief right there at the surface. I wish she wasn't going through this, but she can't run from it forever. Though, one night of numbing the pain might have been a good idea had she not overdone it.

"Your hair," I say. "I'm guessing you don't want to end up with something nasty in it?"

She shakes her head, then winces from the movement. "Too tired to bother."

"Do you have one of those hair-tie thingies? A brush?"

She opens a drawer and plucks one out, complete with a hair-tie wrapped around the handle.

"Can you stand for a little longer?"

She grips the top of the vanity and carefully nods.

I start at the bottom of her hair, brushing it cautiously as I work my way up higher and higher. There aren't too many tangles, which I guess is the result of it being in that tight ponytail all day. She's watching my every move in the reflection, so I keep my eyes trained on the task at hand. Finished with the brush, I place it aside and part her hair into three sections. As it slides between my fingers like silk, the sensation is so intoxicating, I want to stand here all night and run my fingers through its buttery softness.

When I begin working on the plait, I glance in the mirror. Her eyes are closed, a look of peace and pleasure on her face. There's a deep satisfaction in making her feel that way. Finishing, I wrap the tie around the bottom of the plait to secure it. I haven't done too well. One section's too thick, another too thin, but it'll do the job of keeping it clear of any more bouts of retching.

Even with that unpleasant thought, my mind manages to conjure up images of that braid wrapped around my hand, tugging on it as I sink deep inside her.

She sways against me, and I catch her, realising she's almost asleep on her feet. I scoop her up, carry her into her bedroom and lay her down, resting her head on the towel-covered pillow. She groans softly as I force her onto her side so she's facing the edge of the bed and the bucket I've placed on the floor within easy reach. Leaning over, I position a few pillows behind her so she can't roll onto her back. I'm not taking any chances on her throwing up and choking to death on my watch.

I'd love to get her out of her dress and make her more comfortable, but I won't. She'll be mortified enough when she wakes up in the morning and finds herself panty-less. Not to mention all the other humiliations she's endured. Hopefully she won't remember anything, but I'm sure her absence of underwear will be a question I'll have to deal with.

Believing she's out for the count, I cover her with the throw rug at the end of the bed. Just as I straighten up, she snags my hand.

"Gavin Lake, I do not hate," she murmurs. "Not any …" and her words fade into sleep.

My heart swells with relief. Hearing her say it, even in her inebriated state, means the world to me. It can't be easy to turn sixteen years of hatred into something else. But she's not just anyone. To me, she's everything. Even when she *did* hate me.

After grabbing a spare throw rug and some cushions from the couch in the living room, I make myself comfortable on the old wing-back chair in the corner of her room. Not that I plan to sleep. I'll just watch over her in case her stomach protests again.

It breaks me that there's no one here for her in her time of need. But there's a little niggling part deep inside that's all warm and fuzzy because it's me who gets to care for her.

Maybe I'm not worthless after all.

Chapter 17

Jamie

LIGHT BLEEDS THROUGH my eyelids, but I don't move. I get the feeling that'll cause a great deal of pain. I can't remember why, but I trust my instincts. Instead, I crack open my crusty eyes.

And immediately close them again. Clearly, I'm not awake at all because I'm having a vivid dream about Gavin Lake. I suppose it makes sense after the emotional visit with him yesterday, but why I'm dreaming about him asleep in my grandfather's wing-back chair, I can't comprehend.

Well, maybe a part of me does. The man I met yesterday wasn't the ugly, violent monster I've always believed him to be. He was … what? Gentle and considerate, and definitely not ugly.

Ugh. That's not what I should be thinking about. Frowning, I realise I must be awake to be thinking at all. Especially since my head's throbbing in time with my heartbeat.

Prying my eyes open to mere slits, my pulse quickens, doubling the thumping pain in my head. He's still there, his back propped into one corner of the chair, the side of his face resting against the wing. Opening my eyes a little wider, I stare at him. What's he doing here? In my *bedroom?*

I remain motionless as my brain ticks over, slowly accepting the reality that he's obviously been here all night.

The first thing I notice is that I'm not afraid of his presence, just curious as to why he's here at all.

The second thing is how peaceful he looks with his facial muscles relaxed, one leg hanging over the chair's arm, the other sticking straight out, a hand resting on his stomach.

Glancing down at myself, I discover I'm on top of my comforter, a throw rug draped over me, and best of all, I'm still in my dress.

Dress? Why am I wearing a—

Oh, *shit.* I close my eyes and let out a soft groan as I remember heading out to the club. Though I can't remember what any of that has to do with Gavin Lake's presence in my home.

When I shift my gaze to him again, he's watching me with hooded eyes as tired as mine feel. I try to sit up, and instantly crash back to my pillow, my head about to explode. Closing my eyes, I take long, deep breaths while I wait for the pain to subside.

After a moment, something cool and damp touches my forehead. My eyes fly open and meet his. He's standing over me, his face full of concern as he presses a washcloth to my brow.

"I hope I didn't scare you," he says, his voice gravelly with sleep, yet so gentle.

Swallowing, trying to get my thick, dry tongue to work, I croak out, "What … why are you here?"

He gives me a lopsided grin as he turns the washcloth over, letting the cooler side rest on my skin. "You called me last night. Well, you got the bartender to."

"Oh, God. I did?" I whimper.

"Yeah. Good decision by the way."

"I don't remember any of that."

"I think that was your plan."

I swallow again and close my eyes, trying to block out reality. The reality of what I did last night and the reality of why I did it.

"How're you feeling?" he asks, still using that gentle tone. For which my pounding head is eternally grateful.

"Like someone filled my mouth with kitty litter until it absorbed every molecule of moisture, then bludgeoned me over the head."

He chuckles lightly. "That's one way to put it."

My eyes snap open. I want to see that smile. Jesus. How can he look so good after sleeping in a chair all night?

"I have your Panadol, but ibuprofen might be better for your headache if you have any."

"Kitchen cupboard above the microwave," I mumble.

When he leaves the room, I try to sit up, but my head protests so much, I ease back onto the pillow again. Thank God I don't need to pee, because I have no idea how I'd make it to the bathroom.

Before I know it, he's back with a bottle of pills and a glass of water. I groan, place the back of my hand on the washcloth and try not to think about how I'll get those pills down my throat.

"You'll have to sit up, Jamie."

"Don't … think I can," I whimper, disgusted with myself.

The mattress dips at my waist as he sits beside me, and when he leans in closer and closer, my heart stutters. Yet I don't feel afraid or anxious. I'm … curious.

But my curiosity quickly gives way to realisation when he reaches under my armpit and splays his warm hand between my shoulder blades. With such care and tenderness it brings tears to my eyes, he eases me upright.

The new position has my head pounding in protest. Then I feel his thumb at the nape of my neck, making slow, calming circles on my bare skin, just the way he'd done when he held me in his caravan. And it's working. Again. How I'd longed for someone to take care of me like this on the rare occasions I'd been sick. But after my mother died, I became the caregiver, never the recipient.

He holds up the bottle of ibuprofen and I turn my palm up, waiting while he tips out three pills. I pop them in my mouth, and he leans even closer as he reaches for the glass of water on the nightstand. God, he smells so damn good … and familiar. Before I can comprehend why, he encourages me to pop the pills in my mouth, then offers me the glass. After swallowing them down, I relax my muscles, but he keeps me upright.

"More," he says, indicating the water with a nod, his thumb still making those lovely circles.

I take careful sips, acknowledging how wonderful that cool liquid feels gliding down my dry throat. When he tries to take the glass from me, I raise it to my lips again, unsure if I'm drinking because I need more, or because I don't want him to move. Either way, I don't have a choice once the glass is empty. He takes it and carefully guides me down to the pillow, our faces closer than ever. That's when I realise the state of my breath must be beyond vile. Horrified, I slap a hand over my mouth and twist my head away.

He chuckles, extracts his arm from behind my back and stands.

"I'll leave whenever you say the word, but I'd like to get you fed, if that's okay."

I groan. "I can't even think about food."

His faced drops with disappointment. "You want me to go?"

"No, I …" I cover my face with my hands. "I don't know. I don't think I can decide on anything right now."

"Then don't. Let me make the decisions."

I peer at him through my fingers. Not having to decide on anything sounds like heaven right now. I'm so tired of being responsible for others, even myself. "That depends on what you have in mind."

"You should rest until the ibuprofen takes effect. Then, when you're ready, I'll make breakfast. I know you don't want anything right now, but you'll feel a lot better once you eat. How does that sound?"

"That sounds … perfect," I mumble as I let my eyes drift shut.

When I open them again, it's only due to my bladder screaming for release. I glance at the clock. Almost midday. I've haven't slept past 7am since my mother died. Since my father murdered her.

Pushing the thought away, I ease up until I'm sitting. This time, I only feel a slight ache in my head. Grateful, I slide my legs over the side of the bed and wait a few moments. As I do, the faint sound of the TV drifts in from the living room. He's still here, then. Waiting for me.

The thought gives me a sense of comfort and warmth. He seems to have a natural, nurturing demeanour I apparently crave.

Brushing aside the thought, I rise and cross the room to my ensuite. Halfway there, I notice something doesn't feel quite right. It's not until I turn my back to the toilet, slide my hands beneath my dress, and try to pull down my undies, that I realise I'm not wearing any.

Mind reeling, I lower myself to the seat. As I pee, I soon discover they're not missing at all. They're on the floor, over by the shower screen. How the hell did they get there? Had I taken them off? Had Gavin? Oh, God. What the fuck had I done last night?

Some vague, wobbly memories of Gavin being in here with me break through, but none explain my discarded undies.

I guess he can explain what happened, but I'm not sure I want to know how badly I've humiliated myself in front of him.

I've gone from smug superiority and hatred of the man to feeling like I'm a mess he should be running from. Yet, he's still here in my house, willing to take care of me.

As I clean my teeth and wash my face, I decide the real reason he hasn't fled probably has more to do with avoiding that depressing caravan than me. Who can blame him? Why not soak up some ducted air-conditioning and the space a normal home provides?

When I look at myself in the mirror, I notice the messy plait draped over my shoulder. The image of Gavin standing behind me slams into my brain. His concentration and the deliriously amazing feel of his gentle tugs on my hair as he braided it. How many more little kindnesses had he afforded me last night?

Back in my room, I clumsily slide on clean undies, a pair of shorts and a t-shirt. After taking a deep breath, I head down the hallway toward the living area.

Gavin quickly rises from the couch when he hears me.

"Take a seat," he says, indicating the breakfast bar while he makes his way into the kitchen and opens the fridge. "Feeling any better?"

I nod as he slides a plate of orange wedges over to me. They're not cut into quarters, but eighths. My mouth instantly waters.

He tells me to take it slow as I pick up a wedge and suck the sweet juice into my mouth. I try to, but each slice seems to taste better than the one that came before. After popping a couple of slices of bread in the toaster, he leans on the kitchen side of the breakfast bar and takes an orange slice for himself.

I watch as he licks the juice from his lips and smiles.

"Good?" he asks.

My eyes snap to his, jolting me out of thoughts of how delicious that mouth of his would taste. "Yeah, really good. Thank you."

His grin widens as he takes the second to last wedge and returns to the toaster. The moment it pops, he slathers on butter, then scrapings of Vegemite, before he brings it over and takes a piece for himself. "Eat up. Plenty of vitamin B there for you."

Before I even take my second bite, he heads over to the fridge and pulls out some bacon and a carton of eggs. As I watch him grab a frying pan and utensils, I realise he's made himself familiar with my kitchen while I've been asleep. As long as he hasn't done the same thing with my nightstand, I'm surprisingly fine with it.

"How do you know all this?" I ask. "When's the last time you had a hangover?"

"I'm sure you know the answer to that," he replies as he places bacon in the frying pan. "And I know all this from the internet."

"Oh." I pop the last bite of toast in my mouth and work up my courage as I chew. "What happened last night?"

He meets my eyes, and I see a hint of worry there. Great. I definitely humiliated myself. I suppose, if I'm going to help him clear his name, I'd better know how.

"Where would you like me to start?" he asks, flipping the bacon.

"From the moment you saw me."

As he starts frying the eggs, he tells me everything from the phone call in the middle of the night to getting me comfortable in bed. He makes it all sound so civilised and normal, even when he reveals he stayed because he was worried I might choke on my own vomit. But I know he's giving me the highly abridged version, and I need all the details.

When he serves up a plate of bacon and eggs for each of us, I choose my words carefully. "When I changed, there was … an item of clothing missing. What happened there?"

He keeps his gaze firmly on his plate, but the knife and fork in his hands are motionless, and when I glance at his face, he's blushing.

Oh shit.

"It's nothing you need to worry about," he says.

"Which makes it sound like it is."

He lets out a sigh, lowers his utensils and meets my eyes. "You could barely stand and were busting for the toilet. So I … helped. And thankfully you were wearing a dress, so I didn't see anything."

As awkward and humiliating as it is for me right now, I can only imagine what it must have been like for him.

"Sorry," I mumble before staring at my own plate.

"Well, no reason to be."

We eat in silence until I've devoured every last morsel on my plate.

Then, as he takes the dirty dishes over to the dishwasher, he asks, "How about some coffee? I couldn't quite figure out how to use that contraption."

"Good idea." Missing my morning coffee is probably half the reason I can't quite shake this headache. Slipping off the barstool, I make my way around the breakfast bar and get the coffee machine going. When it starts to fill the first mug, I turn to watch him stack the dishwasher. And notice a smudge on his neck.

On autopilot, having done a similar thing a million times when Anika was younger, I reach toward him. He freezes in the middle of closing the dishwasher door, and I hesitate.

"You've got something …" I touch my thumb to his skin and rub, trying to clean away the dark smudge. When my attempt fails, I stare. It's not a smudge at all. It's a bruise. Or more accurately, a hickey.

"I … I'm sorry, I thought it was …" I let my words trail away when I realise what that bruise on his neck means. It hadn't been there yesterday, when I left his caravan.

As the colour in my face deepens, so does his, but his gaze remains unwavering.

"Oh," I say. "I'm so sorry. I interrupted you last night."

"No, you didn't."

"But, you were with someone." I imagine a faceless woman latched onto his neck in the throes of passion, then the phone call interrupting them. I turn back to the coffee machine, trying to distract myself from the ugly feeling in my stomach. What do I care if Gavin Lake has a girlfriend, or whatever she may be?

"The only person I was with last night, was you."

I whirl around, my breath catching. "Are you trying to tell me I did that?"

He tilts his head slightly and shrugs his broad shoulders. "That's what happened."

"I would never—"

"Well, I wouldn't know about that, but I do happen to remember what happened last night."

As the coffee machine falls silent, we stare at each other while I try to will my useless memory into a movie that'll explain what I can't even comprehend. I had my lips on Gavin Lake's neck? I sucked on his skin? It makes no sense.

Except something about him tasting like salt flies into my muddled brain and as it does, his gaze drops to my lips. Only then do I realise I'm running my tongue over them, trying to recall that taste.

I quickly take the sugar out of the cupboard at my knees, slide the mug over to him and grab the milk from the fridge. When I turn around, I ask, "How?"

He locks eyes with mine. "I was trying to find the right key to unlock the door … and you just started … tasting me."

I gape at him, suddenly recalling my arms around his neck, him holding me, how right it felt to be in his arms. Then nuzzling into his neck.

As my face burns, spontaneous combustion seems like a welcome option right now.

"So, you do remember," he says, clearly aware of the state I'm in.

I watch him scoop sugar into his mug and stir. "I … but … I don't understand … why didn't you stop me?"

"I told you, I had my hands full just trying to get in the door."

I scoff, "You're telling me, with all those muscles, I overpowered you?"

When he rubs a hand over the bruise on his neck, I get the distinct impression he's reliving it.

"Gavin?" I wait until his eyes reluctantly meet mine. "I think you owe me an explanation. And if we're going to work together to clear your name, there can't be any secrets between us. There can't be any lies. Or it simply won't work."

He scratches the back of his head. "I agree. It's just … the truth might mean you no longer want to help. And that scares the hell out of me."

My heart picks up pace. What the fuck had I done last night? What had *he* done? "Did we have sex?" I blurt before I can stop myself.

His eyes widen. "Christ, Jamie. I'd never take advantage like that. Ever. The closest contact we had was this," he says, indicating his neck.

And when you took off my underwear, I don't say. But he doesn't look guilty, just flustered and embarrassed. "Well, then, how did you let that happen?"

Releasing a long, reluctant breath, he finally says, "Because if felt so fucking good … I just … let you."

I blink, not quite sure I heard that right. I watch a multitude of expressions pass behind his eyes, but the one thing I don't see there is a lie.

"Oh," I murmur, my heart thundering as I turn to the coffee machine again and get another mug going.

That hadn't been what I'd expected him to say. More excuses are what I'd thought he'd come up with. Instead, he told me the blatant truth. Even though he truly believed I'd be so disgusted by his admission that I'd want him out of my life, he hadn't lied to me.

He places his coffee mug on the counter and stands a little straighter, waiting for me, I think, to tell him to leave.

"What else?" I ask. "What else happened that you've left out, that you haven't told me because you think it's better left unsaid?"

"Jamie, you were intoxicated. I know what happened last night had nothing to do with who you really are."

"Tell me."

"You tried to kiss me, and I stopped you. You also recited a little poem about hating me."

My eyes widen in horror. I'd forgotten all about that idiotic poem. He must see the shame written all over my face, because he takes a step toward me.

"Then you told me you don't hate me anymore. I'm hoping that those words, at least, were true."

I'm too shocked to say anything.

"I should go," he sighs.

I nod, my focus dipping to the floor. I need time to process all this. I tried to kiss him? I recited that awful poem? And still, he'd stayed, made sure I didn't choke, gave me painkillers and made breakfast. Why?

He grabs his phone from the counter and shoves it in his pocket as he walks around the breakfast bar toward the front door.

When he opens it, I find myself right behind him, grabbing his elbow. He freezes on the threshold.

"I'm sorry," I tell him.

"I don't blame you. I understand that you don't want to help—"

"No," I say, realising he's taking my apology the wrong way. Tightening my grip on his arm, he finally turns and looks at me. "I'm sorry because I'm the one who embarrassed *you*. My behaviour … God, I'm awful and I'm so sorry I dragged you into my crap, that you had to witness any of it."

"It's actually nice to know you're not perfect."

I blink at him in confusion. "You thought I was perfect?"

"I was beginning to." I don't miss the way his eyes fill with hope as he smiles. "So, you'll still help me?"

"Of course. I just need some time to process my father's death, to deal with everything that entails. I'll call you, Gavin. I promise."

His eyes flick to my grip on his arm, then back to my face. Just as I try to release him, he covers my hand with his and squeezes.

"Thank you," he says before crossing the threshold and heading down the porch steps.

"Gavin?" I call after him. He turns and looks at me questioningly. I take in the brightness of his expression, the way the sun lights up those deep blue eyes and warms his skin. "I did tell you the truth. I don't hate you anymore."

Before he can react, I close the door, lean against it, and let out a long breath. Then I cover my face with my hands and groan. *Jesus. That poor guy. He must wonder what the hell he's struck.*

One minute I'm giving him great news, the next I'm crying in his arms. Then he brings me home because I'm embarrassingly drunk and I reward him by giving him a love bite and trying to kiss him. And let's not forget about reciting that hate-poem.

Have I missed anything?

Fuck.

I really am a total mess. And he was worried I'd never want to see *him* again? He's the one who should be running for the hills, getting as far away from the crazy lady as possible.

Hurrying over to the couch, I flop down face first and let another groan of humiliation. When I try to force the memories of last night into my stupid, damaged brain, they refuse to surface.

Instead, I'm forced to imagine myself standing before him in the bathroom as he dragged down my underwear. He's right. Wearing a dress meant he didn't have to see anything, and I believe him when he said he didn't. Closing my eyes, I can almost feel his fingers on my thighs, skating upward, searching for the lace. God, I wish I could remember how that felt, how he looked when he touched me. I want to know if he liked my skin, if it turned him on when he slid my panties down.

Scrambling to sit up, I realise it's me who's turned on by the mere thought of him doing that.

Jesus, what's wrong with me?

Needing a distraction, I grab the remote and click on the TV. Gavin Lake's presence in my home had filled up all the empty spaces, and now it's far too quiet.

Which brings me right back to Dad. Although he hadn't been home for a while, the fact that he'll never, ever return hits me like a tonne of bricks. As a band of tension squeezes around my head, I can't grasp onto one single thought or emotion to explain how I feel about his death. All that alcohol last night solved nothing. Even now, it's too much, too hard.

While I try to focus on the TV, my mind drifts, playing a memory featuring a certain man making breakfast in my kitchen like he belonged there. The thought warms me up inside, makes me feel like someone really cares. About me.

A harsh scoff scorches my throat. I shouldn't go there. What's the point of wishing I had someone who cares enough so, for once in my life, I don't have to shoulder every responsibility all on my own?

There is no point. Because I'm just fine alone.

Or is that a lie I tell myself is true?

Chapter 18

Gavin

RETURNING TO THE tin-can I hate referring to as *home*, I plug my battery-depleted phone into the charger, grab a glass of water and down it in one hit. After I stare through the grimy window at the depressing caravans beyond, I turn and take in the space I've been assigned.

Last night, for the first time since my incarceration, I entered a real home.

Unfortunately, it'd been like a fucking dream I never wanted to wake from. Along with the welcoming atmosphere of Jamie's house, the amount of space alone was goddamn paradise. Not to mention that blissfully cool, thin air. While she rested, I snuck a peek at her backyard and that sparkling jade swimming pool. Staring out there, the vague memory of the freedom to open a door and step outside without having to be on alert, tightened my chest.

Fucking heaven, all of it.

But more than all those material things, I relished being there for Jamie. Caring for and doting on her because she needed me, tugged at my heart, proving that's what I'm made for. To care for others. I've spent far too long worrying about myself. I'm over it.

Having her sit at the breakfast bar while I cooked and talked to her … Well, to me, that's something special I want a hell of a lot more of.

She's promised to give me my life back, the idea of a real future. One with meaning. Christ, I want that so badly it hurts in a place deep inside, a place I'm scared to let see the light. As wonderful as hope is, I know all too well how it can also devastate when it crashes and burns.

But it's damn hard to tamp it down when the idea of a life worth living has been dangled in front of my face.

And even though I try not to think about wanting that life to include Jamie Evans, it's impossible. A stupid fantasy. It's just … being around her, looking into her eyes again after all this time, makes me want more than simply a career and a home.

Spending time with her to secure my future as an innocent man will be torture, but worth every punishing second.

A couple of sharp raps on the side of the caravan jolt me out of my head. The moment I swing the door open, Benny barrels inside.

Over the couple of weeks since his release, we've spent most afternoons together. Although I've grown accustomed to being alone, Benny's struggling. I'd lived with him twenty hours a day for fifteen years. He's had forty years of never being alone. When I was released, it'd felt like I'd lost a goddamn limb without his constant presence. I know he feels the same. I also know only time helps reduce that loss. So, I'm trying to ease him into it without making it too obvious.

The same way I've continually delayed the little plan he cooked up in prison.

"Where the hell've ya been?" he grumbles as he flicks on the kettle, then slides onto the bench seat at the table like he's right at home. I suppose he is. His tin-can's identical to mine. "Well?"

Grinning, I lean against the kitchen counter. "You won't believe me. Have a guess."

"Fuckin' Mars?"

"It's far more unbelievable than that."

He narrows his eyes and shrugs. "Can't play stupid guessin' games without me coffee."

Beside me, the kettle clicks off as it boils. I grab a couple of mugs from the cupboard and unscrew the cap off the instant coffee. "You know you can make your own, right?"

"Pfff. Course I fuckin' know that. Bloody milk's off. Came over ta get some of yours once I knew ya'd be back from work, and since ya were nowhere to be found, I'm havin' withdrawal symptoms."

Work. *Fuck!*

So consumed with Jamie, my shitty job hadn't even crossed my mind. I'd missed a whole fucking shift, and I hadn't called in. I stare at my phone on the charger, dreading turning the damn thing on. I'm actually surprised my Community Corrections officer isn't banging my door down.

I add a sugar to my coffee and three to Benny's, top his off with milk, and place it in front of him before I take a seat. I'll deal with my failure to turn up at work later.

"So, spill," Benny says, then raises his mug and takes a sip.

"I spent the night with Jamie Evans."

Yep, I'm an idiot. A fine mist of milky coffee sprays across the table as Benny chokes on the hot liquid.

"Fuck, Benny," I grumble, sliding out from the table to grab some paper towels. By the time I wipe myself down and clean the tabletop, he's finally gained some semblance of control.

"Your fault," he huffs. "Don't go tellin' stupid jokes when I'm tryin' ta get my fix."

"It's not a joke."

"Bullshit. You know ya go anywhere near her, she'll have the cops on ya like you're a terrorist. Ya need to stop with this fuckin' obsession."

"*She* came to see *me*."

"What?" He sits up straighter, the frown lines on his forehead deepening.

"She told me … she knows I'm innocent."

He blinks, and I realise he's having the same reaction I had. Disbelief. Then he grins, and those missing teeth at the back of his mouth make a rare appearance. He knows what someone else believing I'm innocent means to me. He also knows what it means coming from Jamie Evans herself.

"You're not shittin' me?"

"I'm most definitely not."

"But how?" he asks, leaning forward.

"Seems my theory was right. Her father confessed on his deathbed."

I recount her visit, and Benny is just as surprised and impressed as I am that she didn't keep it to herself. Leaving out anything she'd find embarrassing, I fill him in on last night and this morning, wrapping up with her genuine offer to help clear my name.

"And that changes everything we planned," I say, dreading his reaction, but relieved to the bottom of my soul that Jamie's visit might be the very thing to finally put an end to Benny's crazy idea. And hopefully get me out of the lie I told him without ever having to reveal I lied.

Agitated, he gets up and paces beside the table.

"Don't ya see?" he finally says. "This changes nothin' when it comes ta Reid. He still fucked ya over. He still deserves what's comin' his way."

I don't dispute any of that, but although I'd agreed to Benny's plan, I only did so to placate him. I never, ever intended to go through with it. It's the one and only lie I've ever told him. I'm ashamed about that, but he'd been so distressed about his release, I'd had a horrible feeling he might do something drastic to keep himself behind bars. That's why I gave him something to cling to. A purpose. That's why I lied.

I've never been a killer, and I never will be, no matter how much Benny thinks Reid deserves to die.

"Think of it this way. Getting my conviction quashed means Reid'll get what's coming to him. It just won't be the way we thought it'd be," I try to reason. "I'm sure it'll mean the end of his career. He'll probably face charges. Hopefully end up in prison himself. So, we stand back and let the law do its thing."

Benny scoffs. "What? Like the way the law did its thing when it convicted you of a crime ya didn't commit? That way?"

"It's usually more right than wrong."

"Fuck off!" he shouts, his eyes burning into mine. He's coming across angry, but I know it's really disappointment. And fear.

"Benny, I've decided. I'm giving this a shot. I want a life. I *need* a life. And if there's even a microscopic chance she can give that to me, I'm taking it."

His fist strikes the table beside me. "And what about me? Huh? What life do I get?"

Keeping my cool, I stare up at him. Whatever I say will be meaningless when he's in this state. He paces again before slamming his open palm on the table.

"I can't live like this, Gav. Prison's my home. Not this … whatever the fuck this is. I don't want it. The freedom … it's—"

"Terrifying. I know. I felt the same way when I first—"

"No! You don't get it. Forty fuckin' years is a lot different than sixteen. I just wanna go back. Ta what I know. Ta where I'm comfortable. Killin' that prick Reid's my ticket to what I want. I helped ya survive inside, now it's your fuckin' turn ta help me. We made a deal."

He's right. If it hadn't been for our chance pairing in a cell, I know I wouldn't have survived. Benny was my rock. My teacher. My fucking *father*. I wouldn't be sitting here now if it wasn't for him. And we both know it.

In his eyes, what he's asking for isn't unreasonable. The plan was to get Benny sent back to prison after his release. But he can't just commit some victimless crime. Unlike me, he isn't out on parole. He's out because he's served his time, which only leaves one option. He has to commit a major crime to end up in supermax again. His home. But like me, Benny's not a cold-blooded killer. He'd just been unlucky. Twice. He hadn't *meant* to kill anyone. After years of listening to me rant about my conviction being Reid's fault, Benny had come up with what he thought was a fool-proof idea. We'd find a way for me to get my revenge and kill Reid, then we'd make it look like Benny did it. He'd go straight back to supermax, and I'd continue to try to build a life on the outside. But for me, it was pure fantasy, a way to let off steam. I'd played along, never believing he'd actually want to go through with it. That fact hadn't sunk in until a few days ago, when he showed me the gun he'd managed get hold of. I've been wracking my brain ever since, trying figure out how to convince him that it's not so bad out here.

But unlike Benny, I have hope.

Maybe, that's all he needs too.

"You've only been out for a few weeks. I'm not about to stop helping you acclimatise."

"A-fuckin-climatise? Is that what we're talkin' about? Not loyalty, not promises?" He finally takes a seat across from me, runs a hand through his hair, then pounds it down on the table. "Ya remember how my loyalty served you, right?"

"I remember. But there's something else we need to consider." I have no idea what he'll do if I tell him I outright lied. And I sure as hell don't want to lose him.

His eyes flash with anger. "What?"

"Change. Life is change, Benny. And wanting what's best for those you care about, for those you're loyal to. Sometimes, others can see what's best for us, even when we can't."

"Psycho-fuckin'-analysis-bullshit, is what that is."

"You don't want me to have a life? You'd rather I rot out here or rot in prison?"

He glares at me. "That's not fair."

"We both know life isn't fair." I sigh heavily, the guilt of owing him so much weighing me down. "I want to see if it's even possible for her to clear my name. Maybe she can't. I don't know. But I want to find out. And to do that, I'll need time."

"And I just need ta *do* time. It's who I am."

He's right and he's wrong. If he wasn't so damn stubborn, he'd see that and give this new world he finds himself in a chance.

"The moment I stepped foot in this caravan, all I wanted was to be back inside. Which was nuts after wanting to be free, but there it was. That feeling of being an outcast was almost crippling. All I can give you is experience, Benny. And experience has taught me that, just like being hurled into prison, you can get used to it out here, too."

He leans back and crosses his arms.

"I'll help you, Benny. You know I will."

"Six months," he says.

"Six months what?"

"That's what I'm givin' it. Just like you. Six months. If I don't feel any different by then, we go back ta the plan."

"You could take out someone else," I joke.

Unfortunately, Benny doesn't catch onto my humorous tone. "I'd never hurt anyone who doesn't deserve it. Ya know that."

"Yeah, I do. That's why I was joking."

"Not funny," he grumbles, then holds his hand out across the table. "Deal?"

"Deal," I lie again, and shake, hoping like hell he won't even remember this conversation in six months.

After he takes a long sip of his cooling coffee, he looks me in the eye. "I'm happy for ya, Gav. Hope she can do what she's promised."

I give him a nod, not quite sure whether to believe him or not.

Reaching into his back pocket, he pulls out a phone and places it on the table. "They gave me this useless thing when I got out. Only decided ta give it a try last night. Can't even turn the fucker on. I've pressed all the buttons and nothin' happens."

My whole body relaxes. He's actually reaching out, trying. Stubborn old fart that he is, I hadn't expected that.

Picking up the phone, I hand it to him. "See that smaller button on the side?" He looks at it and nods. "Press and hold it down."

He follows my instructions, his face lighting up like the screen. "Well, will ya look at that. Now what?"

I get up, slide onto the seat beside him and begin his first lesson.

Once he leaves, I power on my own phone with dread. Sure enough, I'm greeted with a plethora of missed calls and angry texts from my Community Corrections officer. I call him immediately. I actually like the guy, he's always treated me fairly, but even after I explained that I had to take care of a friend in need, it doesn't change the fact that the poultry farm fired me.

With one of my parole conditions being that I hold down a job, he's given me two weeks to find another, or I'm headed back to prison.

For the next few days, I search for work. Unsuccessfully. I try not to panic. I've been here before. There are plenty of shitty jobs no one else wants.

After dinner, I scour for work on my phone. When it rings in my hand and Jamie's name appears on the screen, my stupid heart does a double-beat as I answer. "Hey."

"Hi," she says, a slight hesitancy in her voice. "I just … well, I wanted to say thank you … for the other night. And the morning. I'm not sure I did, so …"

"Anytime, Jamie," I tell her simply. Because it's true. She could call me for help every night for the rest of my life and I know damn well I'd be there. Although I might try not to lose my job while I'm at it.

While I wait for her to say something, I take in the clinking of cutlery on plates, the low murmur of a multitude of voices. She's out somewhere. I can only presume she's alone since she's on the phone with me.

"So, how are you?" she finally asks.

"I'm fine. And you?" I groan internally at my riveting conversational skills.

"No," she says, "I want to know, Gavin. That was … is some pretty big news for you. So, I really *do* want to know how you are."

For a long moment, I can't breathe. I just sit, unmoving, unable to form words.

"Gavin?" Her voice is soft, gentle, and a little concerned.

"No one's asked me that, and actually wanted an answer, in a very long time." How does she manage to extract little truths from me so easily?

"Well, I'm asking."

"I guess it's sinking in. The rush of it all when you told me, and now the reality that it'll take time. Feels like I'm in limbo. But a good limbo, if there is such a thing. I'm not complaining."

"I know. Nothing's changed for you except for the fact we know the truth. Which doesn't help you at the moment," she says with empathy.

"True, but that's the way it is. Thanks to you, where I am now is a million times better than where I was a few days ago."

"And soon you'll look back at this moment and realise your life's a million times better than it is today."

Damn. She knows exactly what I need to hear. "I believe you."

"Good," she says with a sigh. "Anyway, my dinner date will be here any second. I should go. Night."

The call disconnects, leaving me gripping the phone so hard I'm surprised I haven't cracked the screen. She's on a date? While she's grieving and trying to come to terms with her father's confession? Of course she's on a fucking date. Sure, she told me she doesn't have anyone in her life, but that doesn't mean she's not out there looking for that significant other. My gut churns. I want to be the one taking her out, buying her dinner and making her forget about everything she's dealing with.

I'm a goddamn fucking idiot to have ever let it cross my mind that she might see in me something more than a wrong she needs to right.

Chapter 19

Jamie

AFTER I HANG up, I take a quick look around the busy restaurant. Still no sign of Pete, so I go straight back to staring at the name on my phone. Gavin Lake.

His surprise that I'd really meant it when I insisted he tell me how he was feeling, had my heart constricting. My head's still a bit of a jumble when it comes to him. I need to vanquish the opinion I've held for half my life and create something new. Already it's becoming all too clear that I'm dealing with a man of depth and compassion. A man that the rest of the society sees as a useless ex-con. And will continue to unless I fix what my father has done to him.

Checking my watch, I discover my long-time mentor is now fifteen minutes late, no doubt held up by the investigation he's working on.

Tonight, I need to pick his brain on next steps for Gavin. Then, when I return to work after the weekend, I'll be armed with the knowledge I need to approach my boss.

As I wait, I think of the bereavement leave I've just taken. As lovely as it is to know that society views the loss of a close relative worthy of two whole days off work, I can't actually pinpoint what I've been doing during that time. I just don't know how I'm supposed to grieve for a man I apparently never knew.

However I spent those past few days, I don't want to push it when it comes to work. The firm has always frowned upon any sort of leave. Criminals don't take days off, so neither should we, no matter what's going on in our personal lives.

Pulling up a brief on my phone, I soon discover I can't concentrate. Not when I feel empty about going back to work. Cringing at the thought, I push it aside as a gentle hand squeezes my shoulder.

Pete stands beside me, that sympathetic expression he gave me when I told him of my father's cancer diagnosis plastered on his usually happy features.

He indicates for me to get up, so I slide out of the booth and into his embrace. I suppose the occasion calls for it, because he's never hugged me before. Unlike the other day when Gavin Lake held me, I don't feel any overwhelming surge of emotion. I suppose I might be numb, but I have no interest in mulling that over. There are more important things to worry about.

Pete pats me on the back, releases me and looks into my eyes. "I'm sorry, Jamie. It's a big loss."

"Thanks," I mumble as I slip back into the booth. Pete plonks down across from me, rubs his belly and lets a ghost of a grin touch his mouth.

Although he never met my father, I'd often talked about him when Pete and I got together. I'd always meant to introduce them. Now, I'm glad they never met. That'll make this much easier.

"Hope you've already ordered. I'm starving," he says.

"You're always starving," I point out.

He shrugs. "You got me there."

"Well, never fear. Your favourite's on the way."

He sighs heavily, taking me in. "You're a good person, Jamie. I think your only fault is that you work too hard."

I scoff and take a sip of water. "You work way more hours than I do."

"That's because I'm an old fart with nothing else to do with my time."

"So, the only difference between us is that I'm a young fart. What's the problem with that?"

He takes a sip of the diet coke I ordered for him earlier. "Ugh, still trying to poison me with that artificial sweetener, I see."

"Of course," I grin. Ever since my father's decline, I've been a thorn in Pete's side every time we see each other and food is involved. That belly of his hasn't shrunk one bit, so my efforts to keep him healthy are clearly futile, but that won't stop me trying.

"Anyway, the problem with you working too much, is you're not leaving any time for the important things in life. Things I'm sure your father would want you to have."

"What's more important than putting away criminals?"

"Family … Love," he says so matter-of-factly, I take another sip of water and pointlessly move the cutlery back and forth. When I don't respond, he continues, "Don't you wish you'd taken some leave to spend more time with your father before he passed?"

"Nope," I say, meeting his gaze.

"Nope?" He leans back and folds his arms across his chest, resting them on his protruding belly. "Why the hell would you say that?"

"That's why I asked you here. So you'll understand why. And because, as usual, I need your advice."

As he opens his mouth, the waitress places salads in front of us. Pete stares down at it, then across to mine, assessing.

"Let's trade," he says, reaching for my bowl.

I hold on tight. "Nice try." We have the same thing, only his is sans bacon, croutons and only half the usual amount of dressing.

"Well, I guess I could just leave, go to KFC and not worry about what it is you need from me."

Bastard. That's the problem with people who get to know you too well. "Fine," I relent, and swap bowls with him. "I think they call that blackmail."

"Not when you're trying to deprive me of the simple pleasures in life." He stabs his fork into the salad and comes up with a chunky piece of bacon. "Would you like some? Maybe to go with that rabbit food you tried to pass off as a meal?"

Since he hasn't realised this is just the entrée, I ignore his sarcasm and jump right in. "The reason I don't feel bad about not spending more time with my father is because he's a lying, deceitful fucking prick."

Pete's fork stops an inch from his mouth, frozen for a moment before he lowers it. Staring at me with surprise, he waits for an explanation.

I tell him everything, then eat my salad while he takes it all in.

"Jesus fucking Christ. Are you okay?"

"I'm fine. But I do need your help. If you're okay with that, of course."

"I'm always okay with that. But … is your sister around? How the hell're you coping?"

"I'm dealing with it."

He stares across at me, his food forgotten. The sympathy in his eyes sends my gaze to my half-finished salad.

"Gavin Lake," I say, "I want to get his conviction quashed. How do I go about that?"

When he lets out a deep sigh, I meet his eyes again, sending him a silent plea not to try and tell me what I should and shouldn't be doing. Only I can decide that, and I've made my decision. With or without his help.

"You want to help the man you've hated all these years?"

I nod. "One hundred percent, yes. He's a victim of my father's lies, Pete. The only thing Gavin Lake's guilty of is telling the truth. Always. And no one believed him."

Pete drums his fingers on the table, then stops. "But he *has* lied, hasn't he?"

"What?" I frown. "When? He's always maintained his inno—" And it hits me. My meeting with him six months ago. He told me he was sorry for what he'd done. He'd told the parole board the same thing. That's why he's out. Because he showed remorse for a crime he didn't commit. I'd been so distracted about Dad's confession, I'd forgotten all about Gavin's.

Only one thing makes sense. "I guess he figured out the law's an ass."

Pete gives me a reluctant nod. "He never would've been granted parole without admitting what he … never did."

"It's a sick fucking world, Pete."

"You don't have to tell me. But, Jamie, it's not your responsibility to help him. There are plenty of lawyers who specialise in overturning convictions. You don't have to concern yourself with his side of things. You've got enough to deal with."

I take a long drink of water. "My father stole the life he should have had. Nothing's ever going to make up for that. But I can make sure the life he has going forward is one of a completely free man. That won't happen if he's still seen as a convicted murderer now, will it?"

"Let someone else deal with it. Doesn't have to be you. In fact, you should be distancing yourself from this. Can't you see how triggering it'll be?"

"I'm the one who heard my father's confession, Pete. The *only* one. I'm involved whether I like it or not."

He leans forward. "I don't think you've thought this through. It's not just about your father's confession. The detectives who investigated your mother's murder will come under scrutiny. They're not going to like that."

I stare at him, utterly confused by his resistance. "So, you're telling me, an innocent man has to remain guilty to prevent ruffling a few feathers?"

He sighs heavily. "No. I just want you to understand that this isn't going to be all rainbows and sunshine."

I slam my fork against the salad bowl, causing a few heads to turn. "I'm not an idiot."

"I'm all too aware of that. But I'm also aware that you're going through a major emotional life event. Whether you want to admit it or not. I don't want you ending up broken from this, Jamie. I really think you should take some time off so you can come to terms with everything before you make any promises or decisions."

I swallow, suddenly doubting myself. Pete's the most upstanding person I know. Ethics and integrity through the roof. He taught *me*, for fuck's sake. "I've already promised."

"I doubt the guy's going to hold you to it."

"I'm holding myself to it. Live with it. Now, what's the first step?"

He digs into his salad and chews before he finally answers. "First step is submitting an application to the Court of Criminal Appeals."

"And a Dying Declaration will be enough?"

He shakes his head emphatically. "No. You can draw up an affidavit swearing to your father's confession, but as you said, you're the only witness. When Gavin Lake's confession to the parole board comes into play, that'll be the end of it. I know it's not what you want to hear, but I'd say it's game over before you even start playing."

I stare at him, unable to hide my disappointment. How the hell am I going to tell Gavin I've made a promise I can't keep, no matter how much I want to?

"Maybe," Pete says with sympathy, "just knowing you believe him, and were willing to fight for him, will be enough. Without any solid evidence, you're wasting your time, and getting the guy's hopes up for nothing." He takes another bite of salad and chews thoughtfully. "If something new comes up, something solid, bring it to me. We'll go over it together and make sure it'll be enough to get you over the line. Until then, I wouldn't go mentioning this to anyone else. Okay?"

"Fine." I don't bother confessing that I've already told Jarrod. What does it matter? If I can't gather more evidence, the point is moot. As far as I know, my father's confession is the only evidence at my disposal.

When we're served our main course, I can't stop trying to figure out if there's something else the police missed during their investigation. Jarrod Reid clearly had tunnel vision. Things get missed when the police believe they have the offender wrapped up in a pretty bow. The more I think about it, the more convinced I become. There has to be something.

Because, apart from me, it seems no one else is interested in helping an innocent man.

Chapter 20

Gavin

AFTER GIVING BENNY another lesson on how to make the most of his phone, I trudge back to my caravan to make some lunch. The moment I enter the stifling oven, my phone rings.

Jamie.

My heart thrums in my chest as I grin. As my thumb trembles over the answer button, I tell myself not to get my hopes up. These things take time. A lot of time. For all I know, she's calling with bad news.

"Hey," I answer.

"Hi. I … I'm here, in the parking lot. You said to call, so …"

"Right. Be there in a sec—"

"Wait," she interrupts. I freeze, suddenly very afraid she's here with news I don't want to hear. "If, ah, you haven't had lunch yet, I could use some. I think I passed a little place on my way here."

"Sounds great."

It's not until I take the phone away from my ear that I realise I have a death-grip on the damn thing. With my pulse thumping, I clean my teeth, shrug on a clean t-shirt and brush my hair. When I glance in the tiny mirror, I'm convinced it looks like I'm trying too hard, so I run my hands through my hair to muss it up a little.

"Dick," I tell my reflection. This isn't a fucking date. She's here with bad news. That's why the lunch invitation. To soften the blow.

Steeling myself against the negative thoughts swirling around in my head, I shove my feet into my runners and hurry out to meet her.

By the time I get to her car, the strong possibility that she's about to cut me loose forms a pit in my stomach.

The moment I slide into the passenger seat and close the door, that intoxicating scent hits me. She smells like … I want to say *home*, but that's such a distant memory, I'm not sure if it even exists.

Fighting the urge to close my eyes and breathe deeply, I glance over and flash her a smile as I clip on the seatbelt. "Hey."

"Hi," she says, looking down at the centre console and turning a dial.

As I take in her long ponytail and pretty dress that ends halfway up her toned thighs, the car moves backwards. Which wouldn't bother me if she was looking over her shoulder.

I clutch the seatbelt, convinced she's about to hit something.

She stomps on the brakes and stares at me with genuine concern. "What? What is it?"

"You're backing up without looking." The second the words are out, I want to take them back. Here she is taking me out to lunch and I'm criticising her driving. Especially since I've become such an expert over the last sixteen years. In fact, apart from the occasional Uber ride—something that didn't exist when I went inside—this is the first time I've been in the front seat since my conviction.

Instead of kicking me out, she chuckles. "You think I'm some crazy, reckless female driver?"

"Unless you've got eyes in the back of your head, I don't think it matters what sex you are."

“Damn, you figured out my secret.”

Her eyes glint with amusement, releasing my tense muscles.

“Right,” I say. “I’ll need proof of that, I’m afraid.”

She giggles. It’s such a sweet, melodic sound, I lose myself for a moment. Hearing her laugh like that, as if she doesn’t have a care in the world, does something fucking wonderful to my soul. I want to make her laugh like that *all* the time. Then she points at a screen mounted in the middle of the dash, angled slightly toward her.

I’m an idiot. And now she knows it. “A camera?”

“Yep. The eyes in the back of my head.”

“I’m definitely behind the times.”

“Not your fault,” she says as she reverses. This time I watch her concentrate on that screen. It feels strange. The urge to look over my shoulder is still ingrained after all this time, but I resist.

She grins as she turns that dial on the console again and we move forward.

Out on the road, fifty or so metres in front of us, a car decides to pull out instead of waiting a few seconds for us to pass first. At that precise moment, Jamie takes her attention off the road to stare at me. When I glance into her footwell, I discover her foot isn’t even on any of the pedals, let alone the brake.

“Jamie!” I blurt, slamming my hands against the dash, sure we’re about to plough into the back of the other car.

“It’s fine,” she laughs, her eyes sparkling with amusement.

And then I feel it. Even though she’s done nothing to hit the brakes, her car slows down. Studying the vehicle in front, I realise we’re neither gaining nor dropping back, but keeping pace. When I let out a breath, my heart decides it’s safe to beat again.

Too soon, apparently, because now she’s taken both hands off the wheel to stretch. I snap my eyes back to the road, watching as we approach a bend.

I don't like this feeling at all. No control and no escape from this travelling projectile. My life is literally in her hands and she's not even using them.

Gripping the seatbelt, I wait for us to cross to the other side of the road. Instead, the steering wheel turns on its own, navigating the bend perfectly, never losing pace with the car in front.

Once we straighten, she put her hands back on the wheel and shoots me a smug glance, her eyes dancing with delight.

"What?" she asks, all innocent, like she hasn't almost given me a bloody heart attack.

"Jesus, woman. What the hell?"

"Not scared of how I drive, are you?"

"How can I be when it appears you aren't driving at all?"

She laughs, clearly having fun at my expense. As much as my heart's jackhammering, it's lovely to see her like this. I never thought I'd have the pleasure of witnessing this playful, carefree demeanour, let alone be the reason for it.

But it worries me, too. She suffered a huge blow only a few short days ago. I can't see how this happiness is genuine. I think she's using it to cover up the pain deep inside. And that never comes to any good. Though, God knows, I want more of her laughter and those smiles that reach her eyes.

"I hadn't thought about you never travelling in a car like this. Not until you freaked out when I started reversing."

"I didn't freak out," I lie.

"Ha! Sure you didn't. Naturally, I had to give you a demonstration."

"You could've warned me first."

She shrugs. "I'm not sure that would have been quite as much fun. But, fair enough. Wait until you see what's next," she says with a little too much glee.

I groan. "Please, no more."

When she glances at me, I can't help but catch her contagious smile. Shifting in my seat, I become aware of something I hadn't noticed before. Probably because I was more concerned with making it out of this car alive. "Why does it feel like my arse is getting colder?"

"Fear?" she chuckles.

"Very funny."

"It's probably the ventilated seats."

I stare at her, waiting for the punchline. It doesn't come.

"They must have had cars with heated seats before …"

"Yeah, I remember," I say before she gets too uncomfortable. I don't want to lose this playful side of her.

"So, same difference."

"Does it clean up after you scare the crap out of your passenger too?"

"Not yet."

After a moment, Jamie slows the car, and with practiced precision, she presses a few buttons on the dash display before coming to a full stop. Checking the rearview mirror, she looks at me.

"Ready?" she asks, mischief sparking in her eyes.

I shake my head. "Nope."

"Too bad." And with that, she takes her hands off the wheel and her foot off the brake.

To my astonishment, the care reverses perfectly into a rear-to-kerb parking spot.

"Unbelievable," I murmur. "Does anyone even need a licence anymore?"

"In a hundred years, I bet people will think it was crazy to allow us fallible humans control over such a lethal missile."

I shake my head. "Don't you remember the joy of actually driving? I used to lie in my cell and relive my short driving experience."

The spark in her eyes dies a little. "You haven't driven since you were released?"

"Can't afford a car."

Her hand covers the fist resting on my thigh. And just like every time she's touched me, my body comes alive. I want nothing more than to uncurl my fist and entwine our fingers. Before I can, she opens her door.

"Come on. I'm starving," she says, and she climbs out.

After deciding on a couple of burgers, we head across the road to the river while we wait. Walking along the grassy path, I barely glance at the tannin-stained water flowing past.

I suppose the river's beautiful in its own way, but all I see is Jamie. Her long ponytail bounces against her back, her flowing dress brushing against those smooth thighs, her toned calves flexing with every step. I'd like to run my fingers over every inch of those legs. Then there's that damn ponytail driving me crazy with thoughts of wrapping its length around my hand, my wrist, my forearm.

"Thank you," she says softly, giving me a sideways glance.

I clear my throat. "For what?"

"Making me forget for a while."

I let out a long breath, pushing down my depraved, animalistic urges.

As I suspected, the hurt's still there inside her, lurking beneath the surface. That I'm the one to give her some relief has my chest swelling with pride. We all need a distraction every now and then, but she'll need to face the gravity of everything that's happened sooner or later. I'd love to be there for her when that happens. Last time was just the tip of the iceberg.

"Were you really worried?" she asks, her eyes squinting a little with genuine concern.

"Let's just say, when you're least expecting it, I'm going to make your heart pound that hard."

She gives my bicep a playful whack. "Good luck with that."

"Sounds like a challenge."

Her eyes flash with defiance. "I don't scare easily."

"Scaring someone isn't the only way to make their heart pound."

She stops walking. So do I, suddenly afraid my stupid mouth has thrown up her walls. As she gazes at me, I take in the way the sun shines on the strands of hair that have freed themselves from her ponytail. Fluttering in the breeze, they're lit up like a bright aura of fire around her face. I swallow. She's a goddamn angel.

"We'll see," she says, then before I can read her expression, she glances at her watch. "Burgers should be ready by the time we walk back."

We'll see?

Definitely a challenge, but I shouldn't get my hopes up. Hope might have been all I had in prison, but hoping this woman might ever be interested in me, beyond clearing my name, is probably a reach too far.

After we collect our burgers and find a picnic table along the river, I peel back the wrapping and take a huge bite. Blocking everything else out, I relish the burst of sweetness from the beetroot, the savoury hit of onions, the juicy beef, the tomato sauce.

When I groan with appreciation, Jamie's curious gaze sweeps over my face, locking on my mouth as I swallow. Plucking up a napkin, she reaches toward me and gently dabs the corner of my mouth.

My need to touch her is so strong, I cover her hand and hold it there. Our eyes clash, and I'm sure she feels the intensity of our connection the way I do.

"You've got some … sauce," she says, her voice husky as she retracts her hand, leaving me with the napkin.

I swipe it over my lips, and sure enough, I leave a red smear behind. Jesus, she must think I'm a grub.

"So," I say, resisting the urge to take another humungous bite, "I'm starting to think you're buttering me up for some bad news."

I wait for her to chew her delicate little morsel, and as I do, she avoids my eyes.

Oh, fuck. I'm right.

That's why I'm sitting here. She's about to tell me there's nothing she can do. I glance at my burger and decide to devour it before my world comes crumbling down.

When I look at her again, she's watching me. "Why did you lie to me?"

I almost choke. Chewing fast and swallowing, I grab my can of Coke and take a long swig, fully aware of her unrelenting stare.

"Telling the truth hasn't gotten me very far in life, but I don't lie, Jamie."

"At the Restorative Justice meeting … you lied to me. You confessed."

Ah shit. I shouldn't be surprised. I knew she'd eventually ask.

"I never confessed," I say, looking into her eyes so she knows I'm telling the truth. Well, the partial truth. I did confess, just not to her.

She puts down her burger. "Yes, you did. You told me how sorry you were for … everything."

"That wasn't a confession. That was the truth from right here." I tap my chest. "I wanted you to know that I understood. I've wanted you to know since the day I saw you in court."

"No. You said—" she cuts herself off, her mind racing, remembering. "You manipulated me?"

"No. I'd never do that to you."

I wait for her to jump down my throat, but she only stares at me expectantly. All I can do is give her the truth.

"Before you walked into that meeting, the only thing on my mind was trying to convince you of my innocence. Even my cell mate told me I was crazy if I thought I could do that. He said that wasn't what you wanted to hear. That all you'd want was to know how sorry I was. I thought he was full of shit, that with everything I'd learnt, I could convince you it wasn't me."

I take a deep breath and wait for her to say something. She doesn't. My chest constricts with the thought that I might be about to lose her help, but I push on.

"I was all set to bombard you with the truth … then you walked into the room. The moment I looked into your eyes, I knew I couldn't do that to you."

She frowns while she takes that in. "Why?"

"Because I could see you were still haunted by what happened to your mother, that it was almost as raw as it was when we were in court. You looked … stuck. And I knew, that by continuing to profess my innocence, I was hurting your soul, keeping you stuck. My cell mate was right all along. You were there to get closure, and as far as you were concerned, I was the one denying you that. I was everything that was wrong in your world. So, I decided to put it right. I gave you what you needed so you could move on."

She stares at me for the longest time. Finally, she shakes her head. "But the way you said it … the way you meant it … it felt so real, like you completely understood."

"Of course I understood. I lost my own mother not long before you did. I knew everything you were going through, everything you'd lost. Because I'd lost it all too."

She does that rapid blinking thing, and I know she's holding back tears. Hoping to distract her, I grab her half-eaten burger, wrap it up and place it in its bag. "Come on, let's walk this off."

Apparently accepting my explanation, she nods.

After walking in the opposite direction along the river for a while, I say, "I was actually surprised you didn't grill me about every little detail in that room, that you were satisfied with what I said. I think, if you'd pushed for more, I'd still be inside right now. Why didn't you?"

Silence drags on for a long moment before she admits, "You took me by surprise. I was ready for a battle and you just … deflated me. Every word cut right into me. That's all that seemed to matter. Going over the details felt so … clinical. There was nothing clinical about what you said to me. It felt right to leave it there."

"And you still want to leave it there?" I ask gently.

She nods. "For now. I don't think I'm … ready to hear it all yet. One thing at a time."

We walk on for a little longer before she stops and faces me.

"So, you didn't lie to me. But you did lie to the State Parole Authority."

"I did. That part of it … I listened to my cell mate. And he was right again. Claiming my innocence never once worked for me."

She shakes her head. "I get it. But … you've made it a hell of a lot harder to clear your name. What's the court to think? Here's this man, wanting his conviction overturned, yet he's officially admitted he's guilty. You've handed them the fact that you're a liar. You either lied about being innocent, or you lied about being guilty. Either way, there's a lie in there and they'll latch onto that. The court doesn't like overturning convictions, so any excuse not to will do. You see where I'm coming from?"

My stomach drops to my feet. Why the fuck hadn't I thought of that? Probably because I believed confessing was the only way out, and because I never imagined her father would tell the truth.

"*Shit.*"

"Yeah." Her eyes search mine. She's not even trying to hide her own disappointment. "I want to help you, Gavin but, as we agreed, I won't lie to you. It's not looking great. Unless there's some solid evidence or another witness the police report doesn't mention, then—"

"There *is* another witness. That arsehole detective buried it."

Chapter 21

Jamie

I FREEZE AS Gavin's gaze sweeps over my face. Though I can't quite read his expression, something's shifted inside him.

"You're talking about Detective Jarrod Reid?" I ask, needing to be sure.

"Yeah. That's him. The prick who led the investigation and made sure I was convicted."

Moments ago, those blue irises had emanated warmth, now they reveal an anger so ice-cold a shiver runs up my spine and settles at the nape of my neck.

"Are you saying he knew there was another witness?"

"Yeah," he says, his voice low with barely controlled rage, "he fucking knew."

"It's just … he, ah, was always so helpful, so kind during the whole thing. Even years later, he …" My voice fades away at the mask of stone staring at me, his eyes hard and unforgiving. I take an involuntary step away. The added distance lets me take in the fists at his sides, the muscles flexing in his arms.

Suddenly, I see the man he must have been in prison. His size, the look on his face, in his eyes. Add to that a shaved head, he'd have intimidated the toughest of the tough. This, I realise, is how he survived. Keeping this side of himself present at all times to avoid conflict. It's certainly working on me. But unlike the inmates, I've experienced the real person behind the shield in front of me. The one who oozes compassion and a gentleness I never knew could exist in a man.

There's no way I'm telling him I briefly dated the man he clearly hates. If Gavin's right, if Jarrod buried a witness, then the detective's reaction to my phone call last week makes perfect sense. But I can't tell Gavin that either. By calling Jarrod the night of my father's death, I royally screwed up. And I'm fucking embarrassed by my stupidity.

Scratching the back of his head, Gavin lets out a long sigh as his gaze softens and his muscles relax. "Sorry, I didn't mean … just the mention of that guy fills me with something so vile I don't want it anywhere near me, let alone *in* me."

That admission makes me wonder what soul-crushing terror the detective's interrogation had on that innocent, eighteen-year-old boy.

"He hurt you?" I ask gently.

He shakes his head and sighs. "The lies are what hurt. I kept insisting my kid neighbour, Liam, saw the whole thing. But Reid categorically denied there were any witnesses besides Liam's mother and the security guy. Said I was making it up. Said he had me dead to rights and he'd make sure I was put away for the rest of my life."

"I had no idea."

"Of course you didn't. No one knew but me and Liam. Obviously, I was in no position to demand someone speak to the kid. Even my useless lawyer thought I was full of it because Reid made sure there was no record of Liam seeing anything. That feeling … of being trapped, deprived of any ability to prove what really happened … That was not a fun fucking time."

The palpable stress and anguish bubbling out of him at the memory has the veins in his arms protruding, his whole body tense again.

But why would Reid do that? What could he possibly have to gain by arresting the wrong person? This whole thing is more screwed up than I imagined.

But it's exciting, too. We might just have a new witness.

For the second time today, I reach out, my hand landing gently on his upper arm. I've never been a touchy-feely type of person, but something about Gavin Lake brings it out in me. I can't seem to help myself. Which, for someone who's always in control, is more than a little unsettling.

"Forget him. For now, anyway. This witness … Liam? Do you know his surname? Where he is now? Anything?"

"Liam Thompson. He was only six or seven at the time. I knew him enough to say hi when we saw each other on the street, but I was too old to be hanging out with a kid his age. You think, after all this time, it'll help?"

"Oh, it'll do more than help. It'll show corruption, or at the very least incompetence. As long as we can find Liam, it's not over, Gavin."

He nods, his eyes briefly flicking to my hand resting on his arm, which I realise is squeezing a little too hard from my excitement over this new possibility. As I let it drop away, my fingers briefly dust over his forearm. My heart jolts at the contact. And the way he's staring at his arm, like he's never seen it before, I know he feels it too.

When he lifts his gaze and our eyes hold, I want to touch him again. While I battle to resist the urge, he glances away and runs a hand through his hair. I have the strangest feeling he's trying to stop himself from touching me.

"But, ah," I swallow, trying to concentrate. "Thompson's a common name. You have any clues as to where we might find him?"

"Last I saw him, he was watching what happened from his bedroom window."

"Why don't we go for a drive? Maybe he or his parents still live there." My heart suddenly picking up speed as the significance of that suggestion resonates through me.

"I suppose we could, but—"

"Great. Let's go," I say, already marching toward the car before I change my mind.

"Now?" he asks, catching up.

"Oh, I'm sorry. You have other plans?" I glance at him quickly enough to see his lips twitch.

"No, I don't have anywhere else to be. I thought, maybe you do?"

"Nope. So, looks like we're doing this."

"Looks like it," he agrees, though I don't miss the reluctance in his voice.

Once we're in the car and on the move, the rustle of paper catches my attention. I look over to see him peering into the open hamburger bag. When he spots me watching, he holds it out. I shake my head.

"Any objection if I eat it?" he asks.

"Go ahead."

From the corner of my eye, I watch him demolish the remaining half in a couple of bites. Satisfied, he wipes his mouth and balls up the paper bag.

"What a guts," I say in an effort to lighten the tension that's developed since we started toward our destination.

He lets out a contented sigh and rubs his stomach. "I know, but feeling full like this is so … strange. I kind of love it and hate it at the same time."

I shoot him a serious glare. "Do not throw up in my car."

"I promise not to, as long as you promise not to scare the crap out of me again."

"Deal."

Resting his head on the headrest, he watches me. "Have you ever been there?"

"No, but I know where it is."

A sudden thought pops into my head. My fingers clutch the wheel as the statement I made to the police all those years ago disperses dread into my blood stream.

"Jamie? Are you okay?"

I need to get that night straight in my head. When I pull up at a red light, I glace at him. "Sorry?"

"Last time we were in the car, you barely had your hands on the wheel. Right now, I don't think Superman could pry them off." He pauses for a moment before continuing, "Seeing where your mother died … maybe we should just turn around."

I know what he's trying to say, but right now, what has me in knots is so disturbing, I can't keep it in.

"Have you ever believed something so entirely that you'd swear your life on it," I ask quietly, "only to have your world thrown off-kilter, revealing it to be a lie?"

He doesn't push me. He simply waits.

"I remember the police asking me if Dad had been home all night. And I truly believed he was. But I just realised, he wasn't actually *with* me the whole time. I was upstairs, giving Anika a bath. For at least an hour, I didn't see him, but …" *God, how do I say it?*

"What're you thinking?"

"There's no way my father could have driven to your house and back. The garage door, it always made a hell of a racket every time it went up or down. I never heard it."

When I glance over at him, he's facing front, his jaw clenched, hands fisted on his thighs. "You don't think he did it?"

"Gavin …" I wait until he turns and meets my eyes. "I *know* he did. I just don't know how."

A car horn beeps behind me. The lights have changed. I get moving again, hating the way he's doubting me. I suppose, after a decade and a half of no one believing him, he's finding it hard to trust. And I want him to trust me.

"The cops never bothered to even look at your father, let alone how he might've done it." The bitterness dripping from his words sound nothing like him. "They had their man and that was that."

"Clearly the police failed in their duty to conduct a thorough investigation. If we can prove that they literally let the real killer walk free right under their noses, that they buried the fact there *was* another witness, well … you're not only going to get your conviction overturned, Gavin, you have a strong chance of receiving compensation as well."

He scoffs in disbelief.

"I'm going to do everything I can to make sure you get what you're entitled to."

His intense look of gratitude has tears threatening, forcing me to blink rapidly to keep them at bay.

When we're about five minutes from the scene of the crime, he asks, "Did you live around here?"

"We did, but after Mum's death, we moved to where I am now."

"It's taken almost an hour to get here."

I glance at the clock on the dash. "And?"

"Just … it took you an hour to drive out to me. Now an hour to get here. There's no way you're taking me home. I'll get an Uber back once we're done."

I almost protest about that costing a fortune, but think better of it. He won't appreciate being reminded of how little money he has, especially since I'm the one who had this bright idea. Instead, I say, "I love driving."

He lets out an amused snort. "If you can call it that."

I grin as I take the turn into the Sharman Grove Estate.

When I glance his way, he's tense again. *I'm such an idiot.* He's worried about how I'll react, but he's so strong and resilient, it hasn't even occurred to me how being back at the crime scene might affect *him.* As he stares blankly through the windscreen, I remind myself that he's just as much a victim in all of this as I am. Instead of blindly focusing on facts alone, I need to keep that in mind.

"I shouldn't have rushed you into this," I tell him. "I didn't think. We can turn around."

He hesitates only a moment. "As long as you're okay with it, so am I."

After he directs me through the rabbit-warren of streets, I pull up to the kerb. When I look at him, he's staring straight ahead. I follow his gaze, taking in the way the road doglegs in a sharp bend a little further ahead, causing a row of homes to face us. Anyone looking through those windows have a clear view of the street where I've parked.

We climb from the car into the scorching heat. When I meet Gavin on the footpath, he's tense and uncomfortable, but he forces half a smile my way. This isn't going to be easy for either of us.

"Can you show me where … you found her?" I hate myself for asking, but I know I'll never come back here again and, even though it's not *why* we're here, I can't leave without seeing where my mother took her last breath.

Clearly struggling, he turns his back to the house he's been staring at and glances down the street before meeting my eyes. "You sure?"

I nod, but when he takes a few steps past me, I freeze. Glancing over his shoulder, he offers his hand. I stare at it, the concept foreign. Apart from when I was a kid and when Anika was little, I haven't held anyone's hand in a very long time.

Swallowing over the lump that wants to creep its way into my throat, I step forward and take it. Studying me, he gives a gentle squeeze, and I tighten my grip. As we walk along the footpath, the comfort of his kindness almost undoes me.

Then he stops, gently places his hands on my shoulders, and turns me toward the nature-strip.

"Just here," he says softly, squeezing my shoulders. "If you want me to, I'll tell you every detail I remember. Just ask."

When I nod, his hands slip away and I feel him step back to give me space. I wish he hadn't.

As I stare at the nature strip where my mother died, for some reason I expect it to hold the indentation of her body, as if the continuous growth of grass throughout the years should remember what happened here. It's a stupid thought, but it rattles around in my brain anyway.

Blinking fast to ward off the threatening waterworks, I raise my face to the cloudless sky. Now that I'm standing in this spot, I know it's meaningless. If she's anywhere at all, she's not here.

I take another moment to get myself under control before I turn toward Gavin.

"So," I say, "since we're here, are you okay to walk me through how you found her?"

He nods and I follow him further along the footpath toward the end of the street.

"I'd been out running, but by the time I came around this corner, I was walking. That's when a guy wearing a baseball cap and dark clothes came rushing out of the shadows, knocked me down, then disappeared around the corner."

"He ran into you?" I ask, astonished.

"Yeah. Of course, no one believed me."

Anger ripples through me from the injustice of it all. What the hell were the police doing that night?

I follow him halfway to the spot where my mother died.

"About here, I heard someone yelling. When I looked up at Liam's window," he points to the first house on the bend that faces us, "he was waving his hands around like crazy."

I wait while he takes a breath, clearly lost in the memory.

"He opened his window and frantically yelled my name. The moment I realised something was very wrong, I saw her."

Not ready to hear those particular details yet, I turn back to the corner where my father fled and ask, "Where does that go?"

"If you turn right out of here, the road runs alongside the golf course."

I stare at him, my mind racing with possibilities. "Golf course?"

"Does that mean something?"

"You might have just solved how my father did it."

"Don't keep me in suspense."

I explain that the house we shared a back fence with sat across the road from the golf course. On the outside of this estate. My father could easily have left home on foot when I was giving Anika a bath, snuck through that neighbour's yard and then the golf course.

Gavin runs a hand over his face, the relief sweeping over his expression unmistakable. "The missing piece of the puzzle."

"Yes, but—" I stop cold, realising what he's telling me. "You … you thought my father … before I told you it was him?"

He grips the back of his neck. "Yes and no. I had a hell of a lot of time on my hands to run through every scenario. Obviously, I knew I didn't do it." He shakes his head and gazes into the distance. "The rage I felt when I discovered my father'd been cheating on my mother … well, I imagine that's nothing compared to a spouse finding out his wife's cheating on him."

I swallow over the tightness in my throat. He's right. The spouse is usually the most obvious suspect. For sixteen years, Gavin's been tormented by that fact. A fact the police didn't bother looking into at the time. Because of me.

"Or," I say, guilt churning that hamburger in my stomach, "they didn't look into it because they relied on the alibi I gave them. The false statement I made."

Gavin's eyes lock with mine and he steps forward, placing his hands on my shoulders. "Even if you'd told them he *wasn't* home, do you think they'd have cared? They were convinced they had their man. Don't you see? If they were interested in looking for other suspects, Reid never would have buried Liam's eyewitness statement. Do *not* blame yourself, Jamie."

I stare up at him, wishing I could stop the guilt from crushing me. "But, I—"

"It wasn't a false statement. It's what you believed to be the truth."

Just like I believed his guilt was the truth. Jesus. I don't care what I have to do, I need to set this right for him.

"Tell me you understand, Jamie. What happened to me was Reid's doing, not yours. Okay?"

One of his thumbs rubs over my clavicle, and when it accidentally brushes my bare skin where the neckline of my dress ends, a delicious shiver skates through my nervous system. Trying to ignore it, I realise he's right again. I'd told the truth as I knew it. It was their responsibility to test that truth, and they never did. Slowly, I nod.

I know he's assessing my reaction, checking for signs that I'm lying, or about to fall apart.

Apparently satisfied, he releases me and steps back. "Should we go knock on Liam's door?"

After discovering the house has been sold several times since Gavin's incarceration, leaving the new owner with no knowledge of who once lived there, we head back toward the car.

"When I'm back in the office, I'll do a historical title search," I tell him. "That way we can track Liam's parents down, then find him."

As we draw closer to my car, Gavin's pace slows until he comes to a complete stop in front of the house where he told me to park.

"This is where I grew up," he says, a strain in his tone I haven't heard before. Stepping a little too close to him, our arms brush while I study the house. Ignoring the foreign sparks scattering through my body, I concentrate on the only home he's ever known.

"Do any of your family still live here?"

"I don't know, and I don't care. I lost my mother a month before … you lost yours. And I lost my father that night."

I take in a sharp breath. "What do you mean you lost your father?" He closes his eyes and swallows hard. I knew that he'd assaulted his father that night, knew his father testified against him. But he wouldn't have had a choice.

"I didn't know it until the next day," he says, staring straight ahead at the house again. "Didn't believe it until the next week. He thought I killed her too. I haven't seen or heard from him since he testified."

My own throat tightens painfully, his words bringing up everything I'm trying to suppress. I can't help but wonder how painful losing his father in that way must have been. At least comparable to my mother's death, if not worse. Mum didn't decide to get murdered. Gavin's father made a deliberate choice to cut his only son out of his life.

The damage my own father has done to this man is almost unbearable. Before I know it, I'm blinking fast again, tamping down on all that emotion bubbling under the surface. That's when he chooses to finally look at me.

"Don't fight it, Jamie."

I shift my gaze to the house he once called home. My chin trembles and I'm so fucking close to completely losing it, I blink harder, faster and draw in a deep breath until the quivering subsides.

"I wish you wouldn't fight it," he says, "because … I can't."

When my eyes snap to his, I catch sight of a tear sliding down his face just before he turns his head away and places his hands on his knees. His back heaves as he tries to breathe through it.

"Ah fuck, I'm sorry," he manages to get out, his voice thick and ropey with raw emotion.

I stare in awe at the bravery of this man. I don't see his vulnerability as anything but strength, even though I berate myself for being weak when I break down. There's something different about a man unafraid to let go, and I wonder if this is the first time he's cried over his father's abandonment.

Overwhelmed with the need to hold him and give him the comfort he gave me, I move closer, but the way he's bent over makes it too awkward to wrap my arms around him. Instead, I place a hand between his shoulder blades, absorbing the slight tremble vibrating through his body. Rubbing in slow circles with the heel of my palm, I gradually work my way down his spine, wanting to show him that I understand, that I feel his pain. Right now, I want to connect with him on a purely emotional level that has nothing to do with trying to clear his name.

When my fingers reach the bottom of his t-shirt and connect with bare skin, his body stills, the shudders beneath my palm calming until they stop altogether. This is what he needs. Contact. To be touched. To be shown the kindness and understanding he's shown me.

Wanting to give him just that, I slip my hand beneath his shirt and glide my palm back and forth across his warm, muscular back.

"Fuck, Jamie," he murmurs on a long breath.

He straightens, forcing my hand to slip away.

Oh, God. I've done the wrong thing. I shouldn't have presumed to know what he wants, what he needs. I shouldn't have touched him like that. It crossed a boundary, it—

He wraps his arms around me and pulls me to his chest. I'm so surprised, I grip onto the sides of his t-shirt. "I … I shouldn't have—"

"Please don't say that," he murmurs.

So relieved I haven't offended him, I remember a hug is what I actually wanted to give him in the first place. Leaning in, I wrap my arms around his waist. Why does this feel so damn good? Really, I can't even tell if I'm comforting him, or if he's comforting me. This time, though, I want to be here for him. He's hurting and I want to ease that pain.

Can I? My heartbeat doubles. It doesn't mean anything, it's an act of giving, that's all.

Before I can talk myself out of it, I slip my hands under the bottom of his t-shirt and splay my fingers wide. Beneath my cheek, his chest rises on a shuddering inhale, and he tightens his hold a little. This skin-to-skin contact is an unfamiliar intoxication I had no idea I craved. And clearly, so does he.

My fingertips explore his smooth skin, the restrained strength of his muscles on either side of his spine. Although my intention is to acknowledge what he's going through, I hadn't counted on how wonderful it feels to be the one doing the touching.

Against my ear, his heart thunders. Wanting more, I move a little closer. And bump up against his erection.

He instantly steps back and turns away. "Shit," he grunts. "I didn't mean for that—"

"It's fine," I blurt. It wasn't his fault. If it's anyone's, it's mine. God, I'm so embarrassed with myself. What was I thinking? "Come on, let's get going."

I hurry around the rear of the car and climb in. Only when I start the engine does he follow. He won't look at me. Which I'm thankful for, since I'm sure my face is about the same shade as a Red Delicious apple.

After I follow his directions out of the estate and onto the main road, I finally brave a glance in his direction. He's tense, his hands fisted on his thighs, his gaze fixed on the traffic ahead. This can't go on for the hour-long drive ahead of us.

"Gavin, I didn't—"

"I'm sorry," he says, his voice thick and strained. "You must think I'm a total creep."

He's apologising? "Gavin, that's the last thing … What I think, is that you haven't been touched in so long … the sensation … well, your body just reacted. I understand." Though I don't know if that's true. For all I know, he's probably been making up for lost time since he got out.

He's quiet for a long moment and I know he's looking at me. I keep my eyes on the road.

"How is it you understand that?"

Now I'm the one who tenses. The answer to that question is pathetic. Worse still, I care what he thinks of me. So, I simply shrug and leave it at that, hoping he won't push for more.

"Who *are* you?" he asks.

I give him a quick glance, noting his fingers are now splayed on his thighs, his body relaxing.

"Sorry?"

"You're the first person on the outside to treat me like I'm normal, not some disgusting piece of gum that requires scraping off the bottom of a shoe. That makes me wonder … who you are."

"I'm just me."

"You're not *just* anything. The more time I spend with you, the more I want to know. Have you ever felt like that about anyone?"

I catch my bottom lip in my teeth. He wants to know more about *me*? No one's cared enough to be interested in me since Mum died. Dad saw me as his daughter and someone to look after Anika, and Anika saw me as a pain in her arse most of the time. I was there for them, but I'm not so sure they saw me as a real person with my own hopes and dreams. Which, I admit, wasn't their fault. When did I ever really let them in?

Apart from my family, I haven't come across anyone I'm fascinated with.

Until now.

I want to give him the truth. And I promised not to lie.

So, I simply nod.

Chapter 22

Gavin

WAITING FOR JAMIE to arrive, Benny and I stand in the parking lot and try not to melt. It's only 8am and already hot as hell.

After Jamie called me late yesterday afternoon to let me know she'd located Liam, and that he'd be thrilled to have her draw up an affidavit for him, I wanted to cry with relief. Not only has she followed through on her word, but it actually looks like I might have a shot at clearing my name.

She also explained that Liam needs to fly out tonight for a two-week stint in the Western Australian mines, so she's taken today off work to hightail it up the coast.

In an effort to get Benny out of his little box, along with the fact that I want him to meet Jamie, she's agreed to him coming along.

While we wait for her, I wonder again why this two-and-a-half-hour trip up the coast isn't happening over the phone or online, but I'm not stupid enough to question it. This way, I get to spend most of the day with her.

"Thanks again, Gav. I'm pretty fuckin' grateful ta be gettin' outta that hot-box. Not ta mention finally meetin' your obsession."

"Jesus, Benny. You've already forgotten?" I snap.

"Think I'm gettin' dementia," he chuckles.

"I mean it," I say, turning to face him. "Do *not* embarrass me. This is nerve-wracking enough without you spouting off your nonsense."

He rolls his eyes. "Christ on a cracker. No fuckin' fun, are ya?"

"Remind me," I demand, my heart juddering in my chest at the thought of Benny saying something that'll have Jamie believing I'm a crazed stalker.

"Fine. Don't tell her 'bout ya sketches. Don't tell her how much ya stared at them. Don't tell her you're all mushy inside for her."

After his simplified version of my rules, he gives me a quick one-two in the stomach. Fortunately, I'm so fucking tense, I barely feel it.

Then her car pulls in and drives toward us. "Here she is. Behave."

Benny puts both hands up in surrender. "I gotcha back, Gav. Relax."

I've never witnessed Benny's behaviour around a woman, so I have no idea what I'm getting myself into. But the guy needs to get out of this caravan park, do something different for once, and meet someone other than the scum living here. And I don't know anyone besides Jamie.

When her car pulls to a stop, I reach for the passenger doorhandle and open it. But before I can get in, she climbs out.

I watch over the roof of the car as her ponytail swings behind her, sunnies blocking my view of her eyes. When she rounds the rear bumper, my heart wants to leap from its cage.

She's wearing a pretty summer dress that dips in a low V-neck, cinches in at her waist and flows loosely a few inches above her knees, caressing her bare thighs. When my gaze reaches her toes in strappy sandals, I notice they're painted a delicate shade of pink. I'm sure she wasn't wearing polish the other day. But best of all, when she places her sunnies on top of her head, her eyes radiate warmth.

Fuck, she's sexy.

"Lovely to meet you …"

"Benny," I jump in.

"*Bennie and the Jets*," she mumbles under her breath as she offers him her hand. "Lovely to meet you, Benny."

To my horror, he bats her hand away. "None of that," he says, and wraps his arms around her in a bear-hug. "The way this bloke goes on about ya, feels like I've known ya for years."

If I had the power to disintegrate into a million pieces, now would be the time. As Jamie hugs him back, her eyes find mine over his shoulder, and she smiles. Her eyes sparkle with a brightness that hadn't been there the other day. Hope, maybe. Or purpose. I'm not sure, but I like it a hell of a lot.

Giving Benny's back and affection pat, she pulls away. "Well, the fact that you've always believed he's innocent, makes me like you already." She glances at me. "Ready to go?"

"Sure." I make a move toward the passenger door.

"Shouldn't you let Benny sit in the front?" she asks as she heads around to the driver's side.

I shoot Benny a death glare that hopefully withers his insides. He's along for the ride, not to steal my seat beside her.

"Nah. I'm shorter than Gav. He'll be all cramped back there."

Once we're all in the car, Benny scoot across the seat so he's positioned directly behind Jamie. I glance back at him, and he gives me a smug wink. Which I'm sure Jamie catches in the rearview mirror.

"Now," Jamie says, flicking her gaze to me, "you're not going to freak out again, are you?"

Right. Seems I'll be contending with two smartarses today. I might have made a big mistake introducing these two.

Benny's head appears between the seats. "You freaked him out?"

I catch the cheeky grin on those perfect lips of hers. "I did."

Benny smirks. "Looks like we've got our first road-trip story, 'cause I haven't heard a word about that."

As we get going, Jamie takes great delight in showing Benny what her modern car can do. Only difference is, she explains what it does before actually demonstrating, preventing Benny from having the same heart failure she subjected me to. They crack up when she tells him all about my reactions, and I laugh along with them. The fact that she's comfortable enough to rib me, and lights up while doing it, makes me all warm and mushy.

"So, Gav," Benny says, "I keep meanin' ta ask what that is on ya neck there."

My gaze snaps to Jamie. She flicks a look at me, then glances in the rearview mirror as a bright flush colours her cheeks.

"It's nothing," I tell him, a warning in my tone. Of course, he's not deterred. He leans in even closer.

"Doesn't look like nothin'. Kinda looks like—"

"Caught myself on the corner of a cupboard, that's all." I catch Jamie's eyes for a split second, her relief at my lie evident when she loosens her grip on the wheel.

I know I shouldn't, but I glance back at Benny. He's grinning from ear to ear, his eyes darting between us before he gives me an eyebrow waggle.

"You're a terrible liar, Gav."

"And you're a terrible guest, *Benny*." My death-stare does nothing to stop his chuckle rumbling through the car as he slumps back in his seat.

When we finally arrive at Liam's, my chest constricts the moment I lay eyes on him. Seeing that little boy all grown up only serves to cement how much time I've lost.

With genuine guilt and remorse on the poor guy's face, Liam hits me with a firm handshake. "Gavin, man. I'm so sorry. No one'd listen to me and I—"

"Liam," I say. "Not your fault, buddy. There're a few people to blame, and you're not one of them. Got it?"

He gives me a nod, but I don't quite believe it. "Right, well, hopefully I can set the record straight now."

When he leads us through to the living room, Benny snavels one of two armchairs and Jamie takes a seat on the small, two-seater couch, leaving me in the wonderful predicament of having to sit next to her. After Liam provides refreshments, Jamie gets permission to record the interview and explains she'll also take notes on her laptop. On the drive here, she expressed her concerns about how much Liam might remember, but the guy seems confident.

"I was in big trouble that night," Liam begins. "I'd cut off one of my little sister's pigtails and Mum totally lost the plot. Sent me to my room without dinner and told me to get in bed and stay there. It was way too early for me to go to sleep, and I wasn't allowed to have my light on, so I just stared out the window, waiting to get tired.

"Wasn't long before I saw a guy in black clothes and a baseball cap come round the corner and walk a up the street toward my house. I was so bored by then, I paid close attention to him." He takes a breath, his gaze unfocused. "He stopped in the middle of the footpath, staring at Gavin's place for a bit. Then he hid between a couple of cars on my side of the street. I mean, I was seven, so I didn't know what was going on. I just knew it was weird. Weird enough that I wanted to go get my mum. But before I could, a car came round the corner and parked close to Gavin's house."

Knowing what should come next, my heart speeds up, terrified Liam might remember things differently. If our stories don't match, I'm fucked. Jamie made it clear that I need either evidence or a witness, and Liam's my only shot.

"It was kinda like a movie. She got out of her car, then headed toward Gavin's."

I glance at Jamie as her fingers freeze on the keyboard, her expression tight. Discreetly, I press my thigh against hers. Her gaze shifts from Liam to me.

You okay? I mouth.

She gives me a faint smile, then nods before focusing on Liam again.

Knowing what's coming, I keep my leg where it is, hoping the contact gives her some comfort.

"The guy in the baseball cap was suddenly on the footpath, flying towards her. He had his back to me, so I couldn't see his face. I remember how shocked she looked when she saw him. She didn't even scream. Just bolted. But he was faster. Grabbed her, threw her on the nature strip and was on her, forcing her onto her back, and …" Liam hesitates, his attention shifting to Jamie.

Her thigh presses hard against mine. I push back enough to let her know that I'm right here. I'd rather hold her hand, put my arm around her and protect her. It's killing me that I can't.

"Keep going," she tells Liam, a barely noticeable hitch in her voice.

"I saw him raise both hands above his head and bring them down, but his back was blocking my view. Then he was up and running. It happened so fast." Liam drags a shaking hand over his face, his eyes locked on the coffee table between us.

"Did you notice if he had the knife in his hand when you first saw him?" Jamie asks, her tone professional, detached.

It's surreal, hearing someone else tell the story of how her mother was attacked before I came on the scene.

"No," Liam answers. "I didn't see it until he took off … when he left it sticking out of her chest."

Jamie nods and types. "Keep going."

"Then Gavin came round the corner, and I started waving at him, screaming, trying to get his attention. The other guy knocked Gavin down, then legged it.

"That's when Gavin saw her. He was shocked, but he didn't hesitate. He ran right up to her, tried to help. Then Mum was in my room. Obviously, she heard the racket I was making. She screamed when she looked out the window, then she dragged me away."

Liam lets out a long, shaky breath and leans back in the armchair. Beside me, Jamie does the same. My heart's pounding. I'm not sure if it's from re-living that night through Liam's eyes, or if it's the thrill of knowing his story matches mine exactly.

"Do you need to take a break?" Jamie asks.

Liam shakes his head. "No, I'm fine. Just haven't really thought about it in that much detail for a long time."

"That's understandable," she reassures him. "When you're ready, what happened next?"

He picks at the leather on the arm of his chair for a moment. "Well, my mum thought what everyone else thought. That Gavin had stabbed someone. I kept trying to tell her what really happened, but she was hysterical, wouldn't listen to me."

"And when the police arrived at your house?" Jamie asks.

"A detective interviewed mum. I kept interrupting him, but he shut me down. He was only interested in what Mum had to say. He acted like a kid couldn't possibly have eyesight, couldn't have possibly seen what I was trying to tell him."

Jamie pulls out her phone, scrolls for a moment, then shows the screen to Liam. "Was this the detective?"

Liam nods. "Yeah, that's him."

"So he made no attempt at all to interview you?"

"Nope. Then when Mum told me Gavin was going to jail for a long time, I just didn't understand. But I was seven. I was powerless."

"You tried," I tell him. "There's nothing else you could've done."

He meets my eyes and nods. "Do you think this'll help?"

"This is huge, Liam," Jamie says as she stops the recording app on her phone. "It's proof the police didn't conduct a proper and thorough investigation. And it's proof that Detective Reid perverted the course of justice by purposely ignoring your eye-witness account. This statement will go a long way to giving Gavin his life back."

After I thank Liam profusely, and we promise to see him in a couple of weeks so he can sign the affidavit, we head out.

Jamie digs her key fob out of her handbag, and as we approach her car, all four windows lower and the car rumbles to life.

Benny shoots a look over his shoulder at us, grinning like a kid in a toy shop.

"Show off," I grumble as I nudge her with my arm, managing to get a brief smile out of her.

Once Benny slips into the back seat and shuts the door, I touch Jamie's elbow and stop her before we reach the car. "You okay? That couldn't have been easy."

She shrugs. "I'm fine. I appreciated you … letting me know you were there for me." She glances down the street, then back at me. "What about you?"

"Just relieved Liam remembers what happened. I'm fine hearing about it. I'm sure you can imagine how many times I've been over it in my head. That probably helps keep the emotion out of it."

After giving me a sad little smile, we get in the car and drive away. As I glance over at her, the need to bring a genuine smile to her eyes, to take care of her in every way possible, hits me like a fucking freight train.

Chapter 23

Jamie

AS WE DRIVE out of Nelson Bay and begin the trek back home, the signs for Anna Bay call to me. When the turn-off appears, I take it and head toward the ocean.

"How long since you've been to the beach?" I ask, glancing at Gavin.

He rubs a hand over his chin as he considers his answer. "I was seventeen. Drove Mum to Manly the day I got my Ps. The views from the Fairfax Lookout were amazing. She loved it."

I hope I haven't upset him, but when I catch his eye, he's smiling. I envy him. He must have known by then about his mother's illness, giving him opportunities to make happy memories together before her time came to an end.

"What about you, Benny?"

"Forty-odd-years. You gonna break the drought for us?"

I nod. "Crazy to be so close and not check it out, don't you think?"

"Didn't bring any swim-trunks," he points out.

It's a shame I hadn't put more thought into this trip, but I hadn't planned on it turning into anything other than a necessity.

I glance over at Gavin's strong, tanned legs below his cargo shorts.

"We can still dip our feet in." I suggest.

"Yeah, I'd like that," Gavin says, smiling at me.

"I'm easy," Benny agrees. "Is this the beach that's thirty-somethin' Ks long?"

"That's that one," I say, pulling up to the unusual concrete pyramids that cordon off the carpark from the beach.

"Got a feelin' ya gonna love it, Gav."

The guys decide to ditch their shoes, and I do the same with my sandals, popping them in the boot, along with our phones and my handbag. Locking the car, I shove the key fob down my bra and look up to find Gavin staring at my boob.

His eyes snap up to mine, and I'm not quite sure, but I think his face turns a little red.

"You really shouldn't put electronic devices so close to your, ah … delicate parts," he mumbles.

Nope, no mistaking it. He's blushing. Behind me, Benny snorts.

"This dress doesn't have any pockets," I explain.

Gavin indicates his shorts. "I've got plenty. Let me take it."

I shrug, and as I reach into the top of my dress and fumble around in my bra, he makes no effort to hide the fact that he's watching my every move. *Is he imagining it's his hand down my top?* I find that idea surprisingly appealing.

When I pass the fob over, he turns it in his hand a few times, like he's absorbing the warmth left behind by my body. Catching me staring, he quickly shoves it into the front pocket of his shorts.

"Did you just put it right next your … delicate bits?" I ask, unable to keep the grin off my face.

He smirks back at me for a moment, then reaches into his pocket and pulls it out. "Well, that was stupid."

"Christ on a cracker, give me the bloody thing," Benny grumbles, snatching the fob from Gavin. "No one's gonna care what happens to my *delicate bits*." He shoves it in his back pocket and strides off toward the beach.

"He seems a bit grumpy."

Gavin tries to suppress a laugh, but I'm not quite as successful. "Only when he thinks I'm being an idiot," he says, indicating that we should follow.

As we stroll side by side, I find myself waiting for that reassuring hand of his to rest against my back, and when it doesn't happen, I want to kick myself for being disappointed.

After we make our way from the soft, uneven grains to the damp, firmly packed sand at the water's edge, he moves closer, our arms brushing against one another. And I can't be sure if my heart's beating a little harder because of the contact, or the exertion of walking through soft sand.

"So," he says, "*Bennie and the Jets.* You know that's a song about a woman, right?"

I glance at him, surprised he heard me, let alone took any notice. "Oh, it's not that. When I first started work, I had a hard time remembering everyone's names, so I learnt to use those word association tricks." I shrug. "It's become a habit."

This time, the bump to my arm is deliberate. "Bet you didn't have to do that with me."

Along with my smile, my stomach drops. He knows as well as I do that you don't forget the name of someone you hate.

From out of nowhere, the sea breeze hits me with a forceful gust, lifting my dress up around my waist. Mortified, I spin away from Gavin and flatten the dress over my crotch. Fumbling to cover my backside, the buffeting wind seems determined to keep the material out of reach.

Gavin's hands suddenly grasp my hips, then travel down the outside of my thighs, bringing the dress with them as the gust peters out to a steady breeze.

Holy shit, he just saw my undies. And for the life of me, I can't remember what pair I put on this morning.

He's still standing behind me, his hands hot on my thighs, the front of his body so close to mine his chest brushes against my shoulder blades.

"I think it's safe now," I tell him, rattled by the thudding of my heart.

He releases his hold and steps to my other side, placing himself between me and the water. It's only when we start walking again that I notice his hand resting on my back, almost as if he's been waiting for an opportunity to naturally place it there.

"Well, that was humiliating," I say, trying to laugh it off.

"I think you mean *exhilarating*."

"Absolutely not."

He shoots me a mischievous grin. "I guess it's a matter of perspective. And nice …"

Was he about to say arse? "Nice what?"

"Legs," he says. "Mine. They're nice, right?"

I whack his upper arm, forgetting my embarrassment, loving the way he has no problem making a fool of himself. Going along with him, I pointedly stare at his legs before I nod. "They're not too bad. Good enough for shorts, I suppose, if that's what you're worried about."

"I wasn't, until now."

"Okay, I'll admit it. They're spectacular."

"Now I know you're lying," he chuckles, his eyes dancing with happiness. "Come on, we should catch up to Benny."

He grabs my hand and breaks into a jog, tugging me along until we reach his friend. Before he releases me, he gives a tight little squeeze, then pulls his wallet from his back pocket and hands it to Benny.

Benny grins as he takes it, apparently knowing exactly what's going on. "Go, ya big goofball."

Go? Where's he—

And then go he does. He takes off at a sprint, his feet kicking up sand, arms pumping, his backside magnificent as those long, muscular legs almost become a blur.

"What's he doing?" I ask Benny, the distance between us growing rapidly as Gavin flies along the beach.

"Running."

I let out a huff. "I can see that. Why?"

"Coz that's what he was meant ta do," he tells me, a wistful look on his face.

"He was?"

"Ya don't know he was destined ta be a great soccer player?" he asks, shifting his gaze to me.

"No. I had no idea."

"Yeah, star of his high school. Had a few offers from some scouts he was still deciding on before the shit hit the fan. Paid gig and everythin', right off the bat. No doubt he woulda ended up playin' for the Socceroos."

My eyes water before I even have a chance to try and stop the sorrow pouring out of me.

"Hey." Benny gives my shoulder a comforting pat. "Didn't mean ta upset ya."

Unable to speak, I shake my head. The more I discover about Gavin, the more I understand what my father took from him. Like the fact that he really could have been someone, could have had an amazing career. Instead, he has to start from scratch and find a place for himself in a world that thinks he's a killer.

When I search for Gavin, I can no longer see him up ahead. "Is he going to run the entire length of the beach?" I joke when my voice returns.

Benny chuckles. "Well, if he does, it'll be your fault."

"I made him want to run away?"

"Yup," he says with a wink.

"Okay, I don't feel like that's a compliment."

"Sure as hell is."

Confused, I stare at him. "You'll have to explain that to me."

"And I thought lawyers were s'posed ta be smart."

"Spit it out, old man."

That gets a laugh out of him. "Seein' all this wide-open space, I knew exactly what he'd wanna do. 'Specially since I've never seen him as happy as he is right now." He shakes his head. "Well, not just right now. Since ya first turned up at his caravan."

"Great news tends to have that effect."

Benny does nothing to hide his smirk. "It's not just the great news that has him full of beans. Guy's got a heart so big, I think it physically hurts him not ta have someone ta share it with, so he's gotta burn off all that excess energy. 'Specially when that someone's right here, within reach."

His insinuation has my pulse tripping over itself. Completely flustered, I blurt. "He's … well, I think he's pretty amazing. I just—"

"Amazin' huh?"

Shit. "I meant, it's pretty amazing that he came out of prison the man he is. Knowing no one believed him and probably never would … I can't even imagine."

Benny's smile fades as he stares at the endless stretch of beach before us. "I believed him."

"I've wondered why you did. The cliché that every prisoner claims they're innocent exists for a reason."

"I s'pose, at first, I didn't. But when I got ta know him, it was obvious. That kid didn't have a murderous bone in his body."

Though I don't know Gavin all that well, that statement rings true. "How did he survive all those years?"

"He did it himself without even realisin'."

I cock my head as something darkness drapes over Benny's eyes when he glances at me. I don't want to push, and maybe it's Gavin I should be asking, but if Benny's right and Gavin doesn't even realise how he made it through, then Benny's my only link to that information. "How?" I ask.

He sighs heavily and shoves his hands in his pockets. When his gaze returns to the beach, I'm sure he's only seeing the memory that's playing in his mind.

"He'd been transferred from remand ta the supermax for about a week. Found him in the showers. Three arseholes had him cornered. Good lookin' guy like Gav … was bound to happen sooner or later."

"Oh, God," I gasp, clamping a hand over my mouth. Fuck. Remembering how I once hoped something like that would happen to him churns my stomach. I'd thought he'd deserved it. The terror he must have gone through. And he shouldn't have even been there in the first place.

Benny pats my shoulder, bringing me back out of myself. "Haven't finished the story yet, so don't go gettin' ya knickers in a knot."

I remove my hand from my mouth and stare at him with wide eyes, desperate for him to continue.

"Was just about ta go get some mates, when I saw somethin' come over the kid's face. Think he knew right then that he wouldn't survive what they were gonna do to him. Better he die then and there fightin' those pricks. This wildness came over him, like he wasn't human. He turned into somethin' feral, and he fought those arseholes like a savage beast. There was no skill in it. Just pure fuckin' determination and craziness. Don't get me wrong, those guys put up a fight, but they saw what I saw. Fuckwits didn't stop, though. Gav ended up puttin' them all in the infirmary. He took a goddamn beatin', but that's all he took. After that, and after I convinced him ta shave his head and grow a beard ta hide those pretty-boy looks, no one ever touched him again."

"Jesus," I mutter, blinking at the tears that threaten. I can't even imagine the strength it must have taken to fight off three men. From what Benny just described, it sounded like he wouldn't have stopped until he was dead. His resilience astounds me. "He told me it was you who got him through it."

Benny shrugs. "He earned my respect … everyone's. That's how he survived. And by learnin' to hide who he really is on the inside."

"Except from you. I don't think you're giving yourself anywhere near enough credit, Benny."

He gives me a sideways glance and a crooked smile. "S'pose I can take some of it. But not all. There was someone else who got him through it, too."

"Oh? He's only ever talked about you."

"Then that's where we better leave it. Can't go tellin' ya all his stories. Gotta leave some for him to tell ya himself, right?"

A little disappointed, I nod. I don't think Gavin will ever tell me the story I just heard. Benny's right, though. They're Gavin's stories to tell.

After walking in silence for a while, I ask, "So, what about you? Gavin told me you were convicted of two murders, but both were in defence of another. I'd love to hear what happened."

"Happy to talk ya ear off, love. Second prick I killed was tryin' it on with a newbie. I ripped the arsehole off the skinny runt. Idiot tripped over his own feet and smashed his skull on the edge of a toilet. No one believed it was an accident, so I got another twenty."

As we walk along the wet sand, I listen to everything Benny's been through in his life. It's harrowing and unfair, but he doesn't seem bitter. To him, it's just the way his life turned out. But hearing his story makes me cringe inside. I'm the person who tries to keep people like him in prison. Listening to the reasons why he ended up incarcerated in the first place, then his second conviction, has me feeling dirty about my career again.

After listening to more of Benny's prison stories, I finally spot Gavin walking toward us in the distance. The first thing I notice is the sheen of sweat shining in the sunlight on his bare chest. Why disgusting man-sweat has me intrigued just because it's all over *him*, is baffling.

When he draws a little closer, I notice something dark over his left pec. From this distance, it's just a blob with no definitive shape. So, he does have a tattoo after all. And the fact that it appears to be the only one he has, tells me it holds significant meaning.

Eager to see what it is, my eyes remain riveted as the distance between us narrows. But just as the tattoo begins to take on a distinctive shape, he unfurls his t-shirt and shoves it over his head. I know he's hiding it from me, because he hadn't bothered covering up when other people passed him. It definitely means something. Something he doesn't want to share with me. And for some reason, that hurts.

Which is ridiculous. We barely know each other.

Close now, he breaks into a jog and sails straight past Benny and I with a smirk on his face.

"Now what's he up to?" I ask Benny.

"Beats me."

Glancing over my shoulder, I see Gavin racing toward us,

veering into the breaking waves. As he closes the gap, he kicks at the shallow water, sending a spray of cool droplets misting over us. I gasp, raise my salt-speckled sunnies, pop them on top of my head, and glare at him.

"Bugger off, Gav," Benny warns, inching away from the water until he meets the soft sand.

Gavin's roguish eyes lock with mine. He's not done, and I'm the closest target.

With a rush of lightness bursting through my chest, I take off. As my bare feet fly over the compacted sand, I feel free, like a kid again, and I realise that's probably the last time I actually ran anywhere.

When I hear his footfalls over the waves, I put on an extra burst of speed. I run and run, my dress plastered to the front of my body, my ponytail whipping my back. Grinning, I revel in the spontaneity and unexpectedness of this moment. When I left the house this morning, I never imagined I'd be chased along a beach by a man I hope catches me.

Then the show-off shoots past me as if I'm running backwards.

Once he's far enough ahead, he stops and turns, a mischievous gleam in his eyes. I swerve toward the soft sand, but he mirrors me, and when I veer toward the water, he scoops me up and tosses me over his shoulder. Squealing like a little girl, I pummel his back with my fists as he carries me into the waves.

His body shudders with laugher as I watch the back of his knees disappear beneath the swirling foam. When the next wave crashes into him, he stumbles, and we almost go down, the jolt sending my sunglasses into the ocean.

"My sunnies!" I shriek.

He twirls around, his laughter vanishing. "Hold on! We're going under!"

"Gavin! Don't you dare!" I buck and squirm, kicking my legs. "Please! The salt water'll ruin this dress," I shout, not having the faintest idea if that's true or not.

"Okay, okay," he grumbles, heading to shore. When the

water becomes shallow, one of his hands releases the back of my thigh, and he dips low as if he's about to put me down. Before my feet touch the sand, he straightens up. It's not until he clutches my thigh again, that I tune into the position of his hands.

Holding down my dress, they curl around each thigh just below my backside. I should be grateful he's not giving the whole beach a view of my undies, but my concentration is on the way his pinkies graze my bare skin below the hem of my dress, the heat of his hands and the firmness of his grip only centimetres from my arse. I should be screaming that this is highly inappropriate, but the way my body's reacting drowns out all rational thought.

Trying to distract myself, I accuse, "I can't believe you lost my sunnies."

"You can have mine."

As he steps free of the water, I watch the damp sand turn dry. He needs to put me down before those hands of his turn me into a puddle of mush.

"Can't … breathe," I whimper.

In a whirl of movement, he catches me in his arms, hoisting me close to his chest. I instinctively clutch his shoulders and stare straight into his grinning face. A face wearing my sunnies.

"You bastard!" I laugh, snatching them from his eyes and shoving them back where they belong.

"Well, that's not a very nice *thank you*."

"Ha! You're the one … where're we going?"

"I want to show you something," he says through laboured breaths he's trying to mask. As he walks halfway up a sloping sand dune, I take in the effort on his face, feel his feet sinking into the loose sand.

Just as I'm about to insist he put me down, he loses his footing. I squeal, wrap my arms around his neck and hold on tight.

With lightning reflexes, he pivots, landing on his butt with me in his lap, the arm around my back holding me tight to his chest. While I wait for him to release me, I realise I'm not letting go either.

Heart thundering, I lean back a little.

"Sorry," he mumbles.

When I meet his eyes, there's not an ounce of apology in their striking blue depths. "No, you're not."

I get a bullshit hurt expression in response. "You don't believe me?"

"You're having way too much fun to be sorry."

"And I love that you are too."

He's right. It's been so long since I've felt free and happy, since I've had *fun*. Maybe as long as it's been for him.

But I'm pretty damn sure that's not why my face is on fire. Because, oh my *God*, I'm sitting in his lap, and his fingers on my waist keep gently squeezing and releasing, as if he can't decide what to do with them.

"I should …" As I make a move to free myself, his restless fingers tighten on my waist.

"Don't go yet," he says softly, like he's making a wish.

I freeze, our eyes locking. The way he's looking at me … it's pulling me in.

"I want to show you something, remember?"

I nod dumbly, afraid my voice might crack if I attempt to speak.

He shuffles me around until I slide between his bent legs. My butt hits the warm sand as he rests his forearms on his knees, his chin hovering over my shoulder.

Although he's no longer touching me, his presence is everywhere, encapsulating me in an embrace of pure energy. It buzzes with life, warmth and promise in the miniscule space between us. I don't think I've ever felt so protected, as *whole* as I do right now.

Right beside my ear, he murmurs, "How long since you've stared out as far as the eye can see?"

I don't have to think about it. "When I was a kid."

"Yeah? Beautiful, isn't it?"

Although I'm looking at the ocean, my mind's only aware of what's directly around me.

Him.

Pushing the thought aside, I take in the horizon, the sun sparkling on the water, the different shades of emerald as the waves swell, then break. Seagulls hover on the stiff breeze, the sounds of their squawks mixing with the crashing ocean.

He's so right. In this moment, absorbing all these sensations, the stress in my life ebbs away. "It's truly stunning."

"In prison," he says, his breath tickling my ear, "you can never see the horizon. There's no space, no beauty. Only walls and fences and razor wire. The exact opposite of this."

Tenderness floods through me. He's letting me in again, revealing an important lesson he had to learn in the most atrocious way. And he's passing it on, reminding me what shouldn't be taken for granted when it's freely available.

The heat of his chest radiates into my back, and I can't resist the temptation anymore. I ease into him just a centimetre, as if it's a total accident, and warmth spreads across my shoulder blades as I connect with his hard chest. I hold my breath, waiting for him to break the contact. He doesn't. In fact, I'm sure the pressure against my back increases. As if he's pretending it's unintentional, too.

I long to take his hands and wrap his arms around me, let him rest his chin on my shoulder, and just hold me as we stare out at the amazing expanse of ocean before us.

But I don't move. I can't. I don't really know this man. The problem is, my instincts are screaming all sorts of crazy things, and none of them are the usual warning signals I've come to expect on the rare occasion a man shows me any interest. What I need to do is what I always do. Analyse and pick apart every thought, emotion and reaction I'm having.

And once I do that, I'll be able to reason away these ill-informed instincts.

"Alright, love birds. What's so fascinatin'?" Benny asks from behind us.

Gavin's pecs turn to stone against my back. As I leap to my feet and brush the sand from my backside, I glance at Gavin. Jaw clenched, the amusement in his eyes gone, he's clearly avoiding my gaze. And … is he blushing?

I bring a hand to my cheek, the radiant heat there almost burning my fingers. Thank God he won't look at me.

When I glance at Benny, he's grinning like the cat who ate the canary.

"We should, ah … probably head back, beat the traffic," I say.

"Be right behind you," Gavin mutters.

"Somethin' up, Gav?" Benny chuckles.

Apparently unimpressed, Gavin grabs a handful of sand and flings it at Benny's legs. The older man only laughs harder.

"C'mon, love, let's leave grumpy pants alone for a bit." Benny takes a wide arc around Gavin until he reaches me, then holds out his elbow. I curl a hand around the inside of his arm and let him guide me in the direction of the car.

When we reach the hard-packed sand, I take a quick glance over my shoulder at Gavin. His forehead rests on the arms he's crossed over his knees. I know Benny's *love birds* comment has everything to do with the sudden change in his demeanour.

"Don't worry, love. He just needs a few minutes."

"For what?"

His gaze turns curious. "Why else would a man not want to stand up right after snugglin' with a girl?"

I gape at him. "We weren't *snuggling*," I protest. He chuckles and shakes his head. That's when understanding thumps into my dumb brain.

Somethin' up, Gav?

I'm instantly thrown back to the other day, outside his childhood home, when the same thing happened. He'd been mortified. My heart speeds up. I don't have to imagine how much he craves physical affection. Because with every look, every smile and every touch, he's making me feel it, too. And I'm no sure how much longer I can keep that longing buried deep inside, no matter how much I want to.

"Young people. Totally oblivious ta what's right in front of 'em," Benny says, patting my hand. "Hopefully, by the time he catches up, he'll have stopped wantin' to strangle the livin' daylights outta me."

Turning my face away from Benny so all I can see is the ocean, I smile, so glad Gavin has this man in his life. The fact that they rib each other shows how close they are.

It's not until I drop them off at the caravan park, that I realise I've had one of the best days of my life.

The next morning, I explain to my boss what I'd like to do for Gavin. He agrees that if I'm successful, it'll be great publicity for the firm and, as long as it doesn't interfere with my current cases, he gives me the go-ahead.

When lunchtime arrives, I meet Pete and tell him the good news, eager for more advice now that I have what he claimed I needed. To my surprise, he's not enthusiastic at all. He's doubtful the recollection of a seven-year-old boy, sixteen years ago, will be enough to convince the court of Gavin's innocence. Before I get a chance to go through the details, Pete cuts lunch short when he receives a call, leaving me wondering why he's behaving this way. I'm not buying that he simply wants me to step away from acting for Gavin because I don't need the added stress.

Early that evening, I place my laptop on the dining table, eager to get to work on Liam's affidavit so it's ready for him to sign when he returns from the mines. In an effort to remain professional and detached, I don't bothered changing out of my work clothes like I usually do.

While I sit there, staring at the blinking cursor, the house ticks and cracks as the wind outside picks up, amplifying the silence of my empty house. Reminding me again how alone I am.

Getting up, I pour a glass of wine, hoping it might help while I type out the details of my mother's murder.

Glass in hand, I stride over to the living room and flick on the TV for company while I work. As I toss the remote on the couch, something by the front door catches my eye.

A piece of paper lies on the floor. As if it's been shoved under the door. I hadn't seen it earlier because I always enter through the garage.

Frowning, I hurry over and pluck it up. It's crisp and white and folded in half. An innocuous piece of A4 copy paper.

Until I unfold it.

Three words stare back.

And I'm startled by how fast a harmless piece of paper can turn sinister.

Chapter 24

Gavin

CLIMBING FROM AN Uber after yet another failed job interview, wind whips at my hair and thunder rumbles in the distance as I hurry to my caravan. When I let myself inside, the humidity's so thick it's an effort to draw a breath.

The moment I collapse on the bed, my phone rings.

Jamie.

Instantly forgetting about my zero employment prospects, I grin. "Hey."

"Hi."

Did I hear a tremor in that single syllable? Unsure, and when she doesn't offer anything further, I say, "Okay … so I could say *hey* again, but that might make you say *hi* again and then I think we might get stuck in some weird sort of loop that has no—"

"I'm here. In the carpark," she interrupts. Unfortunately, there's no mistaking the lack of amusement in her tone.

"Be right there." As head to the parking lot, I try to blame the oppressive humidity for my sudden lack of energy. But who am I kidding? She has bad news. It was right there in her voice.

When I reach her car, she glances up at me through the tinted window. Even though thick storm clouds darken the sky, she's hiding behind sunglasses. When she climbs out, I notice her work clothes and the severe ponytail. It's almost 8pm but it appears she's come straight from work.

"Can we talk?" she asks, as if I might tell her *no*.

"I'm all yours. Whatever you need, whenever you need it."

Though they need no adjusting, she pushes her sunnies higher on her nose. She's flustered. But there's something else there too. Something I can't pinpoint.

"I might have to hold you to that," she says quietly.

My heart beats a little faster. *What does that mean?*

"Well, let's get you out of this sweltering heat and into the sauna."

She gives me a tight little smile, though none of the tension emanating from her eases. "Sounds inviting."

Intrigued, I motion toward the path leading to my caravan, step up beside her and place a hand on her back. I really have no need to touch her. Unlike when Fletcher had been mouthing off and I needed to show him she was protected. This time, I expect her to move out of my reach, but she doesn't. And that's goddamn dangerous. Hope is a treacherous beast.

We reach the hot-box without Fletcher or anyone else throwing insults at her, and I usher her inside.

Right away, she toes off her heels, tosses her handbag on the small bench seat and slides in after it before she removes her sunnies.

I want to smile at how at how she's made herself at home, seeing it as a clear indication that she's comfortable with me, but as soon as I catch her eye, I deflate. Sliding into the seat opposite, I forget to make an effort not to brush my knees against hers.

"Something's wrong," I state.

"Not really. Maybe. I'm not sure," she rushes out in one breath.

"Right. Well, let's see if we can figure it out."

"How do you like it here?"

The question's so unexpected, I wonder if it's a tactic to delay what she's really here to tell me.

"As in, here in this tin-can?"

She nods, glancing around. Though she shows no distaste, it's obviously not the nicest place on earth.

"It's wonderful," I say. "The sauna's free; I can pretty much reach everything without having to take more than a step or two; there's a free reality show provided by the other guests on a regular basis; strict rules, so you never have to wonder where you stand; the air-conditioning doubles as a white noise machine—well, that's not true, white noise is its only function—and, of course, let's not forget the cosiest bed ever known to mankind."

"That's what I thought," she says, the faintest smile forming on her lips.

"Why do you ask such an intriguing question?"

She grips the edge of the table in front of her and takes a deep breath. "I have an idea."

Whatever's going on, she's nervous. "Okay, let's hear it."

"There's … there's a place that has plenty of room. A place that has a swimming pool, and a bedroom with an amazing mattress. A place that doesn't feel like an oven, but does actually have one in the kitchen. There's ducted air-conditioning—which I'm afraid to say, doesn't act as white noise. There's also a large TV and a proper dining table and—"

"Jamie," I interrupt, my heart thudding, unable to believe what she's offering. Because I'm either dreaming or completely misinterpreting her. "Be direct."

"It just makes sense," she continues, as if she hasn't heard me. "We're going to have to spend time together to get everything done for your case. And with my workload, I'll only have time for that after work. And, like you pointed out, there's the time it takes to drive here, then drive home. And this isn't the best working environment. It's so hot, I can barely breathe, let alone think. We need more room … and I've got a whole house that's empty. It just seems crazy not to …" she trails off when her eyes finally meet mine.

I'm not sure what she sees, because apart from being stunned, the stifling air seems to be caught in my throat.

I agree with everything she's said. Although she's right about my inconvenient location, and as much as I want to take her up on her generous offer, I can't fool myself into accepting. She's tried to present it as if it's for her benefit, but I think she just feels sorry for me. And I don't want anyone seeing me as a charity case or taking pity on me. Especially her.

"If you're suggesting what I think you are, it's not a good idea."

"I disagree," she says firmly. "My father was responsible for you going to prison, for you living here right now. He owes you. And since he's gone, I owe you."

"You owe me nothing, Jamie. Helping clear my name is more than enough. Above and beyond, actually." If there's even the slimmest chance she might see me as more than the guy her father fucked over, I have to prove I deserve her, that I hold something within me she needs. Having her believe she's indebted to me makes me feel about as useful as a mozzie. If I accept her offer, that's what I'll be. Nothing but an annoying insect bleeding her dry. And that's only one reason.

She shakes her head emphatically. "This place … it's just another prison. If my father hadn't done what he did to you, you'd have a career, your own house. Until we get your conviction overturned, a real home is the least I can give you. Please let me."

The thought of living under the same roof has my body reacting in all sorts of ways that try to weaken my resolve. "I don't think—"

"It's no different from taking in a boarder. At least you're not a stranger. It's a logical solution, Gavin. To say *no* is illogical."

"Not everything has to make sense." What I really want to say is *please don't push this, because I'm so close to caving, it's pathetic.*

"Explain that to me."

"For one, don't we have to keep this professional?" I point out, hoping that'll make her come to her senses.

"Nothing will change. Except we'll have more time to work on your affidavit, and you'll get to live in an environment you deserve. You don't belong here, Gavin."

"I don't feel like I do either. But you're wrong about it not changing things," I argue, realising she's not about to drop this.

"Why? I can't see—"

"What about your boyfriend or … whatever?" I interrupt.

She frowns in confusion. "There is no boyfriend."

"Okay, but there's a high probability that might become an issue at any given moment."

She scoffs, like it's the most ridiculous thing she's ever heard. "There's no danger of that. Whatsoever."

"I find that hard to believe," I tell her honestly. "You were on a date when you called me the other—"

"No," she interrupts. "I was having dinner with Pete. He's sixty-five and about to retire. He's my good friend, a mentor. So, unless some amazing guy comes knocking on my door, it's not an issue. Next reason?"

I could be that guy. The guy who knocks on her door. Shaking my head, I dismiss the notion almost immediately. She said *amazing guy*. That, I'm definitely not.

But to live with her? Just being in her presence is too tempting. Well, even then, I haven't managed to keep my hands off her. I don't think I'd survive the torment of being under the same roof. The need to touch her, kiss her, ravish her would be impossible to resist.

Fuck. How the hell can I convince her without telling her that.

So, I move on to reason number three.

"Jamie, you know how long I've been locked up. And how long Benny's been inside. He needs me right now. I'm not sure if you can imagine living with someone that long, locked in the same cell for twenty hours a day. Then suddenly you're alone. It's like you've been ripped in half. Without that other person, there's a gaping hole that takes a little while to get used to, then a little while longer to fill in. I can't leave him here alone. He's not ready."

She stares at me, taking in everything I've said. The compassion in her eyes squeezes my heart so hard I want to take every word back and just tell her *yes*.

She opens her mouth, then closes it, trying to come up with a rebuttal, I think, but she won't find one.

"Okay," she finally says, nodding. "Of course. I … I hadn't thought of that."

"This won't affect us working together?"

"Gavin, I'm here for you. I'm not going anywhere. I made you a promise, and that means something to me."

"It means *everything* to me."

I see something in her expression I can't quite decipher. And I don't like the fact that I can't figure it out.

I know I shouldn't, but that look in her eyes has me reaching out and placing my hand over hers.

Our eyes hold and, to my surprise, she turns her hand, wraps her fingers around mine and squeezes. I squeeze back, and we sit like that, staring at each other, neither knowing what to say or do next. All I know is that her clutching fingers, her palm against mine, fills me with warmth and comfort. Her affection makes me feel like I'm more than a waste of space. It makes me feel like I matter to someone. And that person happens to be the very one I want to mean something to.

Her fingers twitch around mine as that elusive look in her eyes flashes to the surface again.

"You're a good friend. To Benny … and to me," she says softly.

For a long moment, I'm completely dumbfounded. Jamie Evans sees me as a friend? A *good* friend. Not just someone she's taken pity on or feels indebted to. "Yeah," I croak, then clear my throat. "Ah, you too."

Fuck. I need to do a hell of a lot better than that. I need to be *that good friend.*

"There's something you're not telling me," I say, watching her eyes skitter away from mine.

"It's fine. It's nothing," she says too quickly.

Brushing my thumb over her fingers, I lean forward and wait until she looks at me. "You just said I'm a good friend, and now you're trying to hide something from me? Remember what we agreed? No lying."

"I really should leave," she mumbles, yet her grip on my hand doesn't loosen. "But you're right. There's something … though now that you've given me a satisfactory reason as to why you can't—"

"Jamie. What is it?" I interrupt, all too aware of the tremor in her hand.

Hesitant, she bites her lip as she thinks. "I really hoped you'd accept my offer, but the thought of going home without telling you … you should know … in case anything happens. It's just … I didn't want you to think I only offered my house to you because of this."

My heart jolts. "Because of what?"

I miss her touch the moment she slides her hand from mine. Then she reaches into her handbag and pulls out a piece of paper. Unfolding it, she places it on the table between us.

BaCK OfF BiTCH

I stare at the crude, cliched letters cut from a magazine.

"When I got home, that was under my door."

And now I know what that elusive look is.

Fear.

When I glance up, she won't meet my eyes. "Jamie …"

"I think I fucked up," she whispers.

I'm stunned into silence for a moment. "How is this you fucking up? Do you know who did this?"

Her eyes flick to mine for a second before they focus on the threat again. "I'm not a hundred percent sure … I could be wrong. It could be a threat from someone I'm trying to convict in court. But, I don't … no one like that should know where I live."

"So, you've got a theory?"

She nods. "That's the fucking up part."

Christ. A long, low rumble of thunder vibrates through the caravan. I want to hold her hand again, but she's hidden them under the table.

"The night I got drunk, before I went out … I rang Detective Reid."

Hearing his name on her lips again contracts every muscle

in my body. I put my own hands under the table before I smash something and terrify her. I prefer she doesn't witness the hatred that lives dormant inside me until his name is mentioned. Not after the fear I saw in her eyes last time it snuck out.

"What made you call him?" I simply ask.

When she finally meets my eyes, hers widen. Her posture straightens. She even leans back a little. She sees it. I can't hide it no matter how hard I try. It's in my body, my eyes, my soul. And she sees right into me. She came here asking for my help because she's scared. Now I'm the one she's afraid of.

But she doesn't run away. She sits there and faces me.

"It's just … my father always thought he was a great guy." She scoffs at the irony of that statement. "I thought he should know that Dad had died … and about his confession." She swallows, glances at the threat, then back at me. "I … You have to remember, when I called him, I had no idea I was talking to a man who deliberately buried a crucial witness. I believed I was talking to a man who'd simply missed something, who'd made a mistake. I thought he'd want to right that wrong."

My fingers almost tear off my kneecaps. "And what did he have to say?"

"He thought my father must have been delirious. He reminded me that I sat through the trial and saw what the jury saw."

Jesus, I wouldn't mind betting she'd felt sorry for the fucker. Sorry that he'd have to own up to a mistake. No wonder she froze that day I told her about Liam.

I need to hit something, move, run, expend this energy that desperately needs out. Instead, I stare at the piece of paper between us for a long moment.

When I lift my gaze to hers, I see a strong, independent woman who's afraid to go home. It twists my gut, and the need to protect her becomes so strong, it overpowers the hatred.

"So, you think Reid put this under your door." It's not a question.

"I can't be sure. But he knows where I live. And that I know he screwed up. I never told him I was planning on doing anything about it. But … when he told me to put it behind me, I hung up on him. Then I blocked his number."

"Fuck." I slide out from behind the table, take one stride over to the sink and grip the warm stainless-steel. Letting my head drop, I take deep breaths. I need to calm the fuck down.

"I'm sorry," she whispers.

"I'm not angry with you," I grit out, rubbing at the back of my neck. "It's … *him*. It's *me*."

"You?"

"If it's Reid, then I'm the reason for that threat. Because you're helping *me*."

"Don't you dare say that," she snaps.

As I stare through the grimy window, I hear her moving behind me.

"I should never have told you. You don't need this on top of everything else." Her vulnerable tone doesn't just tug at my heart, but threatens to rip it from my chest.

I turn to find her standing a foot away, her shoes on, handbag over her shoulder, the menacing note nowhere to be seen.

She's leaving.

Ready to return home. Alone. Where she doesn't feel safe.

Every molecule, every cell, every beat of my heart demands I go with her, protect her. But the memory of Benny's reaction when I revealed I wanted to put his plan on hold surfaces with a sting. He needs my support and loyalty. And if that involves being here for him every day, well, I don't think that's too much to ask.

But how do I choose between the man who taught me how to survive on the inside and the woman who wants to give me my life back on the outside?

Thunder cracks overhead, startling us both.

With her gaze firmly plastered to my chest, she says, "I better get going before the rain hits." Then she's gone, the door slapping shut behind her.

I stare at the empty space she occupied, my heart caught in

a vice, my gut in knots. I've hurt her, let her down, right after she called me her friend. She hadn't even wanted to tell me that what she really needs is my protection.

Bolting out the door, I catch up to her short but fast strides. Thunder booms overhead again, the downdraft swirling up dust, leaves and the odd bit of rubbish. When I place my hand on the small of her back, she speeds up. I'd like to think it's to avoid the storm, but I know the truth.

"Jamie. Wait."

She doesn't stop. As her car comes into view, she reaches into her handbag. Her vehicle's mirrors glide out and the indicators light up in the descending darkness.

As she wrenches the door open, I slam it shut and place both hands on the window, caging her in. She whirls around, her chest rising and falling rapidly, her back pressed against the car.

Lightning flashes. Her eyes flare with defiance, the tension between us crackling with as much energy as the approaching storm.

"Jamie, don't—"

"I'll be fine. More than likely it was just neighbourhood kids having some fun."

"You don't believe that." It's only now I realise how close I am to her, how menacing I must appear. *Fuck*. I'm doing a great job of making her feel safe.

"It doesn't matter," she says. "I've looked after myself my whole life. This is no different. I'll be fine." She stares up at me, waiting. When I don't move, she places a tentative hand in the middle of my chest and adds a little pressure. "Gavin, I need to go."

Not wanting to add to her distress, I take a step away. She quickly turns and opens the door. Before she can slip inside, I wrap my hand around her firm little bicep. She freezes.

"Promise me something." She's stiff as a board but doesn't pull away. "Give me a little time. Don't go home until you hear from me."

Beneath my fingers I detect the slightest relaxation in her

muscle. When she gives a slight nod, I release her.

Once her car disappears, I remind myself that last time I asked her to promise me something, she kept her word. All I can do is trust she'll keep this one, too.

By the time I'm inside Benny's caravan, the first fat raindrops tink against the thin metal.

Pacing back and forth in the tiny space, I quickly explain Jamie's visit. When I finally calm down enough to stop moving, Benny cocks his head. And smirks.

"I don't see how any of that's amusing," I grit out as I take the seat across from him.

"For someone who's s'posed to be smart, you're as thick as a fuckin' brick."

"What the hell're you talking about?"

He leans forward, eyes sparkling. "Let's go back to before she told ya about the threatenin' letter for a second. So, she comes to ya, offerin' a place to live, 'cause she doesn't think ya deserve to live like this." He gestures around the caravan. "And she just hoped ya'd take her up on it?"

"And I told her why I can't do that."

"Ha! Usin' me as an excuse. Pathetic."

"You're not an excuse."

Waving a dismissive hand in the air, he continues. "*Dickhead*, she wants you."

I let out a harsh scoff. That's *not* what she'd been thinking.

"Fine," he says, leaning back. "Guess women these days think nothin' of askin' ex-cons to come live in their homes. Yeah, I'm the idiot here. Not the dummy sittin' across from me who told her *no*."

I drop my head in my hands and fist my fingers in my hair. The thought of abandoning him gnaws at my gut, but if I tell him that, he'll feel like a burden, and I knows that's the last thing he wants. I want to tell him what he means to me, but he's from an era where men don't reveal how much they appreciate one another, so I keep my mouth shut.

He doesn't.

"If the threat's from Reid, how're ya gonna feel if he does somethin' to her?"

My head snaps up. He looks me dead in the eye and raises his eyebrows.

Fuck.

He doesn't need to say another word. He knows me too well.

Even though I've lied to Benny about the plan to kill Reid, if that prick tries to harm a hair on her head, he *will* be a dead man.

Chapter 25

Jamie

I'M PATHETIC. I'VE done exactly what I promised. Instead of going home, I'm sitting in a McDonald's ten minutes from my house, staring through the rain-speckled window, wondering what the hell I'm doing.

And wondering why, more than being afraid, I'm disgusted with myself. It hurt when Gavin rejected my offer. But once he explained why, it made perfect sense. After spending the day with both men, it's easy to understand how much they mean to each other. And Gavin's loyalty to the older man only adds to the respect I have for him. He'd put Benny's wellbeing over his own wants and needs. When I think of the men I work with every day, I know not one of them would do the same.

Gavin Lake is special.

He proves it every time I'm with him.

Which explains why I'm disgusted with myself. After he explained his rejection of my offer, that should've been the end of it. But, oh no, I had to go and make him feel guilty.

Believing he'd jump at the chance to get out of that caravan, my plan had been to show him the threat after he agreed. There was the risk he might not want to put himself in a situation that might turn dangerous, but I thought I had a pretty good handle on him when it came to protecting me. According to Gavin, even a simple walk from my car to his caravan requires an escort. *Protection.*

When he accused me of trying to hide something from him, my brain went into overdrive, and I made a quick decision. I wouldn't lie to him. I couldn't disguise how that threat rattled me, but I hadn't told him about it to make him feel guilty enough to change his mind. I'd told him because that's what friends do. Right?

But is that the only reason? Or does it have something to do with the way he looks at me like he actually sees me? The way he studies my eyes, my expressions, as if he's trying to learn the meaning of every reaction? I usually keep everything locked in tight, but the fact he can read me so easily means there's no hiding from him.

Butterflies take flight in my stomach, and I can't decide if that's terrifying or incredibly attractive.

I need to get a grip. I shouldn't be sitting here, keeping my promise not to go home until I hear from him. As far as I can gather, there's only one reason he'll believe it's safe for me to go home. He's trying to find another lawyer to represent him so I won't be a target.

Staring down at the salad I've barely touched, I can't see how he can accomplish that feat at this time of night, let alone find a lawyer willing to take him on so quickly, or without having to pay a retainer.

After checking my phone again, I turn my attention to the noise and chatter around me. Families. Everywhere. As I scan the restaurant, I discover I'm the only one sitting on my own, the only idiot who comes to McDonald's and orders a crappy salad. I wonder, if my mother had never been murdered, if my life might resemble the people around me. Would I be married and have a couple of young children by now?

An aching loneliness I've kept buried for far too long pierces my heart. Blinking rapidly to stop the sudden tears from falling, I stare through the water-streaked window into the darkness, forcing myself not to alter my focus. I don't want to see the miserable reflection of that lonely woman staring back at me.

I should go home. Really, I try to convince myself, I'm not that scared anymore. But when I think about climbing into bed and lying alone in the dark, my skin crawls and my heartrate kicks up a notch.

My heart kicks up another notch when my phone dings.

GAVIN:

Go home, Jamie.

That's it?

I stare at the message for a full minute, waiting for more. Nothing.

I consider calling him and asking what's changed, but I don't think I want to know the answer.

After making a short dash to my car through the torrential downpour, I drive home.

When I pull into the garage, I stay in the car with the doors locked, scanning every mirror to make sure no one slips in before the garage door reaches the ground.

Satisfied, I hurry inside, turning on every light I pass until I'm in the bright kitchen.

I almost scream when a loud knock comes from the front door. Hand to my heart, I wonder if it'll stand up to a few swift kicks.

The knock comes again. It doesn't sound threatening, just loud. Slipping off my heels, I silently cross to the door. I don't dare look through the narrow glass panel beside it. Instead, I rise on my toes, inch toward the peephole, and pray there isn't an eye staring back.

Soaking wet, with a large duffle bag at his feet, Gavin stands on my small porch.

A wave of utter relief sweeps through me as I drop my heels and rest my forehead against the door. But it only takes a few seconds for the guilt burn a hole right through my chest. What has he sacrificed to be here? What about Benny?

Taking a deep breath, I unlock the deadbolt and open the door.

We stand there, staring at each other for a long beat.

Finally, he says, "Benny and I came to an arrangement. If

that arrangement suits you, too … I'd like to be here for you."

His deep, gentle voice engulfs me like an embrace.

My throat tightens painfully, forcing me to stare at my bare feet as I take a step back, silently inviting him inside. After wiping his shoes on the mat, his damp sneakers squeak on the floorboards as he steps past me. I close the door and turn the key in the deadbolt.

But I don't release it, don't turn around. I can't.

No matter how fast I blink, tears slide down my cheeks.

He's here. I'm safe.

So why am I losing all control? What is it about him that makes me feel so thoroughly secure and protected that I can unravel? I'm supposed to be the one who's strong, who holds it together for everyone so they don't have to.

When I try to inhale, my breath catches in my throat, sending a shudder through my body.

A dull thump comes from behind me, then he's at my back and it's like the beach all over again. He's not touching me, but I feel him everywhere.

Without a word, he covers my fist, gently pulls it away from the key, and turns me around. Through blurry eyes swimming with tears, I stare at his chest, unable to meet his gaze. If I do, I'll turn into a blubbering mess. And I'm sure he's had enough of that by now.

"Jamie …" he murmurs, the tenderness and concern in his voice everything I know I'll find in his eyes.

Lurching forward, I wrap my arms around his waist, bury my face in his chest and turn into that weeping mess anyway. As he pulls me in closer, my fists bunch so tightly in his wet t-shirt, water trickles between my fingers. Slipping one large hand beneath my hair, he finds the nape of my neck.

Letting his gentle caress calm me, I tell myself not to feel bad about seeking solace in his arms. The first time I burst into tears, he came to me. The second time, he needed comforting. I might not know too much about men, but this one clearly doesn't shy away from a much-needed embrace. After being deprived for so long, why wouldn't he take advantage every time the opportunity presents itself?

Focusing on the warmth of his body seeping into mine, I gradually realise my sobs have faded away. Then I zone in on his thumb doing that calming rotation he does so well. Only this time, that gentle pad isn't situated against the nape of my neck. This time, it's performing lazy circles behind my earlobe.

God, it feels amazing. And incredibly intimate. Apart from having never been held by anyone the way he holds me, no one's ever touched me the way he does. *Is.*

As warmth pools between my legs, my heart starts jackhammering.

I'm not sure if he feels it, but he murmurs, "You okay?"

I nod against the hard pec beneath my cheek, and find I'm either unable or unwilling to let him go yet.

"Contrary to recent evidence, I swear I'm not a crier."

A low rumble vibrates through his chest. "Jamie, crying and laughing are the rawest, most honest reactions we have. They're what makes us human."

His hold on me tightens and, ever so slightly, I'm pressed a little bit firmer against him. Through his wet clothes, all I feel is warmth. I want to look up at him, but I definitely don't want him to see my puffy eyes and red nose. Not again.

"The amount of stress you're under," he continues, "well, if you didn't release it every now and then, I'd be worried. It's either that or go crazy. And I can't have you going insane. I need you."

He stiffens slightly, then quickly clears his throat, as if realising how those words might be interpreted. But his hold on me doesn't change.

"I'm getting you wet," he says, his breath tickling the fine hairs at my hairline, telling me his lips are so close they're almost touching me. That, coupled with what he just said, sends heat straight up my neck. Even though I know he means nothing more than the fact that his clothes are soaking into mine, he's not wrong on the other front. Keeping my burning face lowered, I pull away.

The moment I release him, he leans in so close I freeze, my

breath catching in my throat, my head spinning. But all he does is remove the key from the door and press it into my palm.

"Never leave a key in the deadbolt. Someone puts a fist through that glass panel, they can let themselves right in," he explains.

Unable to look at him, I nod like a fool. "Right. Of course. I mean, I should've thought of that."

"I wish you didn't have to."

My gaze rises until I'm staring into those intense blue eyes. And I wonder if I've made a terrible mistake inviting him into my home. Because while I attempt to change his life, I think he might change mine too.

"I should find someone else to take up my fight," he says, still holding my gaze, "If that threat is about me, then—"

"If it *is* about you," I interrupt, "that'd be pointless. Going elsewhere would simply change the target."

"Better than it being you."

Lost in those denim depths, at the genuine concern right at their surface, I shake my head. "No. I'm not letting anyone intimidate me. I'm fixing this for you, and I won't stop until your name's cleared. So, you can forget that idea. Permanently." I wipe my damp hands down the sides of my dress and sidestep around him. "Right, come on in. I'm sure you'd like a shower."

He follows me through the open-plan living area, then along the hallway. I open the first door on the right. "Here's the laundry. The internal access to the garage is right through there," I explain, pointing to the other door.

Further along, I enter the spare room. There's a freshly made double bed pushed against one wall, a small desk, a chest of drawers and built-in-robe. Turning, I find him hesitating on the threshold.

"This is yours. The bathroom's directly across the hall. Fresh towels, shampoo, soap, whatever you need is in there. It's all yours. I have an ensuite, so you don't have to worry about sharing with me." *God, I'm babbling.*

He nods as he takes a step inside and lowers his duffle bag to the floor. It's then I notice a dark patch on his t-shirt where

I'd rested my cheek. For a second, I think I've smeared mascara on him. Then I realise the darkness is coming from beneath the damp, semi-transparent material. The tattoo.

"Jamie?"

My eyes snap to his.

"Thank you," he says, his gaze darting around the room, taking everything in.

I shake my head. "No. Thank *you*." When his eyes settle on mine, I ask with trepidation, "You're absolutely sure about this?"

"I might not know much about protecting you … but I know I want to." He runs his fingers through his wet hair. "Anyway, I'll do a sweep of the house, check the locks. We'll talk after I have that shower."

I take that as my cue to get out of his room and give him some privacy. "Sure. I'd better get some work done."

He makes room for me to pass, but when I reach the threshold, he says, "You already know this, but you need to call the police. Just to make sure there's a record of the threat."

I nod before heading into the kitchen to get a much-needed glass of wine.

Once I'm sitting at my laptop, I reach for my phone when I hear the shower start up.

I don't dial the police directly. Instead, I call Pete and tell him about the threatening note and who I believe is responsible.

He's quiet for a long moment before he says, "Accusing a Detective Inspector of threatening you without any evidence isn't a smart move. You can't know for sure it was him. Your profession alone makes you a target for threats."

"I know that. It's just … the timing seems too coincidental."

"But is it? Reid has no idea you're on this mission to get Lake's conviction quashed, so from where I'm sitting, it's highly unlikely."

Now it's my turn to remain quiet. I'd rather not fess up to my mistake, but what I don't understand is why he isn't backing me up like he usually does?

"Jamie?" he asks, his tone that of a parent already suspecting their child's done something wrong.

"You're right. He doesn't know that's what I'm doing, but … I, ah, might've called him the night my father died. I know you told me not to tell anyone about Dad's confession, but it was too late by then. I couldn't take it back." When I hear a long sigh, I add, "At that stage, I had no idea he'd buried a witness … so it's possible he's put two and two together."

"Right. Let me think."

Damn. He's as happy about that little admission as I am.

"Listen," he says after a moment. "Meet me tomorrow for lunch with the note. I'll look into it myself. Discreetly. Any whiff that he's involved, we'll take it further."

"Okay," I agree, feeling a scrap of relief.

"Good." Another sigh. "So, how're you feeling? Do you feel safe? Want me to get a patrol car to cruise by every now and then? Is there anything I can do?"

It briefly occurs to me that those questions should have been the first he asked, but I brush it aside. First and foremost, he's a cop.

"I may have convinced Gavin to stay with me. For protection," I add quickly.

"You trust him?"

"I do. I've spent a fair bit of time with him trying to put the pieces together."

"Well, then, I think it's a good idea. Can't hurt to have a man around the house."

I pull the phone away from my ear and stare at it. Now *that*, I thought he'd protest.

"He's advised his Community Corrections officer?"

Shit. I'd forgotten about that. I might know he's innocent, but the rest of the world still sees him as a criminal on parole. "Well, no, it's only just happened."

"Make sure he does. And Jamie … if something else happens, you call me, and only me. Deal?"

"Deal."

By the time I start Liam's affidavit, Gavin appears in the

kitchen dressed in jeans and a black t-shirt that stretches across his broad chest.

"Mind if I grab a water?" he asks.

"Of course. You don't need to ask. Make yourself at home. That's where you are now."

He pauses halfway across the kitchen, his eyes pinning me with a look of such gratitude my insides flutter.

"That means …" He scratches at the back of his neck. "Well, thank you."

He grabs a glass from the first cupboard he opens and fills it at the sink, reminding me that he already knows his way around the kitchen.

As he brings the glass to his lips, I say, "Wait. The tap water's not great in this area."

After I take his glass and tip the water down the sink, I show him how the freezer dispenses ice, then point out the other tap positioned at the corner of the sink.

"Still or sparkling?" I ask.

He looks at me like I'm having him on. "Sparkling."

I show him which lever to hold down, fill his glass and hand it over. He raises it to eye level and inspects the bubbles. "Unbelievable."

"I like my little luxuries. Since Dad refused any rent, I've made some upgrades over the years."

As he takes a long drink, I actually hear his stomach rumble.

"Oh, God. You're starving. What would you like?" I rush over to the freezer and open the door to reveal a plethora of frozen meals.

He steps up beside me and stoops down to take a look. Straightening, he gently closes the French doors. "Let me cook something."

When he reaches for the fridge doors, I slap a hand over them, embarrassment burning up my neck.

"I, ah … haven't been shopping since last time you were here."

He gives me a curious glance, then opens the fridge. A carton of long-life milk, tomato sauce and a bottle of wine sit in the fridge door. Other than some eggs, butter, cream and cheese and a few random cans of soft drink that Anika left behind, it's basically bare.

Glancing over his shoulder at me, he asks, "You don't like cooking?"

"Actually, I hate it," I tell him truthfully. "I've been the only cook in this house since Mum died."

Understanding passes across his face before he turns back to the fridge and begins removing items. I watch with curiosity as he places the carton of eggs, then the cheese, cream and butter beside the induction cooktop. Opening the pantry, he extracts some dried mixed herbs and spices.

My stomach dips at the sight of him completely at home in my kitchen. As he grabs a frying pan, I'm reminded again why that is, and warmth spreads through my chest.

There's a man about to cook a meal in my kitchen. A man who took care of me when I couldn't do it myself. A man who made me laugh and squeal like a little kid at the beach when I'd forgotten how to have fun. A man who's here now because I let him see behind the wall I put up to hide my vulnerable side.

A man who should be so bitter and mean after the cards he's been dealt, his selfless compassion and gentle nature leave me in awe.

Liam's affidavit forgotten, I sidle up beside him and lean a hip against the counter as he cracks eggs into a bowl.

His hands freeze, his eyes on mine. "Ah, shit. I should've asked if it's okay to use all these. You probably want them for breakfast."

"I don't eat breakfast. It's fine." I wait for him to continue what he's doing before I ask, "So, Benny? What's happening there?"

While he makes a massive omelette, he explains that they came to an arrangement where he'd Uber over to Benny every second day. Apparently, if he didn't agree to keep me safe, Benny threatened to cut ties with him completely.

I laugh. "You don't really believe that?"

"You never know with Benny," he says, throwing me a smile

as he folds the omelette in half over the cheese and herbs. "Wasn't worth the risk. Much as he likes to pretend he's fine, he's still a fish out of water."

"It's sweet how much you care about him."

"Yeah, well, I just want him to be happy." He turns toward me as the omelette cooks, the aromas filling my nostrils and making my mouth water. "So, will seeing Benny every other day be a problem?"

"No. No, of course not. It's the nights, really. Being here on my own … it's never worried me before …"

He gently places a hand on my shoulder and squeezes. "I'll be here," he promises. Turning away, cuts the omelette in half, grabs two plates from a cupboard, and serves it up.

"Oh, you don't have to cook for me, I—"

"Yes, I do. And you wouldn't want to insult me by not trying it, right? It's only plain, but—"

"Sold," I interrupt. "God knows, it smells amazing."

Placing the plates on the breakfast bar, I take a seat as he grabs some cutlery and joins me on the stool to my left. Unlike when I'd sat in McDonald's and couldn't stomach a bite, my appetite's well and truly back. Digging in, I groan in please when the cheese and creaminess hit my taste buds.

Gavin gives me an appreciative grin before popping a bite in his own mouth.

"So, you can cook," I say, trying not to think about the reaction my heart has to that smile. "How did that happen?"

"Mum taught me. Once she found out she was sick, it became her mission to make sure I could fend for myself, especially since my father was useless in the kitchen. Those nights with her, following her instructions, all the little tricks she showed me, the conversations we had … they're some of my fondest memories. Being able to do that again … well …" he trails off, extra moisture shining in his eyes.

"Another thing you went so long without."

"Yeah," he agrees, his voice a little strained.

Resting my hand on his forearm, I brush my thumb over his skin. "I'm sorry."

He stares at his plate and simply nods. But I catch the solid bob of his Adam's apple and feel the tightening of his muscles beneath my palm. Which reminds me I'm still touching him. Again.

Removing my hand, I concentrate on eating. He finishes quickly, and by the time I'm a little more than halfway through mine, I discover the rich ingredients have me full to bursting. Remembering how he devoured my leftover hamburger, I slide my plate over to him.

He quirks an eyebrow. "You sure?"

"Definitely." I pat my stomach. "Another bite and I might explode."

"I'd love to cook every night, to contribute to the accommodation upgrade."

Suddenly, I recall what I'd said to him earlier. I'd told him that unless an amazing man turned up on my doorstep, I didn't have time for a relationship. And tonight, a man turned up on my doorstep. And he wants to cook. Every night. If that's not an amazing man, I don't know what is.

Okay. I need to get a grip.

"I'd love that," I say, "but only do it because you want to. You don't owe me anything, Gavin."

Pushing the now empty plate aside, he fixes his eyes on mine, his expression serious. "Obviously, I don't know what it's like for a woman, but for a man—at least, the way I was raised—I need to contribute. But I can't even get a fucking job."

Confused, I tilt my head. Why hadn't it occurred to me before now that this new situation might interfere with his job? In fact, why hadn't he mentioned it when giving me the reasons he couldn't stay here? "I thought you had a job."

He squeezes his eyes shut and, as he does, I notice his hand fisting on his thigh.

"Gavin?"

Staring at his empty plate, he nods. "Yeah, I did. I lost it recently."

Suddenly closed off, he won't look at me. I can't imagine

him losing a job through incompetence. With what I know about him, I'm sure he'd be the best employee anyone could want.

"How did that happen?" I ask.

"Doesn't matter," he mutters a little too quickly.

"That sounds an awful lot like my answer when I didn't want to tell you about the note under my door. What was it you said? That friends don't hide things from each other?"

Without looking at me, he sighs heavily. "I unintentionally took the day off. And completely forgot to call it in. They don't give people like me a second chance."

Unintentionally took a day off? "Was this the day we went to see Liam?"

"No. It was about a week ago."

As the pieces fit together, I stare at him in horror. About a week ago he'd been here, looking after me. And he hadn't left until around midday. My drunken, irresponsible behaviour resulted in his unintentional day off.

I'm the reason he lost his job. Guilt and humiliation crash through me. I'm supposed to be making his life better. Instead, I've made it harder.

"Oh, God. I'm so sorry. Why didn't you tell me?"

He shakes his head. "I knew you'd feel responsible. And you're not. It was my decision to stay with you, not yours."

Damn this man. I'm making this up to him whether he likes it or not. I close my fingers over the fist resting on his thigh. I really need to have a serious conversation with my hands. They seem to believe he's the magnetic north pole to my south.

"Gavin, I can fix that for you right away. Because now you *do* have a job. I've just hired you as my bodyguard."

Finally, he meets my eyes. "Can't tell my Corrections officer that. Not an occupation I'm allowed to enter into."

He's right. He can't have a job that involves the possibility of violence. That'd break his parole conditions.

"Oh, I know! You can be my personal assistant. It's totally normal for a professional to have one these days. I'll pay you a wage, of course."

He shakes his head adamantly. "No fucking way."

"Yes, fucking way. If employment is one of your parole conditions, that means you need to prove you're earning an income, right?"

I know he hates the idea, but the moment he realises it's the only way this will work, his shoulders slump in defeat, and my heart breaks a little.

"Having you do all the things I don't have time for … well, I don't think you understand how much of burden you'll be lifting from my shoulders. That's quite a gift."

"People don't pay for their own gifts."

Stubborn man. "True, but it *will* be a gift when you pay me back. And I expect you to." I give his hand a reassuring squeeze. "No matter how long it takes."

"I don't know," he says. "Paying me doesn't make me feel like I'm contributing. It seems more like taking advantage. And that makes me feel … less than."

"You *are* contributing. Just by being here. Do you know how it felt to not want to come home? To be afraid of the one place I should feel safe? It's …" Opening up like this goes against my nature, but if he can do it, so can I. "It's unsettling. To know that, in a heartbeat, your sanctuary can be snatched away. And now that you're here … you've given me back my home. To me, that's something that's *more than*, not less than. Please don't put yourself down like that."

The corners of his lips twitch as he suppresses a smile. Averting his gaze to my hand, he slowly uncurls his fist until his fingers wrap around mine and we're palm to palm. "Besides cooking, what do you need assistance with?"

The way he's running his thumb over my knuckles has me thinking about all the assistance those fingers can give me.

Like touching me.

Everywhere.

His eyes search mine, as if he's trying to read my thoughts. Flustered, I quickly withdraw my hand and reach for my phone.

"Well," I say, trying to keep my voice even, "give me your phone. I'll set you up with my grocery app so you can do all the food shopping. That'll save me time."

Although he's reluctant, he lets me install and log into the grocery app. When he gets up and clears the plates away, I log him out of his Uber app and log in as myself, so whatever trips he has to make will be charged to my account. He might be mad when he figures that one out, but it's nothing to me. I don't live an extravagant lifestyle, and I've never had to pay any rent, resulting in quite a large savings account that barely gets touched. I'm more than happy to spend some money.

Especially if it keeps him close.

I'm just unsure if I need him here because I want to feel safe, or because I want to feel something else entirely.

Chapter 26

Gavin

KEEPING MY EYES closed, I stretch in the double bed, loving the fact I can do that without my feet hitting a hot tin wall. I haven't slept this well since I was a teenager. I'm just not sure if it's due to the comfort of a great mattress, or because I'm needed.

Eager to start the day, I throw back the covers, sit on the edge of the bed for a moment, and curl my toes into the thick carpet. As I glance around the room, I take in all the space, including a desk where I can sketch in private. Standing, I roll my shoulders and stretch my arms overhead, pleasantly aware that my hands don't come anywhere near the ceiling. Total luxury.

As I go over everything Jamie said to ease my battered pride last night, I wish the circumstances where different. If I was here because … well, if I was her partner, I'd still do everything she needed me to, but I'd also have a real job. That's what would make me feel like I have any goddamn worth.

I release a long sigh. I can't entirely kid myself. It's pretty fucking awesome not having to endure another minute sweltering in that oppressive oven, though that comes in at a distant second.

It's the knowledge that I'll see her every day that has me buzzing with hope. Hope that I shouldn't entertain.

I'm simply here to make her feel safe in her own home. And cook for her. And do whatever she wants. I just need to get over myself and believe her when she tells me I'm *more than*, that my presence has given her back her home. That's something. Not enough from where I'm standing, but it's all I have.

Grabbing my duffle bag, I unpack my clothes, and as I place them in the chest-of-drawers, I'm hit with a wave of relief. Relief that I stood my ground when Benny tried to convince me to pack the gun. I don't believe for a second that he's eager for Reid to try to hurt Jamie, but he left me with no doubt that he thinks there's nothing wrong with taking advantage of the situation.

It took one of our most heated arguments to convince him that secretly bringing a gun into Jamie's home was not only a violation of her trust, but would land me back in prison and her in a shitload of trouble. My Corrections officer can conduct a search of the home I reside in at any time. While I don't know the consequences of finding an illegal firearm in a lawyer's house, I imagine it wouldn't be good. And for me, it's a serious parole violation. Benny eventually relented, but he sure as shit wasn't happy about it.

After transferring my sketchpad to the desk drawer, I pull on a t-shirt and pair of track pants, grab my shaving kit, and open the door.

A little uncomfortable, I pause on the threshold and listen, not sure where she is, or if I'll be invading her privacy or routine while she gets ready for work.

When only silence greets me, I pad across the hallway and close the bathroom door. After brushing my teeth and tidying up my beard with the clippers, I clean up the mess, then head down the hallway, eager for a coffee.

The moment I step into the kitchen, I freeze.

She stands at the coffee machine, her back to me, wearing a white figure-hugging camisole and matching boy-leg boxer briefs. Which completely throws me. When the wind at the beach had whipped up her dress, she'd worn lace panties that were on their way to disappearing right up her crack. Deciding to help her instead of standing back and enjoying the show that day, was quite a battle. Though I've pictured that incredible arse in those lace panties a million times since, what she's wearing now is just as sexy. They might come down to the tops of her thighs, but fuck me, they cup her arse like a second skin, showing off every muscle flex as she flits about the kitchen counter, blissfully ignorant that she has an audience.

I should announce my presence, but hold off, unable to stop observing her while she's unaware, while she's moving freely without an ounce of self-consciousness. I mean, it's not really my fault. She invited me to live here with her, so she's aware we'll run into each other. And she has every right to wear whatever she wants in her own home. If she likes getting around dressed in next to nothing, who am I to complain? She can't expect me *not* to look.

Unfortunately, I'm not a total creep, so I lean against the breakfast bar and clear my throat.

She startles, whirling around to face me. And holy fuck, her breasts sway beneath that tight camisole. Damn. No bra. It's impossible to drag my gaze away, impossible to miss her nipples tighten beneath the thin fabric. I wonder if they're reacting because I just scared the shit out of her, or because I'm staring right at them.

When she crosses her arms and cups her breasts, my mind goes straight to how they'd feel in my hands. It's one hell of an effort to keep from grinning like a fool. While my mouth manages not to betray me, the sight of her tight little body and the way she's touching herself like that, has my dick ratting me out.

"Sorry," I mumble, finally raising my eyes to hers. "Didn't mean to scare you."

She lets out a huff and gives me a sheepish grin. "Not your fault. I didn't think you'd be …" Her eyes flick to my crotch, "up yet."

Clearly the thin track pants I'm wearing aren't doing anything to hide my growing erection. Shit. Trying to cover myself now seems a little pointless and a little too much like it might matter. Thank fuck the boxer-briefs I have on underneath prevent the embarrassment of a full-on tent situation.

When her eyes meet mine again, her makeup-free face flushes a lovely pink. Yet, she doesn't move, doesn't run away, doesn't make an offhand comment to diffuse the tension between us. She doesn't even avert her gaze.

Benny's words come flying at me. *Dickhead, she wants you.*

The thought that the old man might very well be right, blows my mind. If only it were true, that'd make me feel like a king instead of the worthless man standing before her.

Turning around, she fiddles with a few switches on the coffee machine before facing me again. "It's ready for you."

"Thanks," I mumble.

Then she walks toward me, making no attempt to cover herself. I keep my eyes on her face, but it's impossible not to catch every bounce and sway of those full breasts. My heartbeat pounds in my ears as she stops right in front of me. It's only when her eyes shift to the side, that I realise I'm unintentionally blocking her exit. Turning sideways, I let her slip past.

As she walks down the hallway toward her bedroom, I watch those perfect little arse cheeks tense and relax. Then remember, "Oh, I ah … couldn't find any instant coffee last time, and I'm not sure how to use that complex machine."

"I'll be back in a sec," she calls out as she disappears into her room.

Resting my elbows on the breakfast bar, I shove a hand in my hair and will my disobedient dick to deflate. *Christ. How the fuck am I going to survive the torture of seeing her every day, fully clothed or not?*

Except … she certainly didn't seem offended by my reaction to her.

No. I don't know that. I know nothing. The last time I had anything to do with a girl, I was a stupid teenager. I wouldn't have a clue if I'm reading her right.

If I make a wrong move, she'll kick my arse out.

I can't risk it. Not if I want to keep her safe.

Besides, how can I trust Benny's reasoning? What the hell does he know?

And there's the cold hard fact that my dreams never come true.

Okay, she turned up on my doorstep. She believes I'm innocent. She seems to have fun with me. She asked me to move in with her, for fuck's sake.

All of them dreams. All of them now a reality.

None of which means the ultimate dream will eventuate.

If I screw up or overstep boundaries, not only will she drop my bid to have my conviction quashed, I'll lose *her*.

Hearing her footsteps padding down the hallway, I make a beeline to the coffee machine. As she sidles up beside me, I discover she's put on a light summer robe. Only she's failed to tie the sash that keeps it closed. And although those amazing breasts are now covered by another layer of material, what I failed to check out last time, entices my gaze lower. To that sleek V between her thighs.

"Beans are in here." She takes a step back and opens the cupboard at her knees. "I filled it up this morning, so you won't need to worry for a few days, but this is where they go." She flips a lid on top of the machine to show me.

"I'm happy to have instant. You don't—"

She gasps, bringing a hand to her chest as if I just insulted her. "Don't you ever, *ever* bring instant coffee into this house. I take this liquid gold seriously. Got it?"

I chuckle. Apparently, she's not amused.

"Right," I quickly say, and focus on the machine as she shows me where to put my mug and which button to use depending on what I want. I choose a long coffee and start the griding of beans and flow of dark liquid.

"Sugar?" she asks.

"Yeah, just one."

She reaches into the cupboard at her knees again and produces a clear container filled with raw sugar.

"Oh, spoon," she says. Her warm hand grips my waist as she reaches around to my other side, opens a drawer by my hip, and plucks out a spoon.

I stand stock-still, trying to remember how to draw breath into my lungs.

Touch.

She's touched my hands and arms a number of times. Hell, she's cried against my chest more than once, too. But does any of that mean anything, or are they simply things friends do?

Yeah, because I've held Benny's hand and hugged the guy … never.

Then there's the time she slid her hands under my shirt so she could touch my skin. And I'd ruined that by getting a fucking hard-on. I don't know if that'd happened because her touch felt incredible, or because it's been so damn long since anyone has touched me that way. Which she was kind enough to say she understood.

Maybe that's why she wasn't fazed by my reaction earlier. But, if she believes it's an expected response because I've been deprived for so long, why take the risk of me seeing her barely dressed?

"Gavin?"

I wrench my gaze from the coffee that's now waiting for me, and stare at the spoon she's offering.

"Everything alright? You were miles away." Those mesmerising eyes stare up at me, perfectly portraying curiosity. I know I'll be adding that new expression to my collection of sketches when she leaves.

"I'm right here," I tell her with a smile. "So, that's it?"

"That's it. Give it a try."

I stir in a teaspoon of sugar, bring the mug to my lips and sip. The rich flavours sliding over my tongue have every tastebud standing up and cheering.

"Damn it," I grumble, shaking my head.

"Do not dare tell me you like instant over that."

"I don't have a death wish." I take another sip to make sure I'm actually awake. "You know you've ruined me for life.

There's no going back after this."

"Ha!" She beams at me with satisfaction. "Okay, so I should get in the shower and head into work. Text me your Correction officer's number. I'll get hold of him and explain everything."

I nod, taking another sip as my eyes follow her until she disappears into the hallway.

Now all I have to do is get the image of her standing naked under a cascade of skin-caressing water out of my head.

Yeah, living here's going to be a goddamn fucking breeze.

Chapter 27

Jamie

AT WORK A few days later, in a rare moment of quiet, I bring up Gavin's electronic file in the system so I can finish off Liam's affidavit. Only it's not there. I can see a few notes and my own affidavit regarding my father's Dying Declaration, but not Liam's. Of course, Liam's affidavit holds far more weight than mine. I should have made a backup. But our entire firm operates in the cloud. Without a username and password, no one but staff can access it, which is why I believed it was safe.

My first thought is that I've saved it in the wrong file. Not something I usually do, but not the end of the world. I perform a total system search of Liam's name, but get no results.

Positive a file can't be deleted from the server permanently, I query the IT department. They have no luck either.

Annoyed, and worried this could happen to any document our firm saves on the server, I rise from my desk to go and tell Eric, my boss, what's happened. Before I take two steps, Simon saunters in and plonks himself down on one of the chairs reserved for clients.

"I was just on my way to see your father," I tell him, my skin crawling as his eyes snake up and down my body.

"Something I can help you with?" he asks my breasts.

"No," I say, using my usual impersonal, but not impolite, tone with him.

Finally, his eyes meet mine, a slick smile parting his thin lips. "You haven't even told me what the problem is. Maybe we could barter? I help you out …" he waves a hand in my direction, "you help me out," he points at himself. At his crotch to be precise.

I'd like to tell him to fuck off, but that probably wouldn't go down too well with his father. Which is the only reason I keep my mouth shut. None of the other lawyers want him around either, but here he is and now we all have to navigate with care.

"As lovely as that offer is, I'll pass. *Again*." I stride around my desk and make a dash for the door. As I move past him, I feel the slightest brush against my backside. When I spin around, one arm dangling at his side, like he's just let it drop.

I want to confront him, but I have no evidence, no witnesses. He's always careful that way.

With an ick lurking in my stomach, I have an unsuccessful chat with Eric about the permanent deletion of files. Leaving the mystery unsolved, I give myself an unprecedented early mark so I can get home and start Liam's affidavit from scratch, grateful I have the recording on my phone.

As I pull into the driveway and wait for the garage door to rise, I study the security camera Gavin and Benny installed. It's now one of many covering every angle on the outside of the house. As Gavin pointed out, they can't stop a crime, but they're a deterrent, and evidence should something happen. He's also booked in the installation of an alarm system, but that's still a few weeks away.

Pulling into the garage, I press the remote to lower the door and instantly notice that the usually squeaky door is almost completely silent. Yet another thing Gavin's fixed.

As I grab my laptop satchel, the buzz of a small engine revs to life. Glancing into the corner where I store the mower, I discover it's missing. Warmth and gratitude wash over me. I'd been dreading mowing the lawns again. It's lovely having someone do a chore I hate. And I didn't even have to ask.

Apparently, I'm not the only one Gavin's made an impression on. When I spoke to his corrections officer and not only explained the situation, but also told him about my father's confession, he wasn't surprised at all. Of all the parolees he's dealt with, he knew Gavin was different. Which is why he'd been surprised when Gavin hadn't shown for his job. I'd set him straight, explaining it was all my fault. By the time I hung up, I had the distinct impression we probably wouldn't be seeing too much of him.

Heading inside through the internal garage door, I'm hit with the smell of something delicious. By the time I make it along the hallway, my mouth is literally watering. I dump my satchel on the dining table, slip off my heels and head into the kitchen to investigate.

Opening the oven door, I'm blasted with heat and the unmistakable aroma of lasagne. Covered with foil, a pan sits on the middle shelf. Last night it'd been steak, the night before a Thai stir fry.

An unexpected lump grows in my throat. I can already feel myself getting far too accustomed to this. For the first time in my life, I actually look forward to coming home, to being surprised by what's for dinner, to being cared for.

But more than that, I look forward to coming home to Gavin.

Because we get along, I tell myself, that's all.

Grabbing a couple of bottles of water from the fridge, I carry them into my bedroom, zoning into the sound of the mower. As I slip out of my work dress, I stare at the two bottles of water on my nightstand. I really should head back to my laptop and get started on Liam's affidavit, but it seems like I've already made other plans. If Gavin's mowing the lawn in this heat, he'll need a drink.

Slipping into a pair of cute shorts and a loose V-neck t-shirt, I pad out of the bedroom in bare feet and head toward the back of the house.

As I carry the bottles through the family room where Anika spent most of her time when she had friends over, I reach for the sliding glass door, and freeze.

He's almost done with the lawn. Only a strip of long grass

remains and he's making the turn for the final leg.

I take a step away from the glass, knowing he can't see me in here where it's darker.

As the mower eats up the lawn, I take in his sunglasses, the sweat trickling down the sides of his face and neck, the damp t-shirt clinging to his shoulders and chest.

Before I can study him further, he reaches the end of the grass strip and cuts the engine. But he doesn't head back to the rear of the garage to put it away like I expect. Instead, he leaves it where it is and strolls over to one of the sunbeds.

Now's the perfect time to go out there and hand him a bottle of water. He certainly looks like he could use it. But I wait, anticipating what he'll do next.

Sure enough, he toes off his runners and peels off his socks, tossing them on the sunbed. Turning his back to me, he yanks off his t-shirt, his sweat-slicked back shining in the afternoon sun. My heart picks up pace when his thumbs dig beneath the waistband of his shorts and draw them down with his underwear, giving me an excellent view of his tight backside.

Shit. I shouldn't be ogling him in secret, let alone having those thoughts. It's just not me. Even though I'm standing here all alone, the burn of embarrassment climbs my neck. But it's not because I'm spying. It's the memory of the time I'd been making a coffee in the lunchroom at work and some of the lawyers started a discussion. A discussion about how long someone can go without sex before being seen as either pathetic or a frigid bitch. With my back to them, I'd listened with dread when the consensus came back. Needless to say, I qualified as both.

And I'd shrivelled into myself as they'd laughed and joked, paranoid they somehow knew how long it'd been since I'd had sex. Paranoid the whole conversation was aimed at me.

I remind myself that they'd never understand the trauma of not only suffering the murder of a parent, but discovering the secret that parent had kept. Learning that my mother cheated on my father taught me something I found hard to shake. My father's confession only reinforced that belief. Relationships are filled with lies and deception.

All my life I'd been told how much I look like my mother, how similar our personalities are. The thing about that is, I'll never know why she wanted to leave us for a new life with another man. If I could only understand why, I might understand *me.*

As Gavin strides toward the deep end of the pool, I'm thrust back to the present when his perfect, unmarked skin and rippling muscles gain my full attention.

Reaching the deep end, he turns toward the water, giving me a full-frontal view. Although I want to take in everything that makes up his spectacular body, I pause at his chest.

Damn. He's still too far away to decipher that one and only tattoo. If I had any guts, I'd march out there and hand him the water so I get a proper look at what he's permanently marked on his skin.

Instead, for the few seconds I have remaining, I study him in awe, running my eyes over that strong chest I've rested my face against far too many times, over the light smattering of brown hair and the way it thins as it travels down his torso. As he steps to the pool's edge and curls his toes over the tiles, every movement he makes shows how profoundly comfortable he is in his own skin. If only I could be like that.

Raking my eyes over every part of him, I appreciate the fact that he's not covered in tattoos. He's raw, naked, exposed. He's not trying to hide his true self behind ink. He's bare, and beautiful. He doesn't need to be blanketed in inked art. He *is* the art. At least on the surface. It's up to me to find out who he is beneath that amazing exterior.

And I think the key to knowing what's going on inside him is that single tattoo.

Drifting down, my gaze stops on another fascinating part of his body. His thick, flaccid cock. He's clearly studied the latest trends regarding manscaping, because everything seems neatly trimmed down there.

I've never been excited about the male body. I've never

bothered looking. I just didn't care.

Well, suddenly I do. And I can't stop staring, because watching him is doing things wonderful things to *my* body.

He's so fucking hot. Both literally and figuratively.

As my grip on the plastic bottles tightens, one of them crackles, making me jump. My eyes snap to his face, terrified he's heard it, but he's reaching up, taking off his sunnies and placing them on the tiles beside his feet.

Then he dives, every muscle tense as he hits the water and disappears beneath the surface.

Only then do I remember to breathe.

Surfacing at the shallow end, he stands, swiping his hair back with both hands as water cascades over his exposed torso. It's like he knows I'm watching, knows he's making my blood buzz with his spectacular show.

As soon as he dives under again—and before I can think better of it—I slide the door open and step into the heat.

By the time I slip my feet into a pair of thongs, he surfaces at the deep end. Not wanting to startle him, I call out, "How is it?"

His head jerks toward me. The moment I take a step forward, he swims to the side of the pool to meet me.

"It's perfect," he replies. As I move closer, he gives me a curious look. "You're home early."

I stop beside the large, potted Ficus at the pool's edge. He stays low in the water, his arms crossed on top of the tiles, effectively blocking the view of his naked body, and the tattoo I want to know all about. Of course, I can't ask him about it without revealing I've just seen him naked.

"Sorry, I should have called to let you know," I say, tucking a bottle beneath one arm while I unscrew the cap on the other.

He squints up at me. "You don't have to do that."

"I probably should. I wouldn't want to walk in on …" I trail off, realising I might have given myself away.

"Walk in on what?" he asks, eyes bright with amusement.

Shit. Does he know I've seen every hot inch of him? "Anything I wouldn't want to walk in on, I guess."

He grins. "Are you going to offer me that, or just tease me?"

I quickly pass him the bottle, disappointed when he reaches for it with his left hand, leaving his right firmly covering the tattoo.

Turning, I pull the sunbed closer to the pool, making a show of sliding his clothes aside so I can sit on the towels he's left there. His gaze snaps from his clothes to my face.

"Don't let me stop you from enjoying your swim," I say.

"Why don't you get in?"

I smile. "Why don't you get out?"

He holds my gaze for an intense moment, sending heat racing through my bloodstream at the thought that he's contemplating doing just that.

"Smartarse," he grumbles with amusement before taking a gulp of water.

"Did you do something to the garage door?"

"Just needed a little WD40."

"Thanks. And for mowing the lawn. I really hate that job."

"It's the least I can do. Speaking of which, I'd love to tidy up the garden, do any maintenance around the house you might need. Looks like it could use a lick of paint."

He sounds so hopeful, like it's something enjoyable. "You don't need to—"

"It'd make me feel a hell of a lot more useful."

My heart swells for him. All his worth seems to be contingent on what he can contribute. Already, I know he's so much more than that. "I'm happy for you to do whatever you want. Although the inside was renovated not that long ago, the outside's definitely been neglected. Just let me know if you need anything." I make a mental note to give him one of my debit cards, knowing he'd find it demeaning to ask for money every time he needs to buy something.

"Would you mind if Benny helped out?

"Of course not." He's so sweet, always thinking of ways to not only stay close to Benny, but make him feel useful as well. "Benny doesn't have a job?"

"He's not on parole, so it's not required. But he does still need to look for one to get his government assistance payment. Problem is, he's a twice convicted murderer and he's sixty. It'll be one hell of feat for him to actually land one."

"Well, I think it's a wonderful idea to keep having him over to help you."

"Great. Now, get in here. Water's amazing."

That look in his eyes tells me everything I need to know. He's baiting me. Putting my hand on top of his clothes, I decide to call his bluff.

"I'll need to get changed. Should I take these inside for you?"

"Sure," he says without missing a beat.

I stand and scoop his clothes into my arms, then pick up the towels. "And these?"

"That's totally up to you …"

Oh, he thinks I'm kidding. I take a few steps toward the house.

"And whether you want me traipsing through the house dripping wet," he says, the smirk in his voice all too easy to hear.

Now he's calling my bluff. I consider the reality of being confronted with him in the house, naked and wet. Heat shoots between my thighs. It seems too real, too possible, too tempting. I quickly drop the towels on the sunbed and dash toward the house.

I don't want to ruin what we have here. He needs my help, and I've discovered over these last few days that while I might not *need* his help, I desperately *want* it.

There's something simmering between us. But I don't know him well enough yet to figure out if he's genuinely interested in me, or if he's just interested because I happen to be female. After being deprived for so long, he probably looks at all women the way he looks at me.

I don't even trust what's going on inside my own mind and body. It's possible that our shared connection—the shitty hands we've been dealt—is the reason I feel this way. To find someone who completely understands what I've been through is, after all, an attraction all its own.

Letting anything happen other than friendship might ruin everything. I can't let emotion get in the way. I want to provide him with a life that doesn't involve living in a caravan and searching for mediocre jobs only a convicted murderer can get.

Until his name is cleared, I want him to have some luxury, to know someone cares about him.

Because once I do my job, he'll be free.

Untethered.

From me.

And already, I'm not sure how I'll go back to the way things were.

I scoff at that thought.

The way things were no longer exists.

Chapter 28

Gavin

THE MOMENT SHE disappears inside, I haul myself out of the pool, grab a towel and throw it over my left shoulder, making sure it covers my tattoo. Only then do I bother wrapping the other towel around my waist. Having her see the state of my heart on the outside of my chest leaves me feeling far more exposed and vulnerable than her seeing my dick.

Did she?

I didn't hear her arrive, didn't hear a car door slam. Nothing. Which tells me she probably arrived while the mower was running. Believing I had hours before she'd be home, that glistening water was a temptation I couldn't resist. With no two-storey houses looking into her backyard, I didn't hesitate. I stripped off and dived into absolute bliss. Slicing through the cool water felt like inhabiting another world. A world I'd been denied for the last sixteen years.

Then there she was, and my only thought was to hide the pain permanently marked on my chest. I know if she sees it, she'll have questions, and I'm not quite ready to deal with them yet. Because the answers I've always believed to be true don't quite fit anymore. I need time to wrap my own head around how they've changed before I can even attempt to explain them to anyone else.

Especially her.

Whether or not she saw me before I dived into the pool, she damn well knew I was naked the moment she moved that sunbed and noticed my clothes.

I grin as I rub my hair with the towel hanging over my shoulder. I loved that she was cheeky about it. If it hadn't been for my bloody tat, I might very well have taken her up on her suggestion to get out of the pool just to see the look on her face.

Which would no doubt have ended in disaster.

I can't do shit like that and expect her to let me stay here. Although, she didn't seem fazed about my obvious response to the sight of her in the kitchen the other morning. She seemed curious, fascinated even. Which left me baffled. Surely she's no stranger to men with hard dicks falling all over themselves to get in her pants.

My hand fists in the towel, the thought of her with another man constricts my chest with jealousy. Which is insane. As much as I want her, I can't have her. Besides, she's told me a few times that she's not interested in dating.

I'll never be good enough for her. Even if I was the last man on earth, she doesn't *need* me. There's nothing I can offer her that she doesn't already have. She's completely self-sufficient, self-reliant and financially sound. What could she possibly get from me that she can't get for herself?

Love.

The most volatile of all emotions. It can be taken away in an instant. It's not tangible, can't be held onto and protected. It's always out there, vulnerable, ready to be snatched away and crushed by the very person it was entrusted to.

I should know. My story of love and hope torn apart is permanently tattooed on my skin. In my soul.

But something's shifting. I can't deny that.

Before I can turn further into my mind and analyse what that is, Jamie slides open the door and steps outside, her face dropping when she sees me.

"You got out," she accuses as she walks over to the other side of the sunbed.

I can't tell her why, so I tell her another truth instead. "Yeah. Just remembered I'd better check on dinner."

But I don't move. I'm too busy taking in her modest one piece. It's a pretty jade that brings out the colour in her eyes. Unfortunately, she has a towel draped over her shoulders, hiding her breasts. Fortunately, it does nothing to hide her slender calves, or the smooth curves of her bare thighs reaching all the way up to the stretchy material between her legs.

My eyes snap to hers, and I'm relieved to find she hasn't caught me ogling her like a desperate ex-con. Seems she's too busy studying my torso and what she can see of my chest.

Dammit.

The way she looks just as hungry as I feel, sends a rush of blood straight to my dick.

There's no denying we're both checking each other out.

Before hope floods my heart and lodges there, I grab the front of the towel around my waist, reposition it, and I step around the sunbed before she sees the effect she has on me.

I don't look back on my way to the door. Not until I'm inside and turn around to close it.

She tosses the towel on the sunbed, her back to me as she walks toward the shallow end of the pool. That one-piece she's wearing might appear modest from the front, but from the back, it's a goddamn sin. And she chose it, believing she'd be swimming with me.

If I thought I was hard before, my dick's bloody throbbing now.

The straps loop around her shoulders, then disappear, leaving her back and the curve of her waist completely bare. Until the fabric covers her firm arse, almost disappearing between her cheeks as she takes another step into the water.

My heart rolls in my chest at the thought of running my hands over that taut skin, cupping and kneading that spectacular backside. Christ, I'm delusional.

She turns her head to the side, as if she knows I'm watching. I take a step backward, into the shadows. Is my need for her so palpable she can sense it from here?

I groan aloud as she bends at the waist before delicately gliding into the water, keeping her head above the surface.

Knowing I won't have any intelligent brain activity until I take care of this aching need, I hurry into my room, shut the door and let the towel around my waist drop. I lean against the wall, close my eyes and run my fingers over the tip of my cock, spreading the leaking pre-come, imagining it's her fingers, her hand. Gripping my shaft, I only get about ten strokes in before I let go, my legs turning to jelly as I spurt into the towel hanging from my shoulder.

God help me if I ever get to touch her the way I want. I'll probably come in my fucking pants.

After getting dressed, I pull the lasagne out of the oven, remove the foil, and pop it back in so the cheese on top browns to a nice crust.

Now all I need to do is wait. Serving it up burnt isn't an option. Every meal I cook for her needs to be perfect. I want her wondering how she ever survived without me.

I also need to finish up outside, but I don't want to invade her privacy.

As I slump onto the soft leather couch and turn on the TV, I know that's not true. She's not worried about privacy. She went out there, wearing that swimsuit, fully expecting me to still be in the pool. What I'm really avoiding is seeing the water slide down her body when she gets out, her nipples no doubt hard from the cool temperature.

Turning the volume up, I try to drown out my thoughts, but it's no use. I was right when I initially turned down her invitation to stay here. This is fucking torture.

The question is, will there be an end to it?

When she comes back inside, I hear her go into her room, then the faint sound of her shower running. After taking the lasagne out of the oven to let it cool, I head outside, put the mower away and sweep up the stray grass cuttings from the pool area that escaped the catcher.

By the time I wander into the kitchen, she's set herself up

at the dining table, files spread out, laptop in front of her, fingers flying over the keys. Clearly in the zone. While I find some containers so I can freeze the lasagne we won't eat tonight, my eyes can't help but return to her slender neck.

Her hair's piled loosely on top of her head with wisps escaping here and there. I want to walk up behind her, trail my fingers over her skin and push those hairs away so I can plant my mouth on her neck and taste her the way she tasted me.

It would only be fair.

She suddenly stops typing, rises and heads around the breakfast bar into the kitchen, where I get busy cutting up the lasagne and placing it in containers.

"I hope I'm not disturbing you," I say as she opens the fridge.

"No, I'm used to Anika. She's not exactly quite." She takes a peach from the crisper and washes it at the sink. "It's the silence I find disturbing."

I watch her as I ask, "Have you told her yet? About me living here? She'll be coming home soon, right?"

She freezes, water flowing over the peach she's holding. "I … I will. She'll know before she gets home." Grabbing a tea-towel, she dries the fruit thoroughly.

Turning toward me, she bites into it, the sight and sound of her sucking on the juicy flesh sending a jolt straight to my groin yet again.

Grabbing the containers, I open the freezer. "You'll ruin your appetite."

When I straighten up, she's smiling, and I want to melt at the warmth in her eyes. Especially since it's directed at me.

"If I don't eat this, I'm going to devour all of *that* right now," she says, indicating the two slices of lasagne remaining in the pan. "It smells amazing."

I pat my stomach and grin like a fool at her compliment. "Yeah, I don't think my stomach's shut up since I started cooking."

"Here." She offers me the peach. "Have a taste."

I don't hesitate. If she wants to share her spit with me, I'm not about to object. Taking the peach, I sink my teeth into it. Liquid saturated with sweetness bursts over my tongue and, just like her, I'm forced to apply suction to prevent half of it escaping down my chin. She's staring at my mouth and as she watches, the tip of her tongue slides along the seam of her lips. I don't think she has any idea she's doing it.

And it's fucking hot.

"Good?" she asks as I hand over the peach.

"Yeah, good."

She bites into it without a second thought, her lips plump around the fruit before she draws the morsel into her mouth, letting out a throaty little groan.

What is she doing? Since when has eating a peach been so sensual? So fucking provocative? I want to kiss that sweetness from her lips until all I can taste is her.

"Forget it," she says, as if she's read my mind.

My eyes shoot to hers. "Sorry?"

"You look like you're about to attack me. Which, of course, would be the only way you're getting any more, since this is the last one."

As she takes another bite, her eyes shine with a teasing challenge. A challenge I can't resist. Playfully, I lunge at her. She lets out a little squeal as she flees, her footsteps pounding down the hallway.

Chuckling, I turn back to the remaining lasagne, knowing without a doubt that if I chase her and catch her, I'm going to fuck up everything, because I won't be able to keep my hands off her. And I need to know with one hundred percent certainty that she wants me to touch her.

Right now, I can't figure out if she's completely oblivious to how seductive she is, or if she's deliberately driving me crazy. Either way, I refuse to do anything to screw this up.

When she returns a few minutes later, I'm in the middle of scrubbing the lasagne pan in hot, soapy water.

"Guess you lose," she says, wandering up beside me, her head tilted. "You gave up way too easy."

I stop scrubbing the pan, my heart thudding. "What do you

think would've happened if I'd caught you?"

She blinks, her cheeks darkening, as if it's only just occurred to her that her little challenge would require physical contact.

Her eyes dart away, the corners of her lips twitching. "I suppose you would have … eaten my peach."

Jesus. There's no way she's talking about fruit. She's not only surprised me with her cheeky subtext, she's pushing me to my limit. And I fucking love it.

"But," she continues, "I won. I'm the one with the lingering taste of that peach on my tongue. Not you."

Wild images of my head between her legs rocket through my brain, making me grateful I'm already leaning against the cupboards beneath the sink so she can't see my growing hard-on. Grinning at her, I can't help but tease, "If I had the taste of that peach on my tongue, wouldn't that make us both winners?"

Her eyes widen ever so slightly before she lets out a huff of a laugh. "I don't see how."

As I watch the blush creep down her slender neck, I'm damn sure she knows exactly how. "Why don't I believe you?"

"You know, seeing you happy like this," she says, her voice dropping to a softer tone, "I … well, it's wonderful. I hope living here is helping with that."

When she pushes away from the counter, I mumble under my breath, "It's all you."

Later, as we sit side-by-side at the breakfast bar, I notice her stealing glances at me while we eat. Or is she noticing *me* stealing glances at *her*? Hard to say, but the next time our eyes meet, I decide to confront her, my curiosity too damn strong to contain.

"Did you see me?" I ask. "Before I got in the pool?"

Her eyes skitter back to her food. "Sure. You were mowing the lawn."

"And?" Staring at her profile, I swivel my stool in her direction and wait until she looks at me. "No lying, remember? Your rule."

Our eyes lock just before her gaze drops to the left side of my chest. Damn. She definitely saw me.

I should be angry. I'm sure she would be if it were the other way around. Problem is, my dick seems to think the idea of her hiding inside, checking me out, is pretty hot. I'd love to know what she thought.

Still staring at my chest, she says, "You have a tattoo."

Clever little diversion on her part, steering me away from the fact she saw me naked to the one thing I don't want to talk about.

Swivelling back toward my meal, I let out a dismissive humph, hoping that'll discourage her from further questions on the subject.

"I could only see that you have one, not what it is."

"Good," I say a little sharper than I intended. From the corner of my eye, I see her open her mouth, but whatever question she had doesn't come. Instead, she concentrates on jabbing different salad ingredients onto her fork before adding a bite of lasagne.

Eager to leave that topic behind, I ask, "You working for the rest of the night?"

"Until I can't keep my eyes open, yeah. I've got a few cases to work on and … Liam's affidavit disappeared from the server, so I need to re-do that too."

She said it so offhandedly, I almost missed it. *"What?"*

"It's fine," she sighs. "I recorded the whole thing, so I just need to retype it. Obviously, I won't make the mistake of saving it in only one place again."

"Has that happened before?"

"Well, no. But there's a first time for everything."

I don't like the sound of that, especially since it means taking more of her time when it's clearly stretched thin already.

"Anyway, what're you up to tonight?" she asks.

"I was planning on reading something, but I haven't spotted

a bookcase around here. You don't read? For pleasure, I mean."

Finishing her mouthful, she nods. "I do. When I'm not stacked up with briefs."

She slips off her stool, hurries into the living room and comes back with a thin rectangular object. Placing it between us, she opens the cover. The screen comes to life, showing what looks like a page in a book.

"This is a Kindle," she explains. "I don't have a bookcase, because this thing can hold about a thousand books."

I stare at it in astonishment. "A thousand?"

Her eyes sparkle. Clearly, she enjoys showing me everything I've missed out on, and I love that she wants to.

After giving me a quick tour of the device, I ask, "So I can read anything already on here?"

She snaps the cover closed. "No. I'll have to get you one and set up an account for you." Grabbing her phone, she taps away at the screen.

"Maybe I can pick one up at the shops?"

She snickers as she puts her phone down. "There is no shop. It'll be delivered tomorrow."

"Tomorrow?"

"Sure. We don't live in the dark ages anymore."

"Unbelievable," I mumble as I take another bite, eyeing the device she won't let me use. I hadn't missed the numerous book covers displaying half naked men during her little tour. "But for tonight, I could just read something you already have, right?" When I reach for it, she slides it out of reach.

"I don't think so."

I raise my eyebrows and smile. "What've you got on there?"

"What've you got under here?" She reaches out and taps the tattoo through my t-shirt. Without thinking, I grab her hand and press it to my chest, the warmth of her palm seeping much deeper than my skin. Her eyes widen a little, but she doesn't try to pull away.

"It's a heart … You feel it beating?"

Our eyes hold for far too long before she pulls her hand free. "Smartarse."

Eager to change the subject, I complain about having nothing to read. She soon solves that problem by demanding access to my phone and moving her stool right up against mine. Naturally, my arm finds its way to her backrest, allowing her to lean in close while she shows me how to get all the books I want for free. I'm not sure how much I take in. It's difficult to concentrate on anything other than the closeness of her body, her scent, and the occasional brush of her bare leg against mine. I'm sure she's paid for something, but she's not letting on. Which makes me believe she understands how it feels to be a man who can't even support himself, let alone someone else.

The thing is, she's having so much fun, is so enthusiastic and animated, I don't want to be the one to take that away by rejecting her kindness and generosity.

When we begin eating again, I say softly, "This is nice."

"It's more than nice. It's delicious." She raises her fork and takes the last bite of lasagne.

"I didn't mean the food. I meant sharing it with someone. Other than criminals. You don't eat with your mouth open and you're much easier on the eye." She stiffens beside me. *Shit.*

"Wow," she says, the change in her tone putting me on alert. "I give you praise, and you give me … what was that?"

She's lost me, her mind ticking over into thoughts I can't grasp. "I was giving you a compliment."

"Is being called better than a criminal a compliment?"

I'm an idiot. She's right. My life experience and hers are worlds apart. I can't change that, but I can change my compliment.

"Jamie?" When she looks at me, the vulnerability staring back stops my heart. I'm starting to realise her self-assured confidence and strength only seem to apply to her professional life. When it comes to what's deeply personal, she's painfully, exquisitely insecure. "I've already told you, but I have no problem saying it again. You're gorgeous."

She lets out a sharp scoff, her gaze riveted to the empty plate in front of her.

"Jamie … look at me." When she refuses, I gently touch her jaw. After a moment, she peers at me from beneath those dark lashes.

And I see it. She doesn't believe me, and I find that absolutely astounding. Has no one told her how beautiful she is? How there's a light that shines from her eyes that's dazzling? There's no way she's been able to avoid being the object of a man's desire.

"How do you not know this?" I ask.

She stares at me, utterly confused. "Know what?"

"That you're the most striking woman I've ever seen … ever imagined. You can stop a man in his tracks and make him forget where he's going, what he's doing, and make him wonder why he's doing anything at all other than trying to get to know you."

Now she's blinking fast, her eyes brimming with water. I may have overshot, but as long as she heard me, I don't give a damn.

"Your rules. No lying," I remind her. "Tell me why you don't know that."

She closes her eyes. I'm not sure if she's trying to avoid mine or trying to invent an answer. Either way, I have all the patience in the world.

Taking a deep breath, she mumbles, "I've never really put any thought into it."

"But you must have had men tell you, show you?"

"No," she barely whispers.

I want to explode at the thought that no one's told her how spectacular she is in every way. "What sort of dickheads have you been seeing, when clearly you could have your pick? You must have men lining up around the corner for a chance to—"

"I don't want men lining up to fuck me." Her eyes flash with anger before she turns her face away.

I dig my fingers into my thigh, intrigued as to why she's so fired up. Since she hasn't told me to mind my own business, I don't.

"I was going to say *date you*." Studying her profile, I note the clench of her jaw, the colour burning her cheeks. Even though she won't look at me, she hasn't run away. "Did someone … hurt you?"

She scoffs. "No. I'm just a pathetic loser."

Relief sweeps through me, and I have to struggle against the urge to pull her into my arms and show her without words that she's not a pathetic loser. Where did she even get that idea?

"You'll have to explain that one to me. From where I sit, you're a successful, independent woman who has her life totally put together."

She stares at my chest. "Not totally. That … dating part of my life … That's basically non-existent."

Unable to help myself, I reach out and cover the hand she has resting on the counter. "Why?" I ask quietly. Finally, she looks into my eyes, her expression pained.

"While you've been in a real prison, I put that part of myself in a prison of my own making. Studying, looking after Anika and Dad, then working. I didn't have anything left to give, let alone the time. I locked that part of my life away and got on with what had to be done." She takes a deep breath. "Let's face it, I wasn't an attractive package. Playing mother to my sister while living at home with my father … What sort of guy wants to get involved with that?"

"One with understanding and depth."

She scoffs. "Exactly why I'm still single."

Surprised by her insight, I rub my thumb over the back of her hand. "You were dealing with a shitload of pressure and responsibility. All thrust on you when you were way too young." She searches my eyes, and I hope she finds the truth there.

"So, you can see why I avoided anything that'd make it even harder."

I shouldn't ask. It's definitely none of my business. "So, you've never …"

To my surprise, instead of telling me to fuck off, she shrugs. "Once. When I was seventeen, just after the trial. I think I was trying to escape the suffocating sorrow and hatred that constantly consumed me. I wanted to go somewhere else … *be* someone else. Even if only for a moment. And it *was* just a moment. I was young and naïve, and so was he. It wasn't good … wasn't anything I had any desire to repeat."

My heart cracks open, amazed she's revealed something so intensely personal, and stunned by her bravery in doing so.

But that's not all, is it? My skin prickles as the thought takes hold. What are the chances we'd be sitting here now, both of us untouched for the same amount of time? Because of our parents' actions. I don't believe in destiny or fate, but this feels a hell of a lot like we've been waiting for each other without ever knowing it.

Until now.

I clear my throat, remembering she'd said she had no desire to repeat what hadn't been good for her all that time ago. "And now? How do you feel about it now?"

"Like I said, I don't give it any thought. So, you see. I *am* pathetic."

I squeeze her hand. "Now you're insulting me. If you're pathetic, then I am too."

That gets a tiny smile out of her. "I seriously doubt that."

Heat rushes to my face, but I want her to know. "I haven't had sex since I was a teenager either." I don't care if she thinks I'm a loser. If it makes her feel better, I'm happy to be the biggest loser on the planet. And I hope she sees my confession as another bond between us.

She frowns, her eyes darting rapidly between mine. "But, that guy, at the caravan park. He said … it seemed like maybe you'd had women there."

"That's not who I am, Jamie. One thing about prison, it has a brutal way of teaching you who you are. I know what I want, know what my values are. So, if it makes me a loser for not wanting to pay a woman just to use her body, then I have no problem being a loser. But I don't think it does. And I don't think you are either."

Rolling her lips between her teeth, her hand slips from beneath mine. I think I've totally fucked up, made a complete and utter fool of myself. Until she covers my hand with hers, reversing their position.

"Thank you," she says softly as she squeezes my hand. "But what about … dating?"

I guess I walked right into that one. Not that it matters. We both have similar excuses. "What do I have to offer anyone? I'm not an attractive package. An ex-con convicted for murder, living in a caravan. What sort of woman wants to get involved with that?"

"One with understanding and depth," she quotes my earlier response. Her eyes search mine for a moment, and as light shimmers brighter on their surface, she quickly retracts her hand. "I'd better get some work done." Swivelling away, she takes a seat at the dining table and wakes up her laptop.

As I stack the dishwasher, I now know why she wasn't shocked by my reaction when she made contact with my bare skin. Just like me, she hasn't experienced anyone's touch or love in all that time either. She completely understands.

By the time I hear her say goodnight, she's gone. Her files are still spread out over the dining table, but the laptop's closed. I'm not sure why she's abandoned her work so early, but I notice that reading device of hers is missing from the breakfast bar where she'd left it.

I smile to myself, knowing she thinks about sex and love and relationships a lot more than she lets on.

Chapter 29

Jamie

WHAT THE HELL possessed me to tell him that? Every time I'm around him, the parts of myself I've kept hidden come out. There's so much energy between us, I don't know what to do with it, so I end up doing and saying things I shouldn't.

Like teasing him with that peach. I hadn't planned to. I'd just had an urge to have fun. When I'm with him, it comes bubbling up and I don't want to push it down. Besides, it's not just about *me* having fun. I want to make him happy. I want to see that beautiful, knee-weakening smile on his lips, in his eyes.

Then, when he started pressing me about dating and men, my walls flew back up. Until I understood he wasn't trying to humiliate me. He was genuinely curious, the way I was curious about him. He's seen me at my worst, and it hasn't made him run away. If anything, it's drawn him closer. So I'd told him the ugly truth, and he told me. Leaving me stunned, and relieved. I'd suspected as much after his obvious reactions, even though that creep in the caravan park had placed doubt in my mind. But Gavin Lake is exactly who he appears to be. A decent, genuine human being.

And then there's his insistence that I'm beautiful. No. *Gorgeous.*

After I change out of my clothes and slip into my pyjamas—one of seven identical sets—I let down my hair and step in front of the mirror. And try to see what he sees.

When was the last time I looked at myself closely? I only bother a cursory glance to make sure I look presentable for work before walking out the door. I don't worry about the attractiveness of my appearance. Why would I? That's not what my life's been about. It's been about raising a little girl, then a teen, and it's been about supporting my father, studying, then building a career.

Even when Jarrod asked me on that date, I hadn't tried to do anything different with myself. He already knew who I was.

So why do I feel differently now?

Staring at my reflection, I try to study myself through Gavin's eyes. That special way only he looks at me, like he's seeing something he wants to devour and possess, but also love, nurture and protect. How he conveys that through his eyes alone, I don't know. But I feel it in that part of me I've kept buried for so long. And I like that he's digging. Because when he looks at me like that, I'm not a daughter or a sister or lawyer or a colleague. I'm the me that's been forgotten.

I had no idea I'd been suffocating until he began breathing life back into me.

The next day, while I eat lunch at my usual café and I scroll through my phone, Pete plonks himself down in the chair opposite.

"I wasn't expecting to see you today," I greet him with a smile.

"Yeah, I wanted to have a word."

He's not smiling back. In fact, I don't think I've ever seen him so tense. I put down my phone. "Of course."

When he leans forward, I not only notice the tension in his body, but the dark circles under his eyes. "I need you to do me a favour."

"Since I owe you a million times over, that shouldn't be a

problem."

"You're going to have to trust me on this, Jamie. Can you do that?"

"You shouldn't even have to ask." The way he's looking at me so damn seriously has my stomach knotting. This isn't like him at all.

"I need you to cool it with Gavin Lake's case. Just for a couple of months."

I blink at him, my heartrate picking up. "Why?"

"I can't tell you. That's where the trust comes in."

He's looking directly into my eyes with such intensity I can barely hold his gaze. He's deadly serious. "But he's waited sixteen years—"

"I really, *really* need you to do this for me, Jamie. You know I wouldn't ask if it wasn't important. It's just a few months, maybe less. That's all. Once I give you the word, you can go hell for leather." He leans back, resting his crossed arms on his belly.

My mind races. What Pete's asking clearly has something to do with his internal affairs work, otherwise he'd tell me everything. What it has to do with Gavin, I don't know. Pete's fully aware of how important getting Gavin's conviction overturned is, so he wouldn't ask me to delay it unless—

"Does this have something to do with that threat?"

"I can't tell you anything, Jamie. You simply have to trust me. Please say you do."

I let out a sigh. It might only be a few months, but Gavin's already waited such a long time. I'm not sure how I'm going to explain the delay to him when I don't have an explanation. But I trust Pete.

"Okay," I agree with a small nod.

"Promise me, Jamie."

Wow. He's beyond serious. "I promise."

The moment the words are out, all the tension seeps out of him, making him look even more haggard than when he arrived.

Rising, he stops beside me, places a hand on my shoulder

and squeezes. "Thank you."

It's only when he leaves me there, that I realise he didn't once try to steal any of my food. He didn't even look at it. A chill runs travels up my spine as I push my plate away, my appetite gone.

A week later, I arrive home from work to find Gavin pouring himself a glass of icy sparkling water. I haven't been able to bring myself to tell him about the promise I made to Pete. I'll deal with that when I'm left with no choice.

After dumping my stuff on the dining table, I watch as he drains the glass. He's sweaty and, along with his old t-shirt and bare arms, his hair is spattered with grey paint. I wish certain parts of my body would get used to the fact that, no matter what he's wearing, he pulls off sexy every time.

"Hi," I greet him from the other side of the breakfast bar.

He wipes the back of his hand over his lips. "Hey. You ready for dinner in about twenty?"

"Sure. That's perfect."

He saunters over, his kind, worried eyes locked with mine. "Did you call your sister today?"

We've talked about this a few times now. I need to tell Anika the truth about our father. About Gavin. I have a deadline. She's due home the day before Christmas Eve. I can't have her arriving to the shock of Gavin living in our house. That'd make for quite a tumultuous Christmas.

The clock's ticking. But I keep putting it off. Because I'm a coward. I don't want to be the one to rip open that old wound for her.

"No, not yet," I say quickly, dropping my gaze to his chest to avoid what I know I'll find in his eyes. Changing the subject, I say, "I'd love to see how the painting's coming along."

When I brave a glance at his face, I only catch the last visage of disappointment before he lets me off the hook with a broad smile. Day by day, he can't wait to show me what he and Benny have accomplished. It's abundantly clear he can't stand being idle, that he's at his best when busy, when achieving something. When feeling useful.

Last weekend we went to the hardware store and chose paint colours, plants, mulch and a bunch of other stuff I can't even comprehend. Ever since, he and Benny have kept themselves busy in the backyard.

After I change out of my work clothes and step outside, Gavin places a hand on my lower back. I love it when he touches me, and I wonder if he subconsciously looks for a way to do so without it appearing intentional. Like I do when we manoeuvre around each other in the kitchen every morning.

"No peeking," he says, guiding me toward the pool, away from the house.

Concentrating on the garden bed that's now been completely demolished and rebuilt from scratch on the far side of the pool, I walk ahead until his hand slides to my waist and gently encourages me to turn.

I stare in astonishment at the transformation before me. Instead of the peeling, chipped cladding, the back of the house appears brand new. Pristine white window frames pop against the light grey wall. My drab 1980s house has been transformed into a modern, Hamptons-style home.

I slap my palms to my cheeks. "Gavin … It's amazing! I love it!"

"Here, I'll show you what we've done."

He beams as he guides me toward the house, explaining with infectious enthusiasm which siding planks needed replacing, how Benny did most of the sanding and how many coats of paint they applied. Then he takes me around to the side of the house and shows me what he plans to start on tomorrow.

"I need to figure out how much I owe you both," I say.

His hand instantly disappears from my back and lands on his hip. "You're *not* paying us a damn cent, Jamie."

"But if I hired someone to do this it'd cost—"

"No," he says firmly. "I want to do it. It was my idea, not yours."

"So? You're still doing the work. Just like anyone else, you and Benny should be paid. You obviously have skills. You can't do all this for free."

"I'm not," he says, his smile returning. "If there's any way at all to look at it, this is me starting to pay you back my wages. Just with my services instead of money."

Damn man. Too proud to let me do what's right.

"That's not how wages work. You're cooking, cleaning, landscaping, replacing gutters and making me feel safe in my own home. You're earning that money."

"Fine. But I'm not taking anything extra from you for something I thoroughly enjoy. So, forget it."

"Fine," I bite back, "then I'll pay Benny. And don't even *think* about stopping me."

He rolls his eyes, clearly exasperated, but this time, he doesn't argue. How can he? He can't deny his best friend a bit of extra cash.

I bite my lip as I look him up and down, taking in his paint spattered clothes. They're old and ruined, but that's not the problem. It reminds me of the size of the duffle bag he brought with him.

"There's something else I need you to do for me. Two things, actually."

He narrows his eyes with suspicion. "Which are?"

"Let me take you clothes shopping."

"No."

"I'm not finished. Part two's contingent on part one."

He shakes his head. "Then I'm not interested in part two."

Stupid, pig-headed man. Well, we'll see about that. "I want you to accompany me to the Christmas dinner for work."

"Not inter—" His eyes flash with realisation, then soften. "Sorry … what was that?"

I bite the inside of my cheek to stop myself grinning. I've got him. "The firm puts on a lavish dinner for employees and their partners for Christmas. I've always gone alone. I'd very much like to *not* go by myself this year."

His searching eyes gaze into mine as he shuffles on his feet and scratches the back of his head. "Yeah, ah … I'd love that."

This time, I don't hide my smile. "And you have a suit to wear?"

He lets out a huff, the quirk of his lips telling me he knows he's fallen into my trap. "No."

"So, it's agreed. We're going shopping on the weekend."

The following week, as we finish dinner, Gavin swivels away from the breakfast bar and faces the bare dining table. "Not doing any work tonight?"

"It's the first day in court tomorrow. Big case. I've prepped all I can, so I'm taking the night off."

Rising, I take our empty plates into the kitchen. Gavin follows, opening the dishwasher, waiting for me to hand him the dishes after I rinse them at the sink. A little routine that's developed over the last week. At first, he wouldn't let me help, but he's relented. Possibly because of the deep conversations we get into while we clean up.

If I happen to get home early enough to catch Benny still here on the days he helps Gavin, we convince him to stay for dinner. Already I've grown so fond of him, it's hard to believe he was in prison for so long. I just hate watching him leave. It's okay for us, we've got each other, but Benny has to go home alone to that same sad situation Gavin came from.

"You don't mind working such long hours?" Gavin asks.

Handing him the last of the dishes, I shrug. "I've been doing it so long, I guess I'm used to it."

"And what's your end goal? To make partner?"

As he wanders over to the breakfast bar with a damp cloth, I shake my head. "That's not likely to happen in such a big firm. But I have been considering what I want lately. And I don't think it's being constantly exposed to so much evil in the world."

He stops wiping down the counter, his full attention on me. "Then don't."

If only it were that simple. "I just feel that … if I quit, I'll be abandoning the people who need help."

"You deserve to be happy, Jamie." He walks back to me at the sink and rinses the cloth. "You've put in a lot of years helping others. Maybe it's time to help yourself, to do what you want. Have you imagined what that might look like?"

It's the strangest thing, having someone ask what I want for myself. I don't think anyone's bothered before. So, for the first time, I put what I want into words.

"What I want is my own practice. Not criminal law. Something people need that doesn't involve dealing with the ugly side of human nature. I'm not sure what yet, but to be my own boss, to be in control of how much work I take on and what that work is … that's the end goal."

His eyes hold mine and I know he's thinking about what I've said. He *listens.*

"I can see that. You like being in control."

I nod. "I've had enough chaos in my personal life. Control at work keeps me … grounded."

"I get it. I've barely had any control over my life. Even when I was getting my degree, I knew it was pointless. I should've concentrated on a trade instead."

I move a little closer and gently rest my hand on his forearm.

Stop touching him.

I don't.

"No. You're too smart, too intelligent in here," I place my palm in the centre of his chest. "You didn't make the wrong decision. You'll be using that degree before you know it. And you do have control. You're here instead of that caravan. You controlled that."

He glances at my hand resting on his chest, then into my eyes. "That decision could only be made because of you. For me, being in control means making my own way, a career, a car, a place of my own."

My heart constricts. Of course he wants his independence. That's his end goal. And I desperately want that for him. That's what I'm fighting for. To free him from the shackles my father ensnared him in.

But as images of coming home to an empty house, of eating alone, of not feeling his eyes on me, burst into my mind, I'm hit with the realisation that what I want for him, will mean losing what I want for myself.

His presence has added a richness to my life I hadn't known was missing. The more time I spend with him, the more attached I grow. I don't want it to end.

Plastering on a smile, I reluctantly remove my hand from that beating life inside his chest. Pushing down a feeling I can't quite grasp, I say, "The day will come when you have all of those things." He tilts his head slightly, like he's seeing straight through me.

"One thing I do have control over is the ability to endure. No matter how long it takes."

"I don't know how you did it," I murmur. "You're so strong, Gavin. I couldn't have … I don't think I could have survived. At least, not the way you have."

"I'm sure you would have. I'm nobody special."

Yes, you are. You're special to me.

I keep my mouth shut and swallow over the lump in my throat.

He might only be in my house because of that threatening note, but that's not why I want him here anymore. Sure, he makes me feel safe, secure and comfortable. It's the other things he makes me feel that have me wanting to get closer to him, to know him on a deeper level. Intimately. In every way.

"So, why haven't you started your own practice already?" he asks, startling me out of my head.

"Oh, I … ah … The timing's never been right."

"Are you waiting for that moment when life stands still?"

I blink at him. "I'm waiting for that moment when I'm not drowning in responsibilities."

Concern clouds his eyes. "I hope I'm not one of them."

"God no." That's the last thing I want him to believe. "You … you make me feel like I can breathe again."

As our eyes hold, a new energy shifts between us.

"That's some compliment," he murmurs.

My face heats as every hair follicle on my scalp prickles.

The moment's so intense, I glance away, my gaze falling on the oven clock. It's far too early to go to bed. He'll know I'm running away. And I don't want to run anywhere. What I want, is to spend more time with him.

"Do you, ah … want to watch something on TV?" I ask.

Half an hour later, we're sitting on the couch, tears streaming down our faces, stomachs aching, as an old Frasier episode comes to an end.

Swiping at his eyes, he turns to me. "You have any photos or home movies? I'd love to see what you were like as a kid."

I smile. I haven't looked at them since Mum's death. I've been too afraid that the filter I'll see her through will destroy the memories in my head. But the idea of revisiting those images with Gavin at my side sends that fear fluttering away.

After retrieving my tablet, I sit next to him, and as it powers up, I try to remember Anika's instructions on how to cast the screen to the TV. Before I get the chance, Gavin rests an arm over the back of the couch behind me, his eyes fixed on the tablet.

Well, maybe I can't remember how to do that casting thingy. Unlike the TV, the tablet demands we sit close. Sliding over a little, I position myself so we're almost touching.

"You're so lucky to have all of this," he says. "We had videos and photos, too. But for me, they're gone. I'd love to see Mum again. She's faded away so much."

My heart creaks on its axis, straining toward him with empathy. Although I haven't looked at these in so long, I've always known they're here, waiting. It's one thing to avoid them, but knowing they were gone forever would be gut-wrenching.

"Your father … wouldn't he have them?"

With his gaze fixed on the tablet screen, he shrugs. "Whether he does or doesn't, I'll never know."

Tension radiates off him and even though he refuses to look at me, I see a hard veneer glaze over his eyes. His father's abandonment hurts him deeply.

"Will you ever forgive him?" I ask gently.

He taps the tablet screen. "Come on, I'm dying to see how cute you were as a kid."

Unlike everything else he's happy to talk through, his father is clearly off limits. So, I don't push it. But I won't forget about it either.

I tap on the first thumbnail, then pause it before it plays. "There's a lot of footage. Just tell me when you get bored."

He grins down at me, warmth flooding back into his eyes. "Settle in. Could be a late night."

I let out an amused scoff and play the video of me, as a newborn, in Mum's arms. It's then I realise that resting the tablet on my lap doesn't allow Gavin the best view.

"Here," he says, taking hold of the side closest to him and moving it on his thigh where we can both see it better. "Well, there's no need to ask if this is your mum. She's beautiful. Or maybe it's that ugly little scrunched up thing she's holding that's making her look so attractive."

"Hey!" I jab him in the side with my elbow.

He chuckles, his hand suddenly on my shoulder, squeezing gently before disappearing to the back of the couch again.

Over the next few hours, we watch, with Gavin pausing the footage frequently to ask questions. He can't get over how much I look like Mum, and how beautiful she was. When Mum's laughter bubbles from the speakers, I gasp. It's been so long since I've heard it, it's almost like her ghost is whispering in my ear, reminding me of the loving, happy mother I lost.

I only wish I could reconcile that woman with the one who cheated on my father.

As the videos go on, showing me growing up, laughing with Dad as he puts me on his shoulders, or spins me around, or just cuddles me, I pause it too, telling Gavin where we were or what the occasion might have been. Somewhere in amongst all the pausing and unpausing, my hand drops away from the screen and rests on his thigh. His muscles tighten, but before I take my hand away, he relaxes again. So, I keep it there. After all, it's much easier to reach the screen.

Soon, the footage shows me at fourteen, holding baby Anika protectively. Images roll forward of me trying to pass her to Dad and him stepping back, of me putting her on my shoulders after he's refused. Another of Dad and I standing with Anika in front of the Kiama blowhole. When the blowhole erupts, Anika gets such a fright, she clings to Dad's leg and cries. He quickly extracts her and pushes her at me before marching toward the camera to take it from Mum.

"Your father," Gavin says. "I don't think I've seen a single video or image of him holding Anika. It's always you."

I'm surprised he noticed. I knew it then, and it became more obvious after Mum died. Even the affectionate hugs he used to give me stopped after Mum's death. I always thought it was his way of protecting himself from further hurt—something I'd followed his lead on. But now I understand it was guilt holding him back. He didn't deserve to hold and comfort me or Anika because he was the reason we needed comforting.

"He was always like that with Anika, but after Mum died, he disconnected even more. That's why I stayed instead of moving out when I was ready. She needed a parent and our father was incapable."

Gavin's soft, caring eyes gaze into mine. "She's lucky to have you."

I scoff. "I doubt she sees it that way."

"I think you'd be surprised. She might not verbalise it, but she'd have to be blind not to know that her sister has an incredible heart. I'm sure anyone you care for feels your love."

The heart he's just mentioned thuds hard against my breastbone. His sincerity tears something wide open inside me. He sees me. Sees behind those walls I've constructed. The walls he's destroying with a sledgehammer.

I look away, blink rapidly and swallow over the excruciating lump in my throat. Before he can say anything that'll tip me over that edge, I press play.

After much pausing, laughter and waves of sadness, we finally reach the end. Emotions flow through me like a whirlwind, but I'm so glad I watched it. With Mum's funeral being so morbidly sad due to the circumstances of her death, I never thought to look at these memories as a celebration of her life.

It's not until Gavin places the tablet on his other side that I realise I'm pressed right up against him. He feels solid, warm, and comforting. Too damn good. In this moment, I understand that it hasn't just been one bad experience and too many responsibilities that have kept me from letting a man into my life. I simply haven't met anyone who makes me feel this way. I've never had my heart jolt or my stomach flutter. I've never been hyper aware of every touch. I've never had an insatiable need to look into a man's eyes.

Until he came along.

Every instinct tells me he feels it too, but I can't stop that niggling little voice in my head that doesn't trust my instincts. What if he's only here because he feels obligated while he waits for his conviction to be overturned? What happens when he leaves?

The thought that I might soon lose him, sends a shrivelling pain through my chest. And I've had enough pain to last a lifetime.

"Hey," he says with concern, "what's wrong?" Dusting a thumb over my cheek, he brushes away a tear I was completely unaware I'd shed.

I don't want to lie to him, but I'm not ready for that level of vulnerability yet. So, since I value his opinion, I reveal another truth instead. "As much as Mum's affair was a shock that I'll never get answers to, my father has me torn in two. I just can't wrap my head around him. That level of violence, of deception. I stood by him, I did everything I could for him because I always believed his grief was deeper than mine. How am I supposed to grieve for a man I never knew?"

Gavin places his hand on my shoulder, angling me toward him a little. "Maybe you can't," he says softly. "Maybe all you can do is grieve for the part of him you *did* know."

Staring at my hand resting on his thigh, I wonder why I can't seem to remove it. I bite my lip and concentrate on his words. "But after watching those memories, knowing he had it in him to kill the very person he claimed to love … doesn't that mean *everything* was a lie?"

"Jamie …" He slides his hand from my shoulder and cups my neck, his thumb grazing my jaw. "After watching him, I can't believe his love for you was a lie. And the pride in his eyes when he looked at you … there's no faking that."

"Then how could he do what he did to Mum, to me, to Anika … to *you*?"

"You'll probably never know. And that's a tough fucking truth to swallow. But … what if he'd done the worst thing imaginable, then—as luck would have it—the opportunity to prevent the second worst thing from happening fell into his lap?"

"You?" I ask, trying my best to concentrate on his words instead of the gentle circling of his thumb behind my earlobe.

"Yeah." The intensity in his eyes holds me captive. "Try and put yourself in his shoes. With me taking the fall, he was safe. And that meant you and your sister were safe."

I frown. "Safe from what?"

"From the very real possibility of leaving you girls parentless, at the mercy of a foster care system that would've almost certainly separated you from your sister. The way he was in those videos, I think he'd have done anything to prevent that from happening. Like letting an innocent man go to prison in his place."

His clear blue eyes gaze at me as I absorb his words. "You're … *defending* him?" I ask in disbelief.

"No, not defending him. *Understanding* him."

The fact that Gavin has taken the time to unravel the motives behind the man who stole sixteen years of his life, overwhelms me.

And it makes perfect sense. The man I knew as my father would have done whatever it took to keep his family together. Well, apart from killing his wife. That'll never make sense. My father must have experienced intense relief when the police revealed they'd caught the killer. He'd have latched onto that the way a drowning man clutches a flotation device. Gavin's arrest had been his chance to make sure his crime didn't make things worse for me and Anika.

The man I thought I knew would have been eaten up by guilt. A slow, hungry monster that destroys from the inside out. Was that what he meant when he told me he deserved the cancer? Had he held on until Anika had her life in order, then just let go, let the guilt consume him?

Images of a different life flash before my eyes. I see my father's arrest. I see myself holding two-year-old Anika, trying to shield her from faceless people ripping her from my arms to take her away. The terror, the extra trauma on top of Mum's death. Who knows what would have happened to us. I might not even know my sister today.

"You okay?" he asks, sliding his hand from my neck to my shoulder, his thumb resting on my bare collarbone.

"Yes … I … Why have I never thought about it like that?"

"Why would you? You've only just found out."

"But *you* did."

"I've had a little longer to think about it. Lying in my cell, staring at the walls, I'd come up with every scenario under the sun. But actually seeing the way he was with you in those videos, that cemented it."

I close my eyes, letting more tears flow. I don't care. I know I'm safe with this man, and even more that, I *want* his comfort.

He squeezes my shoulder before sinking his fingers into my hair at the nape of my neck, and then I feel the softest brush of his lips on my forehead.

"You're strong, Jamie," he murmurs, touching the underside of my chin until my eyes meet his. "You know that, right?"

The need to throw myself into his arms, to feel them around me again, is so damn tempting. But I resist. "When being strong or falling apart are your only choices … well, crumbling wasn't an option when there was a little girl who needed me." Swallowing over the lump in my throat, I release a long breath.

"What else are you thinking?" he asks gently, reading me far too easily.

I hesitate a moment. Even having this thought hurts my heart. "Is it wrong to be grateful that Anika and I didn't end up in the system … when it was at your expense?"

To my amazement, he smiles, his blue eyes the warmth of a flame. "No, it's not wrong. Don't ever feel guilty about that."

I shake my head. "How can I not?"

"That's easy."

"I don't think so."

"Jamie," he says, his voice low and deep with emotion. "How can I regret a second of being locked away, when it meant you and your sister's lives weren't destroyed?"

My heart comes to a complete standstill. Then takes off like a rocket as his fingers brush stray strands of hair behind my ear like I might shatter if he touches me with too much force. And I just might. The kindness and compassion of this man is heartbreaking.

Our eyes hold and, as his palm cradles my jaw, his pupils swallow his irises until only a ring of the deepest blue remains.

There's nothing I can do but sink into his touch. When he inches closer, my pulse stutters. The fraction of air between us sparks and sizzles. He's going to kiss me. And oh, God, I want him to.

So.

Fucking.

Badly.

From the kitchen, my phone shrills, wrenching me out of the moment.

"That's my boss," I say, and his hand drops away from my face, leaving a ghost of an imprint behind. I almost whimper at the loss.

Disappointment flashes in his eyes. "You can tell from

here?"

"The ringtone." Reluctantly getting to my feet, I hurry around the couch.

I regret it the moment I answer, but part of my employment contract demands I'm contactable outside office hours. Listening to my boss ramble on about the court case tomorrow, I watch Gavin head down the hallway to the bedrooms. Without glancing my way.

Is he pissed at me? Why wouldn't he be? *I'm* pissed at me. While my boss drones on about urgently needing a document prepared before tomorrow, I wish I'd let it go to voicemail. I wish I was sitting on the couch kissing Gavin right now.

I also know my boss would have kept calling and calling until I picked up.

As much as I regret answering the damn thing, I'm glad my boss's ringtone isn't the soundtrack to the moment my lips first touch Gavin's.

Though I'm not so sure he feels the same way.

After I tune into Eric's voice and understand what he wants prepared and sent over to him tonight, I unpack my laptop at the dining table and get to work.

When what seems like seconds have passed, a warm hand gives my shoulder a gentle shake. "Jamie?"

I grumble and press my eyes deeper into the curve of my inner elbow. It can't be time to get up yet.

"Come on, sleeping beauty. It's two o'clock," that deep, soothing voice vibrates close to my ear. "Let's get you to bed."

He guides my arm across his shoulders, then I'm weightless, crushed against his chest as he lifts me from the chair. "Hold on."

I burrow my face into his neck and cling to him. I love the way he smells, the warmth of his skin against my forehead. Memories flood through my half-asleep brain, pulling me back to the taste of him, the feel of his skin on my lips, on my tongue.

Then my head touches softness. Cool sheets slide against my skin.

"Thank you," I murmur, not sure if the words slipped from my mouth.

"Goodnight, Jamie."

As I cross the threshold between consciousness and sleep, I swear I feel soft lips touch my forehead.

Chapter 30

Gavin

ALTHOUGH I'M OUT of bed and heading into the kitchen at the usual time, Jamie's already dressed, travel mug in hand as she hurries over to the dining table.

"Morning," I say to her back, taking in the deep plum dress that clings to her figure and stops a few inches above her knees. But it's the zip traveling from the back of her neck all the way to her thighs that has my mind filling with all sorts of inappropriate scenarios.

"Hey." She shoves her laptop into its bag, hooks the strap over her shoulder and picks up her coffee.

She's leaving early. A jolt of disappointment spears through my middle. I've missed our morning ritual. Missed the way we stand side-by-side, me purposely positioned in between her and the cutlery drawer. The way she always touches me to get to that drawer. The way she smells so warm and cosy straight from her bed. How we gaze into each other's eyes and reveal what we have planned for the day. It might only last a few minutes, but it's enough to make sure I'm out of bed on time every morning. Why wouldn't I be? I've never experienced a better start to the day.

Now, as pathetic as it is, a sense of deprivation washes over me.

"Gotta go," she mutters as she hurries past the breakfast

bar without glancing my way.

"Good luck," I call after her.

Not even a glimpse of eye contact. Worse than deprivation, that feels like punishment. And there's only one reason she's different this morning. Because of a kiss that didn't happen. Bit by bit she's been letting her guard down, letting me see the real her, not just the woman who's strong, but the woman who's warm and vulnerable. We'd connected on a deeper level last night and I fucking know she felt it too. She'd wanted that kiss as much as I did.

When I hear the laundry door close, I turn to the coffee machine, check the bean situation, and press the button. While the loud rumble fills the kitchen, I try to shake off my irrational reaction to her cold shoulder treatment.

"Sorry."

I whirl around to find her standing there, her coffee and bag nowhere to be seen, her hands clutching at each other as if she doesn't know what to do with them.

"I … I meant to say thank you, for last night," she says, her eyes just as indecisive as her hands.

My lips twitch. So, while I've been standing here thinking about her, she's been busy thinking about me.

She cares. I *do* mean something to her. Otherwise, why bother coming back?

"You don't have to thank me for that," I tell her. "I enjoyed learning about your family, seeing how cute you were as a kid … and still are."

I expect her to hurry off to work now she's said what she came back to say, but she hesitates, her eyes flitting over my entire body before they finally land on mine. She takes a couple of steps closer, allowing me to see what I couldn't before. Like always, she's the picture of professionalism, but she can't hide the heavy fatigue weighing her down this morning.

"That's not why I wanted to thank you. And it's not why I'm sorry." Now her lack of sleep is coming through in the huskiness of her voice. As sexy as it sounds, it proves she can barely muster enough energy to speak.

I shake my head, and take a few steps toward her, aware that she no longer seems to be in a hurry to get to work. "You've got nothing to be sorry for. And whatever it is you're trying to thank me for, I don't need it."

"It doesn't matter whether you *need* it or not." Her eyes flash with defiance. "You *deserve* it. So, thank you for putting me to bed last night. I feel like an idiot for falling asleep at the table, but I appreciate you checking on me. And—"

"Jamie—"

"Not finished," she says sternly. "And I'm sorry … about the phone call."

I'm stunned she's mentioned it. Then again, maybe I shouldn't be. I hadn't left any doubt in her mind about my reaction to that call. I'd stormed off to my bedroom like a child. In my defence, I'd been crushed when that hateful piece of technology interrupted us. And I can't tell her that the moment I entered my room, I threw open my sketchpad and drew the desire in her eyes, the heat that made me certain she wanted me to kiss her.

Before I can ask why she feels the need to apologise for that phone call, she sways on her feet. Actually *sways*.

That's it. There's no way in hell she's driving to work. I'm here to protect her. Whether that involves keeping her safe from an outside threat or from herself, it makes no difference. She's not going to like it. She'll have to relinquish that control she holds onto like a barrier. Too bad, because when it comes to her protection, I'm in charge.

"Give me your phone," I demand, holding out my hand, waiting for her to flare up. I haven't spoken to her like this before, but I need to make it clear who's calling the shots right now.

Her tired eyes widen. "Excuse me?"

As I move toward her with commanding purpose, she retreats from the kitchen until her back hits the hallway wall. I'm right in her space, bracing myself with a hand beside her head, my other still out, waiting. "Unlock it and give it to me. I'm booking you an Uber."

"I can drive myself like I always do," she states flatly.

"You're fucking exhausted, Jamie. You shouldn't even be going to work, but I know you won't let your clients down, so there's no point trying to keep you home. The best I can do is make damn sure you get there and back safely. Now give it to me."

Her jaw tenses as she glares up at me. "It's in the car."

"You're breaking your rule."

"What?"

"About lying," I remind her. "You'd never leave it somewhere you can't hear the bloody thing." I lean away a little, casting my gaze down her body. She needs to know I'm fucking serious. "I'm happy to search for it."

Her sharp intake of breath draws my eyes up to hers, and defiance stares back.

"So do it," she breathes.

Jesus.

Already feeling the effects of being this close to her, my dick swells. Do I want to put my hands on her? *Fuck yes.* Is it risky? *Also, fuck yes.* If I'm misinterpreting what she wants, I'll be out the door before my dick deflates.

But as I gaze into her eyes, I see it there.

She's daring me.

There's no misunderstanding. She's giving me permission to touch her. What sort of man would I be if I didn't accept her challenge?

I sweep my eyes down her body and back up again. I have a pretty good idea where that phone is. A pretty good idea of which area to avoid if I don't want to find it too quickly.

Leaving one hand braced against the wall, I press my fingertips to the curve of her waist. When she doesn't flinch or tense, I flatten my palm there, enjoying the heat through the soft material.

Heart galloping, I meet her eyes again, confident they'll tell me everything I need to know. And they do. That heat I saw last night is right there.

She *wants* this.

I have to stay in control, deny every instinct demanding I slam my body against hers and show her how much I want *her.*

Restraining myself, I slowly rub my thumb over the tight fabric. She blinks up at me, waiting, reminding me I'm supposed to be searching for her phone. I can't keep her in suspense.

As I slide my hand from her waist to the small of her back, my knuckles connect with the wall. She wastes no time tilting her hips forward, making room for me, giving me permission to keep going.

I touch the cool metal of her zipper and follow it downward until I meet the swell of her backside. Dipping a little lower, I skate my palm over her right cheek where a pocket might be positioned. I know damn well this dress doesn't have any. It's so damn tight, even if it did have pockets, nothing but a credit card would fit inside.

Somehow, I resist the urge to squeeze that firm, round, delectable arse. I'm not here to grope her like a fucking pervert. I respect her too much for that. She might want me to touch her, but it's up to me *how* I do that. And I want to make her feel good. I want to leave her wanting more.

Moving on, I graze my palm down the back of her thigh. When my fingers reach the hem of her dress and touch bare skin, she shivers. I pause, holding the intense eye contact, waiting for her to give me any indication I should stop. After all, I'm not touching her where she can hide a phone.

Apart from that shiver and the rapid rise and fall of her chest, she doesn't move.

With a featherlight caress, I leisurely trace her bare skin just beneath her hem. By the time I reach the front of her thigh, goosebumps rise beneath my fingertips. Her pupils dilate, her eyes widen, and her lips part.

Fuck. There's no denying I'm having the same effect on her as she's having on me. My cock's so damn hard, I know it's weeping with excitement. And I'm pretty confident that if I touched her panties right now, they'd be more than just damp.

Jesus. It'd be so easy to slip my fingers between her warm thighs and find out.

But she needs to get to work, not be fucked against the wall by a feral animal who'll probably last two whole seconds. If I ever get the privilege of sinking into her body, the last thing I want to do is remind her of her first and only experience. I want to show her how good it can be. For *her.* Unlike her first time, I want her desperate to repeat it.

The fact that she's allowing me to touch her like this has my stomach fluttering. This isn't just about how good she feels beneath my hand, it's also about how good she feels inside my heart.

Trembling with the force of restraining myself, I slide my palm up to her hip, pretending to search for another non-existent pocket.

Her fast, shallow breaths match mine, and when I lick my lips, her eyes dart to my mouth and linger there.

Christ, she wants me to kiss her as much as I want to.

But that's not what I'm supposed to be doing. The reason I have her up against the wall in the first place manages to sweep past my need. I'm trying to take care of her, not take advantage of her.

Shit. I need to get a grip.

Which apparently means sliding my hand over her ribs until my thumb brushes the underside of her breast. Her eyes snap back to mine, wide and bright, her pupils almost completely swallowing that vibrant green I know so well. She's totally alive right now, completely immersed in the moment.

I lock onto the rapid pulse fluttering at the base of her throat, and a powerful urge to cover it with my mouth, to feel that life force flowing through her with the tip of my tongue, takes over.

I lean in closer. Then hesitate. If my lips touch her skin, I'll lose the control I'm desperately trying to maintain.

Instead, I move my lips as close to the shell of her ear as I dare. "Told you I'd get your heart pounding," I whisper, remembering the stunt she pulled in the car and my promise to get even.

"Mission accomplished," she murmurs, every ragged exhale cooling against my ear, sending shockwaves right through my body.

I pull back enough until our eyes lock. She's smiling, and I grin back, the look on her face confirming I'm not in this alone.

Spurred on, I follow the curve of her underwire with the pad of my thumb, sweeping it slowly up the side of her breast.

A *ping* sounds from somewhere below my chin.

God-fucking-dammit.

Her smile slips.

Game over.

Almost.

Slowly, I brush my knuckles over her clavicle, lingering a moment before my fingers dip beneath the neckline of her dress and withdraw the phone from her bra.

But I don't move away. Neither does she.

"What did I tell you about putting electronics near your … breasts?" I ask, handing over her phone.

Her thumb trembles as she unlocks it, then slips it into my waiting hand. "I think you said my delicate bits," she corrects.

My eyes meet that cheeky look of hers, then drop to the hard nipples pressing against the thin material of her dress. "Maybe I should've said *sensitive* bits."

Christ, what I wouldn't give to see them, touch them, draw them into my mouth.

Trying to get a grip, I swipe her phone screen with my thumb, find the Uber app and open it.

"Are you going to work, or court?"

"Work first," she says, her voice soft and breathy. *So fucking sexy.*

I select her work address and wait a few moments before I accept a ride, turn off the screen and pass it back to her.

"It'll be here in four minutes."

She stares up at me, blinking slowly. "Thank you."

"You're thanking me again?"

Reaching out, she gives my bicep an affectionate squeeze.

"Yeah. For giving a damn." Her fingertips slide down my bare forearm, leaving a burning trail of fire behind. "It feels nice."

Touching me, or the way I look out for her? Both? There hasn't been a day in her presence when she hasn't touched me. That's why I missed it so much when I thought she'd left. Because my day doesn't start until I feel her on my skin.

She stares up at me, as if waiting for me to tell her what to do next.

What I want, is to kiss her fucking senseless. But she's all done up for work and that lipstick won't stand a chance of staying in place. Not against the type of kiss I want to give her. Plus, her ride will be here in a few minutes. And she's exhausted. I've already taken advantage of her state of mind. Taken it way too far. I'm not going further, no matter how much my body's screaming for it.

When I kiss her, I want time to savour her, devour her, ravish her. I want her fully present.

Pushing away from the wall, I take a step back and watch her gaze instantly snap down to my erection. I won't apologise or try to hide from her. I *want* her to see what she does to me.

"You'd better get your stuff out of your car," I tell her before I lose control. She moves immediately, that sexy arse disappearing into the laundry far too soon.

As blood races through my veins, I press my forearm against the wall and rest my head there. I've learnt something new about her just now. When I take charge, when I leave her with no choices to make, she enjoys it.

Benny taught me how to restrain myself in prison, but out here, in the real world, I don't have any fucking control over my life. At least, I didn't think so. Until now.

The woman who appears to thrive on control, wants to let go. My mind races over our conversations. It's been more than once that she's told me she wishes she could let someone else take the reins, be the one responsible so she doesn't have to make all the decisions.

Although control seems ingrained within her everyday life, there's at least one part where it isn't. Her role in a romantic relationship. Just like me, she's never had one, so she doesn't know who she is inside one. The thought of taking the lead, guiding her and discovering what turns her on right along with her, has my breath catching in my throat.

When she emerges from the laundry with her satchel and coffee, she appears more pulled together than I am, though that fatigue is back.

A horn toots outside. I hurry to the front door and open it for her.

"Have a good day, Jamie."

She glances down at my crotch, then meets my eyes with a mischievous grin. "I'm sure yours will be better than mine."

Cheeky little minx.

I chuckle as she hurries out the door and down the steps. Without turning around, she gives me a little wave, then disappears into the waiting Uber at the kerb.

I consider doing what she clearly believes I'm going to do, but I need to get to work on the outside of the house before it gets too hot. Benny will be here soon, so at least I'll have that distraction for the rest of the day.

But that's only temporary. I have no idea how I'm going to control myself when she gets home tonight and we're alone again. We can't continue denying what's happening between us. And it's all too clear now that she won't make a move. That'll be up to me.

I'll simply have to play it by ear. She's already exhausted. Who knows how today will affect her. She's overworked and her father's betrayal is still weighing heavily on her emotional state.

Maybe now's the worst time to push her. I want so much more with her than just the physical attraction that's sparking between us. The last thing I want is to ignite it, only to fuck it up.

Chapter 31

Jamie

I THINK I might have to kill Gavin Lake for the state he left me in.

The moment I arrived at work, I made a beeline straight for the toilets. After twisting and turning in the mirror to make sure I hadn't left a dark patch on the back of my dress, I hid myself in a stall and decided pantyliners should be my new best friends.

Thank God I took my own advice. Trying to concentrate in court when my mind kept replaying Gavin's touch had been quite a battle. Fortunately, by the time lunchtime came around, the proceedings were adjourned until after the Christmas break.

Being back at my desk proves even less productive. Now that I'm under no immediate obligation to concentrate, my mind goes straight to Gavin's hands on me, to drowning in that incredible eye contact.

When he brushed over my backside, when his thumb traced the outline of my breast, when he simply touched me *anywhere*, it took everything I had to hold back a long, throaty groan.

But most of all, he had every hair follicle on my body standing at attention when he spoke those low, gravelly words into my ear like an intimate secret. I've never been so turned on in my life. The night before I wanted his kiss. This morning,

I wanted a hell of a lot more.

And I wasn't alone. He had a predatory look in his eyes, like I'm his, and I'd better hurry up and damn well realise it. Instead of unsettling me, I'd felt cocooned and unburdened. He'd crashed through the crumbling walls around my heart and joined me on the other side, promising he could take as much weight off my shoulders as I'd allow.

Then my phone *dinged*.

And I start all over again, replaying it on a never-ending loop.

Until I start torturing myself about what I'm going to do when I get home. Pretend it never happened? Throw myself at him? Are those the only options?

As Benny would say, *Christ on a cracker.*

Fortunately, by the time 2pm rolls around, and I've accomplished exactly nothing for the day, the funeral home calls to tell me my father's death certificate has arrived. I duck out of work early, pick it up, then hurry over to the solicitor's office and collect Dad's will packet.

Upon returning to an insanely busy afternoon, I don't get a chance to look at the will. Or slip back into fantasy land.

With last night's lack of sleep oozing into my mind and body, I relax against the headrest in the back of an Uber, close my eyes and think about my father's will resting in my satchel. I suppose I could open it now, but really, I can't imagine that my father would have done anything other than leave half his estate to me and half to Anika.

"Lady? Hey, lady?"

My eyes snap open to the sight of the driver staring at me. As I blink my grainy eyes, I we're parked out the front of my house. Grabbing my bag and travel mug, I exit the car and make my way up the porch steps. Fully aware that I have no idea what might be waiting for me inside my home, my heart hammers so hard it thumps in my ears. Will he interpret what happened this morning as a green light to go further?

Weak-kneed, I step inside, shut the door and lock it with a trembling hand.

He's behind me. I *feel* him.

Taking a deep breath, with nowhere to run from the turmoil in my head and stomach, I turn around.

He stands a few feet away, his handsome face creased with concern as he scans me from head to toe. Before I can figure out what to say, he moves in, slips the satchel from my shoulder and takes the mug from my hand. As he places them on the floor, he drops to one knee and looks up at my utterly bewildered expression.

"Gavin? What're you—"

"Hold onto my shoulders."

Too confused to argue, I follow his command.

When he cups my bare calf, I tense in surprise.

"Lift," he instructs.

My hands bear down on his shoulders as I balance myself and raise my leg until I feel my strappy heel slip free. I do the same when he touches my other calf. As my bare foot returns to the cool floorboards, I groan with relief. "Oh, God. That feels so much better."

Rising with a grin, he picks up my satchel and travel mug, carries them through the living room and places the bag on the dining table before striding into the kitchen.

I take a seat at the breakfast bar, watching as he grabs a glass, dispenses some ice from the freezer and fills it with sparkling water at the sink. After he places it in front of me, he returns to the sink and washes my travel mug so it's ready for the morning.

Sipping at the water, I marvel at the amazing man in my kitchen. Of course, he was the one who made a big deal about how exhausted I am, but to look after me the way he is right now, without me even knowing it's exactly what I need, has my heart melting.

I rest my chin in my hand and continue to watch the show

he puts on every evening. He sets a frying pan on the cooktop, turns on the burner, then removes a plate from the fridge containing two marinated steaks. Despite believing I was too exhausted to eat, the moment the steaks hit the pan with a satisfying sizzle, my mouth waters.

"So, what did you do today?" I ask, remembering all too well the state he was in when I left for work.

"Mostly sanding down the side of the house, interspersed with dips in the pool and some reading." From the fridge he grabs a bowl of salad and begins serving it onto two plates beside the cooktop.

"Mostly, hmm? Sounds heavenly. Almost like a holiday."

I love that he's not pressuring me about what happened this morning. It's sweet and considerate the way he's letting the night unfold naturally.

"Can't argue with that." He smiles over his shoulder at me. "Do you ever go away anywhere?"

I shake my head. "Not really. I had a few days off here and there when I needed to attend a school event for Anika or to care for Dad. The only time I actually went away for a holiday was before Mum died."

He turns the steaks, then leans on the counter and looks at me. "Sounds like you must have a lot of leave owed to you."

"About six months' worth."

"Ever considered using any of it?"

"I haven't really had the chance." And I haven't. Previously, the thought of relaxing on holiday seemed impossible. But just an hour on a beach with Gavin showed me how wrong I've been. Not to mention the effortless way he looks after me. That alone feels like a vacation.

"You should, you know. I think you desperately need a break."

He's not wrong, but with my workload, it's wishful thinking.

As we eat, Gavin recounts his day, his eyes lighting up when he mentions how much happier and enthusiastic Benny seems lately.

After we finish eating, I put down my knife and fork, and

say from the bottom of my heart, "Thank you. That was amazing. Again."

"You have to stop doing that."

"Doing what?"

"Thanking me."

I shake my head. "Not a chance. Every single time you cook for me, I'm grateful. And I want you to know that."

"I'm cooking for *us*, Jamie. It's no hardship."

"Tell me that after you've been doing it for sixteen years."

"I'd love to," he says softly.

My heart fires up like a plane preparing for take-off. When I meet his stare, all I see there is honesty. This morning comes roaring back. His hand exploring, the heat in those eyes focused on mine.

I quickly look down at my empty plate and cross my legs. Goddamn the way he makes my body come alive, reminding me I'm a woman. As much as I've suppressed my sexuality all these years, he's woken it up and it seems to have no desire to go back to sleep.

Not while he's in close proximity. Who am I kidding? He doesn't have to be anywhere near me. All I have to do is *think* about the man.

And it's wonderful, and exciting. And it scares the shit out of me.

"Let me help you clean up," I offer without glancing at him.

My plate disappears. "No way. But you can keep me company while I do it."

"Oh, I nearly forgot. I picked up Dad's will. I suppose I should take a look." I grab the will packet from my satchel and slide onto the barstool again. Prying open the flap, I reach in and withdraw the document.

It's short and to the point, but I read it five times before I understand I haven't misread anything.

"That fucking arsehole," I blurt a little too loudly.

Gavin glances up from stacking the dishwasher. "What's wrong?"

"Dad," I say, my anger rising. "Fucking Dad."

Wandering over to the breakfast bar, Gavin glances at the will in my hand. Furious, I hold it up and flap it around.

"He left his whole estate … to *me*. There's not a single mention of Anika in here! How could he do that to her?"

Gavin frowns. "You're sure?"

"You think I don't know how to read a will?" I snap, then immediately regret it. "Shit, I'm sorry. I didn't mean to—"

"Well, he just keeps delivering the hits, doesn't he?"

I drop my head in my hands and let out a single sob, the exhaustion, the emotional roller coaster, finally overwhelming me.

"Fuck," Gavin mutters.

Then he's at my side, wrapping an arm around my shoulders. I lean against him, taking shuddering breaths as I try to get myself under control. He must be so sick of me using him as a crying cushion by now.

"Christ, Jamie. I'm so sorry. I shouldn't have said that. It was extremely insensitive."

I shake my head. "It's so … fucking true."

"Will Anika be able to contest it?" he asks, rubbing my shoulder.

"No." I look up at him and wipe away my tears. "She won't have to, because she'll never know."

He takes a seat next to me, holds my hand and squeezes. "What do you mean?"

"I'll tell her Dad left her half and, once probate goes through, I'll transfer half the house into her name. The stamp duty will be a bitch, but she'll never know. She *can't* know. It'll hurt her too much."

"You're a good person, Jamie."

I shake my head. "I'm only doing what's right."

"I don't think you understand how many people *don't* do what's right."

"You can't work in criminal law and not know that. It's just, you don't expect it from the people closest to you. That's when it hurts. And I refuse to let him wound Anika ever again."

Taking a deep breath, I squeeze his hand, telling him

without words that I appreciate his comfort.

Then I fold the will and slide it back inside the packet. Only it stops halfway. Withdrawing it, I squeeze the edges of the packet until it yawns open. Inside, there's another, smaller envelope. Shaking the packet upside down, the envelope drops to the counter. When I pick it up, it appears to be empty.

I quick glance at Gavin confirms he's as curious as I am. It's not uncommon for people to leave personal notes or letters for loved ones with their will, but as I turn it over in my hand, it has no thickness, no weight to it.

Until I feel a small, hard object in the corner of the envelope.

Tearing it open, I upend it.

A micro-SD card bounces on the stone counter.

"What the hell?" I mutter, picking it up and turning it over between my thumb and forefinger.

Heart thudding in my chest, my eyes meet Gavin's.

He looks from me to the SD card and back again. "What do you think's on it?"

"Maybe his reason for not including Anika? Let's find out."

I grab my laptop, bring it over to the breakfast bar and start it up. After inserting the SD card in the slot, Gavin rises.

"I should give you some privacy."

As he takes a step away, I grab his arm. "Stay. Please."

Slowly, he sits back down.

On the screen, the contents of the SD card pop up. A single video file. That's not what I'd been expecting. A Word document or a PDF would have been my guess. The only name assigned to the video is a date. A week after my father's cancer diagnosis.

Positioning the curser over the file, I double click.

Footage of the empty barstool I'm currently sitting on fills the screen. After a moment, a hand comes into view and swivels the chair to the side.

My father sits down and stares into the camera.

I gasp and hit the spacebar, pausing it.

Seeing him again stirs up completely different emotions

compared to watching the family videos. Those were memories. This most certainly isn't. Fear grips me. I'm not sure I can handle yet another shock. Not tonight.

"Jamie," Gavin says beside me, "this is private. I should—"

I grab his hand, my eyes locking with his. "Don't you dare go anywhere. I can't watch this alone. I need you."

He swallows hard as his grip on my hand loosens. For a terrifying moment, I think he's going to leave anyway. Then his fingers slip between mine and hold on tight. Profound relief sweeps through me. Having him here, having his support right now, makes me feel fiercely cared for.

"Whenever you're ready. I'm not going anywhere," he assures me, his thumb softly stroking over mine. "Not unless you want me to. Okay?"

I nod, turn my attention back to the laptop, and hesitate. This video might hold answers. But it could also hold more devastation.

"Anytime it gets too hard," Gavin says, "you can stop. Remember that."

When he gently squeezes my hand, I find the strength to hit the spacebar.

My father's eyes dart about the screen for a moment before he takes a deep breath.

"Jamie," he says, looking straight at me, *"if you're watching this, I'm finally gone. And I'm glad."* He shifts on the stool, looks off to the side and shakes his head before he focuses on the camera again. *"Damn this's harder than I thought. Even though I've been over it a million times."*

Dropping his head in his hands, he fists his fingers in his hair for a long moment.

My heart thunders against my chest as I tighten my grip on Gavin's hand. Hope flares through my entire body. If this is what I think it is …

Dad's head jerks up, his face determined.

"Right. Gotta get this over with. I hope I got the chance to tell you the truth face-to-face, or this'll be a shock. But, because I'm a coward, I'm recording it as a guarantee, in case I leave it too late. If I haven't told you, Jamie, I'm sorry for what you're about to hear. Either way, you'll have questions. Here are the answers, as I see them, anyway.

"I fell for your mother from the moment I saw her in primary school, but she didn't love me. Over time, we became best friends, but she never looked at me the way I wanted.

"Then, when we were sixteen, a new guy started at our school. He was a few years older than us, in his final year. Well, she fell madly in love with him, and of course, I was jealous. He stole all the looks I wanted from her. He stole all the kisses that should have been mine. When he was around, I didn't exist. He was everything and I was nothing.

"And then something incredible happened. Six months after his arrival, he left. Apparently, he'd just found out his ex-girlfriend from his old school was about to have his baby.

"While your mother was devasted, I was thrilled. It brought her straight back to me. For almost a year I comforted her, supported her through the initial dark days, her sorrow, then her acceptance that he wasn't coming back. We grew closer than ever, but I knew her heart still belonged to him. Even though he broke her, she admired the fact that he took ownership of his responsibilities."

He glances away from the camera for a moment, a look of shame clouding his expression as he stares at me again.

"So, when she finally gave in to me, I knew she'd also take ownership of her *responsibilities.*

"I sabotaged the birth control we were using and got her pregnant. I trapped her. I needed a guarantee that she wouldn't leave me.

"I'll never regret what I did. She loved you so much, she forgot all about him *and devoted herself to being the wife I wanted and the mother you needed. For thirteen years, we had the perfect family.*

"Until they met again. Both of them married, both of them parents, both of them cheating liars.

"But like the fool I was, when it all fell apart again, I took her back. I believed her when she told me she made a mistake. I believed her promises that she'd never see him again. That she'd never leave me.

"I believed her for three years. Then I found a letter she'd written to you.

"And I snapped. She was seeing him again. And this time, he was free. And she was planning on leaving me. Leaving us, *Jamie.*

"I followed her for almost a month. She wasn't going to her girls' nights out anymore. She wasn't out shopping during the day or taking care of the house. She was meeting him. And planning.

"So, I started planning too. I learnt the routine of her deceit.

"If we couldn't have her, no one could.

"So, that last night, I knew where she was going. I sent you upstairs to give your sister a bath. I used the golf course to get to his house before she did. I knew I could kill her and be back home again without you even knowing I'd left the house.

"I stabbed Matilda Evans. I took her life in a fit of rage so great, I didn't even care what happened to me. Of course, it wasn't until after I got home and calmed

down that I realised the fate you and your sister would face if I was caught.

"When Reid rang our doorbell, the horror of what I'd done to you almost destroyed me.

"You can imagine my relief when he said they had the killer in custody. It was too easy. All I had to do was let someone else take the blame to keep you girls safe.

"When I found out who that someone was—his son—I knew it was meant to be. It takes two to have an affair, to cheat on the ones who love you, to destroy them. So, I went along with it, knowing I was taking his son from him. Tit for tat. That's how I justified it.

"It's fucking shameful. And, Jamie, I never got away with it. It ate at me, gnawed at me, haunted me every waking moment and, when I could *get to sleep, it turned my dreams into nightmares.*

"What I did to your mother, and you girls, and that boy, is unforgivable. So, when the cancer diagnosis came, I wasn't surprised. I deserve it. I don't know how quickly it'll take me. Hopefully, it'll be fast..

"I'm so sorry for what I've done to you girls. And I don't just mean taking your mother from you, but for everything your lives became after that, for everything they could have been, but weren't. I'm sorry.

"And I'm sorry about that boy. I'm sorry I put false hate in your heart. None of this is his fault. He was caught in the crosshairs of a jealous, vengeful man who didn't learn what love meant until it was too late.

"Loving her meant I should have let her go. I should have wanted her to be happy. I should have put her first.

"My beautiful girl, I know you'll do the right thing by that boy. You might think you became a lawyer because of what happened to your mother, but maybe freeing him is your real purpose. Tell my story and get him out of that hellhole. Clear his name. I know you can't give him back what I took, but you can give him the chance at a new life. I know you, Jamie, so I know you'll do what's right. There's no doubt in my mind."

He takes a deep breath, drags a hand down his face and stares at me.

"I mentioned a letter from your mother. I kept it from you and your sister to save our family. Now I'm gone, it's yours. But I want you to read it together. You'll need each other. Anika knows where it is. Just remind her of the time she caught me hiding my cigarettes. She'll know. The code is 4778.

"I don't deserve your forgiveness, so I won't ask for it."

He pauses for a long moment, tears welling in his eyes until they escape and flow down his cheeks.

"I can only hope that one day you'll think of me, and remember something good."

He leans forward and ends the video.

Stunned, I sit back.

Gavin's suspicions about his motives were spot on. Everything we'd figured out matched my father's recount of the events. I know I'll have to view his confession multiple times for everything else to sink in, but one thing—the most important thing—is crystal clear.

Gavin squeezes my hand, and I realise I'm holding onto his so tightly it hurts. Extracting my fingers, I turn to face him, my chin trembling. I want to smile, but those muscles don't seem to be working.

He reaches out and grazes a thumb over my cheek, his eyes full of compassion. "Come here," he murmurs, placing his hand on my shoulder and gently pulling me toward him.

I slip off my stool and fling my arms around his neck, crashing against his chest. The moment his arms encircle me, I let the happiness override everything else. Burying my face in the curve of his neck, I half-laugh, half-sob with relief.

"Jesus, that can't have been easy," he says close to my ear as he rubs my back. "But I've got you."

Realising he doesn't understand the significance of what we just watched, I take a deep breath and pull away enough so I can grip his shoulders. "And now I've got you. Oh, my God, have I got you."

His blue eyes bore into mine, something simmering within them that has my heart skipping a beat. Then my words register. Heat burns my cheeks. I quickly let go of his shoulders and slide back onto my stool. And laugh. Maybe a little hysterically, but I can't help it.

"I mean," I say, getting control of myself, "we have exactly what we need now." I glance at the computer, then back at him. But from the look on his face, he still doesn't understand. He should be grinning from ear to ear, not looking like I've just crushed him.

"Jamie … that must have hurt—"

"No! Don't you get it? This confession is everything. His motive, how he did it, why he let you take the blame. That video is your freedom."

As I grab his hands and squeeze, trying to emphasise the point, I see the moment his focus shifts, the moment it dawns on him. His eyes brighten with hope just a moment before he looks down at our hands. Letting out a scoff of disbelief, he shakes his head. When he meets my gaze, that sexy grin spreads his lips and sparkles in his eyes.

"You really think so?" he asks, his thumbs brushing back and forth over my knuckles.

"There's not a single doubt. We just watched your ticket to the rest of your life."

"Jesus," he murmurs.

"It's really going to happen, Gavin. It's not just a hope or wishful thinking or a maybe anymore. It's an absolute, a foregone conclusion. I'm so, so happy for you!"

Tears pool in his eyes, then spill down his cheeks. After a long moment, he releases my hands and swipes them away. On a shuddering breath, he asks, "So, what happens next?"

"Well, apart from making a million copies of that video so it doesn't mysteriously disappear, we need to finish your affidavit. Liam's coming into the office to sign his tomorrow." The excitement at having irrefutable evidence dampens when I remember my promise to Pete. I hesitate a moment, then say, "The courts close in a few days for Christmas, so we won't make the deadline."

"Good. You need to get some rest."

I'd love to do just that, but I'd rather get it finished so it's ready the moment Pete gives me the go-ahead. "I'm fine. Just because we have to delay a little, doesn't mean we can't get everything prepared."

"Jamie …"

"No. We should do it now." I turn to the computer, open Gavin's affidavit and scroll down to where we stopped last time. That's when I remember why I've been putting off going further. Now that we have my father's confession, I need to face what I've been avoiding.

It's better to know the truth than keep wondering. No matter how painful it might be. And Gavin's the only one who can tell me what I've dreaded knowing since the moment I was told of my mother's murder.

Chapter 32

Gavin

IN THE FACE of all the pain Jamie's father just hit her with, her selflessness floods my chest with a deep warmth that emanates straight from my heart.

While that prick revealed the numerous lies and manipulations in his marriage, my only thoughts were for Jamie, and how his words had impacted her.

I still can't wrap my head around the idea that my life might soon be my own again. It's surreal, too much to take in right now.

Surprising me, she closes the laptop and pushes it away. *Good.* She needs to rest and unwind, to take a moment to absorb her father's revelations.

When she swivels her stool away from the counter so she's looking straight at me, she's suddenly apprehensive. "Gavin?"

I turn and face her, the brush of our bare knees sending a spark right through me. Positioning myself so my legs bracket hers, I give her my undivided attention.

"Your affidavit … We're up to the part where you find my mother on the ground." She takes a deep breath. "I think … well … I think I'd like you to tell me about that … personally. Not as a stiff, formal recollection for a legal document."

Her fingers grip her thighs just above her knees, the tension in her muscles so intense I don't miss the slight tremble in her arms. Any ideas I had earlier about what tonight might hold have gone out the window. Right now, I just want to reassure her, pull her against me and protect her from any more emotional turmoil.

But I don't. I've been waiting for this for a long time. And I know she's been avoiding it. I can only hope it'll be cathartic and not hurt her further. Now that the moment's here, I'm not sure the timing's right. Not on top of her father's video. But it's not my decision. It's hers. And I'm convinced she *should* hear it.

She hesitates, and when I see her struggle to form the words, I grab the edges of her stool and pull her closer. Gently pressing the inside of my thighs against the outside of hers, I cocoon her in a safe space. "Ask me."

After exhaling a long breath, she does. "When you found her, was she alive?"

"Yes," I answer, locking my eyes with hers, watching the surprise and torment as she takes in a tiny gasp.

"She suffered, then?"

"I don't … I can't be sure about that." I wish I could lie to her, but I won't.

She bites her bottom lip with indecision. When she releases it, she says, "Tell me. Every detail. From the moment you found her."

I take myself back to that night. And hesitate. Something shifts inside me, and I suddenly feel like I'm falling down an endless dark hole. When her warm hand blankets the fist I've formed on my thigh, she anchors me to her.

"Gavin? Are you okay?"

I don't know what the hell that was or where it came from, but I have to tell her what she needs to know.

"When I fell to my knees beside her, she was breathing fast, shallow breaths. Like an idiot, I grabbed the knife's handle. I remember thinking that if I could just get it out of her, she'd be okay, the way she was before it went into her. Stupid the things that go through your head."

I take the fist from my other leg and drag it down my face,

as if I can erase the painful memory with such a simple action. At the very least, it gives me a moment to pull myself together. This is about Jamie, not me.

"They kept saying you were strangling her. That's what it looked like in the video, but—"

"No!" I blurt, shaking my head. "Jamie, no. That's not what happened."

"I know, Gavin. I know that. What I don't understand is why it looked that way in the footage."

I stare down at her hand covering mine and I uncurl my fist, turn it over and hold onto her.

"Show me," she says as gently as the squeeze she gives me.

While she grips the hand that once held the knife buried in her mother's chest, I reach for her and cup the back of her neck. Slowly, I brush my thumb back and forth over her jaw. Just the way I'd touched her mother. Then I look into her eyes.

And oh, God, it's like I'm back there, living it again. I swallow hard over the rock in my throat, determined to get this over with.

"When I touched her like this, she turned her head and looked right through me, and I forgot all about the knife. Because I knew she was going. So did she … so I told her, '*You're safe. I'm right here. I'm with you.*' And something changed. She wasn't looking *through* me anymore, but *into* me. This … warmth filled her eyes. All the fear vanished. She knew she wasn't alone. And then … I *felt* her go. I saw it in her eyes, and I felt it in her skin. She just wasn't there anymore."

Jamie stares at me with those incredible eyes. While similar to her mother's, they contain a completely different soul. I shut mine for a moment, needing to escape the intensity of the various emotions passing through her.

Through me.

"Gavin?"

I watch a tear slide down her cheek before I meet her gaze.

"How did you know?" she asks softly.

I tilt my head in confusion.

"How did you know she was going? How did you know to

comfort her? To not run off for help and leave her alone in those final moments?"

I blink at her. That's not what I expected her to ask.

"I knew … because I'd seen it only a month before. I was there, when my mother died … while I was looking into her eyes, holding her hand, wishing I could stop her drifting away."

"Oh, Gavin." She squeezes my hand hard. "I'm so sorry. What you went through …"

"It's okay," I tell her, my voice cracking over the lie. *Fuck*.

"It's most definitely not okay. No lying, remember?" She releases my hand and slips off her stool. Standing between my parted legs, she wraps her arms around my shoulders, pulling me into her, resting the side of her face against mine. It's the most natural thing in the world to circle her waist and hold her close.

"I've wanted to tell you for so long," I say on an unsteady breath. "I've never told anyone. I've held it inside, waiting … because it's for you, no one else. It's yours."

"And yours, Gavin. Don't you see that?"

And then I start fucking crying. All this time I thought it'd be her that needed comforting, but I'm the one falling apart. I'm the one who was there, who experienced the horror that night.

As my body shudders, she tightens her hold on me. Pressing my face into the curve of her shoulder and neck, I sink into her and lose myself. I take her compassion, her arms around me, her fingers in my hair, the tightness of her hold. I take what she offers and let it seep into my soul. Never once does she try to move away, or pat my back in a dismissive, *that's enough* gesture. She makes me feel like she doesn't want to let me go. And that means the fucking world to me.

I should have known, should've seen it coming a mile away. I've never explored the impact of what comforting a dying, violently assaulted woman had on *me*. Almost immediately after Jamie's mother slipped away, I'd been chased down and arrested. I'd buried it deep, locked it away and refused to think about it. Because I'd been waiting for the chance to tell Jamie that her mother hadn't been alone. That the man who killed her wasn't the last person she saw.

There's no doubt the universe can be cruel, throwing that at me so close to my own mother's death. Maybe, on top of everything else, it was just too much for me to cope with, so I shut it down. Or maybe my mother's death prepared me for Matilda Evans. If I'd never witnessed that look before, I wouldn't have known she only had moments to live. I'd have run off to get help and Jamie's mother would have died alone.

As my body begins to relax and my mind clears, I tune in to her fingers gently massaging my scalp, the soothing circles she's drawing on my back.

God, this woman. Her touch is so damn caring and genuine, it's calming my heart, my whole being. I want to stay like this forever.

"I'm sorry," I mumble against her shoulder.

"You know," she says, still holding me, ignoring my apology, "I only ever thought of Mum's death as being all about me and my family. Even after I found out you were innocent, I didn't think about you finding her, what it must have been like, how it affected you. Seeing someone else die so close to your mother's death … I'm the one who's sorry, Gavin. I didn't realise. I'm so selfish."

Though I don't want to, I pull back a little. I can't let her believe that about herself. My hands slip to her waist, but no further. I'm not ready to break the contact yet. When she leans away just enough to look at me, I understand she isn't ready to give it up either.

"Jamie, you're the furthest thing from selfish I've ever known. You didn't have to step up when your mother died. You could've acted like a typical teenager. But you put everyone's needs before your own. Like you're doing right now."

Her eyes flick between mine, searching, probing. When her hands smooth over my shoulders and cup my face, I know she sees the truth there.

"I'm so glad someone was there for her in her final

moments." Her thumbs brush the outer corners of my eyes, tickling my lashes. "I'm so glad she was looking into these eyes when she passed."

Her courage to completely open herself to me, the way she's talking to me, touching me, looking at me … I've never experienced anything like it. She's warmth and safety, unguarded care and empathy. I'm not quite sure, but I think I understand what this is.

It feels like … she's *loving* me.

"Thank you, Gavin. Knowing that means more to me than you can imagine."

"I'm so sorry that happened to her … to you."

"And you," she says, her fingers working a delicate spell at the nape of my neck. "A beautiful act of kindness, and what did it get you?"

My thoughts instantly go to the sorrow of comforting her mother, the trauma of her dying in front of me, then the shock and rage over my arrest and imprisonment.

But as I look into her eyes, I suddenly understand something entirely different. Something that's been lingering inside me for weeks now, an idea I've kept just out of reach. Because, as much as I've wanted everything I've been through to mean something significant, it was downright horrifying to believe it happened for a reason.

Not anymore.

"You want to know what it got me?"

She nods, her gaze never leaving mine.

My heart throbs painfully in my chest, but the revelation is so powerful, I have to share it with her. So I let the truth tumble from my lips. "It got me here. It led me to this moment. With you."

Tears fill her beautiful eyes. But this time, she doesn't try to blink them away. This time, they spill freely over her cheeks. It's exquisite.

And then she kisses me.

I'm so stunned, my heart stops, its next beat suspended as it waits for my brain to catch up.

Her lips are on mine.

Her hands are in my hair, her soft breaths fluttering against my cheek.

Her mouth cradles my top lip, while mine embraces her bottom lip. We don't move. Our mouths simply touch and press. I don't crush her to me or take over. Now isn't the time, but it gives me hope that that time will come. For now, I remain completely motionless. This isn't a passionate kiss. It's a kiss of gratitude and pure affection. It's an intimate acknowledgement of the connection that binds us.

Her heartfelt care feels like a flashlight beam lighting up my insides, destroying the darkness within.

When she gently pulls away and takes a step back, I can see she doesn't know what to do or say next, and neither do I.

Not until my gaze falls to the shoulder of her dress and the dampness I've left behind.

"Well, I guess I finally got some payback," I say, hoping to break the tension.

Startled out of her awkwardness, she frowns. "Sorry?"

I touch her shoulder, waiting until she notices the wet fabric. "Payback for slobbering all over my shirts."

She gasps, her eyes sparking with amusement. "I did *not* slobber on you!"

"Pretty sure you did."

She punches my arm with a laugh. "At least it wasn't man-slobber."

As she steps away, I tug her back. "I'm sorry … if I made you uncomfortable. I embarrassed myself."

"You didn't." She squeezes my hand, her face growing serious. "All I saw was a man not afraid to feel. To me, that's beautiful and brave. And like you told me … honest."

Christ, I want to give this woman the world, but I don't even know where to fucking start when I have nothing to offer her. Though, now that we have her father's video, there's a good chance that's going to change. Just not this instant.

Slipping out of my grasp, she picks up her laptop and retreats to the dining table.

In the bathroom, I wash my face, stare into the mirror, and take a deep breath. I can't deny that I feel a sense of peace after telling her what I'd kept locked inside. Of all the darkness and vile depths that night brought with it, Jamie showed me something positive came out of it.

But it's her reaction to the revelations that has my head spinning. Along with her ability to empathise and comfort, she saw the raw, vulnerable man I am … and kissed me anyway.

I've always felt that indescribable pull toward her, but I've never paired it with a particular emotion. Now it's lit up in my head by a billion neurons that won't stop firing.

Fuck.

I don't just want her. I'm head over heels in love with her.

Chapter 33

Jamie

I STARE THROUGH the laptop screen, seeing nothing but the movie playing over and over in my head.

I kissed Gavin Lake.

I can barely believe I'd acted so boldly. But I hadn't given it any thought. For once in my life, I'd let my instincts take over. The intimacy of him opening up like that, the way he trusted me by unabashedly letting me witness his pain, touched something deep inside me.

When he broke, my heart cracked wide open, and I let him seep inside that fracture. Knowing my mother hadn't been alone, had been comforted when she died, gave my soul peace. So I'd done the only thing that came anywhere near what he'd given me. I'd held him and tried to show him how much that meant to me.

It had been effortless, and it worked.

Although I'd been disgusted with myself for never considering the profound impact finding my dying mother had on him, he'd gone and made that okay, too.

When he told me that his act of kindness toward my mother got him here, with me, something exceptional happened. Those wonderful words revealed his soul stripped bare. He'd taken the most negative thing to ever happen in his life and turned it into something positive.

So, I'd kissed him. It just felt *right*. There had been nothing sexual about the kiss. That's not what the moment was about at all. He'd given me a profound gift. How could words convey what that meant to me?

But I can't keep lying to myself. It's been brewing since he held me so tenderly in that caravan. I've been trying to hide from it, trying to convince myself it's nothing more than attraction. But it is. He's chipped away at my cold, closed heart, finally breaking it wide open tonight. Now he's slipped right in, filled it with warmth and melded it back together. With him captured inside.

There's no doubt anymore. I'm in love with Gavin Lake.

Unsure where he is, I shutdown the laptop, stagger over to the couch, and flop against the soft leather. Trying to get that affidavit done while my emotions are a tangled mess is futile. I'm in desperate need of sleep after last night, and tomorrow there's that awful annual work dinner.

I sigh, grab the TV remote and click it on for some background noise. Getting comfortable on my back, I tuck a cushion under my head and close my eyes. My traitorous brain instantly replays the kiss, but it doesn't stop there. I can't help wondering what it would be like to kiss him in an altogether different way. How would he taste? What would his lips and tongue feel like moving against mine? And just like that, a coil of arousal blooms between my legs. From imagining a kiss.

Ugh. How long has it been since I've had an orgasm? I haven't dared do any such thing while he's been in the house. But before that? Jesus, has it been months? Seeking pleasure hadn't been on my radar with Dad's decline and Anika preparing to leave for the Police Academy.

Pushing those thoughts away, I fill my head with memories of cradling his face, at how surprisingly soft that neatly trimmed beard felt in my hands. How it would feel against my skin, wherever he might choose to place a kiss.

Hearing his footsteps approach, then pause beside the couch, I crack an eyelid and peer up at him through the bars of my lashes. He stares at my feet for a long moment, before beginning a slow perusal up my bare calves. When he lingers on my thighs, I remember I haven't changed out of my work dress like I usually do when I get home. From the trajectory of his gaze, I'd say my hem has ridden up to just shy of my crotch.

I should pull it down. But I don't move. Warmth floods my veins, but my skin seems to have the opposite reaction. It prickles with goosebumps, tightening my nipples to rock-hard pebbles.

It only takes a moment for his eyes lock onto my chest. Peering through my barely cracked lids, I'm captivated by the growing bulge in his jeans. Heat pools between my thighs at the sight of his arousal, at what just *looking* at me is doing to him. And to me.

Before he catches me, I close my eyes and remain completely still.

"You awake?" he whispers.

"Mmm." I blink up at him, careful to keep my focus on his face.

"Mind if I watch something?" he asks, pointing to the remote in my hand.

After I pass it to him, he turns and looks at my feet. I instinctively bend my knees, making room for him as I ease the hem of my dress down to mid-thigh. He sits on the cushion my feet vacated and flicks through a few channels before settling on something.

Then, ever so casually, his hand lands on my foot and draws it onto his lap. I do nothing to stop him when he does the same with the other one.

He cups one foot and rests his other palm on my shin, his thumb ever-so-gently rubbing slow circles above my ankle. "So, what do you think your mother's letter might say?"

"What we watched tonight is enough to think about for a while. I'll just wait until Anika gets home to deal with what Mum had to say."

His thumb pauses. "You still haven't told her about your father … about me, have you?"

Our eyes meet as I tense beneath his hand. "She'll know

before she comes home. I promise." Unable to bear the disappointment staring back at me, I rise onto my elbows in a weak attempt to escape. "I should get back to the affidavit."

"No."

"No?"

"There's only one thing you need to do. And that's relax," he says firmly, his thumb grazing my skin again.

"Gavin, I should finish—"

"Actually," he interrupts, squeezing my foot, "I don't want you even thinking about that affidavit until next year."

"But I want to get everything—"

"No. I catch you working on anything to do with me, I'm firing you."

I feel like such a fraud. He's making it way too easy to keep Pete's promise without ever having to tell him I'm purposely delaying what he wants most in this world. After all, the longer it takes, the longer he'll stay here.

"Fine," I grumble.

With a satisfied smirk, he tilts his head. "Good. Now that's settled, you need to unwind. Can I please help you with that?"

He thinks he's getting everything his own way? "I don't need—"

As he applies pressure to the bottom of my heel with his thumbs, he drags them into my arch and up to my toes.

"Oh, God …" I groan, letting my body drop back to the couch.

"Yeah, that's what I thought," he says matter-of-factly.

Smug bastard.

My eyes flutter closed, and a sigh of pleasure escapes my throat as his fingers work their magic. "Deeper," I murmur.

He digs into my arch, the pressure painfully delicious.

"Mmm … yessss … that's it. Right there," I groan. "Oh God, that feels so … *good*."

"Quiet," he orders.

My eyes snap open at his sudden sharpness. His hands betray nothing, but the rapid rise and fall of his chest and flare of his nostrils tell a different story. He's worked up. A surge of heat burns my face and ignites between my legs as the reason for his abrupt command dawns on me. My verbal reactions to his wonderful fingers sounded like … well, I suppose what I imagine I might sound like during sex. *Great* sex.

"Just relax. Close your eyes, J." That same thick raspiness I heard in his voice this morning turns my insides to mush.

As he begins working on my other foot, I do as he says, relinquishing all control. Literally putting myself in his hands.

He knows I've never been touched like this, and I'm sure he hasn't touched anyone this way either. Damn, he's a natural. I sigh, careful not to let it turn into a moan, even though that's exactly what my throat wants to release.

As he alternates between my feet, working them from tired nubs to clouds of nothingness, I'm lulled into a deep state of relaxation.

Wait. Did he call me Jay?

Then those hands slide under my calves and begin kneading the tired muscles. My eyes spring open, my lips part, and my breath catches as I hold back the sounds wanting to escape my throat.

He won't meet my gaze, his concentration firmly on my bare legs as his fingers glide and grip and knead, never venturing higher than my knees. I close my eyes again, focusing on the sensation of his skin against mine, the way my body reacts to his touch. Another wave of arousal floods to my core, turning my mind to dirty, carnal thoughts I've only ever fantasised about with a faceless man. But now that man's face is crystal clear. I know if I move a millimetre, I'll feel how wet I am, how ready my body is to take him. His touch is turning me into an aching, flaming mess.

No wonder the one and only time I had sex was a disaster. My response back then had been fear, nerves and a hope that the physical pain would take me away from the hurt in my head and heart. And it had. For all of ten seconds.

This is something else entirely. That faceless man of my fantasies can get me worked up enough to orgasm when I need to relieve some stress, but it's nothing like this. Instinctively, I know that this sort of craving can only lead to an orgasm that'll leave me shattered and changed forever.

As if sensing my arousal, the pressure of his palms lightens as he reaches my ankles. When his fingers glide along the outside of my calves with a featherlight touch, my skin puckers with goosebumps, heightening every sensation.

I open my eyes and meet the same intense gaze I witnessed this morning.

Watching me, his sensuous touch rolls beneath my calves until he reaches the sensitive skin behind my knees. His progress stops there, but he continues caressing that velvety, delicate skin, driving me crazy.

My thighs tremble with need as I dig my fingers into the couch, trying to remember the me I know, the one who only acts rationally, who's always in control. But I'm spiralling, losing all sense of who I am. Is it possible to embrace a new me? One who's capable of fully letting go?

Then he runs those fingers back down my legs, over the tops of my feet and toes, until he's no longer touching me. My skin tingles with the after-effects, my core throbbing with unfulfilled need.

"Go to bed, Jamie," he rasps. "You're tired. And I want you wide awake for our date tomorrow night."

"Date?" I breathe on a broken exhale.

"That's how I'm looking at it. Is that okay with you?"

My mind reels with what he's trying to tell me. He wants to *date* me? His blue eyes never leave mine while he waits for an answer. "Yes," I whisper.

Lips twitching with a hint of a smile, he turns his attention to the TV. "Good night, J."

Apparently, I've been dismissed. And I don't even care. I'm so exhausted I know sleep will find me fast. After I have the quickest orgasm of my life. Because he's right, I need to unwind, and he's only succeeded in winding me up tighter.

Legs shaking, I rise, and make my way around the couch, I stop.

"Did you call me Jay?"

He turns enough so I can see the grin on his profile. "Yeah. Just the letter, your initial."

Ridiculously pleased by that, I hurry toward my bedroom, every step confirming how slick I am between my legs.

In my ensuite, I rush through cleaning my teeth, grab a glass of water and place it on my nightstand. Stripping off my dress, I toss it on the wingback chair and throw my bra on top. I don't bother with my pjs tonight. Instead, I slip between the cool sheets and turn off the lamp. That's when I hear water running in the main bathroom. He's cleaning his teeth.

Impatient, I wait until his footsteps cross the floorboards to his bedroom.

Letting out a long exhale, I reach beneath the covers, wrench down my undies and kick them off my feet. When I touch myself, I'm amazed by how slippery, engorged and fucking sensitive my clit is amongst all that wetness.

I could easily make myself come just like this, but I want to imagine him pushing inside me. In the darkness, trying to be as quiet as possible, I reach for the bottom drawer of my nightstand. Feeling for the knob with my fingertips, I inch it open, careful not to make a sound. I might be getting my vibrator, but it won't be vibrating tonight. I'm sure he'd hear it through the silence.

Wrapping my fingers around the silicon, I toss it onto the bed next to me. With my throat a little dry, I blindly reach for the glass of water. And bump it with the back of my hand.

In a panic, I fumble for it. Too late. It crashes to the floorboards, shattering the silence.

Fuck, fuck, fuck!

As I reach for the lamp, I hear hurried footsteps.

Oh God. He's not coming in here, is he?

"Jamie?" his voice booms with concern from the hallway.

"No!" I shout.

Forgetting the lamp, I turn over, frantically searching the bed for the vibrator before he—

My door flies open, the overhead light blinding me.

"Are you—"

"Get out!" I scream at him, hauling the covers up to my neck with one hand while my other desperately tries to find the vibrator before he spots it. To my horror, I see it roll down the hoisted duvet and come to a stop just shy of my feet.

Even though I don't want to look, my eyes flick to his face and, as I suspected, he's locked onto the traitorous pink toy.

Far too late, I use my foot to flip the corner of the duvet over it.

His eyes snap onto my exposed feet. Clearing his throat, he doesn't even attempt to suppress a grin.

"You might want to …"

I follow his gaze, my face burning with mortification when I spot my crumpled undies on display.

"Out!" I yell, grabbing a pillow and hurling it at him. Of course, he catches it.

And has the nerve to chuckle. "Are you sure you don't need my, ah … *assistance* with … anything?"

"I swear to God, if you don't get out …"

Placing the pillow over my undies, he walks out. When he shuts the door, I hear his laughter as he moves down the hallway.

I cover my burning face, utter humiliation invading every cell in my body. Did he just imply that he wanted to *assist* me with my vibrator? And now that I think about it, was that longing behind his amusement?

Letting out an involuntary groan, I clamp a hand over my mouth, all too aware how that probably sounds. Then, like a petulant child, I thrum my heels and fists against the mattress. How the fuck am I ever going to face him again?

I take a few deep, gulping breaths and tell myself to act like an adult and deal with it. Why should I be ashamed? The number of times I've seen him with an erection, he's probably doing it every day, multiple times a day, I reason. He just hasn't been stupid enough to get caught. Of course, I haven't taken it upon myself to barge into his room either.

Letting out a silent huff of air, I realise why he came barrelling in here. He heard glass breaking and thought I might be in danger. He'd been protecting me. Doing what I'd asked him to do. *God!* I can't even be mad at him.

Opening my eyes, I'm almost blinded by the bright overhead light. Leaning over the side of the bed, I inspect the broken glass and water on the floorboards. I'll have to clean it up. I can just see myself half asleep, stumbling to the toilet and cutting my feet open.

Pulling on my underwear, I retrieve the vibrator from the end of the mattress and place it back in the bottom drawer. Then I scoot over to the other side of the bed, slip on my pjs, grab my robe and crack the door open.

The hallway's dark, no light coming from Gavin's room.

Just as I'm about to sneak out, I glance down. And freeze.

There, waiting for me, is a roll of paper towels and a dustpan set.

My heart swells. He's so damn sweet it makes me want to cry.

Up extra-early the next morning, I slip on my robe and silently open my bedroom door. From the kitchen, I hear quiet little noises. Damn it. I'd hoped to leave for work before he emerged. So I could avoid him until tonight, when I won't be able to hide. Because apparently, we have a date.

My heart skips in my chest. Okay. Better to rip the band-aid off now and get the embarrassment over with instead of fretting about it all day.

Right. All I have to do is make the topic off-limits in an attempt to prevent further humiliation.

I head to the laundry first and put away the dustpan and paper towels. Taking a deep breath, I pad into the kitchen to find him filling the coffee machine with beans.

He knows I'm there before I say a word. I see it in the tightening of the muscles and the straightening of his spine.

He casually puts the bag of beans in the cupboard, then

turns to face me with an amused smirk on his lips and a devilish spark in his eyes.

Bastard.

"Morning," he says, his voice an octave or two lower than usual, sending heat curling between my legs. *Jesus*. This early in the morning? I suppose I shouldn't be surprised. I never finished what I started last night.

Holding up a finger, I plaster on a stern, warning glare. "*Do not* say a word."

He tilts his head, acting as if he has no idea what I'm talking about.

"In fact," I add, "don't even look at me. Just … move."

As I stalk toward the coffee machine, he drops his gaze, shuffles a mere foot to the side, and leans a hip against the counter. I refuse to look at him. If he pins me with those gleeful blue eyes, he'll have me blushing to my roots with the dirty thoughts I'm sure are swirling around in his head.

Placing my phone on the other side of the coffee machine, I grab my mug and set it in place. He's so damn close, I feel the heat radiating off his body. Usually I'd find some accidentally-on-purpose way to touch or brush up against him, but that's not happening this morning.

No. Fucking. Way.

Pressing the long-coffee button, the machine fires up, filling the kitchen with the sound of grinding beans.

As I wait, the air crackles with a new tension that hasn't been present during our other mornings. I'm not sure if it's me or him. Or both of us. What I do know is that if I touch him, there'll be a reaction this time. And that's terrifying. And way too exciting.

Work. That's what I need to focus on. Get to work. Concentrate on the job. Don't think about tonight.

I grind my teeth at his unmoveable presence by my side. Not that there's anything different about that. But today I won't touch his back or arm as I reach for a spoon. Instead, I take a wide arc around him to get to the cutlery drawer.

When I reach for the handle, he's suddenly behind me. His

chest presses against my back, his corded forearms caging me in as he places his hands on the counter.

Oh God.

The way he's surrounding me jolts me like a defibrillator. But instead of shocking my heart back into a steady rhythm, he's knocked it completely out of sync.

Minty breath washes over me as he leans closer, his mouth grazing my ear.

"Do *not* shut me out," he growls.

Chapter 34

Gavin

APART FROM HER initial jolt when I caged her in, Jamie's completely frozen. When the coffee machine falls silent, I can almost hear the thunderous beating of our hearts.

Although she shouldn't be embarrassed about last night, I knew she would be, knew she'd try to avoid me by leaving for work early, so I made sure that didn't happen. But the moment she skirted around me to get to the cutlery drawer, I knew she was withholding her usual touch.

Well, fuck that.

I *live* for her touch, no matter how brief or impersonal.

Circling her wrists, I force her to release the death grip she has on the edge of the counter and place her palms flat against the cool stone. Then I hold her there, my hands on top of hers, our bare arms brushing with every inhale and exhale, sending sparks of desire crashing through my body.

She probably thinks this is about what I burst in on last night. Okay, so that had left me with all sorts of wicked images of her pleasuring herself, and all the dirty things I'd like to do to her with that pink toy. Not to mention how she almost undid me with those husky little groans and words of praise when I'd massaged her. But those aren't the things on my mind right now.

That kiss.

It might not have had anything to do with romance or passion, but it communicated something much deeper. A silent contract that said *I want you in my personal space. I want your touch.*

She crossed a line last night. A line, I suppose, that's been blurred since we first held each other in the caravan.

Now that I truly know who she is, now that I've accepted how deeply I've fallen for her, I'm almost certain she feels the same way. But I'm done with wondering. I want confirmation before she leaves this house.

Holding onto every ounce of self-control, I murmur, "You kissed me last night."

"Yes." She exhales without hesitation. Owning it. Surprising me. Spurring me on as her intoxicating scent curls into every breath I take. She smells like a cozy afternoon nap and everything that's uniquely her.

"Don't think. Just the truth," I rasp, barely touching my lips to the shell of her ear. "Tell me why."

Again, she doesn't hesitate. "Because it felt right. Natural. There were no words. Only … instinct."

I slide my fingers between hers and curl them under until the tips are touching her palms.

"I also have instincts that feel right … natural … that are wordless," I whisper, nuzzling that delicate spot behind her earlobe, my heart slamming against her back. "Should I act on those instincts?"

She trembles, and I don't know if it's with anticipation or fear. Releasing her hands, I ever so slowly run my palms up her arms as my fingertips graze the soft, sensitive flesh of their undersides.

Drawing in a sharp breath, she presses into my chest, seeking more contact.

"Yes," she whispers. "Yes, you should."

I spin her around. Our eyes collide with feral need. Before either of us can take a breath, I grasp the back of her head and crash my mouth against hers. Holding nothing back, I unleash all my pent-up hunger on her. It's unshackled and unpractised, exploding with such starving intensity, it scares even me.

Yet she clings to my shoulders, her fingers digging in hard and pulling me closer, not pushing me away like she probably should. There's nothing romantic about this kiss. It's raw, animalistic, driven by my need to devour and possess her. And I haven't even started on her body yet.

As my lips grind against hers too hard, as my tongue ravages and our teeth clash, I wrap my arm around her waist and lift her onto the cool stone countertop.

Just as her knees part for me, she gasps and jerks away, the back of her hand flying to her mouth.

Breath blasting from my lungs, I freeze, wondering how I've fucked this up.

Then her hand comes away from her lips and I see the small red smear left behind.

Oh shit. I've hurt her.

Dread slams my heart to a stop. Releasing her, I step away and grip the back of my neck.

"Jamie … I'm so sorry," I manage to croak.

"It's fine," she says through rapid breaths. After pressing the back of her hand to her swollen, ravished lips, she pulls it away and inspects it again. "It's already stopped bleeding."

As my heart starts up again, I drag a hand down my face and turn away, too ashamed to let her look at me.

"Do *not* shut me out," she demands, throwing my words back at me.

Reluctantly, I turn and face her. She's still on the counter, knees slightly parted, fingers gripping the edge of the stone on either side of her thighs. Her harsh breaths rock her body back and forth a little. Everything about her posture tells me she hasn't closed herself off. But those beautiful eyes stare at me with a million questions.

"I'm a fucking beast," I tell her. "This is what sixteen years deprived of touch has done to me. J, I'm sorry." I swipe a hand through my hair and break eye contact. "I meant to … do that differently."

"Gavin …" When I meet her stare, she holds a hand out to me. "I think you should kiss it better."

I stand motionless, completely bowled over by this woman's kindness and understanding. Taking hesitant steps, I grasp her hand. Her grip tightens with reassurance as she draws me in until I'm standing between her parted thighs.

"Let me see," I demand softly.

She pouts out her bottom lip and I can't help but smile, letting go of the dread curled inside me. Thank fuck I haven't ruined everything.

Gently, I cup her face in my hands and ease her bottom lip down with my thumb. There, just inside, I see the tiny cut. And she's right, it's no longer bleeding.

Relief, mixed with a coiling, primal need sweeps through me as I press my forehead to hers. "I screwed that up. I wanted to—"

She places a finger over my lips. "Don't tell me. Just show me."

When her hand drops away, I lean back a little, watching her eyes search mine before they drop to my mouth. My heart races with anticipation. And fear. Terrified I'll fuck this up again. But I won't let that stop me. I move in and feather my lips over hers. "I've wanted this for so fucking long, J."

And then I capture her bottom lip between mine, gently drawing it in with a soft, tender suction. Christ, it's plump and delicate, and so warm. Apart from her kiss last night, it's been so damn long since I've done this. It's vaguely familiar, yet completely new. As she kisses me back, I drink in the divine sensations we've both been deprived of for almost half our lives.

Sinking a hand in her hair, I angle her head and deepen the kiss, our lips sliding, our mouths barely open. When I brush my fingers delicately down the side of her exposed neck, goosebumps break out beneath my fingertips like braille. And God, do I want to read her with my hands, my mouth, my tongue.

As I slide her thin robe from her shoulders, her exploring hands travel up my t-shirt-covered torso and over my pecs, flaring the fire already raging.

I find the strap of her camisole and gently drag it off one shoulder. Skating my fingertips back toward her neck, she shudders beneath my touch.

This is everything I've wished for, and nowhere near enough.

Her fingers thread through my hair, and when she makes a tiny mewl of pleasure at the back of her throat, I know she wants more too.

Heart on the verge of exploding, I break the kiss, trailing my lips over her cheek until I reach her ear. "Christ, J. I love the way you smell first thing in the morning," I murmur as I nuzzle that sensitive spot below her earlobe. "And when you get home …" I place a feather-light kiss to her neck. "And when you're sitting beside me … And before you go to bed." Touching my tongue to her goosebumps, I kiss a delicate trail all the way to the edge of her shoulder.

"Gavin," she breathes, her fingers curling around the strands of my hair. "Oh, God, that feels amazing."

I lift my head and cradle her jaw in my palm. As I try to catch my breath, I remind myself that this is real, this is happening. And she's just as turned on as I am.

"These lips," I murmur, brushing my thumb across their sensitive plumpness. "I want to kiss them every second I'm with you … every moment I'm *not* with you."

Her fingernails scrape through my beard. "I feel that too. I can't stop thinking about you … wanting you."

"Thank fuck." Desperate to taste her again, I kiss her, running my tongue over the seam of her mouth. She releases that little sound of pleasure again and opens for me.

Sweeping my tongue inside, she meets me halfway and I let go of my own rumble of exultation. She tastes like everything I've been craving my entire life.

Fuck, I'm hard. I need to be closer to her. I want to grab her everywhere at once, but more than that, I want to savour every first touch we share.

As our kisses fill the air with delicious sounds that set my blood on fire, her knees cradle my hips and squeeze. At first, I think she's stopping my progress, until she wraps her legs around my waist, scoots forward on the countertop, and pulls me right up against her.

The moment we connect between her thighs, we groan into each other's mouths. Fuck, she's so hot against my dick, I feel it right through my trackpants. Pressing my hand to her lower back, I draw her even closer, positioning myself right where she needs me. Then I rock my hips into her.

Whimpering, panting for breath, she lets her head fall back, exposing that slender neck, her fingers tugging on my hair, encouraging, demanding. Desperate to mark her skin the way she branded mine, I drag my lips down her throat, but stop short, all too aware that she won't appreciate going into the office like that. Instead, I kiss and nip and lick, devouring every erotic noise I've never heard her make before.

Supporting her arched spine with one hand, I trail my other down her side until I find the swell of her braless breast. Sliding my thumb between our welded bodies, I locate the hard, puckered nipple, and rub.

Her fingernails scrap my scalp, and her heels dig into my arse, pulling me in hard as she grinds against the length of my cock. *Fuck*. She's so much more than I imagined. Bolder, hungrier, sexy as fuck. Always surprising me.

My breaths ragged, I lift my mouth from her throat and lean away just enough to watch her tight little body writhe against my dick.

"Fuck, J … you're so gorgeous … so unexpected."

Her hooded eyes bore into mine before she drags my mouth back to hers. Finding the bottom of her camisole, I slide my hand underneath, up higher until I'm holding the weight of her firm, silky breast. Gently pinching her hard nipple, a thrill surges up my spine when she gasps and bucks against my cock.

Her pussy's a fucking furnace and I'm burning up right along with her. She's so damn close, I can taste it on her tongue. Problem is, so am I. But if I can tip her over the edge first, the embarrassment of coming in my pants will be worth every second.

Wrenching my mouth from hers, I nuzzle her ear and groan, "Fuck, yes … Let go, J … give into it."

I grab her hip and slow our rocking into a sensuous, inseparable rhythm.

"Oh, God … Gavin … yess … oh my God, right—"

Loud and shrill, her phone rings, vibrating on the countertop beside us.

We freeze. I know that ringtone. It's her fucking boss. Again. But I'm not about to get angry at his interruption this time. He may not have done Jamie any favours, but he's probably done me one by saving me from inevitable humiliation.

With my mouth still against her ear, I grumble, "Don't worry. When I fuck you tonight, I'll make you come. Over and over. I guarantee it."

At her sharp inhale, I grab her phone and hand it over.

Pressing the phone to her ear, her eyes never leave mine as we try to catch our breath.

"Jamie … speaking," she pants, her face flushed. "Oh, I was just … exercising."

I grin at her, studying her expressions while she listens intently, her eyes roaming over me, until they fixate on my erection. Stiffening, a deep blush scorches her cheeks as her hand flutters to her mouth.

She's seen my hard-on plenty of times, yet she's never had that reaction. Looking down, I see why. There's a lovely little damp patch on my trackpants, right over my erection where she rubbed her wet pussy. When my dick twitches, she lets out a sharp giggle, quickly disguising it with a cough.

"Of course, Eric. I'll be there right away." She hangs up and reluctantly slides off the countertop.

"I'll make your coffee while you shower," I tell her, reaching into the cupboard for her travel mug.

"Thank you."

As she brushes past, I grab her arm, tug her close and kiss her swollen lips. "You're welcome."

After she leaves for work, I hop in the shower and jerk off, then do it all over again before she arrives home. Getting my hopes up that I'll finally get to claim her tonight is something I shouldn't count on, but I'm sue as hell prepared. I did, after all, guarantee I'd give her multiple orgasms. No fucking way am I letting her down by losing it in my pants like I almost did this morning.

Besides, she may have changed her mind for all I know. Earlier this afternoon she sent me a text explaining she'd be home later than usual, giving her only enough time get ready before we need to leave for dinner. Her concise message left no hint at the change in our dynamic.

She wants me, I remind myself. She did a pretty good job of showing me this morning.

As I head out of the bathroom, I freeze. *Condoms*. Shit. Do we need them? I know I'm clean. And I'm sure she is. But she won't want to risk a pregnancy when she's only just finished raising her sister. Would she bother with birth control if she's not sexually active?

Fuck.

Because of soccer and then spending every spare moment with Mum when she got sick, I'd only had sex a few times as teenager, but always with a condom. The thought of sinking inside Jamie without any barrier has my dick stirring already.

I check my watch. No time. We'll have to figure it out after the dinner.

Of all the nights I've spent here, tonight's the first time I have permission to grab her and kiss her the moment she walks in the door. But I can't.

We have a date.

Even so, I'm determined to find a way to drive her crazy, to tease her and turn her on so the moment we get home, she won't be able to keep her hands off me. I've made her a promise, and I damn well intend to keep it.

From my room, I hear the laundry door close, then the clack of her heels in the hallway. I've shut my door, knowing if I see her, I won't be able to control myself.

"I'm here," she calls as she passes by.

"Just getting ready." Rising from the desk, I strip off, then pluck the first and only suit I've ever owned from the wardrobe.

After buttoning the crisp white shirt, I struggle with the tie until I watch a few YouTube videos and finally get the hang of it. Then I slip into the pants and deep blue matching jacket. The colour intensifies my eyes, but I hate the feel of the tight collar around my neck. But I suck it up, knowing I'd walk through fire to make her happy, so a little discomfort for a couple of hours will be a breeze.

Once I'm ready, I open my door and step into the hallway.

"Gavin?" she calls from her bedroom.

"Ready for me to book our ride?" I ask.

"Yes, thanks."

I grin like a fool. Such a simple, domestic exchange of words, but damn if it doesn't give me a thrill.

With my dress shoes feeling foreign on my feet, I stride into the kitchen and lean against the counter. Casually crossing my ankles, I click on the app, book our ride, and wait.

It's not long before heels tap on the polished floorboards in the hallway. My heart thrums with sudden nerves and anticipation.

"Our ride'll be here in—"

I can't finish, because there she is. Her beautiful, expressive eyes widen as she takes me in. She's wearing a stunning forest green halter dress that hugs the curves of her waist and breasts, dipping low enough to show just enough cleavage to be respectable. My gaze lowers to the gentle flare of fabric over her hips, flowing loosely to the tops of her knees, revealing those bare, toned calves. Her auburn hair cascades over her arms in a mass of waves and curls. She's elegant. Exquisite. Ravishing.

And I'm as hard as the stone I'm leaning against.

When my eyes lock with hers, she releases a ragged breath.

"Holy fuck," she breathes, tentatively moving toward me.

I'll take that as a compliment.

Stopping only inches away, she puts down her phone, then tiptoes her fingers up my tie before lifting my collar. Holding the tie's knot, she frees the tail, slides it from my neck and drops it on the counter.

I swallow, wondering where she's going with this. "Undressing me already?" I half joke.

"Just a little." She undoes my top two buttons, folds the collar down and tucks it inside my lapels. Taking a step back, she examines her handiwork.

"Not too casual?" I ask.

Her eyes sparkle. "It's perfect. It's *you*."

She's right. This feels so much better, freer, like I can relax into my own skin again. How does she know these little things about me already?

"I don't think there'll be a single woman left alive after tonight."

"Why's that?"

"With you looking like this, I'll have to fight to the death to keep them away from you."

I grin at her like a total fool. "Do you have any idea how much I want to kiss you right now?"

She moves in just close enough to brush against my chest. And my erection. "I think so."

"You little tease."

Her gaze dips to my throat as her finger traces my collarbone, sliding lower until it bumps into a button. "Well, I wouldn't want you to ruin my makeup, but a careful, gentle kiss won't hurt."

I want nothing more, but I hesitate.

Her curious, worried eyes meet mine.

"I'm waiting for that damn phone to interrupt us."

She smiles. "I've turned it off. And it's staying off. All night."

Well, *fuck*.

"That's some message." I grab her waist and pull her hard against my arousal, bending my head to meet her upturned face.

She rises on her toes, our mouths almost touching. "I believe you gave me a guarantee this morning. I wouldn't want anything ruining that."

Touching my lips to hers, I kiss her. Gentle and careful, the way she suggested. While I fight the urge to bend her over the countertop and take her right now, I marvel again at this sudden boldness she's only revealed today.

"Do we really have to go to this dinner?" I whisper as I pull back a little.

"Unfortunately. But … we need to keep it professional. Although there's no law that prevents lawyers getting involved with their clients, my firm definitely frowns upon it. It won't look good for me if they know we're living together, that there's something … happening between us."

I run my fingers up her spine, watching her eyelids lower with pleasure as her long hair flows like silk over the back of my hand. "There's something happening between us?" I tease.

She jerks out of my arms, her fist clutching at her chest. "Oh, dear. It seems I've made a terrible mistake."

"Get back here, woman," I demand and pull her right up against me where she belongs. While those cheeky eyes smile up at me, I splay my hand over the cool, naked skin between her shoulder blades. "I'd never do anything to risk your career."

She brings her hands up and cups my face. "I know. It's probably more of a reminder for me rather than you." Her eyes flick to my lips as her fingertips caress my freshly trimmed beard. "So soft," she murmurs in wonder. "I can't wait to discover how it feels in different places all over—"

A horn toots outside.

"Okay, cheeky woman," I grin, "let's get this over with."

Preparing for when we get home, I turn on the stereo, then

the living room lamp before flipping off the overhead lights. When we get to the door, I catch her hand and stop her. "I didn't tell you how stunning you look tonight. When I saw you … you stole my words."

She stares up at me, her lips curling into a delicate, vulnerable smile. "Thank you."

My heart thudding with price, I kiss her. She hadn't rejected my compliment. Now, she believes me when I tell her how I see her. Pulling her close, I marvel at this new reality where I can kiss her, touch her and, when we get home, possess her.

In the back of the Uber, we exchange heated glances, but I keep my hands to myself. It took too long for my dick to deflate after our little exchange in the kitchen. Touching her will only set me aflame again.

"I'm guessing the boss's sleazy son will be there?" I ask.

"He won't dare come near me with you by my side." She shoots me a serious look. "And if he does, please don't do anything stupid. I can handle him."

"Avoiding isn't handling."

"Nor is ending up in prison over that little creep."

She's got a point, and I trust she knows what's best. What experience do I have with work colleagues and how to handle such matters? I doubt it's the same as dealing with inmates.

Once we arrive, I reign in my urge to place a hand on her lower back as we approach the entrance. As if she misses the gesture, she looks up at me, her eyes so bright and full of desire, my pulse accelerates. "Watch how you look at me, gorgeous. You're giving yourself away."

"Right back at you."

Inside, Jamie introduces me to so many colleagues I have no hope of remembering their names.

When I meet Eric, her boss, the younger guy beside him snakes his gaze over Jamie's body. Instantly, I know he's the creep she's warned me about. I desperately want to put my arm around her and pull her in close, so the prick knows who she belongs to. But his father's extending his hand, shaking mine eagerly.

"Jamie told me about the exciting news today," Eric says, tilting his glass of amber liquid toward her. "I must admit, I had serious doubts when all she had was a Dying Declaration and an affidavit from a witness who was so young at the time. But a video confession from her father is sure to mean success. You must be eager to get the whole thing over and done with."

"Of course," I offer, trying my hardest to keep my eyes on her boss and not the smug little shit beside him. "But I've insisted Jamie wait until after Christmas. She's had a lot to deal with lately."

Eric's eyes swing to Jamie. "And you're alright with that? You were so eager to hurry this along."

"I … ah, yes. I'll finish the last of the documents over Christmas. Best to make sure everything's in perfect order rather than rush it."

"Well," he says, glancing between us, "we're looking forward to all the free publicity once you win. Nice meeting you, Gavin." I shake his hand again, noting his son never once acknowledges me, his attention still firmly on my woman.

After we find our table and enjoy the surprisingly excellent food, Jamie chats with the others at the table about an array of past cases. Scanning the room, it's not long before I find the sleaze again. He can't take his eyes off Jamie, ogling her with a hunger I know all too well.

Sensing my stare, the guy's eyes dart to me for a split second before returning to Jamie. Then they bounce back. I heed Jamie's words about the jerk, but I never said I wouldn't threaten him with a look. Which is exactly what I do. Using every menacing nuance I honed in prison, I glare at the fucker, leaving no misunderstanding that death is imminent should he so much as look at her again.

To his credit, he breaks eye contact and downs his drink, but not before I register the pinch of irritation in his expression. By the time he places his glass on the table, that carefully schooled mask falls into place again.

After our plates are removed, I'm drawn in and out of conversations with the people at our table, but with the pressure of my thigh against hers, I let her know I never forget she's by my side.

Mid-conversation, she hooks the foot of her crossed leg behind my calf. And gives it a little rub, letting me know she's fully aware of my presence, too.

While she talks animatedly with everyone, and when I'm not involved in a discussion, I listen to her voice. And I notice something I haven't been privy to before now. She uses a distinctive tone with me. A warmer, more relaxed, intimate voice. Could it be that she sees me as *more than* anyone else in her life? My heart swells at the idea. Glancing at her profile, I'm overcome with the need to touch her.

I know I shouldn't, but I feel it's safe enough with the tablecloth pooling in our laps and the wall at our backs.

As the servers move about the table delivering our desserts, I slip my right hand onto my thigh beneath the tablecloth. Picking up a fork with my free hand, I wait for Jamie to do the same. When the first morsel of tiramisù passes her lips, I slide my palm onto her bare knee.

She stops chewing for a moment, and I wait for her to brush my hand away or give me a warning glance. When she does nothing but prepare another bite on the tip of her fork, I ease my way up her thigh and slip beneath the hem of her dress.

After she turns her attention back to Helen—the woman beside her—I slide my thumb along the silky line where her crossed legs meet.

And *holy hell*, she ever-so-slowly uncrosses them. My hand slips between her barely parted thighs, the velvety flesh burning both sides of my fingers as she tenses and traps me there.

When she slips her hand beneath the table and grabs my wrist, I think I've gone too far. Until she parts her legs, releasing my imprisoned fingers, and forces them higher, inviting my touch. All without missing a beat in her conversation.

The cake on my fork trembles as I bring it to my mouth. While she remains deep in conversation with Helen, she removes her hold on my wrist. Beginning a sensual exploration up the inside of her thigh, I note with each centimetre I cover, her skin grows hotter. When my pinkie finally touches the crotch of her damp panties, I stifle a groan behind a cough.

She continues to talk with Helen, and even though she's pretending to ignore me, she's aware of every movement my fingers make. I know because she's pressing her thigh hard against mine, spreading herself wider for me. Giving me permission.

She's radiating heat all over my fingers, the material between her legs so damp I can't resist any longer. I grip the far edge of her panties' crotch and draw it toward me. Waiting until the moment she places another bite of tiramisù between her lips, I glide the knuckle of my index finger through her hot, wet centre. From entrance to clit, I study her profile, taking in the flare of her nostril, the frozen set of her jaw, and finally, the swallow in her throat.

If she looks at me, I know damn well she'll see me mirroring her reactions. But she doesn't turn her head even a millimetre. I don't move either. Because my mind's whirling with a million thoughts that keep coming back to just one. Apart from the obvious, did my brain correctly interpret what the back of my knuckle encountered? Or more accurately, *didn't* encounter?

Desperate to discover if I'm right, I reposition my hold on her panties and touch my fingertip to her labia. Then I make a slow journey up one side, and down the other until I stop at her entrance. And suck in a silent breath. I'd been right. She's completely bare.

Fuck.

She's so hot and slippery, it takes complete control of my muscles not to sink my finger deep inside her. Instead, I wait. The moment her mouth closes around another piece of cake, I dip into her enough to coat my finger to the second knuckle before gliding up to her clit and circling with a featherlight touch.

Loud enough to hear, a soft groan rumbles in her throat.

I freeze when Helen leans forward, raising a piece of cake on her fork. "It's heavenly, isn't it?"

"It's … something, that's for sure," Jamie says, her thigh trembling against mine.

Helen pins her gaze on me. Reluctantly, I move my hand back to my own thigh. "What do you think, Gavin? It must be quite a treat to taste this sort of thing after …" Her voice fades away, suddenly too awkward to finish the sentence.

I bring my hand out from under the table and, using the finger coated with Jamie's arousal, I press it to the crumbs on my plate. When I glance up, Jamie's feverish eyes watch me from beneath dark lashes. Then, sucking the tiny cake morsels from the tip of my finger, I taste her for the first time in a room full of people.

My gaze flicks to Helen, who's still waiting for my answer. "Delicious," I agree, giving her a warm smile before I catch Jamie's eye. "Leaves a lingering sweetness on the tongue."

As a flush races up Jamie's neck, she rises from her chair and places a hand on my shoulder. Digging her fingers into my muscles, she leans in and whispers, "I'm going to the ladies. Then we're sneaking out of here. Meet me in the foyer."

I'm relieved she's given me some time, because I can't move with this raging hard-on straining at my zipper. I'll need at least a few minutes.

Fortunately, Helen helps out by engaging me in a few tales from previous Christmas dinners she's attended.

As I listen, my gaze travels around the room, catching on that fucking sleaze. That fucking sleaze who's getting up and heading toward the foyer. Toward *my* woman.

Chapter 35

Jamie

SLAMMING AND LOCKING the stall door, I collapse against it and take long, deep breaths.

Surrounded by colleagues and their partners, I almost shattered into a million pieces. The way Gavin just touched me, like no one ever has before, lit me up like the Harbour Bridge on New Year's Eve. But the moment he tasted me on his finger … Oh my God … *that's* what had me almost coming undone. His actions had been so wicked and wildly inappropriate, I should be outraged.

Yet, the only thing raging is the heat between my legs. Closing my eyes, I remind myself that it wasn't Gavin's fault. He'd simply put a hand on my knee. I'm the one who opened my legs like a sex-starved hussy and invited him in.

When I'd walked into the kitchen earlier, he'd raked a gaze over me so searing my panties were practically singed. Was it any wonder I lost my sanity when he touched my knee? Not to mention how incredibly fucking hot he looks tonight in that suit. The moment I laid eyes on him standing oh-so-casually in the kitchen, my whole body roared to life, but that was nothing compared to right now.

Fingers bunching in my skirt, my legs shake as the intense ache begs for release. Release which would only take seconds.

I snap my eyes open. That's not what I want. I want *his*

touch. I want Gavin Lake to make me come. I want him to give me my first male-induced orgasm. And I want that tonight. As soon as possible.

Hurriedly finishing up in the restroom, I burst through the door, hoping to find Gavin waiting for me in the foyer so I can grab him and get the hell out of here.

Intent on finding his tall, powerful frame, I don't notice Simon until he barrels into my personal space and forces me backwards. When my bare shoulder blades connect with the cold concrete wall, I gasp.

Leering at me, his whisky-soaked breath floods my senses with memories of my father trying to drown out what I now know was his guilty conscience.

"Get away from me, Simon," I say firmly, shoving at his chest, wondering why the foyer's empty. "Get out of my space."

He moves even closer and trails a slimy finger down my arm. When I try to swat it away, he grabs my wrist in a painful grasp.

"Didn't look like you minded your *client* in your space," he snarls, trying to force a knee between my thighs. "Or is fuckin' a convict what gets you off? You wanna bad boy, is that it? I'll give you a bad boy, you frigid bit—"

His revolting breath and body suddenly vanish. I watch in horror as Gavin wrenches him away by his shirt collar and forces him toward the opposite wall. Flying toward them, terrified someone might enter the foyer and witness Gavin's aggression, I grip his arm and take in the murderous look on his face.

"Gavin, don't!" I beg, trying to keep my voice down. He shoves Simon so hard in the chest, he stumbles, careening toward the concrete wall behind him. At the last possible second, Gavin grabs Simon's shirt before his face smashes against the unforgiving surface.

When I look into Gavin's eyes, I don't recognise the man I know. He's gone. Replaced by the man who emanated the same rage at the mention of Jarrod Reid's name, and I know without a doubt he could end Simon at any moment.

The sleaze wrenches free and grins. "Come on, convict. You gonna hit me for wantin' to fuck that cock-tease? She worth goin' back to prison?"

Gavin grabs him by the throat and hauls him away from the wall like he's about to slam him against the concrete and crack his skull. Every hair on my body stands on end, my heart stuttering in fear.

"Gavin Lake, the man I hate …" I say firmly, not even knowing where that came from.

Like the flick of a switch, Gavin wrenches free of whatever hellhole he'd disappeared into. When his eyes snap to mine, I glare at him, shake my head and grip his forearm.

"I've got this," I say, tightening my hold, our eyes locked.

Just like that, he releases Simon and takes a step away. Then another and another. Until there's enough room for me to squeeze in between them without occupying Simon's personal space. I feel Gavin at my back, his heat radiating toward me, making me want to press up against that strong wall and forget all about the piece of shit before me. But I don't. I need to stand on my own two feet. Gavin was right. I need to address what I should have over a year ago. I need to stop avoiding the problem and face it head-on.

"How many different ways have I politely told you I'm not interested? Yet you still act like you can take what you want, touch what isn't yours. You have no clue what it means to be a man."

Simon's drunken glare sharpens. "You're so fucked. You just don't know it yet. And Dad's gonna hear about you and this low-life scum, you fuckin' slut. Say goodbye to your career."

Before he shoves off the wall, I block his escape. Then I tap the small handbag at my hip. "I thought you might try something tonight, Simon So, whenever I've been alone, I've activated my phone's voice recorder. Feel free to go ahead and squeal. Tell Daddy whatever you like."

"That's illegal. You can't record—"

"Legal … illegal," I shrug. "I'm not sure it'll matter. Phones get hacked all the time, things get leaked on the net. Who do you think will come off worse? The woman who recorded the scum who's been harassing her? Or the narcissistic prick who thinks he can take what he wants? I might lose my job, but your father's firm won't look too good if he keeps his slime-ball of a son employed."

Stepping away, I give him my best smile. Rage flares in his eyes as they flick from me to Gavin, and for just a moment, I don't think he's going to back down. My heart thunders, knowing that if he continues to come after me, Gavin might very well end the night locked up.

"Fuck you," Simon finally sneers, then slips past me and scurries toward the toilets.

"Merry Christmas," I call after him.

He raises his hand and flips me off before disappearing into the men's room.

Turning to face Gavin, I let out a shaky breath and press a trembling hand to my chest.

"Come on," he takes my free hand, places it on the inside of his bicep and leads me outside. When we reach the kerb, he gazes down at me. "Well, you were fucking brilliant. That was some bluff. For a minute there, I'd forgotten you left your phone at home. The way that dickhead ran off to the loo … I think he might've shit himself."

A laugh blasts from my throat, releasing the tension in my chest. I squeeze his bicep, brushing my thumb over the hard muscle. I want to lean into him, but stop myself, worried someone from work might see us.

Then it hits me. *I don't care.* I don't care if Simon tells his father or if someone else spots us. I don't care about losing my job at all.

I lift my chin, and gaze at the most handsome man I've ever seen. His face tilts to the sky, his eyes closed as the wind riffles through his hair. As if sensing my stare, his eyes find mine.

"You look so peaceful," I murmur.

"Just reminding myself to appreciate the small things. Standing out here in the breeze, at night … it's not something you can do when you're locked up."

I tighten my grip around his arm, close my eyes and let the unnoticed wonders of the night wash over me. The warm breeze feathers my hair against my bare arms, sparking sensations the encounter with Simon had numbed.

"*The man I hate*," he says softly, bringing me out of my reverie. "What made you say that?"

I gaze into his gentle, curious eyes, so at odds with the man from minutes ago. "You'd gone somewhere dark, somewhere I couldn't reach you. That look … like you were made of stone. It reminded me of who I imagined you were when I thought you were guilty."

"The inspiration for your little hate-poem?"

I nod, ashamed of that teenage girl. "I thought a little reminder of who you *aren't* might bring you back before you did something to land you in back prison."

"Yeah," he mumbles, placing a hand over mine. "You're right, I almost fucked up. Hearing you say you hate me was like a bucket of ice-water to the face. Thank you. For bringing me back."

"I was just protecting that guarantee you gave me this morning, that's all."

His lips twitch for a moment before his expression grows serious again. "I'm so sorry, J. My behaviour was totally out of line. It's no excuse, but when I saw him touching you, *hurting* you, I just lost it." His thumb brushes over my fingers, genuine remorse shining in his eyes.

"You scared me," I admit.

"Yeah, I really wish you hadn't seen that side of me."

"No, that's not what I meant. I want to know every side of you, no matter how imperfect. What I was scared of, was losing you."

He lets out a long exhale, his eyes a little shinier than they were a moment ago. "Christ, Jamie. You know how to make a guy feel on top of the world and humbled all at once."

I give his arm a reassuring squeeze.

"Anyway," he mumbles, "I'm sorry. That wasn't much of a

date."

"Who says?"

Beneath the lamplight, his eyes bore into mine. "I kind of blew it at the end there. Not to mention the fact I couldn't look at you the way I wanted to."

Like the way he's looking at me now, reminding my entire body how good he made me feel at that table. "Yet, it still had its moments."

His eyes burn into mine. "You're right. There were moments. Certain moments that prove you weren't lying last time we were standing at a kerb waiting for a ride."

I frown before it dawns on me. "The time I don't remember?"

"Yeah." He's grinning now, a spark of mischief in his eyes.

"But that can't be right. You said you'd told me everything."

"Memory can be fickle."

I poke him playfully in the ribs. He doesn't even flinch. "And what was it you thought I was lying about?"

"You might not want to know," he teases.

I poke him again, but I may as well be poking a rock.

"Last time, you told me I was turning you on."

"I did *not*," I gasp. "There's no way—"

"Oh, yeah, you did. Then you tried to climb me like a tree."

"Now *that*, I know, is bullshit."

His body hitches against my side as he chuckles. "Alright, I might've exaggerated that part, but you were very hands-on."

Even though I don't remember, I'm sure he's right. I don't have to tell him he's turned me on tonight. He's felt it for himself. *Tasted* it.

After our ride pulls up and we buckle in, I ask, "What else have you conveniently forgotten to tell me about that night?"

He grins across the space between us, the streetlights flashing a spark in his eyes every time we pass beneath one.

"Well," he says, his voice low and gravelly, "it was more fun than it is right now."

My mouth drops open. "Excuse me?"

He places his hand on the middle seat between us. "Because

you were sitting here."

My heart thuds. Is it possible to be jealous of the drunk woman who pressed herself up against him?

"And then what happened?" I can't help but ask.

He raises an eyebrow. "If you want to know, we'll have to re-enact it."

I stare at the challenge in his eyes for a moment. He's too damn sexy to resist, and the worst thing is, I think he's utterly unaware of that fact. God, I want to kiss him so badly.

As fast as I can, I unbuckle my belt and slide over to the middle, a warning *ding* coming from the front of the car.

I catch the driver's disapproving glare in the rearview mirror when Gavin reaches across me and snaps my seatbelt into place.

Looking straight ahead, I give myself a minute to adjust to the heat of the entire length of his body pressing against my side. All that pent up tension he created beneath the table comes flooding back with a vengeance. With his amused eyes on mine, I ask, "And then what happened?"

"You rested your head on my shoulder."

I bet I did. A girl would have to be crazy to be in this position and *not* cozy up to him. So, I do just that.

While contemplating what I should do next, I remember I don't have to. He's in control of every single moment right now. And I love it.

"And then?" I breathe, eager for his next instructions.

He slides my hand onto his stomach. "Then I had to hold you like this to stop you roaming all over me." He places his palm on my forearm and caressing my skin with slow circles.

"That wasn't very nice of you," I murmur.

"Yeah, you're right."

Removing his hand, he gives me permission to roam all over him. Instead, I pull away a little so I can look into his eyes, then I rest my palm against his jaw, run my fingertips over his beard and murmur, "Does this feel nice?"

"Having you touch me anywhere at all feels fucking amazing."

"Oh." I let a slow smile spread across my face.

"Yeah, *oh.*" Sinking his fingers into my hair, he eases my head back to his shoulder.

I snuggle in, then, starting at the hollow of his throat, I gently glide a fingertip down his skin until I encounter a button. Over the soft fabric of his shirt, I keep going, exploring every rise and dip of his muscled stomach. As I move a little lower, my elbow bumps over his belt buckle, and abruptly stops against something thick, hard and hot. "Did that happen, too?" I whisper.

"Yeah," he admits on a broken syllable.

I squeeze my eyes shut, trying to imagine the torment I put him through that night. He'd wanted me then, too, and could easily have taken advantage that night. Clearly, my body had been telling him to go for it. But he hadn't. Not because he didn't want to. Because he was with me that night for one reason only. To keep me safe, to protect me. Even if it was from my own stupid self.

"Okay." He moves my hand to his waist and clamps down on my forearm. "I think maybe this position is much safer. Speaking of which …"

I wait, and when he doesn't continue, I lift my head and search his eyes. Easing closer, he presses his lips to my ear. Even before his voice rumbles through me, shivers of pleasure run down my spine.

"Do we need to make a stop … to get condoms? I'm clean, but … I know you wouldn't want to get pregnant … just yet."

Just yet? My heart hammers loud and fast. Is he already thinking about the future? A future with *me?*

"No, I … I've got that under control," I manage to answer.

He closes his eyes, his chest rising and falling with deep breaths, as if he's trying to calm himself.

"Gavin? What is it?"

His eyes snap open, locking onto mine. "That'll be a first for me."

I squeeze his waist. "Me too."

Nuzzling his nose into my neck, he slides a hand beneath

the hem of my dress. When he's halfway up my thigh, the car slows to a stop in front of my house.

After he helps me out, he takes my hand, laces our fingers, and walks me to front door.

"What's been the best part of the night for you so far?" he asks.

Digging my keys from my handbag, I think about it for a moment. "Actually, there were two. Dessert, being my second favourite."

He gives me a devilish grin as I unlock the door. Once we're on the other side of the threshold, my heart beats like a hummingbird's wings. We're finally alone. No excuses. No distractions. Nothing but us. And being alone with him like this, suddenly fills me with nerves.

In the dim light cast by the floor lamp, he slips my handbag from my shoulder, places it on the side table and lays his jacket over the arm of the couch.

When he strides toward me, I brace myself for the onslaught I'm sure is coming. I wait for him to crush his mouth to mine and haul me into the bedroom.

Instead, he gently takes my hands. "And what's your favourite part about tonight?"

I tighten my hold on him, our eyes locked. "Coming home with you."

He stands motionless for a moment, then a full-blown smile lights up his face. "You and your perfect compliments. Come here."

He tugs on my hands, forcing me to take the step that lands me right in his personal space. Brushing my hair over my shoulder, he tucks loose strands behind my ear in such a delicate, loving gesture, I sway closer.

Cupping my face, he gazes deep into my eyes. "Coming home with you, living with you, talking with you, touching you, holding you, kissing you … all of it … I can barely believe it's real." He glances off to the side and shakes his head on a deep sigh. When he meets my eyes again, they're shining bright. "Sometimes, I wake up in the dark and think I'm still trapped in that cell, that all of this is a dream. That *you're* a dream. For those few seconds, I feel like I'm being swallowed by darkness … and I *want* it to swallow me."

Tears prick at my eyes. The depths of this man overwhelm me. But it's the fact that he *tells* me, without an ounce of shame, what those depths are that leaves me in awe.

Placing a hand on the side of his neck, I graze my thumb along his jawline, and it's not lost on me that this is how he comforted my mother in her last moments. "Don't let it swallow you, Gavin. I'm right here. I'm real."

Dropping his forehead to mine, he whispers, "I know, J. God, do I know."

He pulls me into his embrace, and I hold onto him, absorbing his warmth and comfort, allowing myself to feel cherished and protected. He's not pouncing on me like I expected. He's surprising me, taking it slow, showing incredible restraint.

"Remember the day you came to the caravan, dropped a bombshell, and I held you like this?" he asks, his voice rough with emotion beside my ear.

"You were so kind and patient. And sweet. And I didn't deserve any of it."

"Yes, you fucking did."

I smile against his chest. "And I remember your heart … beating so fast. Too fast. Like it is now."

A low rumble travels through his body and into mine.

"That's because," he murmurs, trailing his fingers up my spine, "I had to restrain myself from kissing you here." He places a soft kiss below my earlobe, and goosebumps erupt across my skin. "And here." He trails kisses down the side of my neck, the soft tickle of his beard mingling with the warmth and pressure of his lips. Skipping over the material of my halter neck, he presses barely-there kisses along my exposed shoulder. "And here." I quake in his arms, the ache between my legs becoming so intense a soft groan escapes my throat.

Then the warmth of his body vanishes and he's on one knee before me, his hot palm on the back of my calf coasting down to my ankle. As I lift my foot, I slide my fingers into his thick hair.

"You're always taking care of me," I sigh, letting relief wash through me as the first shoe comes off. "The dustpan and paper towels …"

He looks up at me. "You liked that?"

"So much," I breathe.

His eyes glint in the dim light as my other foot eases to the cool floorboards. I wait for him to rise, but his hands drift up the backs of my calves, his fingertips lingering behind my knees, his gaze locked with mine. He's so incredibly beautiful like this, all raw emotion and vulnerability. And desire.

"This is how I wanted to take off your underwear that night."

Breath rushes into my lungs on a gasp. With a torturously slow touch, his warm palms skim the backs of my thighs, his fingertips caressing my flesh as they rise higher and higher. The anticipation alone drenches my lace panties and curls my fingers around the short strands of his hair.

A quiet groan vibrates from my throat when his fingers reach their destination. Slipping beneath the fabric, he cups my bare backside, exploring the contours, kneading and stroking until my eyelids drift to half-mast. I don't know what's hotter. The way he's touching me, or the hunger in his eyes while he does it.

Our gaze holds as he frees his hands and curls his fingers into the waistband, gradually drawing them down my thighs. The sensation flushes my skin and weakens my knees. When he finally breaks eye contact to help me out of them, my legs tremble. I know without a doubt he can see the dampness I've left behind. But I don't care. Let him see what he does to me.

My fingers slip from his hair as he rises, and it's impossible to hide the tremors as I trail them down his arms.

"Jamie, you're shaking like a leaf."

"Nerves," I whisper, angling my gaze to his chest in the hope he can't see how utterly pathetic I am. Thirty-two years old and I may as well be a fucking virgin. Now that the reality's looming ever closer, how can I not wonder if it's going to hurt all over again? Or if having sex with him will ruin everything that's made our time together so wonderful over the past few weeks.

Gently taking my chin in his grasp, he forces my eyes to his. "Relax. We won't do anything you don't want to. I only want to make you feel good."

Suddenly, he sweeps me into his arms, forcing me to cling to him as he carries me to the couch and takes a seat. Snuggling me sideways on his lap, he sinks a hand into my hair and angles my head, so I have no choice but to look at him.

"Talk to me," he murmurs. "Remember your rule."

God, it feels so good to be this close to him. He's not angry or frustrated with me. He's showing me how much he cares, that it's not about my body, but what I feel and think. He's showing me it's more to him than just sex. "I'm scared. If my parents have taught me anything, it's that getting close to someone only leads to pain."

"Everything bad that happened with your parents was because they weren't with the right person," he states with conviction. "That was between them. This is between us. And we *are* with the right person. So, forget that fear. Anything else?"

I open my mouth to say it's not that simple, but close it again. Because he has a point. We weren't torn apart by fate. Fate has thrust us together, almost as if it's trying to make up for the mistake it made with our parents. I want to embrace that belief, but it's not my only fear.

"I'm scared that this will change things, that we're going too fast."

"What scares me, after living a life where nothing changes, is that things *won't* change," he says, his voice raw with emotion again. "We can't go on ignoring this chemistry between us. The sparks are flying, ready to ignite one way or another. We can't keep asking *what if* … we need to start living and feeling." He presses his palm to my chest. "You can't hide this huge heart of yours from me anymore, J."

My hand tightens at the nape of his neck, his words penetrating the fear.

"And I don't think we're going too fast," he continues. "I think we've been going painfully slow."

"Slow?"

He lets out a huff of a laugh. "Let's see … by my calculations, we've been on about twenty dates and a couple of mini-breaks."

I chuckle. "What're you talking about?"

"Dinner together every night," he explains, his thumb brushing my cheek, "Weekends spent in each other's company. Sound familiar?"

Trailing my fingers from his neck, I glide them down his chest and into the open gap of his shirt. When I stop at the first button, I undo it with steady fingers. As I undo the next button, and the next, I say, "I suppose … that's a pretty convincing argument."

His arm tightens around me, his eyes searching mine. "I see you, J. I saw you when I didn't even know you. But now that I do, I never want to look away."

His words make my heart jolt. "I see you, too."

Before I can register what's happening, I'm flat on my back, one hand trapped above my head in his grasp as he presses his body to my side, his eyes dark with hunger.

"I need some clarification on something," he mumbles, that sexy, lopsided smile sending aching waves between my legs. "I've been wondering about that toy of yours."

I gape at him. "Please don't wonder anything about that."

"I was wondering," he insists, his voice broken with heat, "if your little toy can kiss you like this?"

He lowers his head, and finally, *finally*, our lips touch. Brushing his mouth over mine, he explores my lips, pressing and gently applying suction, then pulling back and starting all over again. This kiss, this pure care and exploration, is the sort of kiss I believe only a man who loves me would be capable of.

My mind spins. I could never have imagined I'd fall so

hopelessly in love with the man I despised for so long. The way he's kissing me, the way he talks to me, all the little touches and looks, makes me believe he feels the same way.

With my love desperate to burst from my chest, I grip his shoulder and crush him to me so I can feel his pounding heart.

And then he opens his mouth, angles his lips over mine and kisses me with restrained passion. I groan, slip my fingers into his hair and lean into his erection, letting him know I want everything he has to offer.

Our mouths, soft and yielding, then firm and coaxing, continue to experiment and explore each other. When his tongue slides between my lips and meets mine, his chest rumbles with pleasure, shooting hot spikes of desire through my entire body.

Lifting his head, his craving eyes stare into mine.

"Well?" he rasps.

It's only then I remember his earlier question "No," I whisper, "it can't kiss me like that."

"Can it make your skin tingle like this?"

He brushes his lips over my jaw, and I tilt my chin up, giving him access to my throat. His mouth sucks and tastes, teeth gently nipping as he makes his way down the side of my neck. And he's right. The way his short beard tickles my skin, has me tingling all over.

"No," I breathe, so turned on, I can't remember why I was ever nervous.

When his hand glides over the curve of my waist, I clutch his wrist, encouraging him higher. He watches my face as he cups my breast. Sighing, I close my eyes and arch into his palm.

I want to touch him so badly, but he's interlocked our fingers above my head, and I'll only interfere with this sensuous game he's playing if I move my other arm.

"Can that toy undress you like this?" he asks, tugging at the knot behind my neck until the fabric releases.

Like he's unwrapping a precious gift, he peels down one side of my halter, revealing one naked, waiting breast.

"No," I answer, my exposed nipple tightening painfully.

Those black pools ringed by decadent slivers of blue, shift from my gaze and take in the sight of my uncovered breast. His chest expands on a long inhale.

"Jamie … you're so, so beautiful," he murmurs, his voice thick and broken. With incredible tenderness, his palm brushes over my tight nipple, sending such a sharp stab of heat between my thighs, I rock my hips into him, seeking more.

"Gavin," I breathe. "I want your mouth … your tongue …"

He stares at me, apparently as surprised by my words as I am. Thank God, I don't have to ask twice. He dips his head, his warm lips grazing over my skin until he cups my breast and brings his down on my nipple. Drawing me in, his tongue swirls over the pebbled flesh, dragging a groan from my throat.

Giving in to the need to touch him, I squirm my free hand between us and palm his erection through his trousers. When his hips grind forward, I curl my fingers around his thick cock, feeling the vibration of his growl on my nipple as I squeeze.

Impatient, I frantically work on his buckle, his button, his zipper. Over his tight boxers, I slide my palm up and down the hot length of him and discover he's leaking into the waistband. A shiver of satisfaction courses through me. It's nice to know I'm not the only one with damp underwear.

While I explore, he draws my nipple into his mouth with more force, sending a spike of pleasure straight to my clit. And I need more. I need him bare in my hand.

When I dip my fingers beneath his waistband, he captures my wrist and raises his head, his breaths harsh and ragged. "I'll come if you do that. You've got me so worked up, I'm way too close already."

I smile, loving that he's barely in control.

Studying me with a glint of mischief, he grumbles, "Think that's amusing, do you?"

I nod.

"Let's see how you like it." Forcing my hand above my head, he secures both wrists in his firm grasp.

Crushing his lips to mine, his tongue delves in a way that shows me it's not the only part of his body that wants deep inside me. And I welcome it, *want* it. Something new and bold is awakening inside me, something that wants everything, that pushes aside all my inexperience and tells me to surrender. And I do. I let go and give myself to him completely.

Turning me on my side so we're face to face, and I'm firmly supported by the back of the couch, he tugs his shirt free of his trousers. Yanking at it impatiently, the last few buttons I hadn't managed to undo suddenly pop into the air, before clicking somewhere on the floorboards. As I let out a giggle, he spreads his shirt wide and crushes his hot, hard chest against my bare breast. The touch of our naked skin fizzes my blood like an electric current. I've never heard the noises leaving my throat before, but I'm not embarrassed. He's making them too, and it's fucking wonderful.

Skating his palm up my thigh, he slides the hem of my dress around my waist. Then he hooks my knee over his hip, leaving me fully exposed.

Grabbing my arse, he rocks into me, grinding his erection against my bare clit, the fabric of his boxers creating a frustrating friction. I writhe against him, needing more, needing everything. God, I could come like this. I *need* to release all this pent-up arousal.

Suddenly he holds me still, his breaths hard and fast as his fingertips tease the bare flesh of my backside with slow, gentle circles that border on painful.

He gives me a devilish grin. "Can that toy of yours touch you like this?"

His fingers gently glide over my slippery centre and through my folds, stopping just short of my clit.

"No," I breathe, my body trembling in anticipation.

"Who do you think can make you come harder? Me or your toy?" he asks, circling my clit with a feather-light tease.

"You. Oh, God, Gavin … *you*."

"Damn fucking right."

Watching my face, he eases a thick finger deep inside me. I groan, incapable of holding back the effect he's having on me as his thumb drags over my slick nerve endings.

His chest rumbles in return and he drops his head, trailing his lips up my throat until he finds my ear. "Christ, J. *Fuck* … I knew you'd feel like heaven."

With his gravelly voice right in my ear, those words are like an ignition switch. No one's ever touched me like this. And I know it's not just his touch. It's *him*. It's everything that makes him Gavin Lake. I shamelessly rock against him, seeking just the right pressure as my release rushes toward me.

Carefully, he slides another finger inside, crooking them just right, his thumb gliding and circling, my arousal soaking him as I ride his hand and whimper.

"Fuck, J, that's it … let go … come all over me. Let me feel it."

His deep, rough voice takes me over the edge.

"Gavin … oh fuck. Fuck … *yes!*"

Undulating against him, I come with such incredible intensity, sparks dance behind my eyes as my muscles contract and spasm around his fingers.

Suddenly, light flares behind my closed lids.

My eyes snap open, my orgasm still roaring through me. Gavin's whole body stiffens, his eyes filled with the same shock and confusion as mine.

"Jamie?" a familiar voice calls, "I'm home."

Chapter 36

Jamie

ANIKA.

Shit!

As Gavin whips my dress over my thighs, I frantically cover my exposed breast. Holding the material tightly in place, I sit up, my head clearing the back of the couch.

Shrugging off a backpack, Anika stands in the hallway outside the laundry door, clearly having entered the house through the garage with her remote. Even if Gavin hadn't silenced the garage door's squeal, I doubt either of us would have heard it. We'd been a little too preoccupied.

When my sister's eyes find mine, she smiles. "There you—" As her hand clamps over her mouth in surprise, I become aware of the emptiness at my side.

My eyes shoot to Gavin, now standing, his back to Anika while he quickly zips up his trousers and buckles his belt. Thank God we aren't naked.

"Well, fuck," Anika chuckles. "You didn't get my messages?"

"Clearly not," I reply, scooting off the couch to stand beside Gavin as he does up what's left of his buttons.

"So, aren't you going to introduce me?" Anika asks.

My heart pounds for an entirely different reason now. I

haven't told her a single thing about our father's crimes, let alone the fact that Gavin's living in my home. *Our* home. He'd been right to push me. I should have done it weeks ago. Now she's here and I've totally fucked up.

Before I can formulate a sentence, Gavin turns around, giving Anika her first look at him.

She makes quick work of scanning his body. When her gaze settles on his face, she grins with appreciation. "Well look at you." Her eyes flick to me. "Nice work, Jamie."

Just like I hadn't recognised him when I turned up at his caravan, neither does she.

I swallow over my closing throat. "Anika … this is Gavin Lake."

It takes less than a second for the name to register. Eyes widening, her mouth drops open.

"*What the fuck?!*" she shouts.

A completely reasonable reaction considering she believes the man standing at my side is our enemy. At the time, she'd been too young to understand what happened to Mum, but as she grew up, I'd made sure she knew exactly who Gavin Lake was. I even made up that obnoxious poem to teach her to hate him.

"It's not what you think," I blurt, knowing how pathetic that sounds, but I have to start somewhere.

"Oh? So you're *not* fucking our mother's killer?"

Gavin's muscles tense against me where our arms touch.

"No, I'm not, Anika." I release one of the hands holding my up dress and reach down, entwining my fingers with Gavin's. "I have a lot to tell you, but right now, just know this … Gavin *did not* kill our mother."

Anika's eyes flick from me to Gavin. "Bullshit."

"I know I should have told you sooner, but I—"

"Why the fuck are you still here?" Anika glares at Gavin, ice in her words. *"Leave!"*

His hand loosens in mine, but I hold on tight. "He's not going anywhere. This is his home."

"What?!" Anika stares daggers at him, then me.

I suddenly feel like the walls are closing in and there's no escape from the escalating pressure to straighten out this mess I've caused.

"She's right," Gavin says, his attention on me. "Let me go for a walk while you two catch up."

"You don't have to do that," I insist.

He squeezes my hand before releasing it. "I know. But it's the right thing to do." Shoving his feet in his shoes, he picks up his phone and keys. When he returns to me, he places a soft, reassuring kiss on my forehead.

"Seriously?" Anika shouts. "Fuck off!"

He flinches away.

"Anika!" I yell at her before turning to Gavin. "I'm sorry."

Instead of the hurt and anger I expect to see, he gives me a lopsided smile and winks, telling me he's okay. He understands.

"Text me," he says softly, then strides toward the front door. Almost there, he swoops down and snatches something from the floor. I catch a glimpse of white lace as he shoves it in his pocket. My panties. Saving me the from the embarrassment of my sister finding them there, discarded and damp.

Anika's glare follows him until he steps outside. The moment the door closes, marches to the back of the couch.

My heart sinks to the floor. This is all my fault. I should have told her the day Dad died. Putting it off has done nothing but hurt the two people I care about most. Although Gavin seems to have taken Anika's abuse on the chin, it must have brought back memories of the hatred thrown at him all those years ago. And now he's out there, alone in the dark, unsure of what he'll come back to. I absolutely hate myself right now.

"I'm sorry," I say, desperately trying to blink back tears. "I should have told—"

"He *lives* here? What the fuck, Jamie? Have you lost your mind?"

"He's my housemate." Is that what he is? That sounds so wrong, so cold and detached.

"More like fuck-mate," Anika spits. "What's wrong with you? You hate his guts!"

I shake my head. "No, not anymore. I've screwed up, Ank. I should have told you sooner, but I didn't want to upset you or disrupt your training."

She looks into my eyes, and she must see something there that takes the wind out of her anger. Shoulders slumping, she asks, "What crazy shit's happened now?"

"Let me get changed, and I'll explain everything."

Grabbing my phone from the kitchen, I turn it on and hurry into my room. As I change, a surge of notifications ping from my phone. Before I face Anika, I quickly check them, seeing I have three missed calls from her, then a message stating she's on her way and a few more asking why I'm not answering.

And there's one last message.

GAVIN:

Take as long as you need.

Smiling, I pocket the phone. The sooner I sort this out, the sooner he can come home.

Home.

My gut hollows, remembering Anika's demand that he leave. I wonder if he feels like he even has a home anymore.

Steeling myself with a deep breath, I walk into the kitchen to find my sister sitting at the breakfast bar, a bottle of white wine on the counter with two full glasses waiting. The sight is so unusual, I have to remind myself that she's not a kid anymore. Knowing her, she's probably been getting drunk every weekend while at the academy. She's always had a wild streak in her I've never possessed. Or had I been denied the chance to develop one?

I stand on the other side of the breakfast bar so I can face her. When she slides a glass of wine across to me, I take a sip, then a deep breath.

"Dad told me something earth-shattering just before he died," I say, hoping to prepare her for the shock.

"What? That he couldn't give a shit about me? I already know that."

"Jesus, Ank. He loved you. He just—" I stop myself, hearing Gavin's voice in my head. *Your rules. No lying.* "I honestly don't know what was going on with him when it came to you. It makes no sense."

She blinks in surprise. "Wow. No molly-coddling bullshit? That's a first." Taking a gulp of wine, she screws up her face and forces herself to swallow. "Whatever he said must've been some jaw-dropper."

"Yeah, it was … *is*." I take a deep breath. "Right before he passed, he told me … he killed Mum."

Completely frozen, she stares at me. And I wait. I know all too well how difficult it is to digest this news. Then she slaps a hand on the counter and laughs. "Good one, Jamie."

She's in denial. I've never been one to joke. At least, not about something this serious. When I don't crack a smile or look away, I watch it sink in.

Face slack with shock, she takes a long gulp of her wine. "Seriously?"

I nod, lean on the counter and tell her all the details of our father's dying declaration, of tracking down Gavin, of taking Liam's statement detailing what he saw that night and how it matched Gavin's story. Then I get out my laptop and sit beside her, my arm tight around her, feeling every emotional reaction in her body as we watch our father's video.

"Fuck. Holy fucking fuck," she mutters when we get to the end.

"That's about the extent of it," I agree.

Suddenly, she's out of her chair and hugging me. I hold her for a long time as I run a soothing hand over her back.

"And you dealt with this all on your own?" she asks, the remorse thick in her words.

"Actually, no," I admit, wanting to unburden her of the guilt she doesn't deserve to carry. "I had all the support I needed."

When she plops herself back on her stool, she takes a swallow of the wine she clearly hates.

"What're you feeling?" I ask.

She lets out a huff. "So many things. But mainly … we finally have some answers."

We sit in silence for a long while, sipping on our wine,

contemplating.

"I'm sorry I didn't come home for you when he passed," she eventually says.

"I didn't expect you to. And I didn't want you to."

"Well, I'm still sorry. I kinda lied to you. Truth is, I didn't know how to deal with your grief over him. Because I felt nothing. And that made me feel like a truly shitty sister. So, instead of coming home after graduation, I hid down there with a bunch of mates … pretty much just to avoid you."

I give her forearm an affectionate squeeze. "You are *not* a shitty sister, Ank. You're entitled to feel however you want."

Sighing heavily, she looks at me. "I just know, deep down, he never cared about me. And I know that because I had the perfect comparison. He loved the shit out of you." She takes a few deep breaths. "Is it wrong that this news is a relief? I'm sorry, but he was a fucking prick. What he did to Mum … At least I don't have to feel bad for not liking him anymore."

"Good," I say, and mean it. "You shouldn't have to go through life with that burden. Needless to say, I have my own issues to work through. Mainly the fact that he lied to us, and let an innocent man go to prison in his place."

"Ugh, fuck," Anika groans, slumping over the counter and burying her face in the crook of her elbow. "And I told him to fuck off."

I give her back a comforting rub. "Good news is, he'll be the one trying to put you at ease about that. He's kind of … amazing."

Her head snaps up, her gaze pinning me. "What's going on there, Jamie?"

"Well, once I knew he was innocent, I told him I'd get his conviction overturned. It was a bit iffy until Dad's video turned up. At least that's one thing our father did right in the end. I was so worried I wouldn't be able to pull it off. The thought of not being able to give him his life back … well, it'll happen now."

She nods thoughtfully as she takes another sip of wine. "Okay, I get that. But why's he *living* here?"

I've learnt my lesson. Withholding the truth hurts just as much as outright lying. "Someone threatened me."

"What?"

"It was just an anonymous note, telling me to back off," I say offhandedly, not wanting to draw attention to my suspicion that it's related to clearing Gavin's name. I know she'll only worry, and I'm not backing off, no matter what anyone says. Besides, as Pete pointed out, I have no proof it's anything to do with that. "It freaked me out a little, and … well, Gavin was living in a horrible caravan, and he's big and strong, and I was alone in the house, and it just made sense," I blurt. "For both of us. He makes me feel safe. And there's been no more threats since."

"Fuck, Jamie. And you didn't tell me?"

"What could you have done except worry? And you were so close to finishing Session Two at the academy. I wasn't going to let anything distract you from that."

She rolls her eyes and gives me an exaggerated sigh. "So typical of you."

I grin and we both take another drink.

"So, he went from bodyguard to boyfriend?" she asks. "Not that I blame you. He's hot as fuck."

I choke on my wine. With great pleasure, Anika thumps my back until I stop. After a moment, I manage to get out, "I … I don't know."

"You don't know if he's hot, or if he's your boyfriend?"

"Of course I know he's hot."

Anika scoffs. "He's sleeping in your bed, right?"

Heat crawls up my face. I suppose if I'd had relationships throughout my time raising Anika, I wouldn't feel so awkward discussing this with her. But this is new territory. "No, he's in the spare room. I … tonight's the first time we've … started getting closer."

"And I interrupted?"

"Yes, you absolutely did." I turn in my chair, take her hand in mine and look into her amused eyes. "When he comes back … when he comes *home*, I want you to treat him with the respect he deserves. As a man who's spent almost half his life in a cell because of our father. As a man who I think really cares about me. As the awesome fucking guy he is." To my surprise, I feel tears sliding down my cheeks.

Anika shifts in her seat, looks around me, then behind her, as if searching for something.

"What?" I ask, confused.

"I'm just wondering where my sister is. Because she never cries. Especially not over a *guy*."

Embarrassed, I swipe at the tears. "You've got no idea. I've cried more in his company than I have since Mum died. And he never once made me feel embarrassed or awkward. When I'm with him, I can just be me. I don't have to hide what I'm feeling or pretend to be strong. He makes me feel …" I trail off, my heart suddenly announcing itself in my chest.

"Loved?" Anika offers, squeezing my hand.

I swallow, more tears breaching the dam wall. And I nod.

Her face breaks into a huge grin. "Holy *fuck*. You're in love with him!"

Then she's out of her seat and hugging me so hard I can barely breathe.

When she lets go, her eyes shine with tears. Tears she's usually as good as I am at holding back.

"So, you two haven't slept together yet?" she asks.

"No."

"And he's been locked up for how long?"

"Sixteen years."

"And you've had how many boyfriends in that time?"

I don't like this line of questioning, but I indulge her. "None."

She nods, her gaze locking on her almost empty wine glass as she twirls it around and around, deep in thought. Finally, she looks at me. "Well, it's late. The ghosts of the past aren't going anywhere, so let's get your man back here and figure things out. We're gonna need some ground rules while I'm here, since this's my house too, right?"

I nod immediately, not wanting to even give her an inkling

of what our father's will says. "Rules?" I ask.

"Yep. Pretty much the rules you instated when I started getting interested in guys."

Oh, shit.

Chapter 37

Gavin

FROM THE PARK bench where I wait, I stare at the empty children's playground before me. The lone swing sways slightly, as if a child's ghost can't quite summon enough energy to really get it moving.

Closing my eyes, I let the warm summer breeze wash over me, feel it ruffle my hair and caress my face and bare forearms. I listen to the gentle creak of the swing's unoiled chains and the rustle of leaves in the trees above me. How many times did I long to be outside at night, in the quiet, with the air in motion all around me? To experience the freedom a prison cell keeps extinguished with its motionless, stale air?

Before I ended up in this park, I'd walked around Jamie's block once before it felt too much like the night my father told me to get out of his house before his new girlfriend arrived. Jamie's mother. Now I've been kicked out because of Jamie's sister. I let out a huff. Not true. Jamie didn't want me to go. But I had to, for her sake. It would be impossible to have the conversation she needs to have with her sister with me in the house.

And I've been beating myself up about my miserable failures. Tonight was the first time we've both been out of the house at the same time, so protecting Jamie should've been at the forefront of my mind. The moment we arrived home I should've checked the house and locks for signs of an intruder. But I was so fucking lost in her, she became my entire world. I'd turned us into sitting ducks. Whoever sent that threat could've been hiding in wait. Or walked in on us instead of Anika.

Now I'm sitting on a park bench waiting for Jamie to tell me to come home.

Their home, I correct myself.

No. It's my home, too. That's what Jamie told her sister. *This is his home.* Even after such a short amount of time, it feels like home, a place where I've been made to feel welcome, appreciated, and far more.

Of course, I'd hoped to meet her sister under better circumstances, but it's hard to blame Jamie. It's not an easy thing to reveal what their father has done.

When my phone buzzes in my hand, I stare at the screen.

JAMIE:
Please come home. She knows. She's fine.

ME:
See you in 10.

As I head home, it vibrates again.

JAMIE:
Be prepared. She tends to say whatever's on her mind.

ME:
Good for her.

JAMIE:
I'll remind you of that when she offends and embarrasses us both.

Before I know it, I'm standing at the front door, suddenly

not sure if I should let myself in.

I opt to give Anika some respect by knocking.

A stampede of feet and what I think is a yelp come from inside. Then the door swings open to reveal Jamie in her usual morning attire before she gets ready for work. Except for once, and to my disappointment, her robe is securely tied in front.

"Why are you knocking?" she asks, opening the door wider.

Anika appears at her side and shoves herself between us.

"May I help you?" she enquires, her lips performing a strange little twist, which I can only presume is an attempt to keep from grinning.

"Hi, I'm Gavin Lake. And I'm hoping I still live here," I play along. Extending my hand, I wait.

Anika gives me the once-over before uncrossing her arms and taking my hand. "Anika Evans."

We shake, and I apply the same amount of pressure she's giving me. It's a challenge I don't back down from. We stare at each other, our grasps tightening, bordering just a millimetre shy of painful. Smirking, she releases my hand.

"Well, since this house is half mine, you'd better come in so we can see about whether or not you'll continue to live here."

I don't miss the fact that she's made sure I'm aware she has one up on me. Although Jamie won't tell her the truth about their father's wishes, I'm mindful that soon enough it *will* belong to them both.

Thirsty, I head into the kitchen, noting the half empty bottle of wine and the two empty glasses on the breakfast bar. By the time I grab myself a glass, add some ice, and fill it with water, I turn to find the two women seated on the other side of the breakfast bar, staring at me.

Anika bumps Jamie's elbow. "He sure acts as if he's at home."

"That's because he *is* home," Jamie says, her eyes on me. "And that won't be changing."

"Don't be shy," Anika says. "Come over here so I can get a good look at you, Gavin Lake." As I lean on the breakfast bar, she sucks in a little gasp. "Gavin Lake," she muses, tapping a finger to her chin before turning to Jamie. "Didn't you make up some rhyme about him? Something like—"

"Don't," Jamie warns.

"No need for a recital. I've already heard it." I look at Jamie and wait for her eyes to meet mine. "It even saved me from getting into some trouble earlier."

In my peripheral vision, I see Anika glancing from me to Jamie and back again.

"Well, look at you two," she croons. "Already having private conversations with your eyes. How sweet." Leaning to the side, she gags.

"For God's sake, Ank. Is that what they taught you at the academy?" Jamie chastises.

I wink at her, enjoying this new mama-bear side of her.

"Alright, alright," Anika says, her eyes sparkling with mischief.

Taking in her dirty blonde hair and brown eyes, I can see the similarity between the sisters, but they're also very different. Even though Anika's a stranger to me, there's something familiar about her. Shaking it off, I put it down to recognising her from those home videos Jamie showed me.

I might not know her, but I already understand something. Jamie had her hands full raising her. She's not some well-behaved, obedient daughter. She's full of spirit and, from what I know about her relationship with her father, she's also hurting.

After she offers to refill Jamie's wine glass, she pours herself another, takes a grimacing gulp, puts it down and nails me with her eyes. Which has a strange, unnerving effect on me.

"So, Gavin Lake," she begins, "I owe you an apology."

Jamie's head swivels in her sister's direction so fast, I'm surprised she doesn't lose her balance and topple off her stool.

"No need," I tell Anika. "Just like I've told Jamie, none of what happened is your fault."

"I know that. I'm talking about how we met. I'm sorry for speaking to you that way. And for kicking you out of …" she gives Jamie a pointed look, "your home."

"Thanks, but you don't have to apologise for that either. You acted exactly how I'd expect, given what you knew."

She glances from me to Jamie. "Well, then, I guess I should apologise to you. For not trusting your judgement."

My eyes flick between the two, understanding that this is something new for them.

Jamie shakes her head. "Thanks, but if I'd told you earlier, none of it would have happened. So, out of everyone here, I'm the one who's sorry."

Anika's gaze falls firmly on me. "Well, Gavin. As much of a shock as all this is, at least it's put to rest one of my questions about Mum's murder. I've always had this niggling feeling about you insisting that you were innocent. It seemed crazy to me that you'd deny it when it was on camera for everyone to see. That was some pretty damning evidence."

I'm shocked when the apparently tough little nugget before me swallows and tears well in her eyes.

"Jamie told me you were only trying to help Mum," she barely manages.

Jamie rests her head against her sister's and puts a comforting arm around her, squeezing her tight.

Trying to distract the poor girl, I say, "I'm surprised you looked into it, since you were so young when it happened."

"I like investigating. And reading," she answers, taking a deep breath before letting it go.

"Like your sister," I point out.

Anika shakes her head. "No, I like to read true crime stories, books and articles. For fun. She likes to read smut. For fun."

Jamie pinches her hard on the arm.

"Ow! That's assault!"

"It'll be more than that if you don't stop trying to embarrass me," Jamie mutters.

"Well, buckle up, big sister. It's about to get a whole lot worse."

Jamie blushes a moment before she buries her face in her hands and groans.

Anika turns an amused gaze my way. "She's told me you two

haven't bumped uglies yet, and I don't wanna be here when that happens. It doesn't take a genius to see that the chemistry between you two is fucking nuclear. I don't want to hear it when it detonates, thank you very much," she finishes, giving a repulsed little shudder.

I glance at Jamie, wondering what the hell her sister's talking about. All I get is a shake of her head and one eye peering out between her fingers.

"She's the one who set the rule, so she's already agreed to this. Now it's your turn," Anika says.

"My turn for what?"

"No fucking my sister while I'm under this roof."

I flick a glance at Jamie. Still hiding.

"Don't bother looking at her. It's her rule. When I turned sixteen, she laid it out. I wasn't to have sex in this house while she was in it and vice versa. It pissed me off at the time, but I understood. She didn't want to *hear* it." She gives a little chuckle and nudges Jamie with her elbow. "Guess she didn't think it'd come back to bite her. And I'm guessing, that since my sister likes you, you must be a man of your word, right?"

"I am," I agree, even though I know I'm stepping right into a trap.

"Then promise you'll keep your dick out of my sister while I'm here."

Christ. She's fucking serious.

"Just so we're clear on these terms," I say, "what about when you're *not* here?"

She throws Jamie an amused glance. "Oh, I see why you like him. Determined to get in your pants, isn't he?"

"Just get it over with," Jamie's muffled voice begs.

Anika turns her gaze back to me. "If you're talking about me going out while I'm staying here, forget it. I'm not going anywhere … unless it's with one of you. Believe it when I say, I'm your cockblocking nightmare."

Well, fuck.

I glance at Jamie, waiting as she slowly removes her hands from her face and gives me a helpless shrug.

"And how long is this cockblocking nightmare lasting?" I ask.

"Well, my first day on the job is Christmas day, which means I'll leave Christmas eve. So, what's that? Three nights? Should be a breeze for you, right?"

"Fine," I grumble, already wondering how I'll survive this new hell. After experiencing the torture of keeping my hands off Jamie when I wasn't sure if she felt the same, now I have to do it knowing she *does* want me? *Fucking fuck.*

"Great!" Anika exclaims. "Now I can relax."

"Not quite," Jamie says. "Dad mentioned Mum left a letter. And that you know where it is."

Anika slowly nods as she glances at her watch. "I think I know where he means, but fuck, Jamie, it's past midnight. Not to mention I need to wrap my head around Dad's confession … and you having a *boyfriend*. That's enough to fry my brain without adding something else right now. Can it wait until tomorrow?"

Jamie gives her an understanding nod.

Pouring the last of the wine into her glass, Anika stands and heads to the couch. "I'm gonna unwind with some TV. Feel free to join."

The moment I enter my bedroom, I drop to the mattress, bury my head in the pillow and groan. Just when we were getting going, her sister's put on the brakes, wielding some sort of diabolical powerplay over us. I can't blame Anika, though. I understand why. And it's a perfectly legitimate reason. That doesn't stop my body and soul aching for what we were meant to have. Right about now, we should be completely satiated and fast asleep in each other's arms.

My phone vibrates in my pocket.

Rolling onto my back, I pull it out and check the message.

JAMIE:
Go get in the shower. Don't lock the door.

I sit up and swing my feet to the carpet.

ME:
I just made a promise to your crazy sister.

JAMIE:
Neither of us will be breaking our word.

ME:
I don't know … I heard you have a boyfriend.

With a stupid grin on my face, I wait.

JAMIE:
If he doesn't get in the shower now, he's getting dumped!

After flinging off my clothes and dressing in a t-shirt and trackpants, I silently open my bedroom door and stick my head out. The TV's louder than usual, apparently the way Anika likes it. I can't see her head above the couch, so I presume she's lying down. Like Jamie and I were. Shaking my head, I grin to myself. How flattered I'd been when Jamie announced she'd turned her phone off for the night. And how that decision ruined her orgasm and my chance of sinking into her. A chance I now won't get for another three days.

I suppose that's my fault for taking things slow. The moment we walked through the door, I could have picked her up, carried her into her bedroom and fucked her senseless. I know she wouldn't have resisted. But when I sensed her nerves, I forgot about my own need. And I don't regret a moment. Taking my time exploring her, tasting her and making her come with just my touch is worth the punishment of having to wait. Though, I could do without the ache in my balls.

Following her instructions, I silently cross the hall, step into the bathroom, shut the door and stare at the small bolt. I've never considered locking it before. After half a lifetime of conditioning, privacy seems like a privilege reserved for others. But now that Anika's here, I guess I'll have to start locking it to avoid any awkward situations.

Not tonight, though.

I undress, leaving my clothes in a neat pile on the edge of the vanity, then I turn on the shower and wait for the temperature to rise. Glancing over my shoulder at the door, my heart races with anticipation. I know Jamie can hear the water running. I can hear her shower from my bedroom. Anika's right, the walls in this house are thin.

With the temperature just right, I walk into the doorless shower and brace my hands on the tiled wall in front of me, a vulnerable position I'd never put myself in on the inside. Dropping my head between my arms, I let the water cascade over my hair and run like a river from my chin.

Christ, the anticipation's killing me. I'm not sure what Jamie has planned, but she made it clear neither of us would break our promise.

Then why does she want me naked in the shower? My dick twitches at the thought of her eyes roaming over my body. Sure, she saw me naked when she spied on me after I'd mown the lawn. But that'd been from a distance. Glancing at my only tattoo, I know I won't be able to hide it from her this time. Of course, I knew she'd see it once we became intimate. But for tonight, I thought our passion would spiral us into another dimension, where our bodies tangled, and questions weren't asked.

Taking a deep breath, I let it out slowly. She can't ask questions in here either. We'll have to be quiet.

When a breath of cool air sends goosebumps over my wet back, I turn my head to find her at the door, her back to me as she slides the bolt home. She lingers there for a moment, still wearing that short little robe and, for a fleeting moment, I wonder if she's naked underneath.

Finally, she turns and our eyes lock. I twist around until water thrums between my shoulder blades, matching the blood thrumming through my veins. Placing one hand on the tiled wall, and one on the large screen, I watch through the glass as she slips off the robe and hangs it on the back of the door. I'm not disappointed at the sight of the skintight white camisole and matching boxer briefs that are clearly her pyjamas. Instantly transported back to the first time I found her in the kitchen, my body reacts the same way now.

Her gaze leaves mine, taking a leisurely journey down my body. I know she's not getting a perfect view through all the water droplets on the glass screen, but I'm sure she can see my hard dick.

Lips slightly parted, she pads across the tiles, her eyes on mine again as she steps past the screen, giving herself an unobstructed view.

She explores me with her eyes, and I feel every caress. First my lips, then the throbbing pulse in my neck. They move from right to left over my chest, pausing for the briefest moment on my tattoo before dipping over my abs, my navel, the dark trail of hair. I know the instant she really takes in my cock. Her eyes grow just a little bit rounder, her lips opening slightly wider.

I'm pretty sure I'm the first man she's ever truly seen naked. Thank God she seems … fascinated. My dick twitches under her gaze, and she gasps, bringing a hand to her mouth to muffle a giggle.

Grinning like a fool, I touch a finger to my lips, the sight of her smiling, when a moment ago she was so serious, floods warmth into my cooling chest.

She removes her hand, flashing her teeth at me before her smile fades, her gaze locking on my tattoo.

Gripping my left shoulder with my right hand, I cover it, silently telling her not to look.

Still wearing her pyjamas, she walks into the shower, right up to me, and places a kiss on the back of that hand. I think she wants me to show her, but she surprises me by gripping my shoulder and turning me until my back faces her.

Having her behind me stutters my heartrate, and I find myself locking my knees to stop the tremble that wants to reveal how much I hate and fear this vulnerable position. The brain is a powerful conductor over the body. Logically, I know I'm safe, but after being in this position fifteen years ago, and learning a horrific lesson, my mind has been trained too well.

Gently, she takes each of my wrists, placing one hand on the glass and the other on the tiles. As I fight every instinct to turn around, I realise she's telling me I'm not to touch her. The way I stopped her from touching me on the couch.

She's in control this time. And I'm to obey. I'm not sure how I feel about that.

Until her lips press a gentle kiss to the middle of my spine. With my back cooling now it's no longer beneath the heated spray, her mouth is warm, her tongue hot when it touches my skin in a tentative lick.

While she kisses a slow descent down my spine, her fingers flutter against the outside of my thighs, delicately inching higher until they stop at my waist. I squeeze my eyes shut, hoping she doesn't reach around and grab my cock, or this'll be over way too soon. And God knows, I don't want her to stop touching me.

A second later, I suck in a breath and hold it as her mouth inches closer to the base of my spine. I tense, and I know she feels it, because she stops. Then she presses a kiss to my tailbone. And her tongue dips into the cleavage at the top of my arse ever so briefly.

Fucking fuck.

Is she showing me she's not afraid to test boundaries?

Before my thoughts run rampant, she presses her clothed body against mine, rises on her toes and whispers in my ear, "Now who's shaking like a leaf?"

I hadn't even realised I was, but she's right. They're no longer tremors of fear, but barely restrained ripples of desire.

Like she's rewiring me.

Christ, this woman.

When her warm body vanishes, I tilt my head, watching her pump bodywash into her palm from the bottle on the recessed shelf.

A moment later, her hands slide along my outstretched forearms, coating me with soap. With her fingers gliding over my skin, she kneads and massages toward my shoulders until the tension gradually eases from my tight muscles. Then she starts the same slow exploration on my back, over the mounds of my arse and up again. Her focused touch, every slide, every gentle scrape of her nails, spreads a feeling of love and care deep inside me.

Finding her way to my shoulders, she applies pressure, indicating I should turn around. I obey. I'll do anything she wants.

With my shoulders blocking the shower spray, I gaze down the length of her body, noticing her pyjamas are damp from where she pressed against my wet back.

She's fucking gorgeous. But I want to see more. Before she touches me, I place a warning finger to her lips and smile. She cocks a questioning eyebrow as I drop my shoulder enough to let the shower spray hit her chest. When she opens her mouth in surprise, I slip my finger past her teeth, straighten up, and block the water once again.

Softly biting down, she traps my finger there, closes her lips around it and rubs her tongue against the tip. When my smile fades into hot desire, she releases me with a smirk.

Cheeky little minx.

As her eyes roam over my body, I take in the soaked camisole clinging to all her curves, her nipples beneath puckering as the water cools against her skin. When I reach her waist, a sliver of exposed skin draws me in, and I can't resist the urge to run my knuckles across her flexing stomach. Releasing a shaky exhale, she clutches my wrists, and stretches out my arms, forcing my hands back to the walls.

Not touching her is torture.

And I'm loving every second of it.

Gathering more bodywash in her hands, she runs them over my chest in slow, sensuous circles, her thumbs teasing my nipples before dipping lower. As she traces my abs, I hold my breath, waiting for her to reach my painfully hard dick.

Before she does, she steps into me, rises to her toes, and wraps her arms around my neck. I'm desperate to get my hands on her, to hold her too, but I obey her rules and keep them where they are. Closing my eyes, I allow something I've never felt before to sear into my soul. Although I already know I love her, there's been that tiny niggling doubt about her feelings for me. Not anymore. With soap and her touch, she's washing away all traces of uncertainty, leaving a clean slate of utter trust in my heart and on my skin. I've never felt so vulnerable and free and in utter reverence at the thought of a future with this amazing woman.

Pressing my mouth against her ear, I whisper, "What're you doing to me?"

She slides an arm from my neck and pumps out another squirt of bodywash. "Learning you," she murmurs as she reaches between us and slides her slippery hand tightly down my length.

I buck forward, burying my face in her the crook of her neck, my mouth opening against her flesh and biting down gently to stifle a groan.

Her hand slides up and down, so fucking soft and different from my own, it turns my mind to mush. After a few strokes, she pauses at the tip, her fingers gently exploring the swollen head, tracing its shape with such tenderness I want to sink to my knees. Testing my limits, she wraps her hand around my shaft and strokes me again. I keep my face buried against her neck as I move my hips, matching the maddeningly slow pace she's set. I don't want it to be over, but I'm at the end of my tether.

Sensing it, she whispers in my ear, "Come for me. All over my hand. I want to feel it, just like you did."

She pulls back enough to kiss me and as her tongue enters my mouth, she strokes me harder, faster. Her hand, her tongue, her words, make it easy to obey her. I let go, jerking and pulsing in her tight grip while she swallows my almost silent groans.

Only when my smothered sounds fade does she break the kiss and look down at my cock in her hand, at the ropes of come on my stomach and her fist. We stand motionless, watching the water cascading over my shoulders slowly wash it away.

Releasing my dick, she cups the back of my neck and pulls me down, pressing her lips against my ear. "You're so beautiful. Inside and out," she whispers. "Now stay here until I'm gone."

Then, with a gentle kiss to my lips, she reluctantly steps away and moves beyond the shower screen.

Turning her back to me, she glances over her shoulder, catching my eye before she peels off her wet top. Captivated, I watch her slide the clinging boxers down her perfect backside. When they stick to her thighs, she wiggles her gorgeous arse until they fall to her feet.

Fuck me.

She's making me goddamn hard again.

As she reaches for a towel, I shift my gaze to the mirror above the vanity, catching a glimpse of her tight, naked body in profile before she covers herself and gets busy drying off.

Resting my forehead to the glass, I watch like a greedy savage when she drops the towel, showing off those beautiful cheeks again before she grabs the robe from the back of the door and shrugs it on.

She scoops her wet clothes off the floor, wraps them in a towel and throws me a cheeky grin before she carefully unlocks the door and inches it open.

Then she's gone and all the air I've been holding rushes from my mouth.

She's going to kill me.

But as frustrating as it is, I think I like this game of enforced denial and sneaking around like naughty teenagers. Seeing how much we can give and take without breaking our word. Proving that our promises mean something, even when they're not given to each other. That we can love one another with looks and touches alone.

The anticipation of waiting to be inside her is torture, but I love that we have that to look forward to. And after her little performance just now, who knows what tomorrow will bring.

Chapter 38

Jamie

SILENCING MY PHONE'S alarm, I continue to stare at the ceiling like I've been doing for the last hour. With so many things swirling around in my head, I have no idea how I managed to get any sleep at all.

I've decided to take a sickie today. I know it won't look good, not right before the firm officially breaks for Christmas tomorrow, but I can't summon the mental capacity to care. Finding Mum's letter is far more important. From what my father said in his video, it sounds like it'll hold the answers I've desperately craved for so long.

But first, I need my Gavin Lake fix. Oh, and some coffee.

As I clean my teeth, I replay that crazy stunt I pulled last night. I'd felt like the worst person on earth when Gavin left the house while I dealt with Anika. Then to top it off, the poor guy had to agree to her ridiculous no-sex terms. He'd given me the best orgasm of my life—well, half-orgasm due to a rude, cockblocking interrupter—and I'd desperately wanted to return that favour. If the number of times I've caught him sporting an erection is anything to go by, he's been dealing with a lot of wrist action over the last few weeks.

I'd actually stunned myself when I devised a plan to make it up to him.

Something else surprised me, too. I've never thought of a

penis as beautiful, but when I saw his, held it and stroked it, and witnessed the pleasure it gave him, that's what came to mind. Along with thoughts of kneeling before him and taking him into my mouth while he watches.

I don't even know who I am anymore.

Spitting toothpaste into the sink, I clench my thighs against the torture of that warm, heavy ache. I really need to clear my mind and make room for more important thoughts.

Like Mum's letter.

Like Gavin's tattoo.

When I saw it up close last night, before he hid it, my heart nearly broke. His reaction left no doubt it holds significant meaning. But it's also clear that *I* need to be significant to him before he opens up and explains that meaning.

Slipping on my robe, I hurry along the hallway toward the sound of grinding coffee beans, eager to lay eyes on the man who makes me feel alive and special.

When I pass the hallway wall, I stop. There he is, making his coffee, wearing his usual tight t-shirt and thin trackpants. Trackpants that now cover areas I've been privileged enough to lay my greedy eyes upon. Like those amazing glutes that, for some strange reason, I'd really like to sink my teeth into.

Padding silently up behind him, I slide my palm over one tight arse cheek and squeeze as I press my body against his back.

"I don't think your big sister would approve of that," he says in a low, gravelly voice. I freeze, not sure if I heard him right. Then he glances over his shoulder at me. And jerks a little, like I've surprised him. "Oh, it's you."

Mouth agape, I glare at him.

I'm not sure where it comes from, but I draw my hand back and slap his butt.

He doesn't even flinch, yet my palm burns from the sting. Chuckling, he turns and grabs my hips as I bring my arms up between us in a useless effort to push him away.

"So easy to tease," he says, eyes sparkling with mischief. "And boy, are you going to pay for that slap."

"You deserved it. I don't."

"That's where you're wrong. If you get to slap me because I teased you with words, then I most certainly get to punish you for that teasing little strip show you put on last night." As my arms soften, he places his mouth against my ear. "That was so fucking hot, it took every ounce of restraint I possess to stop myself from dragging you to the floor and fucking you."

"That would've been breaking the rules," I remind him.

His fingertips slide my robe off one shoulder and brush my hair aside. Kissing my exposed skin, he inhales deeply as he works his way up my neck, sending goosebumps shooting over my flesh when he plants a sweet kiss beneath my ear. "When I was staring at that perfect little arse of yours, I couldn't even remember my name, let alone recall rules." His teeth capture my earlobe and tug. "Lucky you'd just been a very naughty girl."

Flames lick at my face and ignite between my legs.

Giving me a wicked smile, he grazes his thumbs across my burning cheeks. "You're so adorably sexy."

"S-sorry?"

"Blushing like that when I've made you come with my fingers inside you. When you've had your hand around my cock … I think we're past the point of embarrassment due to a few words."

I blink at him, amazed I haven't spontaneously combusted. "Talking to me like that … I—"

"You don't like it?"

"I think I might like it … way too much," I admit.

He beams, releases my face and grips my backside in his large hands, drawing me right up against him. God, he's hard, and I'm wet, and we're stuck in the twilight zone under my vengeful little sister's rule.

"How do you like all those extra functions I have compared that toy of yours?" he asks with a satisfied smirk.

"Hmm, well, I *suppose* they're okay. Though, you forgot to ask if my toy is as big as you are."

"That's because I already know the answer."

Then he kisses me, his lips gentle and sweet, his rapid

breaths telling me he's holding back. And I don't want him to. Fisting my hands in his t-shirt, I swipe my tongue across his lower lip and am rewarded with a deep rumble before his tongue finds mine.

Damn he feels so good, tastes so good, does such wonderful things to my body that I never dreamed I'd experience in my life. Feeling like I'm the one who now wants to drag him to the floor, I release his t-shirt and reluctantly finish the kiss.

"Your coffee's getting cold," I remind him.

Refusing to release me, he grins. "Is that your way of saying we need to cool it?"

"If we don't, I think we might start a kitchen fire."

He drops his forehead to mine, cups my face and nudges our noses. "Just getting to kiss you is a goddamn miracle."

My stomach flips at his words, at the intimate way he's holding me. And I can't help myself. I kiss him again. His needy growl vibrates against my mouth, the kiss deepening as our hips grind and sway, sending sparks flying all over again.

This time, he breaks away first, his chest heaving against mine as he fights for control. "Well, I suppose we shouldn't burn the house down just yet. Not while there's a secret to uncover."

I huff out a frustrated sigh and step back, hating the cool air that seeps into all the places his body kept me warm.

Just like he does every morning, he moves aside, giving me access to the coffee machine.

"So, what's the plan?" he asks. "I'm presuming we'll wait until you get home from work before—"

"Oh, I'm not going to work today."

He lets out a long, relieved sigh and grins. "Thank God. I was kind of nervous about being alone with that sadistic sister of yours."

Smiling back, I get my coffee going, then do what I always do. I reach around him to grab a spoon from the drawer. Only this time, I slip my hand beneath his t-shirt and trail my fingertips across his back.

When I return to the coffee machine, he's watching me with smouldering eyes.

"When can we expect the sadistic one to emerge?" he asks.

I snort out a laugh. "You know, she'd probably get a kick out of it if you called her that to her face."

"Oh, I have no doubt."

"Well, she's still a teenager, and she was up pretty late, so I'd say she'll probably emerge around lunchtime."

He nods thoughtfully as I pick up my coffee and lean against the counter.

"How'd you like to give me a hand?" he asks.

He laughs when my eyebrows shoot up.

"I'm talking about another kind of job. Like helping me prep the side of the house so it's ready for painting."

Sounds like a great distraction. "I'd love to."

"We should get cracking before it gets too hot. Put your swimmers on under your clothes. Trust me, you'll want to dive straight in the pool when we're done."

Ten minutes later, after choosing a pair of swimmers Anika won't have a fit over, then dressing in an old t-shirt and shorts, we make our way around to the side of the house. With Benny's help, they've already completed the rear and the other side, where Gavin and Anika's bedrooms are located, so we won't be disturbing sleeping beauty.

After showing me all the lower parts of the cladding that need sanding back and how to do it, Gavin hands me a pair of gloves.

"You're not wearing any," I point out.

"I don't have exceptionally soft hands to protect." He gives me a wink, then climbs up the ladder to deal with the flaking paint higher up.

Once we've completed all the sanding and we're both drenched in sweat, Gavin unspools the garden hose and blasts the cladding. Then, with buckets of sugar soap, we wash the wall, ending up covered in bubbles as we step back to inspect our work.

"Hot enough for you?" he asks.

I swipe my hand across my wet brow. "I'm melting."

I know it's coming before it happens, but I still yelp as an arc of water hits my hip. When I turn to face him, he's staring at the wall, arms crossed, the hand closest to me holding the hose nozzle.

Another stream of water suddenly hits me square in the chest.

"Oh, you're gonna get it!" As I leap at him, he sprays me with the hose, sweeping it up and down my body without letting up.

Squealing, I turn and flee, his laughter close behind as water relentlessly drenches my hair, my back, my thighs. When I reach the pool, I jump into the deep end and sink to the bottom. A loud splash spins me around. Underwater, I watch as Gavin spears himself straight at me.

His arms wrap around my waist, and we break the surface, laughing as I wrap my arms around his neck and he guides us toward the shallow end until we can stand. When he tugs at my t-shirt, I raise my arms and let him drag the water-logged material over my head. Our eyes locked, he tosses it over to the pavers.

Then he undoes my shorts, and I slip out of them, not giving a damn where he throws them. I simply can't look away from the intensity in his eyes as he pulls me flush against him.

Wrapping my legs around his waist, I snuggle up to his erection, the cool water no match for the heat seeping through his boardshorts. He walks us over to the large potted ficus beside the steps and rests his back against the pool wall. Keeping our bodies low, the large planter effectively hides us from prying eyes.

I spear my fingers into his wet hair and kiss him, his tongue plunging into my mouth and stroking as his hips rock up, his hands tight on my hips.

But as my body slides against his, I realise he's still wearing his t-shirt. And I know why. Pulling back to catch my breath, I open my mouth.

"What happened to those other swimmers," he interrupts,

gliding his fingers up and down my spine. "The ones that leave nothing to the imagination from behind?"

I let a slow, satisfied grin lift my lips. "So, you *were* watching."

"Well, you'd just been spying. Besides, you wore it because you wanted me to see how fucking sexy you are. Damn cheeky of you … driving me out of my goddamn mind."

I giggle, rocking into his erection, a little chuffed that he had that reaction to me back then. Oh so long ago. Twenty-odd dates and a few weekends ago.

"What's going through that beautiful brain of yours?" he asks.

I hesitate, unsure if I want to ruin this playful mood. But it feels right. Sliding my fingers from his hair, I graze them over his chest and down into the water. Bunching the hem of his t-shirt in my fists, I lift a little, then pause, asking him the question without words.

A flicker of uncertainty wavers behind his eyes before he slowly raises his arms. I pull the t-shirt up his torso, over his chest and stand so I can free it from his arms. After I toss it past the planter, I straddle his lap and keep my eyes on his.

Trailing my fingers up his bunched muscles, I flatten my hand against his skin, his hard nipple grazing my palm as I move higher. Until I'm covering his tattoo.

"Will you let me see?" I whisper.

His fingers tighten on my hips before he gives a slight nod.

I press a gentle kiss to his lips and when I pull back, I ease my hand away.

Only then do I look. *Really* look.

A heart. Not a love heart. A real heart.

It's not just broken, but torn apart into four pieces. A few drops of blood fall from the jagged tears and make their way down to his ribs, the red faded and dull, indicating he had this done a long time ago.

Tears spike at the back of my eyes, but I blink them away as I study every detail.

Reaching out, I touch the damaged heart and trace the wounds.

He tenses, the rapid beat of his actual heart tapping against my fingertips. I raise my eyes to his. Brilliant blue stares back, vulnerable and afraid.

"Do you trust me … with your heart?" I ask, my own accelerating wildly.

"Yeah, I do," he answers, his voice rough and broken, reflecting the torment written all over his face.

"Why four?" I touch each quarter with my fingertip. "Why four broken pieces?"

He lets out a long breath and swallows. "Jamie … you don't want to hear all that."

I find his eyes again, the pain as clear as the blue staring back at me. "They're the four things that hurt you most, aren't they?"

He closes his eyes for a moment, then nods. "But it was a long time ago. Those wounds aren't the same anymore."

"I want to know. I want to know *you*. Even though I feel like I already do, I don't know everything. And I really, really want to. This part of who you are is so important to you, you branded yourself so you'd always remember."

He scoffs lightly. "Like I could ever forget."

Touching my finger to the first piece of his torn heart, I trace my nail around its jagged edge. "What hurt you here?"

He swallows, flicking his gaze to my touch on his skin. "My father. When he turned his back on me. As if he hadn't raised me for eighteen years, as if he had no idea who I was. How he could think I was capable of killing anyone, let alone a woman …"

"He never tried to reconnect?"

His expression tightens, and his fingers dig into my hips for a moment. "Once," he forces out. "Took him five years to show up at the prison. I refused to see him. I just …" His throat bobs. "I couldn't."

A tear forms in the corner of my eye. I blink, but not soon enough, because all I manage to do is set it free. He follows its path down my face. When it settles in the crevice between my lips, I drop my gaze to his mouth and watch the tip of his tongue appear, as if he wants to taste that tear. And, oh God, do I want him to. But that would be a distraction. That would be easy. This is hard. And it's the difficult things that have the deepest meaning.

I force my attention back to the tattoo and move my finger onto the next piece. "And this?"

"That was for all my dreams that would never come true. The realisation that my life would never be what I imagined or planned. It's for what I once had, and what I lost forever."

Jesus, this keeps getting worse. I intrinsically know the damage his incarceration has caused him, but actually hearing it in his own words, is heartbreaking. But I'm not stopping now. We're halfway there.

My throat constricts as my finger trails down to the piece below. He says nothing, and from the tension coiling through his muscles, I know he's trying to keep his emotions in check.

After a moment, I press, "This one?"

"Jamie …"

I meet his eyes.

"I don't want you to feel bad about anything I felt … back then. Especially now, since that piece is redundant."

"But it meant something once. Gavin, please tell me."

Sensing his indecision, I wait.

"That one was for every time you looked at me in court. Your life was shattered, never to be the same again, just like mine. And you knew it. I saw it in your eyes every day of that trial. You believed I was the one who did that to you. And you hated me for it. And that hurt. Deeply. The weight of being blamed for ruining the lives of others is a backbreaking burden."

I'm so stunned that I'd had such an effect on him way back then, I can barely breathe. Ashamed, I lower my eyes to his chest, causing more tears to spill over my cheeks.

Ever so gently, he wipes them away with his fingertips.

"I'm so sorry," I whisper.

He presses his lips to my forehead. "No. It was no more your fault than it was mine. We were both victims. You just had no way of knowing that. I wrote you so many letters explaining everything. But you never got them." He touches the underside of my chin and tilts my head up until I meet his gaze. "Jamie, that piece … that piece of my heart is whole again. Completely healed." He wipes away another stray tear with his thumb. "I promise you."

I nod, my throat too closed off to form words. Instead, I wrap my arms around his shoulders, tuck my face into his neck and hold him tight. How is it that his heart's been torn to shreds, yet it's still the warmest, biggest heart I've ever encountered? How is that possible?

He slips a hand beneath my wet hair and absently begins circling his thumb on the back of my neck, as if he's done it a thousand times before.

And it feels that way to me, too. I know I'm right where I'm supposed to be, in his arms, just being loved and loving him back.

After accepting his comfort and giving him mine, I pull away enough to touch the one remaining torn piece. "This one?"

His thumb stills on my neck, then resumes the reassuring circles. But he remains silent and, when I meet his gaze, he seems more hesitant to tell me about this last piece than the others. Just as I think he's clamming up, he takes a deep, resigned breath.

"That one's for the loss of love, for the wife I'd never have, the family of my own that'd never exist. Why would anyone want me—a convicted killer—in their lives? All the things people take for granted … I'd never hold someone I loved or be held by someone who loved me. I'd never touch someone with the love I have to offer or feel a loving touch … that's what ripped the last piece apart."

Now I understand his hesitation. This piece was all about the love he wanted to give and the love he wanted to receive. My heart aches for this beautiful man who deserves all the love in the world. *Doesn't he see that?*

Tracing the piece with my fingertip, I ask, "Why didn't you

tell me … that this piece is redundant too?"

When our eyes lock, his thumb stills on the back of my neck. The utter vulnerability in his gaze wrenches at my heart. "Because I don't really know, with certainty, that it is redundant."

He's right. I'm showing him how I feel, but without the words to back it up, he's left wondering. While I feel loved by the way he looks at me, touches me, holds and talks to me, I can't be certain either. I'm as vulnerable as he is. Without voicing how we feel, we're both flailing around in the dark, relying on hope alone.

I'm just not sure if I'm brave enough to be the one to put myself out there first. But if he doesn't feel as deeply for me as I do for him, isn't it better to know?

"You're holding someone right now," I say softly, "and someone's holding you back. You're touching someone, and you're being touched in return."

He tightens his arm around my waist, pulls me flush against him, and rests his forehead on mine, the tension between us sparking.

Oh God. He noticed. By the look in his eyes, he's not about to let me get away with it. And I don't want him to. I need his words, just as much as he wants mine.

"You skipped over the one word that gives all those things meaning," he points out, his voice strained.

"Love," I whisper.

"Do you love me … the way I love you?"

If I had a weak heart, I think it'd give out right about now.

"I don't know," I answer honestly.

He lifts his forehead from mine, his eyes unguarded and full of turmoil.

"Because," I continue, "I don't know the way you love me."

"I love you," he says without hesitation, "for the way my day can't even begin until you look at me. I love you for the way you care with such genuine affection, it brings me to tears. I love you because you don't judge me when I break. I love you for the way you chase away my darkness. And I love you because you make life look so much brighter than I ever thought possible. I'm so in love with you, Jamie Evans. You're the reason this tiny little fucking life of mine is worth living." He inhales deeply and lets it out. "So, do you love me the way I love you?"

Staring into his beautiful, vulnerable eyes, I don't hesitate either. "Yes. God, *yes*. I love you in all of those ways, and all the other ways I'm in love with you, too."

I want to say so much more, but the palpable relief on his face has my heart pounding like a sledgehammer, smashing against my chest and beating a drum in my ears. Saying those words for the very first time was exhilarating. Especially since I didn't have to risk rejection. That was all on Gavin. His own thundering heart beneath my palm tells me just how much courage it took.

He cradles my face with such tenderness, I'm engulfed by a wave of euphoria. Then he kisses me. And it's the first kiss I gave him, our mouths joined and pressing in that wonderful offering of love and affection.

Chest rumbling, he tilts my head and moves his mouth over mine, his lips full and soft as we drink each other in. When he moves us away from the wall, I wind my legs around him as he spins us in circles, my mind dizzy in this magical moment.

Breaking the kiss, he rests his forehead against mine. "Pinch me," he demands on a ragged breath.

Grinning, I slip my hand down to his backside and obey. "Awake?"

"Thank fuck."

"That makes you happy?"

"You have no idea."

"I think I have every idea," I say.

Crashing his mouth to mine, cool water swirls around us as he moves us back into the shade of the ficus. Once we're hidden again, we kiss until we can't breathe. Being in his arms like this, knowing he loves me in all the ways he said, is a truly transcendent experience. One that, just like him, I never thought I'd find.

After a long moment, I lean away enough to see his torn heart again. Touching each piece in turn, I say, "Abandonment … Purpose … Truth … Love."

He sighs heavily, his eyes locking with mine. "I thought I'd worked through all my crap in prison, but there's something inherently different about revealing the pain inside my soul … to someone who actually cares, to someone who wants to know every part of me. The light and the dark."

I cup his jaw, smoothing his short beard beneath my palm. I know what he means. "Did I tell you the last words my mother ever said to me?"

He shakes his head, his eyes never leaving mine.

"She said '*open your heart*'."

"Sounds like good advice."

I nod and touch his tattoo again. "Maybe … maybe these tears don't mean what they once did. Maybe they're torn so your heart is open. So you can allow love and forgiveness inside. So it can heal. So *you* can heal."

Eyes bright with unshed tears, he pulls me into him and buries his face in my neck. His body shudders against mine as I hold him tight. Once he regains control, he trails sweet kisses up my neck and whispers, "Thank you."

I pull back so I can look into his eyes. "Thank *you* for sharing—"

"Oh, my fucking God!" Anika's voice rings out. "You two better not be starkers. Looks like there's been a strip show out here."

Gavin chuckles as I shout to Anika, "It's safe."

A few moments later, she takes the first two steps into the pool, cooling her short-clad legs. Hands on her hips, she rolls her eyes at us.

"There better not be any bodily fluids floating around in here. That rule applies to the backyard, too."

"Morning, Satan's little helper," Gavin says. "Or is it afternoon?"

Anika lets out a snort and smirks at him. "Afternoon, Shawshank."

"Oh, I like that," I say, giving him a cheeky grin, thrilled that the two most important people in my life somehow, so quickly, seem to get each other.

"Don't even think about it," he grumbles, miserably failing to suppress a smile before he plants a quick kiss on my lips.

Anika makes a retching sound before asking, "So, ready for Mum's letter?"

Chapter 39

Gavin

AFTER POSITIONION THE ladder, I climb up to the manhole and slide the cover aside. Taking another few steps up the rungs, I spot the metal safe to my right. Anika had revealed she'd come home early from school one day to find her father up this very ladder. He'd been shocked to find her home, but had told her he'd finished his final cigarette and was locking the rest away as a symbol of his dedication to quitting.

Their father was one secretive, lying arsehole.

The ladder rattles beneath my feet. I glance down at two sets of expectant, impatient eyes.

"Come on, dickwad," Anika demands, "get a fucking move-on."

About the size of a small microwave, I grab the safe, surprised by its substantial weight. Must be one of those fireproof numbers. Straining a little, and trying not to show it, I descend the rungs without the use of my hands. The moment my foot hits the floor, Anika reaches for the safe.

"Forget it," I tell her, pulling back. Damn thing will rip her arms off. "Where do you want it?"

"The breakfast bar," Jamie says.

"Look at him," Anika snickers, "peacocking the shit out of carrying that safe so he can show off his big-boy muscles for you."

There might be a little truth to her observation, but it's not like the damn thing doesn't weigh a fucking tonne. When I set it down on the counter, I shoot her a shit-eating grin. "Seems like you're the one who noticed."

Jamie smirks, her eyes skipping between me and her sister, apparently pleased with this little ribbing thing we've got going on. I don't know where it comes from, only that it feels … normal.

"He doesn't need to peacock for me. I already know he's hot," Jamie says.

Anika scoffs. "Maybe so, but that doesn't make him any less of a dick."

With that, she tries to shove me out of the way so she can get to the safe's keypad. Rooted to the spot like a statue, I quirk another self-satisfied grin at her. "So, you think I'm hot?"

"I never said that."

"You just agreed with your sister," I point out.

"Did you miss the part about being a dick? Now move before I get you in a cuff-hold."

"I'd like to see you try."

"Okay, okay," Jamie mutters, inserting herself between us. "Let's remember what we're doing. Ank, you want to open it?"

Jamie presses her arse against my crotch, forcing me back a step. As Anika punches in the code, I place my hands on Jamie's shoulders, giving them a squeeze when the door swings open.

Anika peers inside, then pulls out a pink envelope. An envelope that's already been opened. When she flips it over, we all read the handwriting on the front.

For Jamie on her 18th birthday.

Jamie's muscles bunch beneath my palms as she takes the letter from Anika.

"Oh my God," Anika says, reaching back into the safe and pulling out a large stack of envelopes bundled together with a thick rubber band.

My heart thuds hard when I recognise my handwriting, and that every single envelope has been torn open.

Jamie's shoulders rise beneath my hands as she sucks in a sharp breath. Placing her mother's letter on the counter, she takes the thick bundle from Anika. After flicking the envelope's edges beneath the pad of her thumb, she flips the bundle over, revealing the prison's address. Turning, she meets my eyes, her own shining with emotion.

"Your letters."

"Yeah," I barely manage to get out, grateful and furious at her father all at once.

She glances at the bundle in her hand, then back at me. "There must be …"

"Fifty-two," I tell her. "One a week for the first year I was locked away."

She bites her lip, the motion sending a single tear down her cheek. I reach out and brush it away, then take the bundle from her hand and turn her toward the pink envelope waiting for her on the counter. "Go read it."

I shoot a glance at Anika, realising she hasn't made a snarky comment since opening the safe. She stares at the envelopes clutched in my hand, then raises her eyes to mine with genuine empathy. In that moment I know all her teasing and snarks are her way of showing she accepts me. I guess that's why I bite back.

Picking up her mother's envelope, Jamie turns to her sister and grabs her hand. "Ready?"

"You sure? It's addressed to you," Anika points out.

Jamie pulls her into her side. "You're her daughter, too. She wrote this when you were little. That's the only reason your name isn't on it. Now, let's go lie on my bed."

As they walk out of the kitchen, Jamie throws me a sad smile before they disappear into the hallway.

I stare at the fifty-two letters still clutched in my hand. With them all together like this, they seem excessive. Obsessive even. But it hadn't felt that way when I'd been writing one a week.

A wave of memories hit me, taking me back to that hard, uncomfortable bed where I sat while I wrote to her. The gut-wrenching heartache, the desperation to be heard and believed by the one and only person I felt mattered. The only person who showed up to court every single day. It didn't matter that she hated me. What mattered was that she cared about her mother. And in my mind, that meant she'd want the right person punished. But the court got it wrong. That's what I tried to convince her of in these letters. But she never responded.

And now I know why.

I set the bundle down on the counter and stare at all the torn tops. That fucking prick read every letter, then kept them from her. And in doing so, he'd kept Jamie in a perpetual state of hatred. It's not the fact that she hated *me* all those years that's infuriating. It's the fact she spent half her life with such a negative, destructive emotion trapped in her soul. Kept there by the arsehole who caused it all. Of course, once he murdered his wife, all sense of integrity irrevocably changed for him. It's clear his mission after that fateful night was to keep what remained of his family intact by staying out of prison.

Exhaling, I turn to the fridge and busy myself by starting on lunch. As I butter bread, then slice tomatoes and cucumbers, I hear various sounds drifting from Jamie's bedroom. A few gasps, murmured words between the sisters, maybe even some sniffling.

After cutting the sandwiches into quarters, I'm arranging them on a large plate when Anika's voice rips through the house.

"No fucking *way!*" It's not an angry exclamation, but one of anguish, surprise and shock.

And now I hear not only sniffling, but actual sobs.

Fuck.

I force myself to grab glasses out of the cupboard and prepare cool drinks. I need to do something to keep from rushing in there to find out what the hell's in that letter to elicit such a response.

Devouring a triangle sandwich in two bites, I pick up another and eat that, my ears straining the entire time. There's plenty of talking, but I can't make out the words, so I lean against the counter, eat another sandwich, and wait.

Thankfully, it's not long before two pairs of bare feet hurry down the hallway. Then they're standing in the kitchen, looking at me, both of their faces wet with tears.

The crazy thing is, neither of them look miserable. They appear kind of happy in a way I can't comprehend. Yet they're both wiping at tears that keep coming, staring at me like I'm the answer to a puzzle I know nothing about.

"I've made lunch, if you—" I cut myself off the moment Jamie breaks away from her sister, walks toward me and takes my hand. Leading me around the breakfast bar, she sits me on a stool.

As she hurries back to the other side and pulls Anika in close, she removes the pink envelope from her pocket, places it on the counter and slides it across to me.

"You need to read it," she says, her voice straining with emotion I can't decipher.

Even though Anika has tears running down her cheeks, she's bouncing on the balls of her feet in anticipation.

I'm desperate to know why, but I hesitate. "It doesn't feel right to read something so personal to you both."

Jamie smiles through her tears. "Trust us, it's personal to you, too."

What the hell does that mean? "Just tell me," I say, my heart thumping in my ears.

Jamie shakes her head. "No. We want you to find out the same way we did."

I little reluctantly, I pick up the envelope, surprised to find my hand shaking. Slowly, I slide the folded letter free and pause, not sure if I'm ready for whatever it contains, for whatever has these two women in front of me so emotional.

"Fuck's sake, dickwad. Just fucking read it," Anika blurts.

Unfolding the pages, with the sisters watching, I read.

My dearest Jamie,

If you're reading this letter, it's because you hate me and have refused to talk to me for far too long. I don't blame you. I'd hate me too. All I can hope is that what I'm about to tell you will open your heart enough to forgive me, even if it's just a little.

I hope by now you've been lucky enough to experience the thrill and heartache of love, so you'll have an understanding of why I had to do what I did.

I fell madly in love with Lachlan Lake when I was 16. My Lockie. He was new at school, finishing his final year. We were instantly attracted to each other. Neither of us had ever felt anything like it. He was my first love in every way. But months later, the ex-girlfriend he left behind at his old school revealed she was pregnant.

We were devastated. They'd been childhood sweethearts who grew apart and broke up before his family moved. Unfortunately, he left something behind. And being the man he was, he knew he had to do the right thing by her and his child. That's the kind of person he is. And part of the reason I love him. So, he went back to her.

I think I cried for a year. But I was never alone. Your father was constantly by my side. You know most of our story. But what you don't know is that I never felt for him the way he wanted me to. There's something to be said for perseverance and an unshakeable love for another. That's what he had for me. And almost a year after Lockie left, I gave in. And along came you.

A gift that changed my heart. Moving the love I had for Lockie to you helped me accept his loss. You became my world, and I learnt that we don't always get what we want, but like the song goes, sometimes we get what we need. And that was you, Jamie.

I loved your father, but I never had that amazing, all consuming, electric charge I had with Lockie. I yearned for it, but accepted it would never be a part of my life, so I embraced what I did have.

Until fate brought Lockie back into my life.

I'd dropped you at a birthday party and went to a grocery store in that area. And there he was, testing avocado after avocado. The moment we saw each other, time became irrelevant. All those feelings were right there between us, as raw and intense as ever.

Your father and I hadn't had an intimate relationship in years, and neither had Lockie and his wife.

We'd both felt trapped with people we loved, but weren't in love with. Yet when we found each other again, our hearts were set free.

There's nothing like it, Jamie. From the bottom of my soul, I hope you find that kind of love. And that you can enjoy it for as long as possible. We lost so much time.

But the world can be a cruel place. I know, because it stung me again for the second time. Though I wonder, if the second time wasn't karma.

Although we did the right thing for us, we were doing the wrong thing by the people we'd built lives with. We began an affair and started to plan how we would end it with our spouses so we could finally be together.

But like I said, life is cruel.

Because the day Lockie planned to tell his wife, was the day she was diagnosed with a terminal illness.

How could he leave her?

He knew he couldn't. I knew he couldn't. As much as it hurt, if he'd left her then, I'd have known he was no longer the man I thought he was. The man I love.

As vile as it may seem to others—to you—we promised each other that we'd eventually be together again. It was only a matter of time.

So, the wait began. But our carelessness had already led to more heartache, and joy.

I was pregnant.

And a terminal illness trumps pregnancy, right? Still, I had a part of Lockie growing inside me, and I couldn't give that up for anything. And he couldn't leave his dying wife.

So, the lie I'd been keeping from your father by omission had to be revealed. Like I said, we hadn't been intimate in years. I had no choice.

I told him the truth, and I think it broke him. But I also think he loved me the way I loved Lockie. Because he forgave me. As long as I promised never to reveal who the baby's father was, as long as I promised never to see Lockie again, he'd forgive me. We'd put it behind us and rebuild our future as a family.

And so, I lied to him again. I promised, knowing I would break that promise the moment the time was right. The moment Lockie was free.

I'm writing this now, before you get home from school. Before I lie to you both again. The girls' nights out were real. For a little while. Then they became the nights Lockie and I would meet, and plan for the tearing apart of my family. For the death of his wife.

She's been gone a month now and we feel the time is right.

Anika's two. So little, so innocent. She needs her real father. She needs the love he can give her. As much as he's tried, your father can't forget the truth of who she is, what she represents. I know you've noticed how disengaged he is with her. Now you know why. At least, if nothing else, you can now make sense of that.

I truly hope you never see this letter. I hope you understand and forgive me the moment I tell you I'm divorcing your father to be with the love of my life. The love that feels like I've waited for forever. I may not deserve it. But I'm taking it. Life is short.

But I know you too well, my daughter. I know you'll be angry. I know you'll say you hate me for destroying our family. I know you'll say I'm selfish. I know you'll say you never want to see me again.

All I can hope is that life shows you something close to what I feel for the man I believe I'm destined to be with, even if the universe kept saying otherwise. Maybe you're still too young, but you're an adult now. And adults leave childish resentment behind and open their hearts to forgiveness.

I will always be your mother, no matter what you decide. So why not let me be part of your life?

I love you, Jamie. Please forgive me. Please open your heart for me.

Love,

Mum.

I'm almost deafened by the pulse thumping in my ears as I put down the pages. Then I lift my eyes to the two women waiting with bated breath. One, the woman I love, the other … my sister.

From the overwhelming mindfuck crashing around in my brain, two thoughts rise above it all.

Anika's my sister.

Anika's Jamie's sister.

My stomach drops to my feet and flops to the floor, my mind swirling so fast, I can't figure out if it means what I hope the fuck it *doesn't* mean.

Recognising my stricken expression, Jamie leans across the counter and clutches my hand in hers. "It's okay. It freaked me out, too. But it's not what you're thinking." My hand grips onto hers, clinging to her words, desperate to understand. She smiles through her tears. "We don't share any parents, Gavin. Anika's the only one who does."

I slump forward and rest my forehead on our entwined hands. The relief coursing through my body weakens my muscles and relaxes the vice around my heart. For a few terrifying seconds, I thought I'd lost her. And I couldn't even comprehend how I'd survive.

"Hey," Anika pipes up, "what am I? Chopped liver?"

"Ank, give him a chance to absorb," Jamie says softly.

Raising my head, I meet my sister's eyes. And suddenly I know why she seems familiar. Although I have my mother's eyes, she has our father's.

And I'm lost. What do I say to this young woman I've only just met? What do I *do?* I have no fucking idea.

Just as uncertain, Anika stares at me. She glances at Jamie, then me again, and I can't read her expression.

"Right, then," she says, slapping an open palm on the counter before pushing past Jamie and coming around to my side to stand in front of me. "Get up."

To my surprise, I grin as I stand. "Bossy little devil."

"Too fucking right," she shoots back.

Then she flies at me, wraps her arms around my middle and grips me like she's drowning. When I glance at Jamie, she's holding a hand over her mouth, her eyes shining with happiness and tears.

Fuck. This is insane, and so fucking amazing.

I wrap my arms around Anika and squeeze her as tightly as she's holding me.

"Hey," I mumble, as if I'm greeting her for the first time. And in a way, I guess I am. I'm meeting the little sister I never knew I had.

"Hey," she replies, her voice breaking on the syllable.

This is just as huge for her as it is for me. She has a brother. And now she knows that the man who withheld his affection from her isn't her father. If nothing else, I hope that knowledge gives her some closure.

After a long moment, the tension leaves her body, and she takes a step back.

"This is so fucking brilliant!" she almost squeals as she swipes the last tears from her face. "Now I can give you even more shit, *bro*. You *have* to put up with me, whether you like it or not."

I chuckle. "You realise that goes both ways, right?"

"Well, shit." She places her hands on her hips and wrinkles her nose, but her eyes remain bright. "I suppose I'll just have to learn to live with that little fact."

She goes back into the kitchen, places the sandwiches on the breakfast bar and scoffs one down.

Overwhelmed, I meet Jamie's eyes, allowing myself the thought that I've always known in my bones. Jamie Evans is connected to me. And had been well before I went to prison.

When she picks up a sandwich, she mouths, *you okay?*

I nod and give her a wink. I should be asking the same of her. There's a lot to digest when it comes to her mother's letter. It's not all about me and Anika being siblings. It's about *why* we're siblings in the first place.

I shift my gaze to Anika. My sister. *That's going to take some getting used to.*

She catches my eye and asks, "So, I've only got tomorrow left, then I'm leaving the next day. I wanna to meet my father before I go."

My jaw clenches, every muscle in my body knotting with tension.

"Maybe we should allow this to sink in for a while," Jamie says, clearly understanding why I'm now a concrete statue.

"Yeah," Anika says, her eyes flicking from me to Jamie. "That's not fucking happening." Her gaze skates back to me, taking in my frozen state. "What? Please tell me he's not dead."

"Actually, I have no idea," I answer, forcing the truth out

through my constricting throat, realising this new development might force me to slice open that wound.

Jamie puts a hand on Anika's shoulder. "Listen, Ank. This is all a lot to take in. Wouldn't it be best to start your new job, get yourself all settled, then think about connecting with your father?"

"No, I don't think that's best at all." She shrugs free of Jamie's hand, the hurt in her eyes palpable. "In fact, I'll look him up and call him right now." Pulling her phone out of her back pocket, she unlocks it.

It takes everything in me not to lean across the counter and swipe it from her hand.

Instead, Jamie does it for me. "Ank, it's not fair to just spring it on him. And there are other issues to consider before you go barging in."

"Like what?"

"Like he might not be the greatest parent," I manage to contribute.

Anika's head snaps toward me, her brows creasing. "He can't be any worse than the man who killed my mother, then let you take the blame for it. Right?"

I let out a long breath. "My father … *our* father, believes I'm guilty. I was your age when it happened, and he turned his back on me."

She stares at me for the longest time. When her eyes flare with anger, I'm sure she's imagining what that might feel like if she were in that position. Empathy and disappointment quickly follow. "Aren't there any decent fucking people left in this world? Is that too much to ask?"

Wrapping an arm around her waist and pulling her in close, Jamie says, "Well, there's two pretty decent people right in front of you. And we're both here for you, okay?"

Anika deflates with a sigh. "I know."

"So, how about you give Gavin and I some time to discuss it?"

"Now?" she asks, hopeful.

"Yes, now."

Satisfied, she grabs her phone, three sandwiches and her drink. "Fine. I'm going out to the pool." She heads toward the hallway, then turns back. "And no fucking around."

Once we hear the sliding door slap shut, Jamie plucks up her mother's letter, along with my bundle, and tilts her head for me to follow.

In her bedroom, she closes the door and sets the letters on her nightstand. I hover at the end of the bed, aware that we're here, alone. And instead of pouncing on her, I'm stuck in a mindfuck of emotions and new information.

Stacking a few pillows against the headboard, she strides over to me, takes my hand and leads me to her side of the bed.

"Get on," she instructs

I do as she says and settle my back against the pillows.

She climbs on, straddles my lap and cups my face as her eyes search mine. "Overwhelmed?" she asks.

"Yeah." Of course she knows exactly how I'm feeling.

Resting one hand on my chest and the other at the back of my neck, she traces soothing circles. Loving me. The way she did when I told her about her mother's last moments alive. I wrap my arms around her and hold her tight. Already, my mind begins to quiet.

"Whatever you need, Gavin, I'm here. If you want me to give you space, if you want to talk, if you just want to be held, I'll do it."

"You're doing exactly what I want. You always do."

After a few minutes of holding each other, I let out a deep sigh and move my hands to her hips, waiting for her to ease back so I can see her eyes. "I guess we should talk. For all we know Anika's looked up his number. She's probably talking to him right now."

"I think what you told her put the brakes on that."

"I don't want to stop her from seeing him," I say honestly. "I just wanted her to know … well, it was all over her face. She thinks he's some sort of solution to the problems she had with your father. She needed to know he's just as capable of hurting her."

Jamie bites her lip, taking in my words. "But Gavin, every single person we care about is capable of hurting us."

I tuck a few stray hairs behind her ear, reluctant to admit she's right.

"Apart from your new little sister, would you like to hear what else I got out of Mum's letter?"

"I always want to hear what you have to say."

Smiling, she slips her fingers into the hair at my nape and massages as she talks.

"What I read was a tragic love story. I know they were deceptive when it came to the people they were married to, but fate had kept them apart. Even so, if everything had gone the way they planned, Mum was right. I would have hated her. There's no way I would have understood."

"I find that very hard to believe. You're full to the brim with understanding."

"Not that sixteen-year-old girl," she says with conviction. "That girl would've seen a selfish woman who cared more about herself than the family she was tearing apart. That girl knew nothing about that kind of love."

"And you think differently now?"

"So differently."

Even though I think I know the answer, my heart cranks up. "Why?"

"Because now I understand how she felt … how they *both* must have felt."

Damn her. Softly and tenderly, I kiss her, putting every ounce of love I have for her behind it. She melts into me, letting me forget everything in this moment.

When I feel like I've thoroughly kissed her, and all that's left is to go further, I pull back, knowing I can't use her love to hide from the inevitable.

Before I can say anything, she asks, "Do you really feel the same way about your father as you did when you were eighteen?"

"Yeah, I think I do," I tell her honestly. "You have to remember, when it comes to him, I've been in a state of arrested development. Nothing's changed in the sixteen years we've spent apart."

"And the letter doesn't make you think something could?"

"Why should it? It doesn't change who he is."

"Are you sure?" she presses.

There's something in her eyes that's imploring me to understand whatever it is she's read into that letter. "Tell me what you're thinking."

"I don't want to put ideas in your head. Maybe I'm the one not seeing things clearly."

"I doubt that. What do you see?"

"It made me think of the trial. When your father testified that you hit him before you left the house. Knowing what we know now …"

She trails off, her gaze studying me intently as her words hit home. "Jesus," I whisper. "The things I said to him about the love of his life … if anyone said the same to me about you, I'd destroy them. But Jamie, I was his fucking *son*, and I was grieving my mother. He made it sound like he'd just met your mum. He didn't take the time to explain anything."

"And would eighteen-year-old you have listened if he had?"

I scoff. "Course not." Funny how it's so damn easy to see other people's problems clearly, but when it comes to my own, I'm totally blind. "That boy only saw a heartless man who couldn't care less about what was left of his family."

"Sounds a lot like the girl I used to be."

I seriously don't think she understands how amazing she is. She's not making me feel like a fool for the boy I'd been back then. She makes me feel like I was a typical teenager, reacting in a completely normal way. Just like her.

"Well …" she says carefully, "now that we know they were deeply in love, imagine what it must have been like for him to know they were finally going to be together … and then, she gets murdered." Her fingers twist in my hair as she thinks. "I mean, what sort of state of mind would *you* be in?"

My grip tightens on her hips. She's right. "If anything happened to you … Christ, I'd be totally fucked. I wouldn't survive."

She rests her forehead on mine. "So, do you see?"

I swallow over the tightness forming in my throat. Because maybe I do. And I really, *really* don't want to. It's easier to continue to hate him, to just leave things as they are. Isn't it?

But even as those thoughts streak through my brain, I remember telling Jamie the same thing when she found out I was innocent. If she'd thought it was easier just to leave things alone, where would I be now? Not here, that's for sure.

"He wouldn't have been able to think straight," she says. "The police would have bombarded him with questions, timelines, the state of your relationship with him. I bet he barely even knew what was going on. He would have been in shock, if not already in the grip of grief. And the police were telling him they had her killer. That his own son was caught in the act. That there was no question of his guilt. How does someone who feels like they've just lost everything deal with that?"

"I'd say they either shut down, or get fucking angry."

"Yeah, I think so, too." She pauses for a moment, gently smoothing down my beard with her palms. "I wonder if, over time, he realised he'd been wrong to turn his back on you? Maybe he still believes you killed her, and even if it changes nothing, isn't it worth hearing what he has to say?"

She's not demanding anything or judging me. She's simply making me think. Only problem there is, she makes me want to do better, to try harder to see things from a different perspective. And I suppose, most importantly, to get over myself.

"When do you think you'll stop being so damn incredible?" I ask.

For the first time, she looks away and mumbles, "I'm not."

Gently touching her jaw, I force her to meet my eyes again. "Yes. You. Are."

Her gaze skitters away. I wait patiently until it returns to mine.

"Jamie, this isn't just a surface level thing for me. The way I feel about you goes deep. All the way down deep. Maybe even scary deep."

"I'm not scared," she whispers. "Not one little bit."

"I am," I confess.

Unease flickers behind her eyes.

"Not of you, J." I take her hand and press it to my chest. "Of what you do to me in here. I'm scared that you can change my heart and mind about things I resolved to *never* change my mind about."

"Are you saying—"

"Anika should meet her father. Before she leaves."

"And you?" she asks, her hand pressing against my chest.

"I don't know."

"What if … I call him, and put him on speaker? He won't know you're listening. You'll be able to hear his voice, his reactions. Maybe that'll give you a bit more insight into who he is now. But Gavin," she rushes on, "you don't have to do that either. It's totally up to you. Whatever you decide, I've got your back."

Chapter 40

Jamie

"DO IT," GAVIN finally says.

I know those two little words weren't easy for him, but I'm so proud of him for taking this small step. Mum's letter held so many revelations, but hidden beneath her words was a deeper truth. That life is short and unpredictable. I'm sure, if something happened to Gavin's father and he never tried, he might get lost in the darkness I know still lives buried deep inside him. But he *is* trying. And that's all I want for him.

After searching for Lachlan Lake in the White Pages on my phone, we discover only two entries for an L Lake in New South Wales. And one of them is a woman.

Wanting to give him some space for this, I climb off his lap. As I punch in the phone number and pace over the floorboards, he sits on the edge of the bed, watching me. Only when he nods do I press the dial icon, then I put it on speaker.

"Hello?" a man answers above a TV blaring in the background.

I lock eyes with Gavin. "Am I speaking to Lachlan Lake?"

"If this's a scammer, you can bugger right off," he says bluntly.

"No, Mr. Lake. I'm Jamie Evans."

The background noise vanishes. Gavin and I stare at each other for at least twenty seconds. "Mr. Lake?"

A long exhale finally comes through the speaker, followed by an emotionally cracked voice. "Mattie's daughter?"

"Yes," I say gently. "Mattie's daughter."

This time we hear a shuddering intake of breath, and another long silence before he says, "Then I guess you'd better call me Lach. What can I do for you, Mattie's daughter?"

I grin. "Well, then, you'd better call me Jamie, since I think you know Mattie had more than one daughter."

"Anika," he murmurs, the brutal pain of that one word filling the room.

"We've only just discovered the truth, so we're still a bit shellshocked." When he's silent again, I jump in. "Thank you, Lach. For not taking her away from me."

Sniffling seeps through the speaker. I don't miss the brief surprise in Gavin's eyes before he shuts it down.

"… all such a mess," Lach says, "I couldn't do that. Mattie always raved about what a wonderful daughter you were. I knew Anika would be raised right by you."

Now it's my turn to strangle back tears. After a moment, I tell him, "She wants to meet you."

This time an actual sob erupts from the phone. Gavin's jaw tenses, and I can't tell if his father's emotions are pissing him off, or getting under his skin in all the right ways.

When the sound of Lach blowing his nose blasts into the room, I almost drop the phone.

"Goddamn it," he grumbles. "I'd love that."

"Okay … And Lach? There's something else."

There's a brief hesitation before he says, "Go on."

My eyes bore into Gavin's. "It's about your son."

Another large sniffle fills the room.

"Did you know he's out of prison?" I ask.

"No, I … no." I get the impression he can't talk at all for a long moment. Finally, he says, "I'd like to say that's good news, but I'm sure you'd disagree."

I tilt my head, watching Gavin's eyes widen a little at the telling statement.

"I don't disagree with you at all, Lach. That's something else that's recently been brought to light. He's innocent."

"I know," he says without hesitation. "It took me a long time to realise that. By then, it was too late to tell him I'd made the biggest mistake of my life." He pauses again, letting muffled sobs reach us. After a nose blow, he asks, "How did you find out?"

"There's a lot we need to talk about. We'd love to meet with you tomorrow." I say, deliberately being evasive about who *we* is. I don't want to promise this man a reunion with his son as well. It's not my call to make.

After arranging a time and place to meet, I hang up, my eyes still locked with Gavin's. For once, I can't read him.

Cautiously, I ask, "What do you think? He seemed sincere."

"Easy to fake it when no one can see your face." He sounds harsh, stuck in his pain.

"True, but do you think he had a reason to fake it? He didn't know you were listening. He doesn't know how I feel about you."

Avoiding my eyes, he runs a hand through his hair and sighs. "I can't just flip a switch and change my mind. It's not that easy."

I step between his spread legs. Tentatively, I place a hand over the fist resting on his thigh, suddenly afraid he might reject my touch. Doubt squeezes my chest. Am I interfering, applying pressure where it's not wanted? How can I know when I've never been in a relationship like this? But I refuse to clam up. All that matters is communication, and if he wants me to stop, he only has to say so.

"You forget, only a few weeks ago, I had to flip that switch," I remind him. "It wasn't easy, but I'm so glad I did."

His fist unfurls and engulfs my hand, his eyes shining with unshed tears. "Yeah. That's because you're amazing."

I give him a lopsided smile. "I seem to remember a pretty incredible person telling me that while he wasn't defending my father for allowing him to go to prison, he understood *why*. If you can understand my father that way, maybe you can understand yours too."

His eyes flick between mine, then he shakes his head. "Well played."

"I'm not trying to play you."

"I know. I just … don't know if I'm ready. It's all so sudden."

"You don't have to do anything you're not ready for. But," I say, brushing the hair back from his forehead, "would you feel like I'm being disloyal to you if I go with Anika tomorrow?"

"Of course not. You should be there to support her."

"That's not the only reason. I want to meet the man my mother was in love with. I want to meet Anika's father. I want to meet *your* father. Because Gavin … he raised you, shaped you into the man I love. He did all that before he fucked up."

Pulling me in tight, his lips graze my ear. "Like I said … fucking amazing."

We spend the rest of the day absorbing all the new information by lazing about in and around the pool. With Gavin deciding to make up his mind in the morning about coming with us tomorrow, I leave that topic alone.

After taking a shower, I head down the hallway to join Gavin and Anika in the kitchen, ready to help with dinner. As I enter, I'm acutely aware of their conversation coming to an abrupt stop. I glance from one to the other, watching as Gavin busies himself at the stove, while Anika quickly opens the cutlery drawer in an obvious effort to avoid my scrutiny. It's unsettling knowing the two people I love have been talking about me, but I refuse to pry.

Sidling up beside Gavin, I nudge his arm. "Anything I can do to help?"

He presses a pair of tongs against each sizzling steak in the pan. "If you want to get the salad out of the fridge, these're almost ready."

As I move away, I let my fingers trail across his back. When I return from the fridge with the large bowl in my hands, he's staring at me, heat in his gaze. I rest my hand on his back and glance at Anika, who's now engrossed in her phone.

Bending his head, he presses his lips to my forehead. "Damn, you smell good," he murmurs as he puts his free arm around me and pulls me into his side.

"I don't know how you can smell anything over these mouthwatering steaks, but I'll take it."

Reluctantly easing away, I try to concentrate on making drinks, but our gazes constantly clash with longing, our bodies brushing against each other for no reason whatsoever.

Anika suddenly announces, "I'm going out with my friends."

I freeze mid-step, my eyes shooting to Gavin before I turn them on my sister. "Sorry?"

She glares at me. "Oh, so *now* you're listening. Apparently, I've been talking to myself for the last couple of minutes."

"You're going out?" Gavin asks with a spark of hope as he plates up the steaks.

"Bet you'd like that, wouldn't you?" Anika answers.

"Yeah, I'd fucking *love* that. How about you, Jamie?"

"I think it'd be great to catch up with some of your friends," I encourage, knowing damn well she's only baiting us because we were too caught up in each other to notice whatever it was she'd been saying.

"Well, there you go," Gavin says, as if it's all decided.

As I carry the drinks over to the dining table and Gavin follows with the steaks, Anika takes a seat. It's not lost on me that this is the first time the table's getting used for its intended purpose.

Because there's an actual family here to use it.

"On second thought," Anika says, stabbing a steak with her fork and plating it, "I think I should stay in. I mean, I only have two more nights here. I really should spend them with my new brother. And my sister, of course." She nods enthusiastically. "Yep, better to spend time with my brother and sister. That's what families do, right?"

"Please don't say that," I implore.

"Say what?" she asks innocently. "That I'm hanging out with my brother and sister? It's the truth. You wouldn't want me to lie, would you?"

I turn to Gavin. "Please make her stop."

With an amused grin, he shrugs. "You've clearly raised a monster."

She gives Gavin's bicep a hard punch. "And don't you forget it, *bro*."

After dinner, Gavin and I relax on the couch in front of the TV while Anika stacks the dishwasher. Before long, his arm curls around my shoulders and I find myself playing with the inseam of his jeans. Two more nights, I tell myself. Two more nights and I'll know what it feels like to have this man between my legs, thrusting—

"Move over," Anika says, a bowl of ice cream in her hand, her butt positioned right between us and coming down fast. I scoot over, Gavin mirroring me just before she wedges herself in. "That's better. You know, I can really do without seeing my brother and sister getting all lovey-dovey with each other. It's kinda ick."

Gavin's amused gaze connects with my horrified one before he turns his attention to Anika. "So, now I not only have to put up with a cheeky woman, I have to put up with a smartarse troublemaker as well?"

Anika whips her head toward him. "Now you're getting it, bro. Welcome to the family." She shovels in a mouthful of ice cream, then bites her lip, apparently deep in thought. "Are you two sure you're not related?" she asks, blinking at me as if it's all so confusing. "I'm not sure I understand."

"Give it a rest, Ank," I beg, knowing it's pointless. She'll milk this for all it's worth.

"But, if you're my sister, and he's my brother, how can you *not* be related?"

"*Half* brother. *Half* sister," I remind her. But as I stare at the beautiful young woman beside me, I know to the core of my heart that she's a whole, vibrant being who can't be divided into a fraction. There's nothing *half* about her.

She shakes her head. "No, I don't like the sound of that. I'm not introducing either of you two as half of anything."

"You won't be introducing us full stop, since I'm going to kill you," I joke so I don't burst into tears at the fact she feels exactly the same way I do.

Her large round eyes glare at me. "Jamie Evans, are you threatening the life of a police officer?"

"I'm threatening the life of my … sister."

She beams. "See, you can't even say *half* sister, can you?"

I let out a defeated breath. "Fine! It doesn't sound right, even in my head."

Utterly pleased with herself, she wriggles further into the couch. "This's gonna be soooo much fun. I mean, parties, right? Can you imagine the look on people's faces when I mention my brother and sister are totally in love? What a conversation starter!"

Exhausted by a highly emotional day, and with another one coming, I finish cleaning my teeth, turn off the ensuite light and plonk on the edge of my mattress. I wish with every bone in my body that Gavin was here, in my bed. I know we made a promise, but I long to feel his arms around me, his body pressed against mine.

Two more nights, I remind myself.

A kaleidoscope of butterflies sweep through my stomach. This rule Anika's enforcing feels like it's building up unrealistic expectations. What if I'm a useless, terrible lover? I have nothing but a bad experience to go on. This waiting is causing insecurities to surface. Insecurities I wouldn't have had time to think about if we'd been able to finish what we started the night we were interrupted.

Sighing, too anxious to sleep yet, I decide to read to help

quiet my mind. Turning to the nightstand, I'm confronted with Gavin's fifty-two letters. I know I shouldn't. I know those letters won't lull me to sleep.

But I can't resist. Only two, I promise myself.

Wiggling the first and last letter free, I run my fingers over the first one he ever wrote. I hate the fact that I'm not the first to read them. They were supposed to be between me and Gavin. My father had no right to violate my privacy.

I scoff. At least he did one thing right. He could have burnt them all. Yet here they are, sixteen years too late, but here, nonetheless.

Dipping my thumb and forefinger into the envelope, I pull out a single sheet of paper folded in half. And hesitate. The boy who wrote these is the man now trying to get some sleep in my spare bedroom. Written in his first year of incarceration, there's a good chance the words on these pages might hurt.

But he didn't try to hide them or ask me not to read them.

Unfolding the sheet of paper, my gaze instantly drops to the bottom of the page.

Where a sketch of disembodied eyes stare at me.

My eyes.

The graphite pencil's attention to every detail makes them unsettlingly *real*, almost mesmerising.

Even more unnerving, is the expression in those eyes. There's no ambiguity whatsoever. I'm staring into the past, into the utter hatred that consumed me back then.

It appears those vile looks I lasered at him in court hadn't gone unnoticed. They'd impacted him. I'm holding the proof.

He'd had seen me.

He'd understood me.

And he'd captured it with astounding precision.

Closing my eyes, I take myself back to those days in the courtroom, the days I spent spewing my hostility at a man who never deserved it. I imagine the reverse, if it were him looking at me like that. It hurts. I'd caused him so much pain without saying a single word.

I stay in that courtroom and try to remember how he'd

looked at me. My stomach drops as I see him in that dock, staring at me. I'd forgotten how he took every opportunity he could to latch his eyes on me. Every time I turned my glare on him, he'd already been watching me.

Pleading. Desperate for me to see the truth no one believed.

Then I remember the only time he spoke in that courtroom. Directly to me.

I didn't do this. I didn't take her from you!

Determined not to cry, I swallow over the lump in my throat, and read.

Jamie,

I know you hate me. And I don't blame you. You believe what everyone does. But they're all wrong.

I did NOT kill your mother.

Whoever did it is still out there.

I'm scared and alone, and it's hard to get my thoughts straight right now.

That night, my dad told me he was going to start a life with your mum. That hurt for reasons you can't understand, but that just makes me human, not a killer.

There's so much you need to know, but I have to get my head straight. I'll keep writing to you. I'll tell you the truth, letter by letter.

But this one is about you and me.

You see, we're connected.

We're both victims of this crime.

And if your mother had lived, we would have met through our parents.

Instead, we've been introduced in a different way. A way that makes you hate me and a way that makes me desperate for you to see the truth.

However it was supposed to happen, we were meant to meet.

I can't get the way you looked at me out of my head. It's right there, at the bottom of this page, a look I need to release through my fingers, or I think I'll go insane.

One day, I hope you'll look at me differently.

Gavin.

Tears flow over my cheeks as I set aside the paper so I don't stain it with my tears.

That boy breaks my heart so hard, my chest literally aches.

And worst of all, if my father had given me these letters at the time, I would have torn them to shreds and flushed them down the toilet. I would never have believed a single word.

Fighting back sobs, I grab tissue after tissue, uselessly wiping my eyes and blowing my nose.

With shuddering breaths, I slip the last letter he wrote from its envelope.

And once again, I'm drawn straight to the bottom of the page where my eyes stare back at me. Only, they're not quite my eyes.

They seem to be what Gavin imagined they might look like if I were happy.

He was close, but since he never once saw me happy, this sketch doesn't have the accuracy he captured in my hateful expression.

Then I read his short letter.

Jamie,

As I've said many times before, I have no idea if you're getting these letters, or if you're reading them and ignoring them, or if you're throwing them away unopened.

I think I've said all I can. And I can only presume you don't believe me.

I won't write to you again. I promise.

Gavin.

P.S.

Beneath the sketch of my inaccurate smiling eyes, he's written …

The thought that one day I'll get to look into your eyes and tell you the truth—and that you'll hear me—helps me to keep working toward being someone you can believe in and trust. It helps me go on. You give me purpose.

Even back then, his soul was beautiful.

And his words devastate me. I bury my face in my pillow and let loose. To think that my hatred helped him survive, gave him something to stay alive for in the hope he could make me see the truth, rips at my soul.

This man. My God. *This man.*

As sobs wrench from my throat, a flash of memory comes to me. Sitting across from him in that Restorative Justice meeting, he wanted to know if I got his letters. When I'd told him no, something flickered in his eyes. Later, he'd told me he'd been determined to make me hear the truth in that meeting, but when he'd seen the rawness of my pain, he'd done something else.

That must have killed him. All those years, hoping against hope that he'd finally be able to tell me what really happened, and he gave up that opportunity. *For me.* He gave up his purpose for me. He'd wanted me to feel like I had closure by making me believe he'd finally taken responsibility for my mother's death. But what I hadn't realised, was that he'd given up a piece of his soul to do it.

I'm not sure how long I cry, but at some point, a comforting hand rubs my back. Surprised, I turn to find Anika sitting on the bed beside me.

As I sit up, she hands me a crumpled wad of tissues. Thankful, I wipe my puffy face.

"What is it?" she asks in possibly the softest voice I've ever heard her use.

I shake my head and smile, indicating the open sheets of paper on the other side of the bed. "I only read two … they're more than enough to confirm what an incredible man he is. Has always been."

Plucking up his final letter, I hand it to her, calming down as I watch her read.

"Well, fuck," she says, her own eyes shining. Then she looks down at the page again, her fingers delicately brushing over the eyes staring at us. "They're like … Wow. I didn't know he could draw."

"Yeah, neither did I."

Anika pulls me to my feet, gathers the letters and places them on the nightstand. Standing there, I watch as she takes my tear-soaked pillow and leans it against the wall, re-arranges the others on the bed, then pulls the covers back.

"Get in. You're not sleeping alone tonight."

Exhausted, I do as I'm told. Before I can say a word, she pulls the covers over me, snaps off the lamp and leaves, shutting the door behind her.

Figuring she's gone to get her own pillow, I close my raw eyes and try to relax while I wait for her to return.

A few minutes later, the door opens and closes. Footfalls stride across the floorboards, then the mattress wobbles as she gets in and wriggles closer.

Really close.

So close that an arm snakes over my waist and a large, warm hand comes to rest over my heart.

"I hear you need to be held," Gavin whispers close to my ear.

I'm sure my heart swells to the size of Phar Lap's. Although I'd thought I was done crying, my tear ducts have other ideas.

"Can I slobber on you again?" I murmur.

"I'd love that."

Turning to face him, I rest my head in the crook of his shoulder and fist my hand in his t-shirt. He pulls me in tight, tangling his fingers in my hair, his lips and nose nuzzling the top of my head. Absorbing nourishment from the touch of our bodies, we remain silent for a long time.

"Thank you," I finally whisper. "Anika?"

"Yeah. She told me you'd read some of my letters, and that I'd better get in here and cuddle the shit out of you … since it's my fault you're upset."

"It's not your fault."

"Hmm. You sure about that?"

"Okay, it's totally your fault. For being … *you*. Amazing, incredible, wonderful … there aren't enough words."

"And that brings you to tears?"

"Not sad tears," I explain, letting my fist relax so I can feel his heartbeat against my palm. "You just … overwhelm me."

"Is that another one of your exceptional compliments?"

Lifting my head from his shoulder, I find the shine of his eyes in the dark. "Yes, it absolutely is. And speaking of compliments, why didn't you tell me you were an artist? From what I saw, you're brilliant."

He shakes his head. "I'm no artist. Pathetic as it is, I've only ever drawn your eyes."

"I think you're the exact opposite of pathetic." I cup his face, tenderly tracing his ear with my fingertips. Swallowing over the lump rising in my throat, I choke out, "You're my Shawshank."

A soft chuckle rumbles through his chest. "Done with the compliments, then?"

"That *is* a compliment."

"I don't know if being referred to as a prison qualifies."

"I'm not talking about the *place*, I'm talking about the heart of that story … *hope*. My beautiful man full of hope."

He lets out a long breath, and when he draws in another, I feel the hitch through his entire body. "Christ, woman. I don't know what to say to that," he murmurs, "so I'm just going to kiss you."

And he does. One of those loving kisses that promises safety and comfort. I sink into him, this contact between us becoming familiar, yet no less potent. Then he slips his knee between my thighs, and I snuggle right up against him, heat flooding my body as reality seeps in. He's in my bed, holding me, kissing me and, from the hard length pressing against me, most definitely wanting me.

And I can't get close enough.

Just as I'm about to slip my hand beneath his t-shirt, he breaks the kiss and presses his lips to my forehead.

"I had an interesting conversation with Anika earlier," he says, trailing his hand down to my backside and squeezing.

"Oh? When I came into the kitchen and you both stopped talking?"

His lips smile against my skin. "Yeah. Shed a light on why she's enforced this torturous rule on us. She doesn't want to hear her *mother* having sex."

"I don't under—"

"You, Jamie. *You.*" He reaches between us and holds my hand. "She told me how lucky she was, that not many kids who lose their mothers get an instant replacement. She knows how hard you worked to make her feel special; how much of your life you sacrificed for her. Just like me, she knows how extraordinary you are."

"She said that?" I choke out.

"She did. She also said your mother may have given birth to her, but you were the one who raised her, who'll be there on her wedding day, who'll hold her children as if they're your grandbabies."

I squeeze his hand, not sure how much more my heart can take.

"So, if you think about it, her rule's probably valid. No one wants to hear their mother having sex, right?"

I shake my head. "She wasn't just being a pain the arse."

"Oh, I'm sure there's that, too."

I huff out a laugh, my throat loosening. "I never realised she thought of me that way."

"Feel good?"

Knowing Anika appreciates what I did for her, that she feels like she has a mother, creates a deep, warm pool inside me. "I was never sure if I'd screwed everything up when it came to raising her."

"You didn't screw up," he says softly. "She's her own person.

A little spitfire who doesn't take shit from anyone. She has a light in her that you didn't try to extinguish, but nurtured. And it's pretty obvious that made her quite a handful."

I chuckle and nod, and suddenly, I want to let him in and reveal a little piece of me no one knows. "After Mum's funeral, Dad refused to take me to her grave. So, once a month I'd sneak away with Anika and take the bus there. I struggled with the idea that it might not be the best place for a kid, but I couldn't stand the thought of hiding our mother from her. She was so little, I knew Mum would fade from her memory fast. I felt like she deserved to have both her daughters remember her. So, I'd put down a blanket on Mum's grave, and we'd have a picnic. Each time I took her there, I'd tell her different stories about our mother. I think those memories helped make Mum a real person for her, because as Anika got older, she'd remind *me* of some silly thing our mother had done, as if it was her own memory. When that started happening, it made me feel less alone too."

As his fingertips sweep tendrils of hair behind my ear, he stares at me with what I think is adoration.

"J, you're the most amazing person I've ever known. I only wish I knew a billion people so you'd understand how much I mean that. I know, coming from me, it doesn't hold much weight."

My heart melts for this man. "It means everything," I whisper, "*because* it's coming from you."

He kisses me, soft and sweet, with so much meaning behind it, no words are necessary.

"Come on," he eventually says. "Let's get some sleep."

Turning me away, he spoons me, his hand resting over my heart where I hold it tight. I wiggle around a little to get comfy, then have to wiggle a little more so his erection nestles into the cleavage of my butt cheeks. "Is that going to be there all night?"

"I'd say so, since I'm living one of my favourite fantasies."

I give my backside another cheeky wiggle. "This is a fantasy?"

"Not that," he grumbles. "Having a particular woman in bed, spooning her while we fall asleep. That's what I craved the most, what I thought would forever be a just a dream."

I squeeze my eyes shut and take a deep breath.

"Don't say anything. Just know how happy this makes me. How happy *you* make me." He kisses my shoulder, then lays his head behind mine. "Goodnight, J."

Feeling exactly the same way, I smile into the darkness and whisper, "Goodnight, Shawshank."

Waking on my back, the first thing I notice is an arm angled across my torso and a large, warm hand cupping my breast. I open my eyes and look down, loving the way the evident strength in that hand and arm seem to own my body, yet at the same time, touch me so tenderly.

Waking on my back, the first thing I notice is an arm angled across my torso and a large, warm hand cupping my breast. I open my eyes and look down, loving the way the strength in that hand and arm seem to own my body, yet at the same time, touch me so tenderly.

Shifting my line of sight to the side, I find him asleep, lying on his stomach, face twisted toward me, lips pressed to my bare shoulder. With his dishevelled hair and relaxed features, he reminds me of the boy in that courtroom. Back then, my hatred made me see nothing but a monster. Now, all I see is a loving, gorgeous man. Inside and out.

Amazing what a different perspective can do.

What the heart can do.

While I gaze at the man I'm madly in love with, I'm overcome with the knowledge that, for the first time in my life, I haven't slept alone.

Letting my gaze drift lower, I study his broad shoulders and the muscles defined by the t-shirt twisted tight across his back.

I want to roll against him, wake him up, feel his weight on

me and make lazy love with him. Unfortunately, it's not to be. Not yet. Because Anika doesn't want to hear her *mother* that way.

Grinning, I slip out from under his arm, grab my robe and head to the kitchen, shocked to find Anika already up and sipping from a mug at the breakfast bar.

"Hey," I mumble as I make a beeline for the coffee machine. After I get it going, I turn back to my sister. "I can't believe they assigned you to Gosford. That's two hours away. I'm hardly ever going to see you."

Anika waves a dismissive hand at me. "I have a feeling you can keep yourself occupied. Soooo … how was it?"

I grab my coffee and take a sip. "How was what?"

She rolls her eyes as if I'm the stupidest person in the world. "Sleeping with him, of course."

"Oh. It was nice."

"Nice?" she barks. "Well, fuck. That's a letdown."

I frown. "Why would sleeping beside Gavin be a letdown?"

"*Beside* him?"

"What are you on about? You're the one who sent him in to hold me. And thank you for that, by the way. It was exactly what I needed."

She comes around the breakfast bar and stands right in front of me, her face a mask of confusion. "Are you saying you didn't fuck?"

I flinch at how crude that sounds coming from her mouth. When Gavin says it, somehow it has me melting. Then the implication of what she's saying hits me. "We promised we wouldn't."

"Yeah, and last night, when I told him you needed him, I said he could forget about the no-sex rule."

I blink at her, astonished. Gavin could have had sex with me last night, but chose not to. He'd done something else instead. Something more profound. He'd shown me love and support when I was in a vulnerable place. And even though his body clearly wanted to, he hadn't taken advantage of my emotional state. He'd soothed it.

Can he get any more perfect?

Anika studies me a moment before rolling her eyes. Again. "So, you're telling me, I put headphones on and blasted my ears for hours for no reason?"

"He just held me, and we went to sleep."

"Wow," she says, shaking her head, a surprisingly wistful look on her face. "Well, he's either not that into you … or he loves the fuck out of you. No telling which one it is, of course."

I smile at her. And she grins back, her eyes shining. Taking the mug, she places it on the counter, then hugs me.

"I'm so happy for you," she says. "He really is a pretty great guy."

"Yeah," I murmur. "He really is."

Chapter 41

Gavin

AFTER THE BEST night's sleep I've ever had, I wake up thoroughly refreshed. A little disappointed that Jamie isn't beside me, I roll onto my back and stare at the ceiling. I could've made love to her last night, but there are more important things to a relationship than sex. What she needed was comfort, so that's what I gave her. And I don't regret it for a second.

When the sound of the sisters' chatter reaches my ears, my mouth curves into a smile. Yesterday when I woke, I was a family of one. Me. Alone. For sixteen years. Now I have a new addition.

With a sense of hope, my mood light, I decide I'll go with the girls—*my* girls—today. I'll keep my distance, observe, and make a decision about my father when I feel ready.

Before I know it, Jamie's driving and Anika's in the back seat, straining against her seatbelt the whole way as we head to the park where my sister will meet her father for the first time.

Surprising myself, and hoping it'll give Anika a more rounded picture of the man, I recount some amusing stories from my childhood that include my father. When the memories remind me of the pretty great dad he'd been until that fateful night, I hide the hurt they stir up.

By the time Jamie finds a parking spot, the temperature has

already roared into the mid-thirties. I thought I might be able to watch their meeting from the safety of the car, but that's not happening.

We all get out, Jamie coming around to take my hand in hers as we scan the beautiful park. No playground exists here. Just a lovely expanse of neatly kept lawns with leafy English oaks and liquid ambers scattered throughout, providing much needed shade amongst the Australian natives. Park benches rest beneath the dense canopies, and in the distance, I spot my father waiting on one. He's far enough away that his features aren't clear, but I know it's him.

I catch Anika's eye and tilt my head toward him. "He's here."

She snaps her head in his direction, and grabs my upper arm, her fingers curling around it too tight. "Are you coming?"

"I'm not sure yet. Either way, you should see him first. This is about you, not me." Jamie's hand squeezes mine and I squeeze back.

Anika lets out a little scoff. "Why the fuck am I so nervous?"

"You'll be fine," Jamie reassures her.

"*Me?* You're coming too."

"You should meet him one-on-one, Ank. Like Gavin said, this is about you. It's a huge moment for you both. I'll meet him when you're ready."

"Fuck that. I need you, Jamie. Like, *really* need you, okay? Please."

Jamie gives me another squeeze, releases me and holds her hand out to her sister. "Are you sure?"

Anika grabs it like a life preserver and nods.

I smile and give Jamie a wink. Tough little Anika needs her mum for this. It doesn't surprise me one little bit. I tilt my head in the opposite direction. "I'll wait over there."

"Okay." Jamie turns to Anika. "You ready?"

Anika takes a deep breath. "Ready."

Instead of heading off to the park bench I spotted under a dense liquid amber, I find my feet rooted to the parking lot's hot bitumen, watching my girls, hand-in-hand, head toward the man I vowed I'd never forgive, let alone see again.

As they grow closer, my father stands and walks toward them. I notice his gait no longer has that bounce I once knew. He doesn't seem as tall, his shoulders slightly rounded, and even from here I can see his dirty blond hair is several shades lighter.

When they're only ten metres or so apart, his steps falter. I can't be sure from this distance, but I swear it looks like utter shock on his face.

And then his knees give out.

I tense as Jamie and Anika race to his side, their hands on him, supporting him.

Is he having a fucking heart attack?

My legs want to run toward them, but my heart keeps me frozen. What if he dies right here and now? What if he's gone before I even make a decision about whether I want to talk to him or not?

Shaking, I take a few steps forward. Then stop. Jamie and Anika help him to his feet and guide him back to the park bench. They sit on either side of him, both holding a hand each. Since no one's frantically pulling their phones out and calling for help, I gather he's in no danger of keeling over.

Turning my back on them, I head to the kiosk across the road, my mouth dry from not only the heat, but the shot of adrenalin that's ebbing from my system.

With an ice-cold can of Coke in hand, I traipse back across the scorching parking lot and take a seat under the shade of a liquid amber. As I watch, the party of three rise and head off in the opposite direction.

After I open the can and take a long drink, a notification pings on my phone.

JAMIE:
Going for a walk. Once we're out of sight, I'll tell him you're here. I'll call you when we're heading back so you can make a decision. I love you. J.

I concentrate on the positive. My first message from Jamie Evans telling me she loves me. In writing. I grin like a fool, my heart bouncing happily around in my chest.

Then I go over the rest of the message. Once again, she's giving me an out. I can run and hide when I know they're coming back, or I can sit here and face him.

I've already made my decision. The moment he fell to his knees brought all the clarity I needed. I know, deep down, I couldn't live with myself if he died before I hear what he has to say. I'm under no delusion that his excuses will allow me to forgive him, but I won't deny him the chance to put them forward.

Staring at my phone as the time ticks by, I don't see a single thing that scrolls past on the screen. When it vibrates and rings in my hand, I almost drop the damn thing. But that's not what has my heart knocking hard against my chest. It's Jamie. Which means they're heading back.

"Hey, gorgeous," I answer.

"Hey. I'm hanging back so they can't hear me, but you'll see us in about five minutes."

"Okay. I'll be here."

"You will?" she asks, the hope in her voice obvious.

"No promises on what the outcome might be, but I'll try."

"I love you," she says so easily, so openly, as if she's been saying it for years.

"That's one of the main reason I'm doing this."

She's silent for a long moment before she says, "There must be a lot of good in the man if Mum was willing to break apart our family to be with him. Just … try to remember her last words. Open your heart."

"I'll try, J. I really will." And because of her, I mean it.

It's not long before the trio emerge through the trees. When they make their way back to the seat where my father waited earlier, he glances my way, but I don't acknowledge him. After giving Jamie a hug, he holds Anika tighter, and she returns his embrace with enthusiasm.

Good for her.

As the sisters take a seat, my father heads my way.

I don't want to watch him approach. I don't want to look at his face. So, I lean forward, rest my elbows on my knees, and stare at my phone like it's the most fascinating thing in the world. That doesn't stop my heart from crashing against my sternum, my brain tearing in two. Do I keep my distance to protect myself? Or do I put my trust in him and risk that he might betray me again? I'm not sure I could survive that sort of crushing blow a second time.

Too soon I hear footsteps in the grass, then he takes a seat beside me. The silence stretches out as my heart pounds and my hands tremble. Instead of looking at him, I raise my head and stare into the distance at the two most important people in my life. I feel his eyes on me, but I can't bring myself to pull my gaze from my girls. They ground me, stabilise me. Even so, my body's a statue, frozen between what might never be and everything that might be.

After what seems like an eternity, my father says, "Anika's not backward in coming forward, is she?"

Smart. Neutral ground. Probably a good idea. Heart thundering so hard I'm surprised it hasn't scared the birds from the branches above us, I finally open my mouth. "No, she's certainly not."

More silence. I wonder if he's waiting for me to elaborate, or if he's just as lost for words as I am.

"She was angry at me at first," he offers.

"Why's that?" I still can't bring myself to look at him, but I'm finding strength as my gaze connects with Jamie's. Even across this vast distance, I know she's filled with hope.

"Because I didn't claim her as my daughter at the time," he explains.

"And what did you tell her?"

"I told her I'd considered it, but it wasn't the right thing to do. She already had a family. She'd just lost her mother. How would ripping her from the only life she knew, the people she loved, be any good for her? So, I put my selfishness aside. I'm not sure if that decision was the right one or not. She told me how cold Brian Evans was to her, and now we know I left my daughter in the care of a killer. The man who murdered the love of my life … the man who let you take the fall."

Without thinking, I turn my head and look at him. Not for long, just a glance. Enough to see tears rolling down his face as he stares back.

"It seems, though," he continues, "she has a sister whose heart's big enough to make up for the love Evans refused to give her. That's Mattie all over." He takes a deep breath. "Christ, I can see parts of Mattie in Anika, but Jamie … it's like seeing a ghost. For a moment there, when I first saw her, I thought she *was* my Matilda."

"Not the eyes," I say, wanting him to know she's not his dead lover's ghost. She's very much alive, and she's mine.

"Sorry?"

"They look similar. But not the eyes."

"How do you know?"

"Because I'll never forget her mother's eyes … how they looked when I tried to comfort her … how they looked when she died."

I know he's watching me, but I can't find it in myself to look back. I understand all too well what my words must mean to him. I know what they meant to Jamie, and they both loved Matilda.

"Fuck," I hear him mumble, then sniff, and I know that if I look at him, I'll lose it. As he tries to get control of himself, I remain stuck in tough-guy, closed-off mode.

"Anika told me," he begins in a voice heavy with emotion, "it's not too late to start a relationship with her. *Better late than never*, she said. I agree. But I'd love to know what your thoughts are on that."

I'm not ready. I don't know if I ever will be, so I deflect. "Yeah, she's right. For thirty odd years I didn't have a sister. Now I've got one for the rest of my life."

He doesn't pressure me, and I don't glance at him to see if he's disappointed in my answer. Looking might mean I care.

When the silence descends again, I realise he's initiated

every conversation. Maybe that's for the best. I'm not sure what horror show might come out of my mouth if I go first.

"Can't take your eyes off her, can you, Son?"

I tense at his use of that word. He has no right to use it when addressing me. Grinding my teeth, I hold back the anger pushing its way up my throat. "Nope."

"It's obvious you love her."

"Yeah, I love her. I love her so much it fucking hurts." Jesus, of all people, why am I telling him?

"Then you understand?"

The hairs on my scalp prickle. *Fuck*. He has me there. If something happened to Jamie, I'd lose my mind.

"But you stayed with Mum." I curse myself the moment the words are out of my mouth. In a way, that statement feels like I'm giving him the respect Jamie's mother gave him. And I really don't want to.

"Obligation overrode love. My heart still aches for every moment I wasn't with Matilda. But I'll never regret being there for your mother. I'll never regret being your father, Gavin. I can't imagine a life where I wasn't there for every moment of your childhood. Of course, I always thought I'd eventually be with Mattie, that it was just a matter of time. But that time was stolen. And I ended up losing you both."

We're silent again. He's waiting for a response, but I simply don't have one. Yes, his time with the woman he loved was stolen, but the time he could have spent being my father wasn't. He threw that away.

"I'm so glad you're able to love deeply … after what you've been through."

"Yeah," I admit.

"So, imagine being told I killed Jamie. That there's irrefutable proof. Imagine I took her from you. Forever."

Anger buzzes right beneath the surface my skin. *How fucking* dare *he?*

I rise, crushing the empty Coke can and slam it into the bin a few feet away. Then I turn and finally look him dead in the eye. "Except I *didn't* kill anyone. And you never bothered to ask."

Utter shame stares back at me, but he doesn't look away, doesn't hide from me.

So I don't hide from him. I let him see my rage, see how much I despise him for abandoning me, for believing the boy he raised was killer.

Then, before I do something stupid, I walk away.

Halfway to Jamie's car, I realise she has the keys. For a second, I think I'll just keep walking, but the blood flying through my veins, the hurt surging through my heart, has other ideas.

I turn back.

He's standing beside the park bench, staring at me, tears spilling down his fucking cheeks. I stalk toward him, every muscle in my body coiled tight, ready to release what I've kept locked inside. If it didn't mean going back to prison, if it didn't mean hurting Jamie, I'd beat him to a fucking pulp.

But sometimes, words hurt more.

I march right up to him, slam my palms into his chest and shove. "I fucking hate you!"

The idiot doesn't flinch. He steps right back into my space. I shove him again. "I hate you!"

He nods, steps toward me again. "I can't hear you, Son."

The fuck?

Rage throbs in my ears as I shove him again. "I hate you!"

He steps right back for more. "Why?"

"You left me! Left me like I was a piece of shit, like I meant nothing to you. Like you didn't know me. You let those fucking cops pick over what was left of my carcass, like I was nothing more than roadkill. My only parent, and you turned your back on me when I needed you most, when I needed you to stand up and tell them all that I could never do what they accused me of. I needed you at that useless lawyer's office. I needed you in that courtroom. I needed you to explain the context of our fight, not testify like it was obvious I killed her!"

I pause to catch my breath, my eyes on him, watching every emotion flit across his fucking face.

"You're right," he agrees, choking on the words. "And it's the biggest regret of my life. I monumentally fucked up. I know I did, Son. There's no doubt about it. And I've been living with that regret, that heartache, for as long as you've been hating me."

I take in his face, all the sorrow etched there. His cheeks seem hollow, the lines around his eyes and across his forehead deeper, multiplying. I notice now that his dirty blond hair isn't a lighter colour, but mostly grey, aging like the rest of him.

Although his eyes look the same, there's deep regret right at the surface. He's not lying.

"I know it's an astronomical thing to ask, but it would mean everything to have a relationship with you. Any sort of relationship. I miss you so much, Son."

Then, to my shock, he hugs me. Hard.

I'm so stunned, I stand frozen, my arms like concrete blocks. "I hate you," I tell him, but there's no hiding the lack of conviction behind those words. Because now I'm thinking about Jamie, about the hate she had for me, how it lived in her heart, hurting her.

My father's arms only tighten further. "I love you, Gavin. Please … please forgive me."

The last words Jamie's mother said to her rush at me. *Open your heart.*

My brain takes a crowbar to the lock I've kept on all the positive memories I'd buried. The encouragement and support he gave me in everything I did as a kid and a teenager. The affection he showed me that I never saw any other father show my friends. The pride in his eyes when I was offered a spot in three professional soccer teams. The way he treated and looked after my mother when he'd always been in love with someone else. I release everything I've kept suppressed so I could hold onto the one time he let me down.

The concrete encasing my arms shatters, and before I know it, I'm wrapping them around him, holding my father while he embraces me the way I needed to be held the night we were torn apart. As I feel the tension leave his body, a quiet sob escapes his throat.

"I need time," I say, my own throat painfully tight. "But I'll try. On my terms."

"Anything you want, Son. Anything."

After a few heartfelt pats on the back, we release each other. Swiping at his tears, he says, "So much time … wasted because of me. Giving me more … It means everything."

As we take a seat again, Jamie and Anika stand and wave. At first, I think they're coming over, but after I raise my hand in return, they saunter off for another walk.

"I'm proud of you, of the man you've become," my father says.

"How can you be proud of someone you don't know?"

"What I do know, is how Jamie talks about you, how her whole face lights up when she does so. Since she seems like a lovely, bright young lady, I trust her judgement."

My heart stills in my chest as I look at him. "She was talking about me?"

He chuckles. "Oh, yeah. And it wasn't just what she was saying, it was the *way* she was saying it."

For the first time since seeing him again, I grin. "Yeah?"

"Yeah. Looks like you light up the same way she does."

We chat for another half an hour, keeping the topics light and casual, trying to find a way into reconnecting. The more we talk, the easier it gets, though I'm still not in a place where we can discuss the things that really matter. But I feel that, as we get to know each other again, it'll happen down the track. After all, we can't have a meaningful relationship without discussing the hard stuff.

When Jamie and Anika return, I wonder who else my father has in his life now. From the way his eyes water as all three of us put our numbers in his phone, I'm guessing he's not close with too many people. I suppose I'd be overwhelmed, too. Reconnecting with him has been an emotional roller coaster. I can't imagine what it must be like to deal with three of us at once.

As we say goodbye, he hugs Jamie and Anika, then turns to

me. I extend my hand, and he grabs it, pulling me into a man-hug while he promises to seem me soon.

Once we pile into the car and drive away, I let my head flop against the headrest as a wave of fatigue overcomes me.

"Well, holy shit," Anika says, a finger poking at my shoulder. "It looked like you were about to kill him. For a second there, I thought I was gonna have to arrest my brother. Can you imagine if—"

"Anika. For once, shut the hell up," Jamie tells her firmly.

"It's okay." I turn and glance at my sister. "So, how was it for you?"

She's quiet for a long moment before she says, "Weird. Sad. And kinda brilliant. I think I like him already. I mean, I don't know him yet, but there's a connection there." She lets out a little frustrated huff. "Now I don't want to move so far away. He said he'd come visit in a couple of weeks, though. So that's something."

"I'm glad," I tell her, meaning it. She's starting from scratch with him, which isn't easy in itself, but it's a hell of a lot easier than having the history I have with the man.

Her hand comes down on my shoulder and squeezes. Surprised, I meet her eyes. "He's really bummed about what happened with you. Like, I mean, *really* sorry."

"Yeah, I know." I turn and face front again, and as I do, I pat her hand a couple of times. It feels good when she gives my shoulder another squeeze, like we're bonding over this strange moment in both our lives.

As my lips twitch with the urge to smile, Jamie places her hand on top of mine. Something about that simple gesture gets me out of my own head and makes me realise how fucking lucky I am. Sitting here in a car with the woman I love and my long-lost sister. I'm completely present in this moment. I'm not in a cell, not in a prison. I'm out on a sunny day, doing family stuff I never dreamed I'd do.

And I feel it in my soul. This is happiness.

I turn my hand in Jamie's until our palms touch and our fingers entwine. As she pulls to a stop at a set of traffic lights,

I stare into her beautiful, sparkling eyes.

Thank you, I mouth.

She blinks. Fast. And I know she's holding back happy tears. Her eyes flash a gorgeous shade of emerald, but it's not the colour I crave. It's the love I see there. Clear and true, not a speck of doubt to be found amongst the green and copper of those incredible irises I know so well.

I bring her hand to my mouth and kiss the back of it.

Behind us, our sister retches.

And I laugh.

"What's so funny?" Anika pipes up, her head appearing by my shoulder.

"You," I tell her. "The idea that you think you'd be able to arrest me, an innocent man, who happens to be your long-lost brother, for killing our long-lost father."

She chuckles. "I would've done it if you'd gone too far."

"As if Satan's little helper could physically overpower me."

"Oh, I could. I'm a goddamn machine when it comes to bringing down big brutes like you."

I grin at her. "Talk about tickets."

"Fuck off. When we get home, I'm taking you down," she threatens.

"Yeah, we'll see."

As Jamie laughs beside me, Anika punches my arm. Hard.

But I don't feel any pain. All I feel is the incredible sensation of belonging.

Chapter 42

Jamie

AS THE SUN sinks low in the sky, I sit on a lounger by the pool, my stomach aching from laughing too long and hard as I watch Gavin and my sister act out an arrest. When she fails yet again to secure his hands behind his back, they regroup, and I take the opportunity to sip the passionfruit cocktail Anika made me earlier.

Watching them get along like they've always known each other makes my heart feel like it's filled with helium. Apart from when I was a child with no responsibilities, I don't think I've ever felt this light and happy.

Readying for another try, Gavin shifts his attention to me, his face breaking out in a smile so bright it melts my insides.

While he's distracted, Anika sweeps his feet out from beneath him and crashes him to the grass. She's on his back in an instant, yanking his arms behind him and securing his wrists. Not once does he take his eyes off me.

"Bro, you're under arrest!" she shrieks in triumph.

"Fine," he grumbles, "you got me. Eventually."

As Anika releases him, he gives me a wink. Unaware she's won by distraction, my sister performs a victory dance, arms in the air, bouncing on her feet as she spins around.

Taking her completely off guard, Gavin throws her over his shoulder. She squeals and pummels his back as he walks straight to the deep end of the pool and tosses her in.

Giggling, knowing we all needed this release after the tension of the day, I join him at the end of the pool and wait for Anika to surface. She doesn't.

Gavin grips my shoulder, his smile dropping. "Shit. Is she—"

"Don't fall for it," I tell him. "She wants you to jump in and save her. Did it to me all the time when she was a kid."

A huge gasp sounds at our feet when Anika breaks the surface.

"Arseholes," she shouts, splashing water at us. "I'm drowning here and you two are making goo-goo eyes at each other? Real nice!"

"Did you hear something?" Gavin asks me, his eyes bright and amused again.

"Nope."

More water splashes up at us, this time making it to our faces.

Anika grips the side of the pool and stretches her hand out to Gavin. "Help me out, dickwad."

Chuckling, he glances at me. "Look at that. The sadistic one thinks I'm a fool." Then he plants a kiss to my forehead and saunters off inside.

"Prick!" Anika yells at his back. Smirking, she holds her hand out to me.

"Ha! I'm not a fool either." I return to the sunlounge and sip at my cocktail, watching Anika swim to the shallow end and get out. She strides over to me and whips her head back and forth, spraying me with water. "Ahhh," I sigh, "that's so refreshing."

Scoffing, she plonks herself down on the end of my lounger. "I can't believe tonight's my last night. I'm gonna miss this." She reaches for my half-finished cocktail, and I pass it to her. "Don't get me wrong, I'm looking forward to starting my career. But I want to get to know Gavin more. And Lach." She sucks down half my cocktail in one long sip. "I just … everything's changed so fast. I feel like this black cloud that's followed me around all my life has been blown away. Never having to wonder again why Dad couldn't stand me, that it didn't have anything to do with me at all, is weird. But getting a second chance to have a dad, that's just … wow."

"I'm happy for you, Ank." I don't mention the twinge of jealousy in my heart. She gets to start over with a brand-new father. A father who loved our mother deeply. I can't deny my envy. She was conceived by soul mates. I was conceived by deceit, my father the man who took our mother from us. But I would never deny Anika the happiness she deserves.

Finishing my cocktail, she hands it back, her gaze intense. "I'm happy for you, too. He really loves you."

A wonderful warmth settles in my belly. "Yeah, he does."

"Well, don't be too certain about it or anything," she says with a cheeky grin.

"That's just it, though, Ank. There're no guessing games with him. He shows me how he feels, and he *tells* me. He's so open about it. About everything. I love that."

I don't miss the brief shadow that passes across her face. "Just … be careful thinking like that. Everyone has secrets. Look at Mum and Dad."

She's not wrong, but I don't believe for a minute that Gavin's keeping anything from me. That's not who he is.

When I head inside and walk past the guest bedroom, I hear music coming from behind the closed door. I've noticed he shuts himself away sometimes, but I haven't been bold enough to ask what he's doing in there. As I wash the delicate cocktail glass in the kitchen, Anika's words ring in my ears. *Everyone has secrets.*

The thought prickles my skin. I haven't told Gavin about my two dates with Reid, but really, there's nothing to tell. I didn't even let him kiss me. I also haven't told him about my promise to Pete. By keeping that from him, I'm simply saving him from more negative emotions he doesn't need. He's had enough of those to last a lifetime.

But the thought that I've held back has me on edge. If I have, it's possible he has, too.

I catch my bottom lip with my teeth as I dry the glass and set it in the cupboard.

What's he doing in there when he closes himself off?

Curiosity wins. Outside his door, I bring my hand up to knock, then lower it. I shouldn't have to knock, right? We love each other. We've even shared a bed. I wouldn't feel uncomfortable if he walked into my room without knocking.

Steeling myself, I turn the knob, slip inside and close the door. When I turn around, I'm surprised to find the room empty. Frowning, I take a few steps forward until I'm standing beside the bed, wondering if he went back out to the pool while I was washing up.

As I turn to leave, a large notepad on the desk catches my eye. Stopping beside the office chair, I stare at what lies before me.

There's nothing written on the front of the pad It's old and worn, with loose pages sticking out here and there that aren't neatly tucked in with the others. One pokes out far enough for me to catch what looks like eyelashes.

Gently, I slide it free and find myself staring into my own disembodied eyes. Only this time, instead of graphite, the irises are a stunning green with hints of copper framing the pupil.

And they're gazing up at me with desire, the accuracy so astounding I could be looking in a mirror.

Stunned, and overcome with curiosity, I run my fingertips over the battered cover before I flip it open.

Another set of my disembodied eyes stare out at me, the sketch only in the early stages, but already I see deep happiness gazing back. I don't need to look at the date in the corner to know this is what Gavin saw at the pool when Anika took him down, when he was looking at me. This is why he disappeared inside.

Tears prick at my real eyes. He'd seen me, seen the joy in my heart, and apparently, he'd had to capture it forever.

Welling with emotion, I move the loose sheet of paper aside.

And gasp.

Again, my disembodied eyes stare out from the page. Another complete sketch, the green and copper of my irises stunning against the graphite surrounding them.

And the look that bleeds from the page is unmistakeably love. What he must see when I look at him. It's extraordinary.

How he can capture emotion with no facial features apart from the eyes and eyebrows, I don't know. But he does. I can see right through those windows, right beneath the surface.

He's an incredibly talented artist. Why doesn't he know that? Why hide?

With one hand over my mouth, I turn page after page of nothing but my eyes, discovering what he's seen in them from the moment we met, but in reverse.

There's desire, compassion, forgiveness, hope, confusion, sorrow. A plethora of emotions leading all the way back to his first drawings.

Hate.

The glaring eyes take me right back to that courtroom, to the darkness I directed at a young man who had done nothing but find my mother dying on the nature-strip, then offered her the only comfort he could.

My heart breaks.

Tears tickle my jawline, and I swipe them away before turning those hateful eyes over.

My breath catches.

These eyes are different. They're mine, but they're not. They look at me with a mixture of love and happiness. Like the sketch on his letter, it's not quite right. Frowning, I study the drawing, noting the date. Ten years after he was locked away.

I let out a silent puff of air. So, he hadn't stopped trying to get it right after the final letter he sent me.

I can't stop the sob that escapes my throat. The thought of him locked away, drawing all of these, hoping he'd see something in me other than hate.

And now he has.

Here I was thinking he had a secret, but these sketches prove that he's been honest with me all along.

"Jamie?"

I whirl around, startled out of my thoughts, ashamed that I've been caught looking at something he obviously keeps private. I swallow the sobs and choke out, "I'm sorry."

He strides forward, but he's not angry. When he reaches me, he brushes the tears from my cheeks, his eyes soft with concern.

"Jamie? What is it?"

"I didn't … I didn't mean to snoop. I was looking for you, and—"

"I couldn't care less if you snoop. I have nothing to hide from you."

"But you have been," I say, taking a deep breath as I turn back to the desk. "These drawings … Gavin … they're incredible."

He wraps his arms around my waist and rests his chin on my shoulder, looking at the sketches with me.

"I wasn't hiding them from you. They're just scratchings."

"Oh, *please*. That's the first lie you've ever told me. You're a true artist, Gavin. Look at these." I leaf through them, as if I'm showing him something he's never seen before. "They're so … moving."

"You think so?" It's a genuine question. He honestly has no idea how talented he is.

"I more than think so." While I continue to flick slowly through the sketches, I come across one that isn't clean like the others. Smudges and streaks smear the page, lacking a polished finish, though it was clearly on the way there. "Why didn't you finish this one?"

"I was still working on it the day I walked out of prison. I left it like that. As a reminder."

I look closer, fascinated by the process. That's when I notice it. The reflection in the irises. They look like … prison bars. Intrigued, I flick through the pages, seeing the bars on all the others. Until I get to the more recent sketches. The bars are gone, replaced by the silhouette of a man instead. That one little detail shatters my heart all over again. It's him. It's me, looking at him. It's the moment I stopped seeing him as a prisoner and started seeing him as a man.

Taking a moment, I breath through the overwhelming tidal wave of emotion. When I finally have control again, I ask, "Why me? Why my eyes? Why any of it at all if you don't think you're an artist?"

Raising his head, he plants a sweet kiss on the part in my hair. "I don't know."

"Yes, you do." I twist out of his embrace, take a seat on the edge of his bed, and look up at his questioning expression. "I'd love to know that part of you."

A little reluctant, he slumps onto the office chair. After staring at the drawings for a long moment, he drags a hand over his face, then turns his attention to me.

"Although I always hoped I'd meet you, I didn't believe it'd happen. So, when it did, I thought you might see all these," he waves a hand at his sketches, "as kind of … creepy."

I think about that for a moment. "But you drew them on the letters you wrote me. You weren't worried about that."

"They were doodles. Not the same as these."

"Tell me the difference."

He swivels side to side in the chair, his eyes focused on his hands fisted in his lap. Finally, he lets out a long breath and looks at me.

"Unless you've been through it yourself, it's one of those things you think you might be able to imagine, but without firsthand experience, you can't understand what it truly means to be locked in a cage. When you find something—*anything*—that can take you out of there, that can make you feel free for even the briefest moment, you hold onto it. Tight. For me, that was you." He picks up one of his sketches and stares at it. "You have no idea how many times I escaped prison by looking into these eyes."

My heart stills. There's something special in what he's telling me, I just don't quite understand. "But you didn't know me. All you knew, was that I hated you. Why would anyone want to use that as an escape?"

He leans forward, rests his elbows on his knees, and reaches for my hand.

"When I saw you in that courtroom, you stunned me. I tried to ignore you and concentrate on what was happening. I tried. But I couldn't do it. There was something about you that kept reeling me in. I was captivated. And yes, you only ever looked at me like you wanted me to burn in hell, but … all that fierce emotion, all that energy put into conveying how you felt about me … You were alive with it. And since I felt dead, I wanted some of what you had."

My heart stutters in my chest as I squeeze his hand, encouraging him to go on.

"In between court days, I started sketching. And what came out were your eyes. I hadn't even planned to draw anything to do with you. It just … happened. Then it became my meditation. I'd disappear. I wasn't in a prison cell, waiting to be found innocent or guilty. I was with you, bringing you to life so I could see you whenever I wanted. Your eyes were the only image that would flow from my hand onto the paper. Looking into your eyes … that gave me something tangible to hang onto."

Before I can barrel into his arms, he releases my hand, flips the sketchbook over and slides out the last drawing. "At first, I didn't care that you hated me. I understood. But over time, I wanted to change that. I tried to make you look happy. I just couldn't get it quite … right."

"Until recently."

He nods. "I guess I need to see the real thing before I can immortalise it on paper. Once I had you in front of me, giving me all those different emotions, I couldn't get enough. I still can't. I don't think I ever will. You helped save me in there, J. And now you're the one saving me out here."

Rising, I position myself between his spread thighs and cup his face. "They're so beautiful, just like you. You should share them with the world, Gavin."

He shakes his head. "No. They're private. They're mine … and now yours."

"But people would be amazed—"

"No, J. They're my therapy. When I get overwhelmed, drawing them lets me escape."

I study his face, see the sincerity there. As I run my fingers through his hair, I try not to let my own vulnerability show when I ask gently, "You still get overwhelmed?"

He nods, drawing me closer. "Yeah. I do. There's a lot going on right now. But Jamie, being overwhelmed isn't always a negative thing. Loving you as deeply as I do … sometimes, I don't know what to do with that sort of fierce emotion. Drawing your eyes … it's hard to explain. It just works for me."

If my heart expands any further, it'll explode. So I kiss him and try to show him everything I feel for him too, but I'm not sure I know how. This goes deeper than any words or touches can convey. And that's when it hits me.

Breaking the kiss, I gaze into his eyes. That's where it is. I see it pouring from those beautiful blue irises. I saw it when he broke down on me after revealing how he tried to comfort my mother. It's the reason I kissed him.

Flicking my attention to the sketches spread across his desk, I realise it's there in my eyes, too. There's no hiding it, and I don't want to.

His hands tighten on my waist, bringing me back to him.

"I told you, J … I see you. Even when I didn't know you, I saw you. And I never want to *not* see you."

I drop my lips to his. When our tongues meet, his hands travel languidly up the backs of my thighs and beneath my skirt. Groaning, I lift my mouth from his and stare into his blown pupils.

"When you touch me like that … God, it turns me on," I whisper.

"Every damn thing about you turns me on. All the fucking time. You wearing this skirt … I remember the first time I saw you in it by the river. These beautiful legs, all smooth and perfect. Christ, how I kept my hands off you for so long is a total mystery to me right now."

Reaching higher, he cups my arse and squeezes, deepening

that ache for him, making me want so much more.

I take a step back, then another, grasping his hands when they slip from my backside. His questioning eyes gaze up at me, and when my legs hit his mattress, I sit down and pull him forward.

"I need to feel your weight on me," I demand.

Rising from the chair, he towers over me. "Where's the sadistic one?"

"Out by the pool."

Crashing his mouth crashes against mine, he grabs my shoulders and follows me down to the mattress. As he settles himself over me and eases a knee between my legs, I'm not surprised to find him already hard against my thigh. Instinctively, I press up into him, wanting more, wanting everything.

A low groan of frustration slips past my lips as I free my leg from between his so I can circle them both around his waist. The moment his erection makes contact with my damp panties, we being rocking slowly into each other. It feels so natural, so right. So torturous.

Grabbing my wrists, he draws them above my head, then tangles our fingers together so we're palm to palm. Somehow that feels even more intimate than the friction between my legs.

Trailing sweet kisses over my cheek, he sends goosebumps skittering across my skin when his lips brush the shell of my ear.

"Fuck, J. I'm desperate to be inside you."

Heat blasts through me as I squeeze his hands. "You had your chance last night."

"That's not what you needed. It wasn't the right time."

"Oh God, do I want it to be the right time now. This feels amazing."

A low growl vibrates from his chest to mine as he nibbles at my throat, his tongue tasting, lips gently sucking.

"You realise we've been reduced to teenagers sneaking around so we can make out, right?"

I chuckle silently. "Is this what that feels like?"

He lifts his head and looks at me with a satisfied gleam in his eyes, then thrusts against me. Arching my back, I tighten my legs around his hips and dig my heels into his arse.

"Fuck," he grates out. "I need to taste you again. Right from the source this time. Just a little sample."

My breath catches, anticipation and nerves curling through my arousal. No one's ever looked at me down there, let alone put their mouth on me.

His fingers untangle from mine as he trails his lips over my collarbone and between my cleavage, that short beard of his giving me delicious tingles. Cupping my breasts, his hot tongue dips between them, his thumbs grazing across my tight nipples through my tank top. When I suck in a sharp breath and undulate my hips beneath him, he lifts his head and gives me a devilish grin.

"I can't even count the number of times I've imagined fucking these gorgeous tits before I come all over them."

Oh. My. God! My nostrils flare at his words, my core clenching. "Gavin … that's so … *dirty*." He stills, worry in his eyes as he studies my face. I let him off the hook with a grin. "And I love it."

Relief sweeps over his face, his eyes dancing with mischief. "Cheeky little wench."

Then his weight vanishes and he's kneeling between my parted thighs.

I study his every move, my pulse throbbing between my legs, desperate for his touch, desperate to know the feel of his mouth and tongue on me. With a slow, teasing ascent up the outside of my thighs, his fingertips tickle as he brings my skirt with them.

Bunching it over my hips, he draws in a deep breath, his gaze riveted to the sheer lace underwear he's revealed.

"Look how beautiful you are, J. So fucking sexy," he breathes as he runs the tip of his index finger over my pelvic bone and down my slit. "I just hope I don't screw this up."

Lowering his head, he presses a kiss to my inner thigh. "Why would you …" I trail off as his lips tickle slowly upward, his beard adding incredible sensations to his journey.

"I'm guessing …" he whispers, placing another kiss higher, "that we're both virgins … when it comes to this." Through the sheer fabric, his hot mouth covers my clit. My breath hitches as his tongue presses on the lace, right *there*. The air I'd been holding explodes from my lips.

Grinning, he lifts his head. "Shhh …"

"I'm trying," I whisper, slapping a hand over my mouth.

He chuckles as he peppers kisses toward my other knee.

"Where are you going?" I protest.

"To look." Leaning back on his heels, he skates his palms up the inside of my thighs, pressing slightly, forcing me to spread wider. Then he runs his fingertips along the edge of my panties, slipping beneath just enough to move the crotch aside, fully exposing me to his riveted gaze.

"Fuck, J … so exquisite." He touches my entrance, then slides a finger inside. "So fucking wet for me. Yet another one of your amazing compliments." Removing his finger, he sucks it into his mouth, his eyelids fluttering closed as a low hum reaches my ears.

"*Gavin*," I whimper, so turned on my legs tremble.

He opens his eyes, lowers himself, and delicately brushes his mouth over my clit, mercilessly teasing me before the slick heat of his tongue strokes over me. My hips buck up, my fingers tangle in his hair and grip on tight.

"Oh my God," I breathe against the palm pressed to my mouth. I gasp when his tongue moves lower and slides inside me, in and out, until he leisurely licks all the way back up to my clit.

Writhing, I clamp my thighs over his ears and grind against his mouth. When he slides two fingers inside me, I fist his hair so tight, I'm sure I pull strands from his scalp, but his only response is to suck my clit into his mouth and curl his fingers.

I'm so close to coming apart, I almost miss the sound of the sliding door banging shut, the footsteps pounding along the hallway.

Fuck!

I wrench away, scuttling up the bed, my breath exploding as I re-adjust my panties and skirt.

Gavin stares at me with confusion, his lips and beard slick with my arousal.

Standing on shaking legs, I whisper, "Anika."

From the kitchen, a glass clanks against the stone countertop, the slam of the fridge door rattling bottles.

He swipes the back of his hand over his lips, his own breath just as ragged and choppy as mine as he gets off the bed.

"Come here," he whispers, and pulls me close. Then he kisses me, his tongue rubbing against mine, coating me with my taste. When he pulls back, he gives me cheeky grin. "Didn't want you to miss out on the delicious taste of that juicy peach."

"Dirty bastard." Emboldened, I palm his erection through his jeans and whisper in his ear, "I can't wait to taste *you*." His cock jerks in my hand and, with a satisfied grin, I step back and walk out of his room.

Chapter 43

Gavin

JESUS FUCKING CHRIST. *That woman.*

Trying to get control of my pounding heart and straining erection, I slump onto the office chair. When I rub my hand over my jaw, that gorgeous scent of hers fills my nostrils again, not helping the situation at all. God, she's so damn responsive, and so fucking sexy with the way she wants me just as much as I want her.

Swivelling in the chair, I stare in wonder at the sketches of her eyes spread out on the desk. She asked me to heed her mother's words and open my heart. Well, I haven't just let her in. She's speared right through to the other side and wrapped herself around it, making certain it'll never be anyone's but hers.

I suck in a deep breath, reminding myself that even though I can barely believe it, it's real. And tomorrow can't come soon enough. I just need to survive tonight.

Deciding I'd better take a shower, calm my dick down and reluctantly wash this amazing scent off my face, I grab some clean clothes and get to it.

After dinner, we remain at the dining table and play round after round of Uno. With two packs shuffled together. Apparently, that's Jamie and Anika's tradition. We laugh and fight and squabble over the rules like we've been doing it all our lives. The whole time, Jamie and I constantly touch each other under the table with our legs and feet. It's playful and caring and the whole night is another moment in my life where I feel totally at home, where I belong, where I matter, where I'm needed and wanted.

"Well, that's it then," Anika says as she scoops all the cards together and taps them on the table until they come together in a neat, thick rectangle. "My last night as a cockblocker. Until next time I'm here, of course."

I press my knee against Jamie's. "I thought that was off the table?"

Anika scoffs. "That was a one-time deal. Too bad you blew it. Or, more accurately, didn't blow it."

"Anika!" Jamie chastises, her face instantly flushing. She's such a contradiction, loving a bit of dirty talk, then blushing over a little innuendo.

"What?" Anika asks with faux innocence. "Jeez, I'm sure after all this time, you two can contain yourselves for a few more hours. You've got all day tomorrow to go at it. Kinda hurts my feelings, though, that my brother and sister want to get rid of me so they can get down and dirty."

As Jamie shoots to her feet, I scoot my chair back and grab her, pulling her onto my lap before she kills our sister.

"Oh!" Anika says with glee, "I just had a thought. Gav, when you're out with Jamie, you can introduce her as your sister's sister. How cool is that?" With that little nugget, she slaps a palm on the table and cracks up.

Jamie struggles to free herself from my arms, but I hold on tight, then tickle her side until she's giggling and writhing on my lap. When I relent, I find her hand, bring it to my lips and kiss her knuckles.

"Vomit," Anika gags.

I shoot her a wicked grin. "How about this, little sister … The more you talk about us like that, the more we'll make out in front of you."

Jamie smiles and gives me a quick peck on the lips before she turns to look at Anika.

Our sister's eyes shoot back and forth between us. Finally, she lets out a defeated breath. "Fine! But you're not gonna stop me talking about it behind your backs. And with that," she says, standing, "I'm going to bed. Behave."

"I'd wish you sweet dreams, but I doubt Satan's little helper has anything but nightmares," I smirk.

In return, she gives me the finger before disappearing down the hallway.

Jamie snuggles into me, squeezing her arms around my neck. "Nice one, Shawshank."

I pull her in closer. "Give me that cheeky mouth of yours."

And she does, her soft, plump lips pepper me with those sweet little closed-mouth kisses that drive me crazy until I have to taste her. Drawing on her bottom lip, I gently nip at it before soothing it with my tongue.

Sweet little whimpers escape her throat, then her tongue's touching mine and I lose myself in her, in the wonder that I get to do this at all. That she wants me to kiss her and touch her and love her. That she wants to do the same to me. It's a goddamn fucking miracle.

When she wriggles against my hard dick, I reluctantly break the kiss. "Let's get to bed. The sooner we fall asleep, the quicker tomorrow'll be here."

She's off my lap in a flash, grabbing my hand and pulling me toward her bedroom.

Our bedroom.

I smile as she closes the door behind us. The thought that we'll never sleep alone again swells my heart.

As we stand side by side in her ensuite and brush our teeth, staring at each other in the mirror, I take it all in. It's surreal, yet completely and utterly normal. A normal I'm sure most people take for granted. But to me, this is so far removed from my life in prison, it means everything.

Back in the bedroom, she grabs a fresh set of her usual pyjamas. While she changes in the ensuite, I strip down to my boxer briefs and slide into my side of the bed. When she emerges, my dick gets hard again at the sight of her in that skintight camisole and boy-leg undies. It doesn't seem to matter how many times I've seen her like this, I can't get enough. The fact that she's keeping her completely naked body from me until tomorrow drives me crazy. And I love it.

Kneeling on the bed, her breasts bounce a little as she settles back on her heels, our eyes locked.

"Christ, J. Get under the covers before I go insane."

Leaving her lamp on, she does as she's told. Once she settles on her side, she props her head up with one hand and places the other over my heart.

"I was wondering," she begins tentatively, "if maybe you'd like to invite Lach to Christmas lunch?"

Reaching out, I cup her neck and graze my thumb over that tender spot behind her earlobe. "Remember Benny's coming. He's the one who's always been there for me. Now I need to be there for him. He might feel pushed aside if my father's here, and I never want that thought to cross his mind."

She slides her hand from my chest to my chin, her fingers gently stroking my beard. "Another reason I love you. So damn thoughtful when it comes to how others might react. And you're right. We'll make Christmas special for Benny. It is, after all, his first Christmas on the outside in forty years."

I tug her in close, cradling her head until her face is tucked into my neck. "Maybe … we could invite my father over Boxing Day?"

She nods. "I think he'd like that."

Stroking my fingers up and down her spine, I say, "I wonder if he has someone special in his life."

Lifting her head, she props her chin on the hand covering my tattoo. "I asked him about that. He doesn't. He said Mattie was it for him."

"So, I do have something in common with him after all," I murmur, brushing a thumb over her cheek. "You're it for me, J. I know it right down to the bottom of my soul."

She stares at me, her eyes a little wider, her pupils swallowing those emerald jewels. For a moment, I think I've said too much, revealed too much, but that can't be right. I've told her in no uncertain terms how much I love her, *why* I love her. She shouldn't be surprised.

Then she's sprawling on top of me, her lips pressing briefly to mine before she lifts her head, her face alight with love and happiness.

"Seems we both have a lot in common with the way our parents felt about each other. Because you're it for me too, Gavin. I have absolutely no doubt about that."

Although the weight of her body on mine is intoxicating, I roll her over until I'm on top of her. As I devour her mouth, our bodies rock against each other instinctively, our hands squeezing and groping, unable to get enough.

When our air runs out, I stare down at her. "Jesus, woman. You're a wet dream and the love of my life, all wrapped up in this perfect, gorgeous package. How the hell did I get so lucky?"

"I could say the same about you. Only the price you had to pay to get here was far too high."

I rest my forehead against hers. "It was worth every fucking second, J. I'd go through it all again as long as it led me here. To you." The words slide out of me so easily. Apart from believing no one would ever want me, let alone Jamie Evans, it'd crossed my mind that I might be a little too damaged, a little too distrustful when it came to loving someone. Not with her. It's so damn easy.

Eyes welling with tears, she lets them spill down her face.

"Hey," I murmur, "I didn't mean to upset you."

She shakes her head. "I'm not upset. I'm just so happy right now, my body can't keep it contained."

Goddammit. I kiss her. Softly. Tenderly. Trying to convey everything I feel for without words.

She rocks into my erection and grins. "Looks like your body can't contain your happiness either."

I smile down at her. "That's not just happiness. That's euphoria. And a hell of a lot of frustration."

"Hmm … you think it's any different for me?"

I drop my head to her shoulder and groan almost silently,

letting her know just how much she's torturing me. Sliding to her side, I tell her, "Roll over. We're never getting to sleep at this rate."

With a little grumble, she turns off her lamp, then I draw her tight against me until every inch of our bodies touch. Even her feet rest atop mine. Like last night, I position the length of my erection between her perfect little butt cheeks, and let out a half-satisfied, half-frustrated sigh. She responds by wiggling a little too seductively.

"Anika's got nothing on you when it comes to evil," I whisper in her ear.

"Me? You started it."

"Right. Because you wiggling that perfect little arse against my dick is me starting it."

Giggling, she rolls toward me, tucking herself against my side and resting her head in the crook of my shoulder. Then she splays her fingers over my chest and begins a languid exploration of my nipple. "Getting into my bed without a shirt on is definitely starting it."

I let out an amused huff as I trace my fingertips over her arse. "So easily turned on, you wanton wench."

Turning her face into my armpit, she bursts into giggles, her breath making me squirm and laugh with her.

She gapes at me. "You're ticklish!"

I shake my head in denial, but her fingers quickly launch a tickle attack. Chuckling, I grab her wrist, force her onto her back, and use my body to hold her down.

She squirms beneath me, desperately trying to get away until she realises there's no escape.

"Brute," she whispers.

"Bimbo." I playfully kiss the tip of her nose.

"Beast."

"Babe."

"Hmmm," she murmurs. "You've never called me that before."

"Don't get used to it. That was an observation, not a term of endearment."

She frowns with confusion.

"Babe or baby are way too generic for you. You're my J. My unique, gorgeous J."

"Why only the letter J?"

"So many questions," I protest playfully.

"I know you. There must be a reason."

I hesitate, heat scorching my face. "It's corny."

"Now you *have* to tell me!"

"Because …" I draw out reluctantly, "not only is it your initial, it's the only letter in the alphabet shaped like a hook. And you had me hooked the first time I laid eyes on you."

"Wow! What a dork!" she snickers, then gives me a sweet kiss. "Don't you dare take that back. I love it." Growing serious, she asks, "What will it be like tomorrow?"

I rub my nose affectionately against hers. "We shouldn't think about that. Just let it happen. No planning."

"I feel like it's been built up, that it won't be what you expected and—"

I cover her mouth with another kiss. "J. What I expect is that it's going to feel like this. Just us. Comfortable with each other and turned on like fucking crazy. That's as far as I'm letting my expectations go."

"Really?"

I nip at her bottom lip. "Well, maybe there is one thing I expect."

"I'll give you anything you want."

"When I push into you, when our bodies join, I want to look into these eyes. I want to see exactly how they change in that moment."

She curls her hand around the back of my neck. "Thank you. For being so patient. For loving me even though we haven't been able to—"

"I'd love you even if I didn't have a dick. As long as you loved me back, I'd be deliriously happy if all I ever got to do was give you pleasure."

"Well," she says, her eyes brimming with emotion, "that might just beat any compliment I've ever given you."

"You like that?"

"So much," she whispers as her fingers sink into my hair. "But I'm glad you *do* have a dick, because I want to make you feel just as good."

We rock our bodies together, our breaths hitching again. "You already know you do." With every ounce of strength I have, I kiss her lips and roll off her. "Let's get to sleep."

She finds my hand and squeezes without letting go. "Good night, Shawshank."

"Good night, J."

I wake gradually to the sound of playful squabbling coming from the kitchen, reminding me again how well sound travels in this house. Stretching out diagonally across the bed, I let out a long, satisfied yawn, surprised how fully rested I feel after the torture of trying to keep control last night.

Showered and dressed, I head to the kitchen to find Anika at the stovetop, while Jamie flits between pouring orange juice and checking on bread in the toaster.

Neither have spotted me, so I lean against the breakfast bar, just like I did my first morning here, and watch, observing the difference only three short weeks can make. Instead of ogling the woman I was intensely attracted to, I'm now ogling the woman I'm also madly in love with.

And then there's my sister. *Our* sister. Yeah, saying that doesn't exactly make me comfortable either, but apart from twisted minds thinking the worst, it's kind of special. Sharing a sibling with the love of my life only reinforces my view that we're connected, that we were always meant to be.

When Jamie turns toward the fridge to put away the orange juice, she startles a little at the sight of me. Unfortunately, today she's fully dressed and clearly wearing a bra. Damn shame.

Rushing forward, she plants a kiss on my lips. "Morning."

I cup her arse, pull her in close, and murmur. "Best morning ever."

"Okay!" Anika shouts from the other side of the kitchen. "No groping each other until I'm gone."

Releasing Jamie, I ask, "What's all this?"

"A goodbye breakfast for Anika. She'll need some extra energy today," Jamie explains, her eyes sparkling with mischief.

I'm guessing Anika's not the only one who'll need extra fuel.

"For once, you get to relax. Now, go sit," she instructs.

By the time I take a seat and Jamie places a glass of orange juice in front of me, Anika's heading around the breakfast bar with three plates expertly balanced. She sets them down and I stare at the perfectly fried sunny-side-up eggs resting on toast with bacon on the side.

"Seems I should've been pretending I didn't know how to cook all along. I could get used to being waited on by one beautiful woman and Satan's sidekick."

"So fucking funny, dickwad. Only I'm nobody's sidekick." Before I can stop her, Anika stabs her fork into one of my eggs, bursting the silken yolk.

"While you're at it, don't forget the other one. Then you can cut everything up into nice little bite size chunks for me." I only just manage to snatch my hand away before her fork slams into the placemat.

"Anika!" Jamie shouts.

"He started it!"

I hold my hands up in surrender.

"That's right, bro. That's exactly how every perp'll behave when I have them cornered."

"No doubt about that. You're fucking terrifying."

"You bet your arse I am. Oh! I almost forgot," she says, her eyes lighting up with glee. "I was thinking … if you two get married, you'll be my brother *and* my brother-in-law, and Jamie'll be my sister *and* my sister-in-law. How's that for a mindfuck?"

I shoot a glance at Jamie, and we both crack up. What else can we do but laugh? Anika's not wrong. It's a fucking mindfuck.

Way too soon, and nowhere near soon enough, it's time for Anika to get going. Giving her and Jamie some space, I potter around the kitchen, cleaning up the mess I insisted on dealing with.

When I'm almost done, Jamie wraps her arms around me from behind. "We've said our goodbyes. She's waiting for you in the garage. Apparently, she needs help getting her luggage in the car."

I turn in her arms and look down at her tear-streaked face. But it's not entirely sad. She seems content, happy that her sister's starting her own journey in life.

"Help?" I ask. "Since when does she need help with anything?"

"I think it's code for *'I need to say goodbye to the big brother I absolutely adore, so therefore must pretend I need him for something.*'"

We smirk at each other. "Nope, doesn't sound like her at all."

"Okay. What about, '*Get my stupid fucking bro out here so he can use those big muscles for something useful.*'"

"Better," I grin. "You okay?"

"I'm fine. Now go." She shoves me out of the kitchen and into the hallway.

"Don't disappear on me," I warn.

"Oh, we'll see …" she says with a sly smile

I shake my head with a laugh, hoping I appear relaxed. I don't want her to know how hard my heart's beating. Now that we can finally be together, nerves are kicking in. *Idiot.*

Summer heat engulfs me as I step into the garage and squint against the brightness of the sun streaming through the open door.

When I meet Anika at the back of the car, I find she's already placed her suitcases in the boot.

"Thought you needed help."

"Yeah, yeah, sure you did," she smirks.

When I catch her eye, I realise Jamie's not the only one who's shed a tear. "Someone squirt you in the face with a hose?" I tease.

"Fuck off," she bites, then the next second, her arms are around my waist, and I'm hugging her right back.

"She's really going to miss you," I tell her. "Guess I will too. Just a smidge."

She holds me a little tighter, remaining silent for far too long. I don't rush her. I think she's only quiet because she can't speak through her emotions.

Finally, with a thick voice I haven't heard from her before, she says, "Don't you ever tell anyone, but I think you're amazing. I'm pretty fucking happy I have a brother, and that he's you."

Coming from her, that admission lights me up inside. "Right back at ya, kid."

Her body vibrates with a laugh as she lets go. Then she meets my eyes.

"As great as you are, Mr. Wonderful, you do anything to hurt my sister, and I'll hunt you down and put you right back in that cell. Only difference being, you'll deserve it."

"That'll never happen." I take a deep breath, my gaze unwavering. "I love her, Ank. I'll never do anything but love her, protect her and look after her the way she's meant to be cared for."

She nods, quickly wiping at a stray tear.

Placing a hand on her shoulder, I say, "I'm proud to have you as my sister. You're one of the best surprises of my life. And I know you'll be a great cop. Just … be careful, okay?"

A genuine smile blooms on her face, and I pull her back in for a hug. "Now fuck off so I can finally get laid, you little demon."

Laughing, she pulls away and punches my bicep. I grunt and rub at it as if she's hurt me.

Then, without another word, she slams the boot shut and gets behind the wheel. I watch until she's reversed out. With a final wave she drives off and I press the button to lower the garage door.

Alone. Finally.

And my heart's performing summersaults.

Opening the laundry door, I come to an abrupt stop.

There, discarded on the floor, are Jamie's shorts.

Grinning like a fool, I pick them up and head down the hallway, finding her shirt in a crumpled heap in front of our bedroom door. I snatch it up and turn the doorknob, expecting to see her standing beside the bed in her underwear. That's where I want to find her, so I can peel off the final layers of her clothing and fully expose every inch of her incredible body.

But the room's empty. Confused, I hurry over to the ensuite. Not there either.

Doubt sweeps through my mind, a mind that's been trained to expect the worst from people. Has she changed her mind now that Anika's safety barrier has gone?

Heart knocking like a demented hammer, I stride out of the bedroom, stop in the hallway and cock my head, listening.

Then a splash from outside catches my attention. I move, stalking toward the family room. The moment I enter, I freeze.

A lacy bra hangs from the sliding door's handle. Relieved, I have a little chuckle to myself as I open it and step into the heat. Cheeky bloody woman.

Instantly, I spot her discarded underwear on the pavers near the shallow end of the pool. Damn it. She's completely taken away my chance to undress her.

The water ripples and, on her back, she floats out from behind the potted ficus. Moving closer, I stop a few feet from the edge, transfixed. Her breasts float slightly above the waterline, her nipples pebbled from the cool liquid as she leisurely glides toward the steps.

Then she fully immerses herself. I wait, counting the seconds before she surfaces and faces. With our eyes locked, she ever so gradually rises. Water cascades over those perfect breasts and drips from her tight nipples.

And I've lost the ability to breathe.

As she takes the first of the steps, slowly revealing the curve of her slim waist, it hits me. This is a goddamn striptease. If I thought my cock was hard before, it's fucking granite now. I remain glued to the spot, desperate to see the rest of this show.

A beautiful blush stains her cheeks when I meet her eyes again. She's so fucking sexy my heart might stop, but she's also so damn sweet and self-conscious, it might just burst instead. The fact that it's still beating at all astounds me. But it is. And now it's revving up to a thousand Ks an hour.

Because she's taking the next step, revealing the swell of her hips, and her navel. I never knew a belly button could be such a fucking turn on until this moment.

My hands fist at my sides, desperate to touch her, but determined to let her finish this exquisite presentation.

When she takes another step, sunlight glistens on the water as it runs over her bare pussy.

My disappointment at not being able to undress her vanishes. Because *holy fuck*.

That's my breaking point. I can't keep away another second. Releasing an appreciative rumble from deep in my chest, I meet her at the edge of the pool and extend my hand, unable to keep my eyes from travelling up and down her incredible body.

Her cool, wet hand grips mine tightly as I help her the rest of the way out of the pool. She stands before me, dripping all over, her long dark hair slicked back from her face, fully exposed and vulnerable. It's a poignant moment in my life.

"Christ, J. You're stunning. So goddamn beautiful."

Her blush deepens as I step closer, slowly raking my gaze from her feet to her eyes.

"You really like what you see?" she asks, her insecurities surfacing again.

Well, I can't have that.

Reaching out, I cup her face and stare deep into the green I know so well. "I don't like it," I say, my voice rough and low, "I fucking love it. I love you. Every. Single. Part of you." Then I grab the back of her head, fist her wet hair and crash my mouth over hers.

She groans, her fingers gripping my t-shirt over my chest, her tongue slipping and sliding against mine. We unleash on each other, but I'm careful not to cut her with my teeth. I don't want to do anything that'll dampen the passion flaring between us.

Barely able to draw another breath, I tug on her hair, breaking the kiss as her head falls back. Trailing my lips and tongue over her throat, I taste the salt on her skin, feel the vibrations of her moans beneath my mouth. When she arches her back, I kiss my way to a pebbled nipple. And suck it into my mouth. Hard.

She gasps, her fingers in my hair hanging on for dear life. Swirling my tongue, I release her long enough to scrape my teeth against that glorious, roughened texture before soothing it with my mouth and tongue.

"Oh, Gavin … *yes* …"

Christ. Her responsiveness, her wanting me with the same desperation I need her, literally brings me to my knees. Trying to rein myself in, I crush my face against her stomach and nip lightly at her smooth skin.

"What're you doing?" she breathes.

Gazing up at her, she watches me through hooded eyes, her fingernails scraping deliciously against my scalp. "If I didn't fall to my knees in worship, I wouldn't be a man deserving of you."

"You … you can't say things like—"

Rocking her forward, I bury my face in her pussy and drive my tongue hard against her clit. She almost tears my hair out by the roots as she jerks against my mouth, her gasps loud and primal. Cupping those tight little arse cheeks of hers, I soften my tongue and kiss her the way I kiss her mouth. Her hips move with me, her moans growing louder and louder until I worry the neighbours might hear her and decide to take a peek over the fence.

With one final lick, I rise to my feet and sweep her into my arms. Gripping my shoulders, she nuzzles into my neck as I carry her into the cool house. By the time we reach our bedroom, she's nipping and tasting my skin the way she did the night I brought her home drunk.

Lowering her to her feet beside the bed, I make a dash for the ensuite. When I emerge with a towel, she's already flung aside the covers, but instead of waiting where I left her, she's standing at the foot of the bed.

I meet her there, taking in her damp, air-conditioned skin littered with goosebumps. Draping the towel over her shoulders and back, I cup her head with it and try to get as much water out of her hair as possible. While I massage her scalp, her cool fingers slip beneath my t-shirt and explore my heated skin.

"Hey," she murmurs on a nervous little smile.

I grin back at her. "Hey, gorgeous."

"Taking care of me again?"

"Always." I kiss the tip of her nose and gently rub the towel down her back.

Whipping it away, she tosses it to the floor. "Now it's my turn to take care of you."

She drags my t-shirt up my body, and by the time I yank it off and fling it away, she's undoing my belt and turning me until my back is to the bed. Then she unbuttons my jeans and slides down my zipper.

As they drop to my ankles, our eyes lock. She strokes my erection through my boxer briefs, her other hand dipping beneath the waistband and cupping my arse.

"Fuck that feels good," I say on a ragged breath.

Breaking our gaze, she glances down. "Mmmm. Looks like I'm not the only one who's wet." She gives me a wicked grin. "I think I should clean that up for you."

My heart jackhammers. She can't mean—

As she drops to her knees and drags down my underwear, I understand that's exactly what she means.

Jesus.

With my entire body rigid, I watch her wrap her fingers around my shaft and draw my cock down until the tip hovers at her mouth. I think it might be the most erotic sight I've ever seen.

Wrong.

Eyes on mine, her hot tongue licks that pre-come right from my slit. I groan, and as she pulls back a little, a thin string of liquid stretches between us, connecting us. Breaking it with a lick of her lips, she smiles.

"Delicious," she whispers, then takes me into her hot mouth.

As she swirls her tongue around my swollen head, my fingers instinctively sink into her hair, my throat releasing a loud rumble of pleasure when she draws me deeper and begins to suck. "Ah, fuck, Jamie. *Christ.*"

I close my eyes, taking in every sensation while she explores my dick with her lips and tongue. I'm pretty damn sure she's never done this before, but *fuck*, the way she's working her mouth and hand in perfect harmony, she's getting me way too close to the edge.

In an effort to get control, I snap my eyes open. Bad idea. Because now I know why she positioned me with my back to the bed. I'm staring straight at the full-length mirror attached to the closed door. And what I see has my spine tingling. Jamie kneels before me, her perfect bare arse on display, her damp, tangled hair swaying with every bob of her head. The sight of her, the feel of her … it's too much.

"Fuck, I'm gonna come, J." I tug on her hair, trying to withdraw, but she's not having it. Her grip on my shaft tightens and she takes me deeper, moaning around my dick. In an overwhelming rush, my orgasm rips through me and I empty everything I have into her sweet, beautiful mouth.

Chapter 44

Jamie

SWALLOWING EVERY LAST drop, I look up into his dazed eyes, overcome with the knowledge that I can make him feel so damn good he loses all control.

The moment I release him, he tugs me to my feet and into his arms. As I wrap my legs around his waist, he takes a step backward. Still tangled in the jeans around his ankles, he loses his balance, and we fall to the mattress. Only his quick hands on my shoulders prevent our skulls from cracking together.

"Klutz," I say, bursting into giggles.

"Well, it's your fault." He sweeps my hair back from my face. "You made me lose my fucking mind."

"I have no idea what you're talking about." I kiss him, long and slow, and when he slides his tongue into my mouth, I suck on it gently. Releasing a guttural growl, he rolls his warm body against mine.

"That tongue … that mouth … Christ, J. How did you know how to do that?"

"I read," I answer, deeply pleased by the pleasure I'd given him.

"I knew you were hiding your dirty books from me. Even before Anika outed you. Now I'm feeling a little inadequate. I mean, I don't know if I can live up to your standards."

"Well … your previous efforts have left me wanting," I

tease.

He balks at me in apparent horror.

"Because you had to stop," I clarify.

Nuzzling my nose with his, he wriggles against me as he kicks off his jeans. "This time," he says, "I'm not stopping until you come undone."

"Don't torment me," I sigh.

"Like you did with that water-themed striptease you subjected me to?"

I chuckle. "You say that like it was some sort of punishment."

"It was glorious. Something I'll never forget." His denim blue eyes search mine, his fingertips tracing my jaw. "You're perfect, J. Beyond perfect."

Then he's kissing me, stroking my tongue with his, sending that aching need throbbing between my thighs as he positions me fully onto the bed.

When he moves onto my neck, little whimpers and moans escape from my lips until I gasp, "I want you inside me. Please."

"Patience," he murmurs, cupping my breast, gently pinching my nipple.

I grind up against him, wanting him, needing him, loving the way his naked skin feels against mine. "I've been patient way too long."

He looks at me, his fingers stilling on my nipple. "Exactly why I want to make sure you're as ready as you can be. I don't want to hurt you, J."

"You won't," I insist, though I'm not so sure that's the truth. The only thing I'm sure of is that I don't care.

I catch my breath, suddenly realising he might not be able to hurry, that he might be stalling to give himself time to recover. Reaching between us, I circle his cock. It's not soft, but it's not hard either. Squeezable, but plump. Grinning, I tease, "Oh, dear. What happened?"

"Your mouth happened, you naughty, cheeky woman."

Dipping his head, he latches onto my nipple. I gasp at the streak of lightning that spears straight to my core. As his tongue swirls and his teeth nip, he grows thicker in my hand.

"Goddammit, Gavin," I breathe, "touch me … Please."

Like I weigh nothing, he flips me onto my stomach, traps my thighs beneath his and presses his body against my side. Just as I'm about to protest, he sweeps my hair from my neck and places a gentle kiss right at my nape. I shudder with pleasure.

"You want me to touch you," he murmurs against my skin, "so feel it."

Torturously slow, barely there fingertips descend in circles down my back, then over one butt cheek, then the other, the sensation so intense, it borders on painful. When I groan, he cups my arse and squeezes before sliding a firm palm up to the nape of my neck. With the tip of one finger, he traces my spine straight down to my tailbone, then further, skating between my cheeks, teasing me when he stops just shy of where I want him. Instinctively, I try to lift my hips, but his heavy thigh keeps me pinned to the mattress.

A deep, throaty rumble washes over my skin as he grazes his soft beard down my back, kissing my sensitive flesh all the way to my arse. Then, with a gentle bite, he sinks his teeth into one cheek and sucks hard. The thought of him marking me, making me his, has my fingers clutching the sheets as I shamelessly groan.

With my entire back tingling and alive from his touch, he works his mouth up my spine until his lips reach my ear. "I love you, J."

Before I can catch my breath, he flips me onto my back, our eyes locked as he trails a knuckle over my stomach. Stopping at my belly button, he circles it twice before continuing his agonising, downward journey. Ever so lightly, his fingertip touches the top of my slit. And pauses. I glare at him in frustration.

His eyes sparkle with amusement and heat. "Spread for me, J."

Desperate for his touch, I do as I'm told. With his eyes on mine, he feathers his fingertips over me, teasing me to the point of insanity. "I'm going to kill you," I seethe.

He chuckles, then glides his fingers through me, sliding into my wetness, coating me with it until I'm moaning and writhing and desperate for more.

Thrusting his rock-hard cock against my thigh, he says, "You feel what that does to me, knowing you want me?"

"Oh, God … please, Gavin … just fuck me," I whimper.

His eyes blaze with hunger, but he continues to touch me slowly, deliciously, watching my every reaction. Pushing a thick finger inside me, his thumb circles my clit. "We've got the rest of our lives to fuck. There's only one first time, and I'm not rushing it."

Slowly, he withdraws, then stretches me with two fingers. I arch my back as he curls them, gliding his thumb around and around my clit until I'm right on the edge.

When whimpers escape my lips, he removes his fingers at the same moment his warm body leaves my side. An animalistic growl of frustration rumbles from my throat. Giving me a cheeky grin, he reaches for a pillow, slides it beneath my backside, and kneels between my spread legs.

I watch as he fixates on the sight before him, his hot hands gliding up the inside of my thighs until his gaze locks with mine.

"You're fucking magnificent."

Eyes dipping between my legs, he lowers himself, his mouth consuming me, tongue licking, lips sucking me in as he buries his fingers deep. The filthy sounds he's making have me clutching at his hair, shamelessly thrusting against his mouth, desperate for release. When his deep groan sends vibrations right through my clit, that's the end of me. Over and over, I cry out his name until the waves of ecstasy dwindle away, leaving nothing but a panting mess.

Soft kisses pepper up my body until his mouth finds mine in a languid kiss filled with love and the taste of me. Drawing my knees up, I wrap my legs around his waist, the head of his cock sliding against my entrance, ready to so easily push inside.

With his body flush against mine and his forearms

supporting his weight, he breaks the kiss, smiling as he brushes tendrils of damp hair from my forehead.

"So disappointing," I joke.

"Tell that to my fingers," he chuckles. "You nearly crushed them with those contractions."

Digging my nails into his muscled back, I rock my hips and beg, "Would you please just get inside me."

Smile fading, his eyes grow dark and serious. "So demanding."

"I just want you. All of you."

"And I want all of you, too. Nice and slow."

Nuzzling his nose against mine, he shifts slightly, easing forward until I feel the head of his cock slip inside.

My hips rise up to meet him, trying to take him deeper, already excited by how good he feels. Groaning, I run my hands down his back and grab his tense arse. But when he gently thrusts forward, an intense pressure grips me. The moment I gasp at the intrusion, he immediately pulls back.

"J? Look at me."

Having no idea I'd scrunched my eyes closed, I open them and stare into his worried gaze.

"We can stop anytime you want, we don't have to—"

"No!" I say too harshly. "I mean, don't you dare. We're doing this."

"Fuck." He drops his forehead to mine. "I hate the thought of hurting you."

"It'll hurt more if you don't." I roll my hips, showing him with my body that I mean it. "Please."

His eyes hold mine as he eases inside me a little more, and I tense. I know it's not him, that it's my body remembering the last time, remembering the pain.

"J … it's me. Just me. You know who I am. The man who loves you, worships you, adores you. Relax. We're made for each other. Your body just needs to learn how to take me."

His gentle words, the look in his eyes, reminds me how much I trust him. And now he's patiently waiting for his words to sink in. And they are. I relax. Everywhere.

Warmth and relief shine from his eyes. "Good girl. Now give me your hands."

When I rest them above my head, he slips his fingers between mine, the intimacy of his hold and our locked gaze, sends heat rushing between my legs. I let out a long breath, and smile.

"There's my J," he murmurs. Rocking forward, he sinks deeper with each gentle thrust. It burns a little, but the feel of him moving inside me eclipses everything.

I squeeze his hands and moan, my back arching, my hips reaching for more.

Studying me with intensity, his fingers tighten on mine. "Fuck, J. You feel so … fucking … wonderful."

"So do you, Gavin. So do you."

"I'm only halfway there."

Before I take in what he means, he flexes his hips and sinks all the way home. Electricity sparks through my entire body, and I gasp, "Did you feel that?"

Motionless, buried deep inside me, his gaze never leaving mine, he murmurs, "Like a goddamn power-surge between us." Eyes blazing with heat, his control barely restrained, he asks, "You okay?"

"I'm more than okay. You feel like … I don't know … like I'm filled with you. Not just here," I breathe, raising my hips, "but in my head … and my heart."

Emotion simmers in his gaze as he withdraws, then strokes all the way back in. "You're … you're everywhere, J. All around me."

Then there's no more need for words. We say everything with our bodies, our eyes and our lips.

Moving with slow, deliberate thrusts, his pelvis rubs against my clit in a perfect, slippery rhythm. As my breasts roll beneath his chest, the feel of all that naked skin and muscle pressing and sliding against me, forces me to just be in the moment.

Along with all the unfamiliar sounds of sex that are new music to my ears, our moans and ragged breaths fill the room, drawing me closer and closer to another orgasm.

Sensing it, he eases out of me and braces himself on his hands.

"Gavin?" I whimper.

"Getting too close." Kissing his way down my neck, he palms a breast and brushes his thumb over my nipple. "And I want to see it all when you come on my dick."

My face and body catch fire. Clearly, the more turned on he is, the dirtier his mouth gets. And I love it.

When he latches onto my nipple, I raise my head, wanting to see, too. I watch, fascinated by the way his cheeks hollow as he draws me in, the way his long eyelashes flutter against his cheeks. Catching me, he holds my gaze, runs the tip of his tongue around my areola, then flicks my nipple.

This time it's me who groans, "*Fuck*."

Letting out a deep, rough grumble of satisfaction, he kneels between my spread thighs and rests back on his heels.

My gaze sweeps over him, taking in those muscled shoulders, the rapid rise and fall of his broad chest. And those lean abs leading down to that enticing line of dark hair partially blocked by his erection.

And, oh God, is it a sight. Shiny with my arousal, his cock stands tall and proud, veins bulging along the shaft, the bulbous head dripping. Before I can reach out and wrap my fingers around it, he slides his hands under my backside and hauls my arse up onto his thighs, spreading me wider.

"Look at you," I say in awe, trying to figure out where to put my hands.

Leaning forward, he cups my face. "I've got nothing on you, J. I'm the luckiest guy in the world."

After giving me a long, slow, drugging kiss, he eases back, places his palms on the tops of my thighs and watches as he parts me with his thumbs.

I'm raw and exposed, but the way he's looking at me with such rapture, I can't help but grow hotter and needier.

"Christ, Jamie. You're a damn angel in a sinner's body."

As I writhe beneath his steady gaze, he fists his cock, dragging it from my entrance to my clit, then back again before slipping the head inside. His fingers curl into my hips, and he rocks forward, sinking into me halfway.

Eyelids heavy, he finds my gaze locked on him. "That invisible thread that's connected us from the start … now I can see it. And it's fucking beautiful. The way you're stretching around me. Seeing it and feeling it at the same time … Jesus … *fuck*."

Fascinated, I watch him sink all the way into me, that line of hair below his navel like a goddamn arrow pointing straight to heaven. Placing his thumb on my clit, he drives into me, both of us taking in the joining of our bodies, both of us feeling the connection, the pleasure.

I'm getting close, and I know he is, too.

My breasts bounce around so much from the impact, I cross my arms beneath them and cup one in each hand.

"Christ, J. Touch your nipples," he grinds out.

I do as he says, circling them with my thumbs, and when he copies the motion against my clit, I detonate.

"Oh, God, Gavin. Oh, fuck … *yes!*" Ecstasy races through my body, all thoughts gone as I come apart around the one man I thought I would hate until my dying day.

Lurching over me, his rhythm lost, our gazes locked, I feel him swell inside my clutching walls. A thunderous growl from deep within escapes his lips. As I cup his jaw and he drops his forehead to mine, I feel the wonderful sensation of him pulsing inside me, emptying everything he has into me with his cock and his eyes.

Breath blasting, he collapses, burying his face in my neck, his heavy body crushing me in the most sublime way. Lying beneath him, I revel in the beat of his heart pounding against mine.

After a few moments, he pushes up on his elbows and gazes down at me with the goofiest smile I've ever seen on his face. And I smile right back, falling madly in love with him all over again.

Long and slow, he kisses me, and I drink him in, savouring this wonderful afterglow.

"Holy fuck," he murmurs.

"Well, that says it all."

He laughs, his whole face filled with a deep happiness that almost bursts my heart. Rolling us onto our sides, he pulls me in close, tangling our legs until our naked bodies are snug against each other.

As he presses sweet, loving kisses to my forehead, he asks, "You okay?"

"That all depends on what you mean by *okay*. I think you've broken my brain, but my body doesn't seem to care. Or maybe it's the other way around?"

He brushes damp tendrils of hair from my forehead with such tenderness my eyes prick with tears. "I need to know if I hurt you."

I give him a cheeky grin. "You just want to know if you've got a big dick, don't you?"

He throws his head back and laughs, his body shuddering against mine. Taking me by surprise, he flips me onto my back and captures my wrists above my head. "Yeah, that's exactly what I want to know. Now, woman, tell me … did I hurt you with my monster dick?" With his free hand, he tickles my exposed underarm.

"Yes!" I squeal, squirming uselessly beneath his hard body until he stops the onslaught. "Yes, it hurt," I say, catching my breath, "It hurt so good, I can't wait to do it again."

"You little hussy."

Cracking up, we roll onto our sides again, his forehead dropping to mine as our bodies absorb every beautiful laugh that escapes us. When we relax again, he cups my face.

"I thought the happiest day of my life was the day you stepped into that caravan and told me you knew I was innocent. But this, right here, leaves that for dead."

My heart beats hard as I slide my palm over his tattoo. "You say the most wonderful things."

"You deserve the most wonderful things."

"So do you," I whisper.

"I've already got the most wonderful thing." He kisses the

top of my head and squeezes me.

"Stop it."

"What? Don't tell me I'm outdoing you on the compliments?"

"I'm too relaxed and tired and comfortable to try to one-up you right now." Tracing the outline of his tattoo, I ask, "Tell me when you first realised you were falling for me."

"That's easy. It started in that awful tin-can. The day you told me I was innocent."

"Because of the fantastic news I gave you?"

"No. Because that day, we met for the first time … as equals, with the truth between us. And it was how quickly you let me know, how you wanted to help me tell the world I didn't kill anyone. Considering the circumstances, that told me what an extraordinary person you were. But they weren't the only reasons."

My heart soars. I'd only been doing what was right, and he loved me for being me. Running my fingers through the sprinkling of hairs on his chest, I prompt, "What else?"

"When I was laughing with the relief of it all, and I turned around and saw you laughing too. Your beautiful smile, the joy on your face, and the care and happiness in your eyes. I think that was the pinnacle moment."

"And then I ruined it for you."

"Hell no," he argues, trailing his fingers through my hair. "Yeah, you started crying—which you should have done well before that moment—but do you remember what happened next?"

"I told you, I'll never forget. You held me."

"You have no idea the inner turmoil I went through when I saw you break down. My instinct was to hold you, but logic reasoned that was the last thing you'd want from me. And if I tried, and you pushed me away … well, that thought was terrifying."

I prop my chin on his chest so I can look into his eyes. "But you took the risk anyway."

"The moment you held onto me, you had my heart.

Comforting you when you needed it most, made me feel real, like I mattered. Like I was useful. That maybe I hadn't been discarded and thrown on the trash heap. Your body in my arms, your words, the way you cared about me more than the hell you were going through … I'm sure my heart leapt over to your chest and took up residence right then. And I knew I'd never feel it beat with life again unless I was with you. I fell so fucking hard, J, I didn't know what to do with it. So, I buried it. Because I couldn't let myself hope that you'd ever feel the same way." He gently tucks my hair behind my ear, his eyes searching mine. "When did you?"

"The next morning," I answer without hesitation.

His eyebrows shoot up. "It took you that long? I thought it was the moment I walked into that cocktail bar, and you threw yourself at me."

I give his nipple a playful pinch. "I don't remember that."

"Sure you don't," he chuckles.

"It was definitely the next morning. The way you took care of me. The way you didn't once blame me for bringing it upon myself. When you told me the truth about my mortifying behaviour even though you thought it might mean I'd turn my back on helping you. Then, when you left, the house felt so empty. *I* felt empty. So I tried to bury it, too."

"Hmm," he sighs, his palm grazing down my hip before grabbing my backside. "You knew we'd end up here, didn't you?"

I gape at him. "No."

"Breaking your rule."

"No, I'm not!"

He scoffs. "Okay, let me rephrase that. You *hoped* this would happen?"

I hesitate a moment, but what's the point? "Yes."

"So, when you asked me to come and stay here …"

"It might have been at the back of my mind."

He laughs, his whole body hitching against me. "I can't believe Benny was right."

I stare at him in surprise. "He was?"

"I think his exact words were '*Dickhead, she wants you.*'"

"Do you think that's why he came to an agreement with you? So you could give this a shot?"

"Yeah, I do." He rolls me onto my back and presses his erection into my thigh. "And now, I think we should go have a shower"

"But I don't want to move."

"Neither do I but … I think I might've made a bit of a mess of you."

"Oh."

"Yeah, *oh*. Gotta be some downside to not using a condom."

Reluctantly, I let him lead me into the shower, then not so reluctantly, I let him wash every single millimetre of my body.

After we've dried each other off and agree that we need a nap to recharge, we slip into bed. Moving closer to him, I'm greeted by a cold, wet spot against my hip.

"You know," I murmur, "it's not really fair that you have to sleep so far away from the bathroom. I think you should take my side of the bed."

He palms my breast and chuckles. "If you want me to sleep on the wet patch, you only have to ask. You know I'd do anything for you."

And I know deep in my soul, he means it.

Champer 45

Gavin

AS I START to drift awake, a grin pulls at my lips. I don't open my eyes. Not yet. She's pressed against me, her head tucked beneath my chin, her little breaths tickling the hairs on my chest. I'm pretty sure my arm's numb beneath her, but with the delicious sensation of her bare flesh against mine, I don't care. Even with my hard dick sandwiched against her stomach and her naked pussy resting on my thigh, I refuse to disturb her.

No matter what she says, she must be a little sore. And I know if I make a move, she'll let me. She seems to get as much out of pleasing me as I do from pleasing her.

So caring and precious. Such a fucking surprise. I thought she'd be sweet and innocent in bed, and I would've been more than happy with that, but the fact that she's never explored her sexuality is a goddamn turn on. And so far … well, she's blown my fucking mind.

We both have a lot of lost time to make up for, and I'm more than thrilled that I'm the one who gets to help her discover what she does and doesn't like.

But that's only scratching the surface.

She's never been loved. Neither have I. And it's fucking incredible. Like soaring with utter freedom.

It's the truest thing I've ever experienced in my life.

And every breath in me knows she feels it too.

That's the real clincher.

Unable to wait another moment, I open my eyes and drink her in. With the covers tucked under her arm, dark hair tumbles in a glorious mess over her bare shoulder. It takes all my strength not to run my fingertips over that smooth flesh.

I don't want to wake her. Not yet. Not when this tidal wave of emotion is hitting me so hard, I feel like I'm drowning. Tears spill from my eyes, and I clamp down so hard on the urge to sob that I can't breathe. The immense and painful lump in my throat refuses to budge, and there's no way I want her to wake to a sobbing mess of a man in her bed.

Nothing … *nothing* I ever dreamed of or fantasised about in prison compares to the reality of my life right now … the reality of her. I had no idea a love this deep could deliver so much happiness it goddamn wrecks me.

Then I remember what she told me when she couldn't contain her own tears of happiness. When the emotion is so intense your mind can't contain it, your body has to release it.

That's exactly what this feels like.

Very slowly, I draw in a lungful of air, then carefully exhale. Then I do it again and again until I'm back in control. Inching my hand from her hip, I bring it to my face and wipe away the evidence of my tears.

Satisfied I look normal again, I want her eyes. Sliding down the covers, I take in the dip of her waist, the curve of her hip, her breasts flush against my chest. As the cool air seeps into her skin, she wriggles closer and lets out a contented sigh.

"Merry Christmas," I murmur.

She blinks and smiles up at me, her arm squeezing tight around my waist. "Best Christmas present ever."

Christ, my heart melts for her all over again. "You got that right."

I lean down to kiss her, but she jerks away, untangles herself and leaps out of bed. "Be right back."

With her arms crossed, she cups her breasts and gives me quite a view of her backside as she hightails it into the ensuite and shuts the door. Grinning like a fool, I soon hear the flush of the toilet, then running water.

When the buzz of an electric toothbrush starts, I whip off the covers and join her, disappointed she's shrugged on that skimpy little robe. Winking at her in the mirror, I grab my own toothbrush and get to it, realising the other mornings I woke in her bed, she'd already slipped out while I was sleeping.

She finishes first, and after placing her brush on charge, her gaze in the mirror travels down my naked body until it settles on my semi-hard dick.

Her mischievous eyes snap up to mine. "Well, someone's not *that* happy to see me."

Bending, I rinse my mouth out and tell her, "You've worn him out. Probably for a year or so."

She smirks. "Oh, really?"

I straighten and watch her in the reflection. Her cheekiness, the way she's staring at my cock with utter fascination, has me growing hard.

"Liar." She locks eyes with me and grins. "It's like a magic trick."

I pull her in close and tilt her head up. "The magic happens when I'm inside you." I kiss her, our minty fresh breath filling my senses. Christ, I want her, but she needs some recovery time before I sink into her again. Tonight. It's Christmas day, after all. We couldn't possibly *not* make love.

"Okay," I breathe, "let's save it for later, or I won't have the energy to cook, let alone laze around the pool all day ogling you while trying to make sure Benny's not doing the same."

After Benny arrives and we gorge on the roast lamb Jamie and I prepared, we all decide on a dip in the pool. When Benny goes into the bathroom to change, I head to our room. Yeah, I fucking love that thought. Words I'll never take for granted. *Our room.*

I slip in and shut the door, stopping short when I turn to

find Jamie wiggling into that revealing swimsuit. Striding straight up to her, I whirl her away from the dresser and bend her over the bed, planting her hands on the mattress.

"Gavin," she gasps, but there's not a resistant bone in her body. And why would there be? I know she's playing by wearing this particular swimsuit, and I fucking love that she likes to tease me.

My chest on her naked back, my groin against her arse, I nip at the skin along her shoulder and neck until my mouth finds her ear. "You're going to get it for even *thinking* you can wear this in front of another man."

"Oh?" she breathes as she presses into my erection, "What is it I'm going to get?"

Grinning, I tell her in a low, intimate voice, "You'll be quiet while I show you exactly what I wanted to do to you the first time you wore this. Then you'll put on something more appropriate and go entertain our guest. I'll be out once my dick calms down."

I don't waste any time freeing her arms from the straps so I can cup her bare breasts and grind my cock against her arse. Apart from her accelerated breaths, she remains silent.

From the nape of her neck, I trace the beautiful curve of her spine with soft kisses. When I reach that sliver of arse cleavage, I dip the tip of my tongue in. And she trembles. As she begins to push up, I put a firm hand between her shoulder blades, then drag her swimsuit down her thighs and let it pool at her feet.

Dropping to my knees, I find myself staring at heaven. The way she's positioned, she's spread wide enough for me to see everything. *Everything.*

Fuck.

I don't need to touch her to know how aroused she is. She's glistening right before my eyes.

Burying my nose between her cheeks, I slide my tongue into her sweet pussy until I can't go any deeper. When she drops her chest to the bed and presses back against my face, I fuck her with my tongue until it aches, and her muffled groans grow far too loud.

Giving one cheek a gentle, warning pinch, I remove my tongue and feather it teasingly over her clit before I rise to my feet. As I revel in the sight of her back arched seductively, I know this moment will be etched in my mind forever.

Even though Benny's waiting for us, all I can think about is how much she likes rubbing against my dick when it's wedged in that crack, and how she might like something else there. Hands gripping her hips, I lower my lips to the top of her backside and slide my tongue all the way down to her soaking pussy.

She tenses, but can pull away if she wants to.

When she doesn't, I travel back up, swirling my tongue around that puckered hole before I lick and kiss my way along her spine, taking in every shuddering breath until I reach her ear.

"Get dressed," I whisper, "before you make me do something really dirty."

She straightens, her face red, mouth quirking at the corners. Pressing against me, she rises to her tiptoes, grabs my hard cock through my shorts and whispers in my ear, "Don't you dare take care of this. It's mine to take care of. Got it?"

"Yes, Ma'am," I murmur, grinning like an idiot.

By the time I've changed, I find Jamie and Benny chatting in the shallow end of the pool under the shade-sail Benny and I installed. Two beers and a cocktail rest on the edge beside the large potted ficus. I take a seat beside the planter, grab a beer, and take a long swig. Then I slip completely beneath the water, revelling in the coolness as it steals the fire from my overheated body.

Pushing off the side of the pool, I zero in on Jamie, spear toward her and grab her around the waist. As I haul her over my shoulder and stand, her ear-splitting squeals have me laughing. I spin her around a few times, her fists pummelling my back, before I sink down in the water and position her sideways on my lap.

"You're making Benny uncomfortable," she protests, trying

to wriggle out of my hold.

"Nah," Benny says. "I'd only be uncomfortable if you two weren't actin' like idiots. It's about time."

Jamie looks from Benny to me, and back to Benny. "About time? It hasn't even been a month."

Benny picks up his beer, leans against the pool wall and takes a swig. When it drops away from his mouth, the bastard's smirking. I shake my head, but he responds to my warning glare by pointing the neck of the bottle at me. "This guy here's been pinin' for ya half his life. Isn't that right, Gav?"

Prick.

"I wasn't pining over anyone," I say through gritted teeth.

"Well," Benny relents, "maybe pinin' isn't the right word. Which one is, Gav? Obsessed? Infatuated? Love-struck?"

With my spare hand, I splash him. "Fuck off."

"No," Jamie says, her fingers sinking into the hair at the back of my head. "I want to hear this. Which was it?"

"I've told you what you meant to me, how you helped me survive. But that was an *idea* of you. I didn't know you. So how could I be infatuated, pine or obsess over you?"

Benny lets out a snort. "He's pullin' ya chain, girl. I spent twenty hours a day in a cell with this guy. I think I know him better than he knows himself."

"Bullshit," I say, widening my eyes in warning again when Jamie turns to look his way.

"Let me ask ya this, love. At that restorative justice meetin' ya had with him, did he, or did he not, kinda, sorta, make ya think he was apologisin' for what happened to ya dear Mum?"

She grins, her fingers tightening in my hair. "Oh, he definitely apologised. Grovelled, almost."

Benny tips the neck of the beer at her and winks. "So, there ya have it. Told me he was gonna convince ya he didn't do it, no matter what. Took one look at ya in the flesh and melted. I know, 'cause he wouldn't shut up about it. Only peace I got after that was when they let him out. Then I copped it all over again when ya went an' asked him to move in with ya. Well, didn't that send him into a tailspin."

"Benny. Seriously," I warn.

Jamie tugs on my hair. "Let him finish. Go on, tell me everything."

I'd like to hightail it inside, but that hold she has on my hair tells me she's not letting me run away.

Benny shoots me a wink, takes another sip of beer and smiles. "He barged in, actin' like a big baby, tryin' to use me as an excuse. I wasn't havin' none of that. So, then he says he couldn't stand livin' with ya because he'd fall for you. Said he wouldn't be able to keep his hands off ya. I knew it was way too late for that. Day ya took us to the beach … it was crystal fuckin' clear he was a goner."

The burn in my face has nothing to do with the heat. I'm going to kill him.

Except Jamie's fingertips are lovingly tickling my nape, and her palm on my cheek is forcing me to look at her. Giving in, I meet her eyes, but all that stares back is a love so soft and sweet it melts my heart.

"And," Benny adds, "it was obvious you felt the same way, love. Am I right, or am I right?"

"Clearly, Benny's smarter than both of us," she says, her eyes sparkling as she winks at me. We both know he's a little off the mark, but not by much. Bringing her lips to mine, she gives me that affectionate kiss.

Okay, maybe I won't kill him.

Around four in the afternoon, Benny announces it's time to head home. The thought of him going back to that shitty caravan and the suffocating heat just about does me in. I appreciate it when Jamie offers him the guest room for the night, even if it means infringing on all the wonderful things I want to do to her, but he graciously declines.

After he hugs Jamie goodbye, I walk him outside to wait for his Uber.

Surprising me, he places a hand on my shoulder and squeezes. "I'm so happy for ya, Gav. You deserve every fuckin' thing that woman'll give ya. You were right about her. She's a good one … and she's just as damn lucky to have you."

Unable to help myself, I wrap an arm around him and pull him in for a hug. "Who'd have thought I wanted to kill you a few hours ago?"

"Fuck off," he says affectionately as he thumps me hard on the back before releasing me. "You made the right decision … about not goin' through with the plan. I was wrong. I got no problem admittin' to that. You're gonna have a good life, Gav."

I scratch the back of my head and nod. "Yeah, as unbelievable as it is, I think I am."

Slipping his backpack off his shoulder, Benny places it on the ground and unzips it. After he digs through the contents, he comes up with a square gift box, the type that doesn't need wrapping, though he's taken the time to tie a yellow ribbon into a crooked bow to keep the lid in place. Then he shoves it at me.

"Jesus, Benny. We said no presents."

"Yeah, well, I didn't wanna give it to ya in front of Jamie. I wouldn't know what ta get her, let alone be able to afford somethin'. This's just for you. Cost nothin'. But it means somethin'."

I reach for the ribbon, but he places his hand on top of mine. "Wait 'til ya get inside. When you're alone, right? Not in front of her."

Just as I look up from the box with a question on my lips, his Uber pulls up to the kerb.

Clapping me on the back, he opens the car door and tosses in his backpack. "Thanks for havin' me, Gav. Appreciate it."

"See you in a couple of days."

"You got it."

And then he's gone. I stand there and stare at the box. It's about the size of a small, square tissue box, only it's heavy.

Escaping the heat, I hurry inside and collapse on the couch. A moment later, Jamie joins me, handing me a glass of sparkling water. I down it in one go.

"Aww," she says, eyeing the box beside me. "He gave you a present?"

"Yeah. I told him he wasn't supposed to. Said it didn't cost him anything."

She wraps her arm around mine and grips my bicep. "Well, aren't you going to open it?"

I hesitate, remembering his words. *Not in front of her.* I have no idea what he could give me that Jamie shouldn't see. Besides, I don't want to hide anything from her. I don't want secrets between us. She established that early on and I agreed with her then, and I still do. I always will.

Resting the gift on my lap, I tug on the ribbon until it falls away. When I remove the lid, I'm greeted with tissue paper. Jamie leans closer as I brush it aside.

And we both freeze.

After an eternally long second, she hitches in a breath. "Why would he give you that? Why would he even bring it into our home?"

I stare at the silver snub-nosed revolver Benny showed me after his release from prison. The gun we were meant to use to take out Reid. I'd forgotten all about it.

I study the fear and confusion on her face that, just moments ago, was so damn happy. When her eyes meet mine, I'm not sure where to begin.

"Is that … a bullet?" she asks.

I follow her gaze back to the box and brush aside more tissue paper. Sure enough, a single bullet rests next to the gun. Before I can stop her, she reaches in and plucks it out. Holding it on her open palm, her eyes lock with mine.

"Why aren't you saying anything? What's going on?"

I shake my head. "It's not what's going on. It's what Benny *thought* was going on … before you came to the caravan that day."

"I don't understand," she whispers, her eyes wide, her hold on my bicep loosening.

"I'll tell you. But first, I'm just going to take it out and make sure it's not loaded. Okay?"

She releases my arm, but doesn't move away. I take that as a good sign.

Reaching in, I hold the snub-nose by the handle and inspect

the chambers. Empty. Worried there might be more bullets amongst the tissue paper, I remove it all and stare at a folded note at the bottom of the box.

I pluck it out, shove the tissue paper back in with the gun and set it aside. When I glance at Jamie, her eyes are fixed on the note. Letting out a breath, refusing to hide anything from her, I unfold it.

Gav,

You didn't know it, but this gun had two purposes.

A couple of bullets meant for the problem.

Then one for me.

That's how I had it planned out.

Then the plan changed. I looked at that gun every night, ready to put that bullet in my head. Then I'd tell myself 'one more day'. And every day you were either with me or badgering me on the phone. You've shown me I'm not alone out here. Seeing you so happy, so in love, has given me something I never thought I'd have. A sense of peace, like everything's right with the world, and I don't want to miss out on any of it.

So, I don't need the gun anymore.

Just know, you're the reason I'm still here.

You changed my mind without even knowing it.

Thank you, Son.

Benny.

I stare at the note, taking in the words, turning them over in my mind. My gut churns, thinking of all the times I thought he wasn't doing well, that something was wrong behind all his assurances that he was fine.

When I look at Jamie, she's holding a hand over her mouth, tears falling freely down her cheeks. After a moment, she clutches my shoulder, her lips trembling as she forms the words, "You saved his life."

I shake my head. "No. He helped save mine."

She kneels on the couch beside me and cradles my face in her palms. As her thumbs ghost across my cheeks, I notice a cool, wet sensation. *Fuck*. I'm shedding tears, too. "Gavin, he's given you the gun and the bullet he was going to take his life with. You changed his mind."

"No," I tell her, determined she know the truth. "This is the gun Benny believed I was going to kill Reid with. The gun Benny thought he was going to take from me, and shoot Reid again, so it'd look like he did it … so he could go back inside. *That* was his plan. And I let him believe it. I had no idea he was thinking of using that gun in an entirely different way."

"No. Read it again," she says, tapping the note. "It says …" She freezes, her face contorting with confusion as her gaze travels from the note to me. "What did you—"

Her hand drops from my face as she shuffles back, stands and takes a step away from me. Her whole body trembles as she crosses her arms over her chest. My gut's no longer just churning, it's now sinking deep into the couch cushions.

I place the note in the box, set it all aside and wipe my palms on my jeans. But I don't stand. I couldn't bare it if I tried to get close to her and she retreated. So, I remain where I am and look up at her, willing her with my eyes not to flee, to just let me explain.

"You'd better start talking, Gavin, because I don't like the way I feel right now."

Heart hammering, I place my hand on the couch cushion she just vacated. "Will you sit?"

She shakes her head. "No. I'm about to jump out of my skin. Speak."

"Okay," I sigh and drag a hand down my face before finding her eyes again. "First of all, I'm sorry. I should've told you. Right from the start, I should've told you."

"Told me what?" she snaps, her patience clearly wearing thin.

"Years ago, Benny devised a plan, and I made him believe I was on board. He knew I wanted Reid to pay for what he'd done to me, wanted to make sure he couldn't do it to anyone else. And Benny needed to stay in prison. It's been his home for forty years, his comfort zone. He didn't want freedom. I'm sure you know about prisoners being institutionalised?"

She nods.

"So, Benny thought it'd be a win-win. I'd get my revenge by killing Reid and Benny'd be right there with me, ready to take the gun and fire it a second time so forensics could prove he pulled the trigger. I'd disappear and Benny would go back to prison."

Arms still crossed, she turns her back on me. My heart freezes. What else can it do when it feels like hers has frozen too?

Then she moves. She stalks around the dining table, around the breakfast bar and into the kitchen, then back into the living room, stopping in the same spot she started from.

Looking me in the eye, she plants her fists on her hips. "But that didn't happen."

"Because it was a lie, Jamie. I *lied* to him. And when he got released, when he started pushing to get it done, I kept putting him off, finding one lame excuse after another so I didn't have to admit I lied to my best friend. I was grateful to have him with me on the outside. Apart from him, I was utterly alone. So, I wanted to keep him with me. And I figured the longer I delayed, the more he'd come to accept being free. But fate had other ideas. Because you happened."

Her arms drop to her sides, her hands tight little fists. "What does that mean?"

Taking a risk, I stand, but I don't try to get closer. I wait a moment, then remember to breathe when she doesn't back away. "It means, the day you came to my door and revealed the truth, I had a long discussion with Benny, and we came to an agreement. He'd give it six months."

Now her hands are back on her hips again. "So, all that hatred and blame you put on Reid, you never planned to do anything about it?"

"I won't ever deny I hate that prick. And I have no doubt that if he's done it to me, he's done it others. I *want* him to pay for what he's done. Of course I do."

Barely above a whisper, she asks, "That's why you changed your mind about staying here, isn't it? You used me, hoping to get to him."

"No, that's not it at all. When you told me you'd clear my name, at first, that's all I heard, all I saw. My future, my life back in my hands. Then the other implication seeped in. I realised that by clearing my name, that piece of shit would also be exposed as the corrupt cop he is. Being able to humiliate him, strip him of his power … that felt far more satisfying, far more punishing, than anything else that could happen to him. I'm not a killer, Jamie. I'd never allow scum like Reid to turn me into a monster. You know that. You *know* that."

She opens her mouth to say something, but I see the hesitation there, the cogs flying. I take a quarter of a step toward her. She doesn't flinch or move away. It's all I need. In two strides I'm right in her space, my hands on her shoulders, my face only inches from hers.

"Jamie, you have no idea the relief I felt when I suddenly had you in my corner. When I realised I actually had a chance at a normal life. That relief … well it only comes second to how much I love you." I cup her face. "Please don't hate me for lying to an old man to make him believe I had his back. Because that lie meant I *did* have his back."

She blinks at me, then lets out a long sigh. "I could never hate you again. Never. I just … I'm trying to get my head around it all. It's so *fucking* sad that Benny was desperate enough to devise a plan just so he could live the rest of his life in prison. It breaks my heart."

"He had no hope, no life out here. I just needed time to show him it wasn't as scary on the outside as he thought. And, because of you, he knows that now. Because of you, J."

She shakes her head. "None of that has anything to do with me."

As I place my forehead on hers, I feel her fingers curl into my t-shirt. "I told you at the time … you didn't have to reveal your father's confession to me, to anyone. Only you knew the truth, and you could have kept it that way. But because of the person you are, you didn't. And because you didn't, everything that happened after that led to me being here and you welcoming Benny into your life as well. I'm not sure you understand what that means to a man like him. To a man like me."

She rolls her forehead against mine in denial. Suddenly, she pulls away, sending my heart plunging through the floor. "Jamie?"

Fuck. This can't be the end. We've only just started.

For a moment, she won't meet my eyes. When she does, she bites her lower lip, her features tight with worry. "There's something I should have told you, too."

"O … kay," I say cautiously. I don't like the way she's looking at me, and the fact that I'm not the only one who's omitted the truth, has my pulse stuttering.

"Pete … he asked me … well, made me promise to hold off on your application to overturn your conviction. There's something going on, but his hands are tied. He can't tell me anything. I wanted to tell you so many times, but I just … I didn't want you to be disappointed in me."

"Are you kidding me?"

She shakes her head. "I'm so sorry. I—"

"Jamie," I interrupt as I take her hand and pull her close. "You could never disappoint me."

"You're not angry?"

I thread my fingers through her hair so I can cradle the back of her head. "You trust Pete?"

She nods.

"Then I trust you're doing what's right."

"You're sure?"

I kiss her, and drink in her response. Nothing's changed. She's still mine, still wants me, still loves me. When I lift my mouth from hers, I say, "No more secrets."

"No more secrets," she agrees. Turning her head, I follow her gaze to the gift box. "Now, can we address the fact that you saved a man's life?"

I shake my head as she leads me to the couch. Taking a seat, I pull her down on my lap and wrap my arms around her waist. Before I can stop her, she picks up the box and rests it on her thighs. "You saved his life, Gavin. That has to mean something to you."

"But I let him down," I confess.

She gives me a confused blink. "I don't understand."

"I was so excited that you knew I was innocent, so caught up in working with you to clear my name, I ignored an important factor. Benny. He seemed happy for me. But to him, it must have felt like I was abandoning him."

Her fingers fist in my hair as she shakes her head. "Explain to me how spending every second day with him is abandoning him? You've given him purpose. You taught him how to use technology he'd never encountered before. You made him help you fix up this house. And you were right … you gave him another person who cares about him … and you gave him to me, too. And I bet, when you were alone with him, you talked his head off. I think you knew he was struggling, and you used everything you are, and everything you've learnt, to help him."

I stare into her eyes, dumbfounded by her insight. I want to believe she's right. I *hope* she's right. "Maybe … maybe we both saved him."

She lets out a puff of air. "Stop it, Gavin. It was all you. I think you could help a lot of people like Benny. Whether that's something you want to do or not, I'm determined to at least give you the choice." She looks down into the box on her lap. "Now, what're we going to do with this?"

"We need to get it out of here."

"I'll call Pete tomorrow. I'm sure he'll know what to do with it." Suddenly, she lets out a little chuckle.

"What can possibly be funny?"

"Just my weird brain. Now I'm not going to be thinking, *Bennie and the Jets*. Now I'm going to be thinking, *Benny and the*

Gun. Stupid, right?"

"Cute." I nuzzle her neck. "You got a good place to hide it? I'd prefer to never see it again."

She nods. "Why don't you go for a walk around the block, and I'll take care of it? But," she adds, taking the note out of the box and handing it to me, "you should keep this somewhere close to you. It's probably the most precious gift you'll ever receive."

I take it from her and nod, but I can't look at the words. I know if I do, I'll end up a mess.

So, I take a walk, letting everything that's transpired sink into me. I feel torn, like I failed Benny and saved him at the same time. I guess I'll never know if doing everything Jamie mentioned really worked or not. Maybe he would've been fine without my support. Maybe not.

One thing I do know, is that I should look on the positive side. No point beating myself up for something that didn't happen.

As I head back home, I pull out my phone and call him.

"Don't bother, Gav. Everythin's been said. I'm stickin' around. End of discussion."

"Right," I say, trying to hide the crack in my voice. Swallowing hard, I tell him, "Well, I just wanted to say you've outdone yourself with your gift giving skills. Oh, and I love you, you old goat. There's that."

He's silent for so long, I think the connection's dropped out. Then his voice, thick with emotion, comes through the receiver. "See ya in a couple of days, Son."

This time the call ends. As I shove the phone back in my pocket, I let a smile take hold, and I feel it in my heart, too. I'm pretty damn sure calling me *Son* is his way of telling me he loves me. And I'm more than fine with that.

After a light dinner of leftovers and a pathetic attempt to relax in front of the TV, we decide the bed seems far more attractive than anything else in the house. While Jamie stacks the dishwasher, I clean my teeth, climb into bed naked, and pick up my Kindle. Propped against the headboard, I pretend to read as she breezes in, grabs something from her dresser and disappears into the ensuite.

When she emerges, I continue to pretend to read, but in my peripheral, I catch the very short, sheer white negligee she's wearing, her auburn hair tumbling over her shoulders in stark contrast.

Crawling onto the bed, she snatches the Kindle from my hands, places it on the nightstand, and straddles my lap.

"How rude," I grumble through a wide smile. As she nestles on my lap, I take in the lovely view of her cleavage and those pink, pebbled nipples peeking through the lace. Running my hands up her arms, I hook my fingertips beneath the thin straps on her shoulders. "What's this new torture you're subjecting me to?"

"I thought I should wrap your Christmas present."

"Mmm … I do like to unwrap gifts. But we agreed on no presents. I don't have anything for you."

"Yes, you do."

"Oh? Where?"

She cups my face. "Here," she murmurs, pressing her lips to my forehead. "And here." She plants a sweet kiss on my mouth. "Here," she breathes, nudging the stubble along my jaw with her nose. "And here." Her mouth finds the pulse in my neck.

"Mmm. I got you a lot of presents."

"I'm not finished yet." She scoots back on my thighs a little, dips her head and kisses each quarter of my tattoo. "Here." When she straightens, her eyes lock with mine, and she wriggles forward, rocking against my hard dick. "And here."

I run my hands down her sides, grip her waist, and flex my hips, grinding up to meet her. And damn, even through the sheet, she's scorching hot. "That's all?" I tease.

She blinks at me, the corner of her lip twitching, her palms caressing my chest. "I'm not greedy."

"Liar." I clutch the back of her neck and force her mouth to mine. Her tongue glides between my lips and we suck and nips at each other as I run my hands along her bare thighs, slip them under the soft fabric and cup her naked arse.

Maybe this will be old one day, but that day is not today. And I have a sneaking suspicion we'll be doddering, grey haired fools by the time that happens. I hope so.

Breaking the kiss, I squeeze her firm backside. "Cheeky, sexy, wicked thing."

"The only thing wicked," she pants as she reaches between us, slides aside the sheet and grips my hard cock, "is that this isn't inside me already."

Lowering my hand from her arse, I reach around until my fingers brush over her soaking entrance. "You want to ride me, J?"

She nods eagerly. "I like this. We're so close … so easy to look into your eyes."

"Take what you want from me. I'm all yours."

Rising to her knees, she grips my shoulder with one hand and guides the tip of my cock over her clit, teasing herself for a long moment before, slowly, slowly impaling herself with a soft sigh against my lips.

Then she begins to grind against me, and I know she thinks she's in control right now. I'll let her take a little, but not everything. Removing her hands from my shoulders, I slip them behind her back and trap her wrists there. With my other hand, I slide one thin strap off her shoulder. Before the material falls away, I grip her breast, lower my head and scrape my teeth over her hardened nipple, teasing her through the fabric. Only when she moans my name do I jerk the lace down, clamp my mouth over her, and draw her in.

She clenches around my cock. Fuck, she's driving me wild with her tiny glides up and down my shaft. Her attention's focused more on the contact her clit's making just above the base of my dick, on the trail of hair that's giving her all sorts of wonderful sensations.

Releasing her breast, I find her mouth, drive my tongue inside. Then I drag down her other strap until both hard nipples skate against my chest with every rock of her body. Fuck, that feels amazing.

Tugging on her wrists, I ease her away until I have a spectacular view of her tits as she bounces on my dick.

But I want to test her again, push her, discover what she likes at the same time she does. Freeing her wrists, I groan, "You want to be my naughty girl?"

Biting her lower lip, her fingernails scrape against my beard. And she nods.

I grab her arse with both hands, rock her flush against me, and reach lower until I touch my cock. As I move in and out of her, I soak my fingers in her arousal, then drag all that wetness up between her spread cheeks. When she groans and her eyes flutter, I do it again and again until she's a slippery mess.

Concentrating on that tight, virgin hole of hers, I apply pressure, but I don't push in, I just tease those nerve endings, circling my finger around and around. Our bodies tense and strain against each other, dragging out every sensation for as long as we can.

She presses her mouth to my ear, her breaths loud and ragged. "Oh, Gavin, why does that feel so … fuck, I'm going to come, I—"

She contracts around my dick. Hard. "Fuck, J. Ah, *fuuck*." I follow her right over the edge, exploding with long, hot pulses as she continues to clench around me.

After we clean up and slip back into bed, we lie on our sides and twine our bodies together, our heads resting on one pillow as we gaze at each other.

"So, naughty girl," I murmur, "you liked that, hmm?"

So quickly, I don't see it coming, she clamps a hand over my mouth, her eyes wide. "Don't speak of such things."

I chuckle against her palm, then give it a lick.

"Eww," she gasps, snapping her hand away.

"I hope that's not what you're thinking when I lick your

delicious pussy."

Grinning from ear to ear, she pinches my butt. "Okay, hot stuff. Enough."

Laughing, I press my forehead to hers and rub our noses together. "You're too fucking cute."

"Cute?"

I give her lips a gentle kiss. "And sexy and beautiful, hot, gorgeous and sweet and every goddamn thing all at once. I'm spoiled rotten, you little wench." I litter her face with kisses before pulling back so I can see her eyes. "It's like we both waited for each other … we just didn't know that's what we'd been doing until we met."

She caresses my jaw, her eyes watery. "I think you're right," she whispers before planting her mouth on mine. "I love you so much … I don't even know how to describe it."

"It's easy," I tell her. "You're my happiness, my life, my breath. When you stop breathing, so will I."

I startle awake, heart pounding, not sure what brought me out of sleep. Motionless, I listen. Nothing. Reaching out, I find Jamie's back only a foot away. Instinct wants me to snuggle against her, but I don't want to disturb her. Besides, now that I'm awake, I could use a glass of water.

Slipping out of bed naked, I pad quietly out of the room, down the hallway and into the kitchen. With the illumination from the various appliances, I don't bother with the lights as I grab a glass from a cupboard and fill it with water.

When I raise the glass to my lips, I freeze.

At the fringe of my vision, a shadow moves.

I spin toward the breakfast bar as he rounds the end. He stops there, in the hallway, giving himself a view of our bedroom door, while effectively trapping me in the kitchen.

So I can't get to her, can't protect her.

Like I'm fucking supposed to. The very reason I'm in this

house.

And now Reid's pointing a pistol with a suppressor attached right at my chest.

I'm naked, exposed, caught completely off guard.

The fact that he's made no effort to hide his identity sends terror streaking up my spine.

He's here to kill us. And he wants us to know exactly who's ending our lives.

I let the glass slip from my fingers. When it hits the tiles in the silent house, the shatter sounds like a foreshadowing of what's to come. Because all that broken glass is about to hurt.

I'm certain it's woken her. The very reason I dropped it.

Reid chuckles. "Merry fucking Christmas, arsehole."

"Jamie! He's here! Don't come out!" I yell, knowing that's what she'll do. If there's any hope of her surviving this, she'll have to take him by surprise. "Get Bennie and the Jets!"

At Reid's confusion, I launch myself at the fucker who took so much from me. The fucker who's here to take everything.

As I charge at him, the glass slices into the soles of my feet, and I slip on the blood, almost losing my footing. But I don't stop. Over the roar of rage coming from my throat, I barely hear the *pop*, barely acknowledge the burning pain spearing through my shoulder, the acrid smoke filling my nostrils.

Before I reach him, Reid ducks behind the kitchen wall, constricting my heart with renewed terror. *He's going after her.*

But when I slam into the hallway wall, he's not racing to our room. He's facing me, bringing the gun up again.

Launching off the wall, I swing my arm down on his wrist, hoping to knock the weapon from his hand.

Another *pop*.

Heat slices through my torso.

Ignoring it, I ram my uninjured shoulder into his chest. He stumbles backward, raises the gun again, and this time I grab the hot barrel, try to twist it from his grip.

When I rocket my other fist at his face, my sliced feet slip on the polished floorboards, and I only manage to graze his jaw.

"Benny!" I shout, trying to regain my footing. But there's something wrong. Reid's not afraid of me, and I can't be sure, but I don't think my voice is as loud as I want it to be. "Get Bennie and the Jets! Get Benny!"

As my knees hit the floor, Reid wrenches the gun from my failing grip. When he takes a step back, the hallway walls grow fuzzy.

Then the fucker laughs. "I watched that worthless piece of shit leave hours ago, arsehole. Give it up."

I stare at him, my mind drifting, blurring. He's not looking at my face. He's looking at my dick. I glance down. No. Not my dick. At the blood pumping from the hole in my gut. Blood that's running down my leg and slicking the floorboards.

He raises the gun, and as I fall forward, I manage to grab his ankle. With everything I've got, I yank it toward me and hold on.

He crashes to the floor, and I hear that *pop* again. But no pain this time.

"Get Benny!" I yell, barely louder than a whisper.

The pain from the bullet scorches my insides and dims my vision, but I keep going after him, pulling at his jeans, using them to drag myself up his body.

He squirms beneath me, our eyes locking. The only thing looking back at me is determination and hatred.

As a wave of weakness loosens my grip on him, the heel of his shoe connects with my temple.

The foggy world fills with bright sparks, then threatens to thrust me into darkness. I fight it with everything I have. I need to save her. I can't let him take her from this world. She's too precious, too kind, and loving, and good. She'll survive my death, but I won't survive hers. If there *is* any surviving. I'm not so sure right now.

When the world swims into focus, Reid's looming above me, the gun pointed at my head.

"Get Benny," I croak.

A thump comes from the bedroom, sending Reid's attention to the open door. With the pathetic amount of strength I have left, I try to grip his leg to drop him to the floor again.

No longer amused, he shakes me free, raises his foot and brings it down on the bullet wound in my abdomen.

I think I cry out, but I can't be sure. The world's spinning away, darkness descending. Warmth pools at my sides, and I know it's my blood. In contrast, there's a deep cold seeping from the inside of my useless body, radiating outward. I desperately try to draw on the strength I found that first week in prison. The night those pricks cornered me. That feral animal still lives within me and it's fighting like fuck to get out. But I hadn't been shot back then. I'd had complete control of my body. Not this time. No matter how hard I try, it won't cooperate.

With no concept of how much time has passed, feeling like I'm diminishing into nothingness, the last blurry thing I see is the hallway. Empty.

"Get Benny," I whisper, over and over, when all I want to say is *I love you, I love you, I love you.*

As the darkness finally claims me, a gunshot blasts through the house.

Chapter 46

Gavin

LIGHT BLEEDS INTO into the darkness behind my closed lids, creeping in with flashes of memory. Something I don't want any part of.

I'm floating, untethered from my body.

There's no pain.

Just the comfort of nothingness.

And I embrace it.

I can't be sure if seconds, hours or days have passed, but there's something insidious squirming inside me. A foreboding lurking beneath the surface of this floating comfort. The nothingness buries a truth I can't quite grasp.

Dread. Seeping in around the edges, tugging and seeking a way inside. I can't let it. I won't.

When a warm hand squeezes my arm, I let the nothingness take me back down into sleep, into that safe place where there is no reality, no pain. Where my heart doesn't hurt.

The next time consciousness tugs at me, I'm no longer numb.

I move a little, gasping as the pain snaps my grainy eyes open.

I'm in a stark white room. A television hangs suspended from the ceiling, and beeping comes from beside me. Carefully turning my head toward the sound, I discover I'm tethered to various machines. A cannula's taped to the back of my hand, a pulse monitor clamped to my index finger.

An uncomfortable looking padded chair rests close to the bed, but it's empty.

Jamie.

Memories flood my mind. Finding Reid in the kitchen. Being shot. Twice. The struggle, the fight to stay conscious, the drive to protect Jamie. Spiralling into unconsciousness.

The gunshot.

Fuck. *Fuck!*

Jamie.

Where is she? Where—

Searing pain abruptly stops my effort to get out of bed. Slumping back, darkness bites at the edges of my vision as the heartrate monitor's beeps increase.

Where the hell're the nurses? The doctors?

Sliding a hand off my thigh, I touch what feels like a remote control. I jab randomly at the buttons, hoping it'll summon a nurse.

Instead, the TV bursts to life, instantly drawing my attention. I can't hear anything, but I don't need to.

A female reporter stands on the footpath in front of Jamie's house, police tape all over the fucking place. My heart jackhammers, and before I can fumble with the remote to turn up the volume, words scroll across the bottom of the screen.

Female lawyer murdered. Police calling on public for help.

I want to float again. I want nothingness. Darkness. I want to cease to exist, to go to a place where nothing matters, where nothing's real, where nothing hurts.

I close my eyes, shutting out the world, the words on the screen, the sight of Jamie's house surrounded with police tape.

It's all meaningless, because it's just a dream. A stupid nightmare reflecting everything I fear deep down in my subconscious. That's all this is. I'm in bed beside the love of my life and I'm having a nightmare. A nightmare I desperately need. Because I've let down my guard. I've let love overtake me and blind me to the reason I'm in her house. That's what this is. A wake-up call. When I *do* wake up, I'll touch the curve of her hip and wrap myself around her warmth. And I'll remember that I need to stay vigilant, that I'm here to protect her.

When I draw in a sharp breath, pain snaps my eyes open. I'm still in this empty hospital room, the beep of the monitor faster, images moving on the TV, the reporter in front of Jamie's house replaced by a newsreader in a studio.

Onto the next story.

Like the previous one meant nothing.

Like *she* meant nothing.

Desperate, I raise the remote, find the volume and turn it up. Then I change channels, over and over until I find what I don't want to find.

A male reporter faces the camera this time, a slightly different angle of Jamie's house behind him.

"—was shot and killed in her home in this quiet suburb last night. Currently, there are no leads as to the identity of the shooter. Police are canvassing the neighbourhood, hoping someone saw something that will give them the lead they need to track down the offender. Over to you, Ron."

There's a new sound in the room, a keening that hadn't been there moments ago. I turn my head toward the closed door, but no one's there.

And then I realise I can't breathe. My throat's closing up tight, the air barely entering my windpipe. It's me. The sound's coming from me.

I can't … I can't … fucking breathe.

It's not real.

But I still can't draw a breath. And I told her just last night, *when you stop breathing, so will I.*

No. She can't be gone. No, no, no, no, no, no.

As my useless body tries to suck in air, my mind races.

I should have known the life I'd fallen into was too good to be true. Just when I thought I had everything I'd ever need to live a good life with the woman I love, it's ripped away. Again. Like some cruel joke. Giving me a taste of what's possible, then snatching it from me forever.

Her life. Extinguished by a monster who thrives on destroying others.

The knowledge that I can give the police what they need to eviscerate Reid is utterly pointless. What does it matter?

Reid killed her.

That fucker should never have had the chance. I should have killed him. I should have followed Benny's plan. I should never have let her get under my skin. Instead, I let hope for a future that was never meant to be mine blind me. If I'd only done the *wrong* thing, she'd be alive.

Now I can't touch her, hold her, look into her eyes. Everything is meaningless.

My father's face suddenly swims before me. And now I know. I truly know what he felt the night Jamie's mother was murdered. Everything became meaningless for him in the blink of an eye. Including me. And I can't hate him anymore.

But it doesn't matter, does it?

Excruciating pain suddenly tears through my body.

Then I'm falling.

When I crash into something hard and unforgiving, the pain screams. But before I can vanish within that soulless darkness again, the hurt that tears my heart right open obliterates anything my body throws at me.

On some level, I realise I'm on the floor, trying to drag myself to the door that seems to retreat every time I inch closer.

I don't know where I'm going, or why. I just need to leave this room, the truth it holds within its walls. If I'm not in here, maybe the truth can't follow me, maybe I can stop my heart from disintegrating.

Or better yet, maybe it'll vaporise and end the dread that's engulfing me.

Please, I beg. *Please stop beating.*

I need it to stop.

Just like hers.

I'm sinking, drowning, and I want to slip under the water and let it swallow me into its darkest depths.

"Gavin!"

I raise my head. Anika stands in the doorway, her expression horrified as a coffee cup slips from her hand, splattering across the shiny lino.

Beside her, an equally shocked uniformed cop stares at me.

"Get help!" Anika screams at him. "Go!"

As he takes off, my sister races toward me, skidding to her knees, lifting me under my arms until my upper body leans against her. Engulfing me, she rocks me, muttering nonsense words that everything's okay.

But it's not okay. Not if Anika's here. She only just left to start her new life.

She's back because her sister's dead.

Heaving sobs burst from my closed throat. And I hate it. Hate it because it means I'm still here in this nightmare. I'm breathing. She's not. It should be the other way around.

"Gavin," Anika says into my ear. "Gavin, I'm so sorry, I—Fuck!" There's careful jostling, then she's kneeling beside me, my back pressed against something firm. The wall, I guess.

She takes my face in her hands, just the way Jamie does.

Did.

Now she's crying too.

Through my own tears, through the wracking sobs that send shockwaves of pain through my body, she forces me to look at her.

"Gavin!" she screams on a whisper, her trembling fingers tightening on the hinges of my jaw. "Gavin, listen to me." She leans in so close, her breaths cool my tears. "She's okay. She's alive. She's fine."

I know she's only saying that to calm me down. And it's

fucking brutal.

My eyes ping to the TV screen above the bed. She follows my gaze, her face coming back, head frantically shaking.

"No. No, Gavin. It's not true. It's a false press release. The cops are trying to bait … It doesn't matter. Gavin. I promise you, it's not true. She's alive and she's so worried about you."

I stare at her, wanting to believe every word coming from her mouth. One thing stops me.

"If she was alive, she'd be here," I croak.

"She's in protective custody. She can't be here for you until this thing's done."

I don't believe her. Nothing makes any sense. "Then why … why're you here?"

She looks at me with such confusion in her eyes, my heart sinks.

"I'm here, dickwad, because you've been fucking shot. I turn up for my family. Deal with it."

I stare into her eyes, desperate to believe her, but my only family wasn't there for me when I needed him. I can't help but doubt her words, can't help but think she's only here because Jamie's dead.

Before I can argue with her, soft soled footsteps race into the room and someone gasps. I don't look at the source of the sound. Instead, I follow Anika's eyes as they latch onto my torso.

Blood blooms on the hospital gown covering my torso and, even as I watch, it grows wider, darker.

Then a nurse is on her knees, hiking up the gown to inspect the source of the blood.

Anika's gaze snaps back to mine. "Well, fuck," she says, anguish still bright in her eyes even as a glimmer of the girl I've come to know shines through. She scrunches up her nose. "I just got an eyeful of my brother's junk. You realise I'm scarred for life now, right?"

As more staff enter the room, I hear the nurse say I've ripped open my stitches. Then there's a pinch in my arm, and that wonderful floating feeling sings through my body.

Before it overtakes me, I chuckle, watching Anika grin back at me, one hand still on my jaw, the other gripping my hand. There's no way she could crack a joke if her sister was dead.

I stare into her eyes. And I see truth.

Letting it in, I bring it with me into the darkness.

When I wake again, I find Anika sleeping in that uncomfortable chair beside my bed, the TV remote firmly clutched in her hand.

Turning away, I stare at the ceiling, trying to piece together what happened. I suppose it doesn't matter. All that matters is that Jamie's alive.

My heart squeezes tight, remembering all too well the excruciating pain of believing I'd lost her. It's not like I haven't experienced loss before. My mother's death, my father's decision to abandon me. But somehow, the intensity of losing Jamie was … soul crushing.

Even though I know she's alive, the trauma's still fresh and overwhelming.

My mind twists and turns, thinking the unthinkable, then latching onto it anyway. I'm not sure I can go through losing her again. Loving her like I do means annihilation. She might have survived this time, but will she ever really be safe? Is anyone? She could die in a car accident, get run over on a pedestrian crossing, crushed by a falling tree. She could get terminal cancer. Or she might decide at some point in the future that she doesn't love me after all.

The thoughts race around and around until I realise they all lead to one thing, and one thing only.

One day, I *will* lose her forever.

There's only one way to prevent that from happening.

She has to lose me first.

This thing called love is utterly fucked up.

No matter what, it can only ever end in pain. Whoever gets

left behind to endure it is a total crapshoot.

I contemplate the idea of pushing her away, or simply disappearing so I can avoid this inevitable agony in the future.

For about two seconds.

I could never deliberately cause her that much pain.

When I imagine her walking into this room, I know I'll see guilt and fear in her eyes. And I can't have that. None of this is her fault.

When her eyes meet mine, I want them filled with love. It's my job to put it there, to keep it there. I know that's selfish, but I don't care. When she looks at me that way, she makes me soar.

As I close my eyes and drift back to sleep, I know I've learnt something significant about myself.

My love for her far outweighs the pain of losing her.

Chapter 47

Jamie

Sixteen Hours Earlier

SHATTERING GLASS BRINGS me out of sleep like a sharp slap to the face. I sit up, trying to focus in the dark as I reach for Gavin.

My hand finds empty sheets containing only a trace of warmth.

That's when I hear a male voice. "Merry fucking Christmas, arsehole."

Every hair on my scalp rises to attention. I know that voice.

Jarrod.

As quietly as I can, I slip out of bed, my feet carrying me toward the open door.

"Jamie! He's here! Don't come out!" Gavin yells. I freeze. My stomach clenches. He sounds scared. Panicked. Totally unlike himself. Whatever's happening out there, his voice sends chills down my spine. "Get Bennie and the Jets!"

What's he—

A roar of anger fills the house, and something underneath. A *pop*. I hold my breath, heart skittering and stuttering in my chest.

A loud crash comes from the hallway. Next, I hear grunting

and shuffling feet. They're fighting. Then another *pop*.

If I go out there, Jarrod will see me. There's no way I can make a dash for the backyard. And there's no way I'm leaving Gavin.

"Benny!" Gavin's voice quavers. "Get Bennie and the Jets! Get Benny!"

"I watched that worthless piece of shit leave hours ago, arsehole. Give it up," Jarrod says, his voice strong, confident. The voice of a man in control.

Oh, God. Has he shot Gavin? Is that what those pops were?

Get Benny.

Get Bennie and the Jets.

Benny and the Gun.

The gun.

Get the gun.

Oh, fuck.

I turn on my heel, snatch my phone off the bedside table, and race into the ensuite. Shutting the door silently behind me, I turn on the light, flinching at the sudden brightness.

I can still hear Gavin telling me to get Benny, but he sounds so far away now, and I don't know if it's because I've shut the bathroom door, or if he's fading.

With no time to think, I call Pete instead of triple zero. He answers almost immediately.

"Jarrod's here," I whisper. "I think he shot Gavin. He's coming for me, Pete." I hang up immediately, change the phone to airplane mode, find the voice recorder, press record and shove it in the vanity drawer. I trust Pete will get the police and ambulance here faster than emergency services can.

Tears threaten and my throat closes. I want to curl into a ball, put my arms over my head and pretend none of this is happening. Except the man I love is out there, and after all the practice I've had at acting strong, now's the time to draw it to the surface.

Legs shaking violently, I lower myself to the tiles and reach for the edge of the vanity's loose kickboard. Pulling it aside, I flatten my body to the floor, my cheek to the cold tile, and stare into the dark space where I hid the gun.

I'm sure I hear Gavin's faint voice, but I don't want to think about why it sounds so weak.

I grab the gun and bullet, and sit up. Fumbling, I take my mind back to my second date with Jarrod. At the pistol club. He let me shoot a few different types of guns, the last being a six-shooter. Except the one I shot that day had a much longer barrel.

Remembering how to push the lever forward to free the cylinder, I shove the bullet in place and snap the barrel closed.

Silence. No more thuds or grunts. No more pleas to get Benny. I want to scream out to Gavin, but I keep quiet, listening.

My heart pounds in my ears as I rise to my feet. I only have one bullet, literally one shot to survive this and try to save Gavin's life. And I'm up against a cop who knows exactly how to use a gun, how to bring a suspect down.

Backing up to the toilet so I'm not reflected in the mirror, I grab a towel off the rail and wrap up my naked body, securing the soft fabric beneath my right armpit.

That's when I hear his footsteps.

And now I'm not sure if I positioned that bullet correctly. What if I'm one cylinder left or right of the hammer? What if I pull the trigger and nothing happens?

I have to take him by surprise, but there's nowhere to hide in here. If he comes through that door and Benny's gun doesn't fire, I'm dead. And so is Gavin.

I slide my right arm into the gap where the towel overlaps itself, concealing the gun within.

The door flies open. Jarrod points his long-barrelled gun straight at me before he cautiously steps into the room. I understand the *pops* now. He's using a silencer.

I welcome the full body tremor that rattles through me. I want him to see how terrified I am, to believe he has a scared, harmless little mouse cornered.

For a split second I wonder if I can convince him I'm confused, that I still trust him, that I don't understand what's happening.

But he's staring at me with that same look he had when I refused to let him kiss me. My skin crawls. There might be a vile reason he didn't pull the trigger the moment he had me in his sights.

"Jarrod, what's—"

"Shut up, Jamie. This's fucking hard enough. You and your stupid convict's plans to fuck me over end here."

I don't miss the irony of his words, but I'm not about to point it out.

"I don't understa—"

"The only thing you needed to understand," he interrupts, "was to back the fuck off. But you didn't, did you? You kept digging. When you came up with the affidavit from that kid, well, that was easy enough to get rid of. But that fucking video of your father's … It's gone from your work's server now, but I know you're smart, Jamie. After the affidavit disappeared, you'd have made sure you kept other copies. I'll be needing those, and the original."

My left hand trembles as I raise it to my throat. He watches every movement. The urge to tell him I've already sent it to the police bubbles behind my lips, but I hold back. If he thinks it's too late to stop the evidence coming to light, he'll end this right here and now.

"Did you kill him? Just tell me that."

"He's not doing so well, Jamie. He's suffering. So hurry up and give me what I want, then this'll all be over. No more fear, no more pain. Won't that be nice?"

He's still alive. Still alive, still alive, my mind beats in time with my heart. There's hope. That's all I need.

"You're going to kill us? Over a botched investigation all those years ago? It doesn't make any sense."

He lets out an unamused chuckle. "Smart in some ways, dumb in others. It's not about your mother's murder. Such a one-track mind, Jamie. I simply can't have anyone poking around in my business. But you're right about where this is headed. Such a shame. It really is. You're fucking beautiful."

Hearing that from this monster's lips peppers my skin with goosebumps.

"But you never got to see me, did you?" I whisper.

His eyes skate over the towel, down to my bare legs, then back to my face again.

"Drop it," he commands.

I shake my head. "Not while you're pointing that at me."

The gun doesn't waver. "Drop it," he repeats.

I jut out my chin, my heart banging against my chest. "You can either shoot me now and perv at my corpse, or you can put that gun down and look at me while I'm alive. I suspect you've always wanted to see me naked."

He licks his lips, the hesitation obvious. "Even when you were a teenager, I'd jerk off to fantasies of that body of yours."

Fucking pervert.

I remain silent while I stare at him, waiting.

His answer comes when he lowers the gun, his grip still tight as it bumps against his thigh. Eyes ablaze, he gives me a sharp nod aimed at the top of the towel.

Trembling, I reach beneath my right armpit, and in one smooth motion, I yank the tucked corner free, fling it aside and raise the gun.

Aiming at his chest, I squeeze the trigger.

The explosion sends a shockwave through my arm and shoulder. Even with our close proximity, I'm unsure if I've hit him. He's wearing black, so I can't tell if he's bleeding.

Then I see it. A small hole in the fabric over his chest.

But it doesn't matter. He's raising his gun.

Screaming, I launch myself at him, smashing my revolver into his nose as I arc my other arm down on the hand hold the gun.

He pulls the trigger. A *pop*, then a flare of heat sears my right hip, but I don't have time to think, because as his legs buckle, he grabs my throat, and we both go down.

Sprawling on top of him, I try to twist out of his grasp, but it's unrelenting, cutting off my airflow, crushing my trachea. In my scramble to get my legs beneath me, my knee slams his forearm to the tiles. The forearm connected to the hand holding his gun. Frantic, I grab for it, astounded when it slides it free without resistance.

As I stare down at him, his grip on my throat loosens, then drops away.

And I see it. Just the way Gavin described my mother. Jarrod's going. He's still here, but blood's pumping from his chest wound, his skin ashen.

His eyes fastened on my bare breasts.

And that's the last thing he sees. He's gone.

When I look at his chest again, there's barely a trickle seeping from the wound.

His heart's no longer pumping. It's as dead as his eyes. Though, I suspect, it always has been.

Gavin.

Leaping off Jarrod, keeping his gun in one hand, I grab the towel and almost bolt from the room. But my feet freeze. If I don't go out there, Gavin's still alive. If I do, I might discover he's not. And I don't know if I'll survive that.

Turning to the vanity, I take my phone from the drawer and stop the recording.

I stand there, too afraid to move and too afraid not to.

What if he's dying? What if he needs me with him so he can look into my eyes as he goes? How can I deny him that when he gave that gift to my mother?

I don't remember leaving the ensuite or my bedroom, but I'm suddenly in the hallway.

Gavin lies outside the kitchen. Naked. Motionless.

No!

Then I see it. The almost imperceptible rise and fall of his chest.

I sprint to him, dropping to my knees in the dark pool of blood growing at his side. I crush the towel over the bullet wound in his torso, using my weight to keep the pressure steady.

Finally, I brave a look at his face. His eyes are closed, his skin pale. I'm glad he's unconscious. He doesn't need to endure this pain. Concentrating on the rise and fall of his chest, I drift into some sort of disconnected state. All I can do is watch, making sure each breath expands his chest at the same rate as the one before.

When the front door smashes open and armed men storm in, I don't even flinch. Orders and responses are shouted, heavy footfalls pound the floorboards, but I don't see flashing blue and red lights through the windows. I don't remember hearing sirens approach.

Then a blanket's being wrapped around my naked body. I see Pete's kind eyes as he kneels beside me, and I have the ridiculous urge to tell him he's ruining his pants. When he places an arm around my shoulders and pulls me toward him, I try to resist. I have to keep the pressure on the wound. That's my job. My *only* job.

"The ambos'll take care of him now, Jamie. Let them get him to hospital."

I hadn't even noticed them kneeling at Gavin's head, one on each side, an oxygen mask over his mouth and nose, their impatient faces staring at me.

Dazed, I nod as I release the towel over the bullet wound and let Pete help me to my useless legs. Sagging against him, I manage to point at the floor. "My phone … recorded what I could."

He snatches it up, guides me to the couch, and lowers us both down. I catch a glimpse of my knees smeared with Gavin's blood just before Pete drapes a throw-rug over them. Then he calls over a paramedic to examine the wound on my hip from Jarrod's stray bullet.

"I'm sorry," Pete says, his hand tight on my shoulder. "I'm so sorry. We fucked up. *I* fucked up. I let you down. I'm never going to forgive myself."

As the paramedic cleans and dresses my wound, I look into Pete's tormented eyes, not understanding what he's talking about. It's only then that I realise it's not just my whole body that's numb, it's my mind, too.

"Can you ever forgive me?"

I stare at the people going about their business from the fourteenth floor of the police headquarters. Must be nice to be in a hurry to get somewhere and actually be free to do just that. But who am I to judge? I don't know what any of those strangers have been through.

Turning away from the window, I gaze at Pete standing beside the uncomfortable couch he tried to get me nap on last night. "I told you, I can't answer that until I see Gavin with my own eyes." Until that happens, I won't sleep.

He nods, then goes back to studying the ugly brown industrial carpet at his feet.

I should feel sorry for him. He's carrying a heavy weight on his shoulders. But, for now, I can't bring myself to feel anything but anger.

Even so, he hasn't left my side since the moment he found me applying pressure to Gavin's gunshot wound. Under the cover of darkness, he escorted me through the police headquarters' back entrance and up to this room. He's done everything right. Besides what should have been done right in the first place.

I've been in this room for sixteen hours now. Sixteen. Sixteen hours, sixteen years. I hate that fucking number.

Over those hours, Pete filled me in on the operation internal affairs have been conducting on several high-profile politicians and police. Detective Inspector Jarrod Reid being one of them. They've known of his corruption for some time, but had held off bringing him down, wanting to go after the bigger fish they knew, but couldn't prove, he was involved with.

When the fire broke out in the historical building next to the high-rise apartments in The Rocks, the investigators knew it had been deliberately lit. After hidden security cameras across the road revealed the identities of the thugs who ignited it, they crumbled and pointed the finger at Reid. He'd hired them to do the job.

Pete's team knew Reid didn't stand to gain anything from the destruction of the historic building. But they knew of a certain politician who, a few years prior, had tried to get his hands on that land. Greed had set in motion a plan that went terribly wrong. A plan that cost the lives of seven innocent people.

Once Pete's team had the phone taps in place, a false media report stated the fire was caused by an electrical fault. Ever since, the police have been listening and gathering information on the involvement of the suspected high-ranking police and politicians. But it's one thing to know what they'd done, and another to prove it. And those involved were careful not to let anything slip.

While Pete's team waited for the evidence to arrest them all, I came along. Wanting to overturn Gavin's conviction, which would directly lead to an investigation into Jarrod. And I'd alerted him to that fact. To allow such an investigation to take place would risk uncovering links to those in positions far higher up the chain. The people he worked for would eliminate him before they let that happen. So he took action.

First, the threatening note under my door. Then he bribed that snake at work, Simon, who deleted Liam's affidavit, and informed Jarrod when I saved my father's video confession into the file. Unless Reid could eliminate the reason he was about to come under investigation—me—he knew he was a dead man.

But police procedure tied Pete's hands. He couldn't tell me anything. It all made sense now. How he'd discouraging my involvement in overturning Gavin's conviction, then his insistence that I promise to hold off for a few months. I know he was bound by rules he'd vowed not to break, but if I'd only known, we could have taken steps to protect ourselves.

Now, after a second false media report—my death—those involved in the fire haven't been quite so careful with their phone conversations.

"Jamie?" Pete tries again. Before he can continue, his phone rings. "Yeah … Yeah, send her in." He looks at me, his face grim. "Your sister."

I haven't seen her yet, but I'd filled her in over the phone, making it clear that I was safe, that it was Gavin who she needed to be with. So she should be here.

A moment later, the door unlocks, and a heavily armed officer shows Anika in. As soon as she spots me, she bursts into tears and runs at me, grabbing me in a bear hug.

"I fucked up," she cries. "I fucked up, Jamie. I'm sorry."

I hug her tight, fear blooming in my chest. "Gavin?"

She nods, then quickly adds, "He's okay. I just … I'm … I'm so fucking stupid."

Ignoring Pete's questioning gaze, I wrap an arm around my sister and lead her over to the uncomfortable couch. Holding her tight, I wait until she calms down. Finally, she looks at me with haunted eyes that do nothing to calm *me*.

"He … he hadn't woken up yet, and I thought … I'd just go to the loo and get a coffee. A few minutes, that's all."

Her lip trembles as she swallows hard, trying to stay in control. I've never seen her this upset before, and it scares me to death. "Okay," I encourage. "So, you went to get coffee …"

"And when I came back, he was on the floor … bleeding … he'd turned on the TV and seen the news … he thought—"

She bursts into tears again. I cradle her head to my chest. She doesn't have to say more. If he saw the news, there was only one thing he *could* think.

"I had one job," she cries, "and I fucked it up so bad."

I hold her closer, half to comfort her and half to comfort myself. I'd told her on the phone that I needed her to be with Gavin so when he woke up, she could tell him what was going on before he saw or heard something he shouldn't. "But you said he was okay."

She pulls back, swiping at her face with her sleeve. "Yes and no."

"Ank. What does that mean?" My heart doesn't know whether to stop or burst through my chest.

"He ripped his stitches open. They've fixed that up. But … I've never seen someone look like … like all the life had drained from him. It fucking crushed me, Jamie. And it was all my fault."

I place my hands firmly on her upper arms and squeeze. "Now, you listen to me. It's not your fault. It's Jarrod's fault. Not—"

"It's my fault," Pete says from beside us.

We both look up at his desolate face. It'd be really fucking nice to blame someone. Someone who wasn't dead. Someone I haven't killed. Over the last gruelling hours, I've discovered blaming the dead isn't as satisfying as I'd like.

Pete runs a hand over his face and takes a deep breath. "Because I should have trusted our friendship and … told you more."

"Yes," I say without blinking, "you should have. But rules are rules, right?" I ask bitterly.

He nods, his eyes downcast, remorse rolling off him in waves. When I'd tried to discuss it with him earlier, he was stoic on his reasoning and unapologetic. Seeing Anika's distress—distress I've buried—has clearly affected him.

After a moment, he meets my eyes. "I am truly sorry, Jamie. My judgement was clouded. I wanted them all to go down so badly, I couldn't risk screwing it up. It should've been me in that surveillance car watching your house Christmas night, not a couple of jerks who thought it'd be a smart idea to sneak home to their families instead of doing their job. I'm a shit friend."

"Yeah, well. I'll be the judge of that. Just not right now." I know it's harsh, I know it's not what he wants to hear. I also know I'll forgive him. But I'm so fucking furious, I feel no guilt in letting me suffer a little longer.

I don't want my sister to suffer, though. Taking her hands in mine, I look into her eyes and tell her again. "See? It's not your fault. You get that, right?"

She hesitates as a few more tears slip from her eyes. I squeeze her hands and nod. After a moment, she gives me the tiniest of nods in return. "I don't think he's really going to believe you're okay until he sees you." She glances up at Pete. "How much longer?"

"Everyone's almost in position," Pete says, running a weary hand over his face.

"Must be killing you, to be babysitting me instead of out there, making the arrests yourself." I now know how much work has gone into this operation. It's Pete's baby, his last case before he retires.

"Here is exactly where I should be. My team's more than capable."

I call bullshit. "You're not the babysitting type."

"For you, I am. I almost got you killed. I definitely got your boyfriend shot. At the very least, I got you both traumatised."

"I'm fine," I say truthfully.

"You killed a man. You're not fine."

Anika's arms tighten around me. "He's right. We studied this at the academy. Even hardened cops are traumatised when they're forced to take a life. Don't bury it, Jamie. You'll need help."

I rub Anika's arm and give her a faint nod. I won't tell them how I feel about killing Jarrod. There's only one person I'll talk to about it, the only one who'll truly understand. Because I don't feel guilty, or traumatised. All I feel is utter relief.

I'd had no idea I was capable of killing a man. Not until the moment arrived. But I hadn't pulled the trigger to save my life. I'd pulled it in the hope that Gavin's life could still be saved. Jarrod was merely a roadblock to the man I loved. And nothing, *nothing* would stop me from being by his side.

Except I'm not, am I?

But I know he's alive, know he's safe. Although his part in all of this has been hidden from the media, Pete's taken measures to keep him protected.

Patting Anika's arm, I ask, "How're Benny and your father holding up?"

"They're both going outta their fucking minds. Especially since they can't see him until all the arrests have been made.

But Lach went over to Benny's. Apparently, after they had quite a pissing contest about who cares more about Gavin, they sorted things out and are waiting at Lach's house for the green light."

I briefly wonder how long it'll be before she refers to her father as *Dad*. I hope she does. She deserves to have a real dad who truly cares for her.

"You should get back to the hospital. Keep Gavin company, keep him calm. You know what to tell him."

As I stand and encourage her to her feet, she gives me a fierce hug before making her way to the door. Turning the handle, she looks over her shoulder, her expression lighter, a touch of that spark back in her eyes where it belongs.

"You should probably know … I saw your boyfriend's junk."

I freeze, the admission so unexpected, I have no idea how to react.

Anika grins at me, pulls the door open and winks. "Gotta say … lucky you. Not so lucky for me. Now *that* was traumatising." She makes a gagging gesture, then she's gone, the armed officer closing the door behind her.

I glance at Pete, but he seems focused on his phone. Until I notice the corner of his mouth twitching.

"Something amusing?" I ask, struggling with my own battle to keep a smile at bay.

He shakes his head, refusing to take his attention from his phone.

Striding over to the windows, I stare at the street below and let that grin stretch my lips. Anika wouldn't be acting like her usual self if she didn't believe Gavin was out of the woods. Nor would she joke if she still blamed herself for taking a toilet break. We're going to be okay.

Without turning around, I say to Pete, "I know how you can make it up to me. To us."

"Let's hear it."

Nearly forty-eight hours after the shooting, Pete's team have every corrupt cop and politician involved in the apartment fire in custody.

Instead of making my own way to the hospital, Pete drives me himself, sacrificing precious time when he could be interviewing the high-profile suspects.

It's well past midnight by the time I'm standing outside Gavin's room. Before I enter, I message Anika and wait in the corridor for her to emerge. When she does, the prominent dark circles under her eyes speak volumes about the lack of sleep and stress she's been under.

Gesturing to Pete behind me, I tell her to let him take her to Lach's to get some rest before they all come back in the morning. She really must be on her last legs, because she offers no resistance, giving me a weak hug and a wave as Pete leads her away.

When I step into Gavin's room, I close the door and lean against it, taking everything in. A dim light above the bed casts a soft glow over his sleeping features. With his upper body raised slightly, his gown has fallen halfway down his chest, exposing the dressing over his shoulder. The first bullet he took. An IV line adorns the back of his left hand, but none of the machines he's attached to make any annoying sounds.

Slowly, I approach, rounding the end of the bed until I'm standing to his right. I've heard all the details about the second bullet he took, so I know to keep clear of his lower left side. He lost a kidney and a nick to his large intestines had to be repaired, but apart from that, he'll make a full recovery.

I stand there for a long time, just taking him in, basking in the warmth and love I feel when I'm in his presence.

Swaying, the pull of sleep oozes into my bones and brain. Careful not to wake him, I silently lower the bed's safety rail.

Not silently enough. When I glance at his face, his sleepy,

hooded eyes stare at me. Without a word, I toe off my shoes and, as I slip into the tiny space beside him, his arm makes way for me. I feel the railing latch into place at my back, then his arm circles around my shoulders. Secure in the bed with him, I carefully rest my bent leg across his thighs and drape an arm over his chest.

Only then do I tilt my head up so I can look at him. He's still staring at me, and I can't be sure if he's really seeing me, or if he thinks he's dreaming. It doesn't matter. I'm too tired to do anything but lie my head on his chest and close my eyes.

As I listen to the steady beat of his heart, his fingers gently trace up and down my back, and before I know it, I'm drifting.

Chapter 48

Gavin

SOMETHING WARM PRESSES against my side. Keeping my eyes closed, I remember the vivid dream of Jamie climbing onto the bed with me, filling me with such relief I think I slept like the dead.

A twitch against my chest pops my eyes open.

Not a dream.

I stare down at her limbs, perfectly placed to avoid my injuries. Her face is tucked into my neck, her dark, tangled hair fanning over her arm and my chest. The hand resting over my heart twitches again. I can't see her eyes, but I'm sure if I could, I'd see them dancing beneath her lids as she dreams. Her breaths come long and measured, indicating she's deep in the depths of what I'm certain is some much-needed sleep.

Closing my eyes, I lie there, sucking up her warmth, her presence, every tick in her fingers.

She's here. She's alive.

The urge to hold her tight, cup her face and kiss it all over, surges through me like a tsunami. But I don't want to wake her. That'll come soon enough. Along with the reality of what happened. For now, I enjoy this quiet moment with my arm around her and the gentle beat of her heart against my rib cage.

I drift off again, and the next time I open my eyes, a nurse is standing beside me. Care not to move my shoulder, I press a finger to my lips, and she nods as she continues to check my vitals in silence. When she lifts a cup of water with a straw, I nod and take it from her, quickly emptying the contents. Once she leaves, I know it won't be long before breakfast comes around. And I'm certain the gorgeous woman by my side will be pretty damn hungry.

Tracing my knuckles over her bare forearm, I take her hand from my heart and bring her fingers to my lips. I pepper them with kisses, then nibble at the inside of her wrist. Her fingers twitch, then fan out over my cheek, lightly stroking, as if she's testing to see if I'm real.

Placing her hand back on my chest, I touch her chin and tilt her head back.

When her eyes meet mine, when they shine with love, I grin at her like a love-sick puppy.

And she bursts into tears.

"Hey, hey," I murmur as she buries her face against my neck. She shudders and sobs, her hand on my chest finding its way into my hair and fisting the strands like she's hanging on for dear life. That's when I realise I've already done the same thing to her.

"I thought I lost you," she cries, "thought I'd never see you again. Never hold you, kiss you, love you …"

"I know, J. I thought the same thing about you." I hold her as she sobs, and I let my own tears fall as I stoke her hair and relish every bit of her living, trembling body against mine.

After a while, her sobs begin to subside into little sniffles against my neck.

"I think I might have to trade you in," I tell her.

"What?"

"Well, this drooling Saint Bernard routine's getting a little too much. I'm thinking maybe a Chihuahua. They don't slobber, right?"

Her body shudders against mine, a hiccup of a giggle escaping. "I'd punch you, but I'm too scared I'd hurt you."

Craning my neck, I try to see her face, but she's keeping it firmly pressed against my neck. "Look at me."

She shakes her head. "I'm a mess."

"I love you messy." Her lips smile against my skin, but she doesn't move. "Jamie, I need to see you. I need your eyes."

"Tissues?"

Over her head, I spot a box on the bedside table. Managing to reach out and snag a wad, I hand them to her. Only when she's dried her face and blown her nose does she finally look at me.

I cup her cheek in my hand so she can't hide. Staring into her eyes, I see the fear, the anguish, the relief. And love, and desire, and hope. "Give me those lips," I grumble.

She hesitates. "But … morning breath."

"I don't give a fuck about morning breath. We'll cancel each other out. Now shut up and come here, woman."

Grinning, she surges forward and plants her lips on mine. It's that first kiss she gave me, so sweet and filled with comfort and the reassurance that she's mine. I love that kiss, but right now, I need more. While our lips suck and teeth nip, my body lights on fire, leaving me thankful the catheter came out yesterday.

With some sort of sixth sense, the thigh resting atop mine slides upward. When it finds my erection, she gently rubs up and down its length, releasing a groan into my mouth. Christ, I want to ravish her and fuck her into oblivion, but my body's in no condition to achieve either of those activities right now.

Pulling back, her gaze skates down to her rubbing thigh. "How long until you can be inside me again?"

"I haven't quite gotten around to asking the doctor that yet. But I can't see any harm in having you sit on my face. Should we check with him when he does the rounds?"

"Definitely," she giggles.

The door swooshes open and an orderly brings in a tray. Once everything's set up, Jamie takes the lid off the plate.

"Mmm, scrambled eggs and bacon, a muffin, apple juice and coffee. You're not allowed any food, right?"

I squeeze her side, then find the remote to raise the bed. "Feed me, woman. I'm starving."

And she does just that, offering me a bite for every mouthful she feeds herself. By the time we've devoured everything, we're both sleepy again. But I fight it. I need to know.

"So, Reid's been arrested?"

She stares at me, bewildered. "Anika didn't tell you?"

"She told me about the operation your friend was leading, that they were waiting on the arrests before they'd let you come see me." The look on her face sends fear spiking through me. "They got him, right?"

She shakes her head. "They didn't need to. I shot him. I killed him."

I stare at her in stunned silence. Never once did it cross my mind that she'd killed the man I blamed for so long. Shit. My failure to even remember he was a threat almost cost us our lives. Now she's the one who has to bear the burden of killing a man. Because of me.

I tighten my arm around her, the need to protect her from the fallout overwhelming, even though it's far too late. "Jesus, Jamie. Are you okay?"

"I've got a battle wound," she says, a slight smile on her lips as she gently pats her hip. "Just a graze. A couple of stitches. After I shot him, he shot back."

My heart thunders, my eyes never leaving hers. *Fuck.* He could've killed her. It's a miracle she's still here, but I don't want to worry her with my thoughts. I want hers. "I'm talking about how you *feel* about it. The truth, J."

She looks into my eyes for a long moment. I see a hardness there I haven't seen since she glared at me in court. But there's vulnerability within those depths as well.

Hesitating a moment, she says, "I never thought I could do something like that. Not until I was right there in the moment. He was going to kill us both."

"Fuck, I'm so sorry."

"No. Fuck him. No one hurts the man I love without consequences. And I'm not sorry. He was evil. Does it make me a bad person for being glad I've erased him from this world?" Uncertain, she bites her lip while she waits for my answer.

I stroke her cheek with my thumb. "You're not a bad person, Jamie. You're my fucking hero."

Resting her hand on my chest, she shakes her head. "You're the hero, dummy. I know you would've done the same for me. I know he took you by surprise, that you fought him after he shot you. And I know you saved both our lives."

"I was useless, I couldn't—"

"Not finished," she says, placing a finger over my lips. "When I heard his voice, I was operating on automatic pilot. There was nothing in my brain except getting to you. If I'd done that, we wouldn't be here. It was you … you yelling at me not to go out there, to get Bennie and the Jets. It took me a second to figure that out, but when I did, it saved us. *You* saved us."

As I start to deny her statement, she kisses my lips, no doubt to shut me up again. I felt like I'd completely failed her, yet she's not having it. I suppose there's a nugget of truth there. At the time, my words were my only way to try and protect her. As luck would have it, they'd worked. But the credit isn't mine. Not by a longshot.

Breaking the kiss, I rest my forehead against hers. "Benny saved us."

She grins. "Okay, Mr. Won't-take-credit-for-anything, how about we say it was a group effort?"

I grin back. "Perfect. And when we see Benny …" A sudden knot forms in my stomach. "The gun … what's happened with that? Benny can't go back—"

Pressing a finger to my lips, she stops me again. "I had to tell Pete a few lies about that. I told him we found the gun in Dad's safe when we found the letters, and that I was going to contact him after Christmas to find out what I should do with it."

Jesus, how much more amazing can this woman get? After everything she's been through, she still had the presence of mind to protect Benny. "So fucking smart, J. And he believed you?"

"Oh, he knew I was lying, but he went with it. It made sense. And he owes me. Big time. He's agreed to a couple of other favours I've asked of him, too."

"You're busting his balls?"

"Abso-fucking-lutely," she says, sinking her fingers into my hair. "He almost destroyed us. I think it's only fair that he makes up for it."

"Well, I don't know the guy, so I trust you know what you're doing."

She snuggles against me, our eyes locked. "It's almost visiting hours. You know you're about to get swarmed by your family."

"My family?" Those words sound so foreign to my ears, but I like them. A lot.

"Anika, Benny and Lach. They'll be here by now. But before they come in, there's something serious we need to discuss."

I lean back a little and watch her eyes dance with amusement. "Spit it out."

"I heard my sister saw your junk."

I laugh, then groan when pain spikes through both of my injuries. "Yeah. I thought that was kind of funny … until I realised *my* sister also saw my junk. Then it just became disturbing. Do you think she'll be traumatised for life?"

"Let's hope so," she giggles.

Then, just as I'm about to kiss her, a barrage of knocks come from the door, and the rest of my family burst into the room.

One Year Later

Chapter 49

Gavin

I PARK MY shit-box of a car in the empty garage and kill the engine. It might be a piece of junk, but I love it for everything it represents.

Freedom.

Clutching the wheel, I check the time on the dash. Half an hour and she'll be home.

My heart flip-flops in my chest before setting itself to a brisk pace. Thirty minutes to get ready and calm the fuck down so I can act like there's no difference between this day and all the others we've spent together.

I hightail it into our ensuite, get in the shower and think about everything that's happened since last Christmas.

Jamie quit her job, studied estate planning and conveyancing, and has now opened a boutique law firm, freeing her from the constant barrage of evil that criminal law presents. She's put together a great team, which also gives her the option to take time off when she needs a break.

Three months ago, my conviction was officially overturned, allowing me to start my own career. I've been visiting prisons and counselling inmates, which I'll continue to do. But I also want to run a private practice. I've been putting out feelers for an office, though I'm not quite sure if that's the sort of clinical environment I want for myself or my clients. What I'd like, is to operate out of our home. Unfortunately, the layout of this house doesn't allow for a homely office that won't involve taking clients through our sanctuary.

But as of this morning, I don't think that's going to be a problem anymore. We've talked about moving a few times, mainly because of the shadow of Jamie's father and the fact we both almost died here.

We want to make new memories, *our* memories.

And now we can. When I checked my banking app this morning, I discovered I have fifteen million reasons why we can now make that happen.

I haven't told Jamie yet. She knows it's coming, just not when, or how much. Along with getting my conviction quashed in record time, she asked Pete for something else. She demanded he push hard for compensation. Compensation which isn't a forgone conclusion for the wrongfully convicted. It's simply left to the government's discretion on whether or not to offer an ex-gratia payment.

Pete warned me it could take years and, if I was awarded anything at all, it might not be much. Matters such as mine are not, as a rule, public knowledge, so it's difficult to determine who has come before and succeeded.

But I had a number of things on my side. Reid's corruption being one of them. Malice or negligence by a government official are the top factors in a successful ex-gratia payment. And Reid had that in spades. Then there's Pete himself. Though I don't blame the guy, he claimed he was negligent in not supervising the surveillance on Reid, resulting in me being shot. Along with Liam's statement and Jamie's father's video confession, I'm apparently one of the lucky few to succeed.

So says my bank account.

I can't wait to see her face when I tell her.

It marks the end of the past I want to put behind me. And the start of our future.

A future I'm now capable of providing for her.

As I dry off and hurry to the wardrobe, excitement courses

through my bloodstream. With a trembling hand I pull on a deep blue Henley t-shirt Jamie bought me, then find the pair of jeans I hid at the back of the wardrobe a while ago.

Taking a deep breath, I slide them on, check the pockets, then inspect myself in the mirror.

I might not look like fifteen million bucks, but I definitely feel like it. My goofy grin seems to think so, anyway.

Giving myself another quick pat-down, I check my watch and take a few deep breaths. Almost time.

In the kitchen, I transfer the bottle of champagne I've kept hidden at the back of the fridge to the freezer, grab a couple of glasses and pop them in too. As I turn away, I hear the faint rumble of the garage door.

My heart thunders. I don't know why. I'm positive she'll be thrilled, but I guess my heart wants to make sure I'm fully alive and present. It's beating hard and deep because I care hard and deep.

Striding into the hallway, I lean against the wall and wait for her to emerge. I hear the internal garage door close, footsteps, then the laundry door swings open.

She smiles when she sees me. I step forward like I do every day and kiss her. After I slip her laptop bag off her shoulder and place it against the wall, she touches my chest.

"Ooo, the Henley," she says, her eyes sparkling with mischief. "Someone's getting lucky tonight."

"We'll see." Her hair's loose around her shoulders, and she's wearing a pretty blouse paired with tight jeans and cute little heels. Now that she works for herself, she dresses however she likes.

As comfortable as she looks, those heels are coming off.

I drop down on one knee, her hands automatically going to my shoulders.

"Gavin, you know you don't need to keep doing that. I'm fine."

"And you know I love taking care of you. Don't try to deny me that pleasure, woman."

"You're right. So stupid of me. Knock yourself out," she

says with a pleased sigh.

I do just that. First one shoe, then the other. When she drops her hands from my shoulders, I take them in mine and look up at her.

She gazes down at me, confused. Usually, I'd be on my feet, telling her what's for dinner or asking about her day. When she realises this too, her eyes widen a little, and she starts to blink. Fast.

She knows.

And now I know, without a doubt, I have nothing to worry about.

"Jamie," I begin, feeling her hands tighten on mine, "before you, time seemed endless. Sitting in that cell, I wished for nothing more than time to speed up. Every second was an hour, every hour a day. But now, with you in my life, I wish it'd slow down. Now that I've found you, it's like time's making up for its previous error, making every day an hour and every hour a second. Now there's nowhere near enough of it. And I don't want to waste another moment."

Looking deep into her eyes, I release her, reach into the back pocket of my jeans, and produce the small velvet box.

Her hands come up to her mouth, her eyes already leaking rivers as I reveal the ring.

"Jamie, my sweet, sexy, wicked woman … my *you're-it-for-me girl* … will you let me love you and take care of you for the rest of our lives? Will you marry me, J?"

Her knees buckle and she throws her arms around my neck, clinging to me for dear life as her whole body trembles. I wait patiently, and soon enough, she pulls back and looks into my eyes.

"Yes, I'll marry you, and let you take care of me and love me … because that's what I want to do for you, too."

Sitting her on my thigh, I cradle the back of her head and kiss her. Long and slow, taking in all her little noises of pleasure, and her sniffles. Not wanting to suffocate her, I pull back enough to press my forehead to hers. "I love you, J."

"I love you, Shawshank."

"Damn it, I forgot to mention cheeky in that proposal." She buries her face in my neck and holds me tight. That's when I remember I have something in my hand she needs. "Hey, don't you want to check out the ring?"

"Oh," she say, easing away, "it seems so insignificant compared to—"

I bring it up between us. Her eyes widen as I remove it from the box, take her hand and slip it onto her finger.

"Oh my God," she breathes, "it's … so beautiful."

I bring her fingertips to my lips and kiss them. "It is now you're wearing it."

She studies the gold band shaped into the infinity symbol, the intricate pattern of diamonds following the shape around two oval diamonds resting within that symbol.

"But …" She tears her gaze away to look at me. "Gavin … how could you afford this? It's so stunning, I can't imagine how much—"

I press my finger to her lips. "Dad gave it to me. It's the ring he bought for your mother." I swallow hard over the lump in my throat. "Is that okay?" I've been so worried she might not like the sentiment, that maybe she'd prefer I picked something out for her myself. But when I saw the ring, I knew it was perfect. And this way, she'll have a piece of her mother with her always. Dad and I both agree the ring belongs to her.

More tears spill from her eyes as she meets mine, then hugs me tight. "It couldn't be more perfect."

Scooping her up in my arms, I carry her to the bedroom, place her on her feet and begin removing her clothes. We work together until we're both naked. Our hands and mouths intimately know what the other wants and needs. But now that we're truly bound, it somehow feels … *more.*

Ravishing her until she pleads to have me inside her, I slowly and deliberately slide into my fiancée. As I make love to her with the knowledge that she's truly mine and I'm hers, I know our future will be everything our past wasn't. With my body and my eyes and my actions, I vow to never let her down again.

Twining our fingers above her head, I look into her eyes and smile as I rock into her with long strokes. Her pupils dilate as her breaths grow rapid, her pelvis grinding up to meet me. I know all the signs.

"My gorgeous fiancée," I murmur, right there with her. Once she breaks, I follow her over the edge, our eyes never leaving each other's.

After I help clean her up and pull her to my side, I reach for the bedside table and pluck up my phone.

"That's a bit rude," she says, nuzzling into me.

"You won't think so in a second." I find my banking app and log in, then I turn the screen toward her sleepy face. "How does it feel to be the future wife of a multi-millionaire?"

Her head snaps up and she snatches my phone from my hand. She stares at the screen for a long time. Just like I did. All those zeros are quite mesmerising. When she finishes absorbing what all those digits mean, she puts the screen to sleep and rests it on my stomach. Then she gazes at me and caresses my jaw.

With a smile spreading her lips, she says, "I'm so happy for you. You deserve every cent." She blinks at me, her expression growing serious. "But it's kind of anti-climactic."

I want to chuckle at her choice of words, but her expression stops me. "I thought you'd be thrilled."

"I am … but having you love me, having you want to marry me …" She taps the phone. "Money's only value is what it can buy. And it can't buy that."

Damn woman. She's so fucking right.

As we gaze at each other, that burst of true happiness surges through me. I'm here, in this moment. A moment that not long ago I never thought would be a part of my life. I have so much to be grateful for. I'm indebted to not only her, but Benny and my sister and my father. And I'll make sure they always know how important they are to me. To us.

"We're in this life together for the long haul. A team. A united front. You and me, J."

"You and me, Shawshank," she whispers as she kisses me.

And that's all I need.

The End

If you enjoyed this book, the most wonderful thing you can do is leave a review letting other readers know. Even a few words are so appreciated.

ALSO BY DARCY DANIEL

These Hands

Deceivious

The Devils' Cradle

Playing the Part

ABOUT THE AUTHOR

Darcy Daniel enjoyed reading from an early age and fell in love with many genres, but was drawn most of all to romance. Darcy enjoys life in a picturesque, small historic town just outside Sydney, Australia.

Printed in Dunstable, United Kingdom

76575990R00298